A HEART FOR TWO

Daddies Who Love Their Daughters

Volume 1

Nona Gallien

ISBN 978-1-957220-83-3 (paperback)
ISBN 978-1-957220-84-0 (digital)

Rushmore Press LLC
1 800 460 9188
www.rushmorepress.com

Printed in the United States of America

Contents

Acknowledgments

I want to thank my family and the many friends who have listened and supported me. A special thanks to my mother, EGT, who always told me I'd accomplish great things.

Chapter One

*R*oyce Hawthorne left Louisiana at eighteen when he graduated high school and moved to Detroit, Michigan. He'd heard stories about the Motor City and that the auto industry paid well. Unfortunately, that wasn't the case anymore. The auto industry was close to folding up when he got there. After struggling for a few years with odd jobs, working at fast food joints, and doing construction work. He started looking for something else that didn't require working outside in the cold.

Eventually, after finding a better job, he worked his way to an assistant manager position at a Starbucks. Until one day, he was fired and accused of stealing a large sum of money. He knew he hadn't taken anything ever in his life. Now, he was reduced to working as a cashier on the night shift at a corner gas station. His dreams of becoming someone had faded. He was sure that it was one of the two people working with him that night that stole the money, but he didn't have any way of proving it. His name had been on the receipts for the night deposit. Somehow, the bag he put in the night deposit box had been emptied of all the cash—three grand was missing.

For months, he replayed that night over and over in his head. He'd been in the office counting up his shift's receipts while the others were cleaning up. He left the bag on the desk for a few minutes, and he remembered locking it. No one other than management had access to the keys that opened the bank bags. So, it had to be either Cindy or Freddie that had stolen the money. Again, he had no way of proving it. The office camera had been turned off, and he was securing the other doors for the night. They all walked out together. Two days later, he was standing face to face with a district manager, asking him why he would steal from the company. He'd worked there for almost three years and was working toward a manager position. The district manager listened to his story, but she didn't have a choice. She'd liked him for his mannerism, even though he looked like someone who should be a bouncer at a nightclub.

Royce was scrawny when he graduated high school. He hadn't been a jock or a geek, and he'd been average height and weight until he turned nineteen. It seemed overnight that he grew taller, putting his height at six feet, four. He only bulked up when he started working construction. And he never cared for working out in gyms or pumping iron. Royce hated working outdoors in the elements, but he'd needed it to survive. He wasn't going back home in defeat.

Every day, he watched the men coming into the Starbucks wearing their expensive suits, and he was in awe. He didn't see himself as a college student, even though he had that option at one time. His parents had begged him to go to college. He wasn't the smartest student in school, but he wasn't the dumbest either, doing just enough to keep a B average. The only thing he was glad of was that the bullies never found their way in his direction. He was neither popular nor sociable, and he didn't attend dances or any school activities.

Daily, his mother told him he had a beautiful smile to go along with his perfect set of white teeth. So he always wondered why the girls would hug the other side of the wall when he walked down the hall. He had the darkest set of eyes. Add those deep-set dark eyes with a face that never smiled. So a girlfriend was *definitely* not in his vocabulary.

After his growth spurt and his added construction-built muscles, he was sweet-talked, whistled at, and often propositioned by plenty of women. It didn't help any that he rode a motorcycle and obtained a few tattoos along the way. Now he looked like a bad boy. Except how many bad boys do you know that are night cashiers at a corner gas station?

One night, Royce was checking out a customer who loaded the counter with junk food. The customer asked for ten lottery tickets and a pack of cigarettes. He rang up his purchases and gave the man his total. The man started arguing that he'd been overcharged. Royce exhaled, and then politely went over each item with the customer. The customer asked for ten lottery tickets and didn't realize that they cost $2 each. He'd overspent by $10. Royce huffed because he didn't like canceling transactions with the crazy lottery machine. He held up the tickets and asked the customer to pick which ones he wanted, and he'd revoke the unwanted ones.

There was a line forming behind the irate customer, so Royce threw down the customer's extra unwanted tickets. He worked his whole shift each time forgetting, to cancel the additional tickets. When his replacement showed up the following day and counted up his drawer, he found the tickets at the bottom of a pile of dollar bills.

Damn! He didn't want to waste any more time at the store. He pulled $10 from his wallet and added it to his receipts so his drawer would balance out. Stuffing the tickets in his wallet, he left the store.

About a month later, Royce showed up to work during his usual shift. There was a large sign outside. It read: *Winning Lottery Ticket sold at this location.* And beneath it was a smaller sign, *unclaimed.* Royce read the note twice and sighed to himself. If only he could be the winner, he never considered himself to be lucky. He felt more like he was the character Schleprock from the cartoon "The Flintstones." You know the poor guy that nothing good ever happens to.

That sign bothered Royce all evening. Something kept nagging him. The store stayed busy all night, selling more junk food than gas. Several customers bought lottery tickets throughout the night, with comments that a win could happen again. He was the only person that worked the night shift. The manager thought it was quite funny when he hired him, making jokes that nobody would try and rob a guy of his size. Royce hoped and prayed the same thing, except he wasn't bulletproof. He'd worked there for six months, and no one had attempted to rob him, thank God. Royce looked at the clock on the back wall. His shift was almost over, and he was dead on his feet. The store was empty. Cleaning up was one of his responsibilities, so he wiped the counters around the soda fountains. He heard the ding of the bell, letting him know that someone had entered the store. Looking up, he saw the last person he wanted to see.

Jamie was one of the store managers, and she strolled in like she was a queen. His shoulders dropped, and he exhaled loudly, hoping that he wouldn't run into her anytime soon. The last time he'd seen her was when he was running from her house with his pants in his arms, weeks ago.

She'd teased him and openly flirted. She also left out the part about a boyfriend during all the flirting and phone conversations they'd had. After baiting him for over a month, he finally caved and asked her out. On his one night off, he asked her to go out to dinner and a movie. Pulling up on his bike, he parked across the street. She walked out dressed in a flimsy dress and heels. Her hair looked longer than it had two days prior, and she wore entirely too much make-up. He didn't think it would be gentlemanly to let her drive, so he called a cab. Royce listened to her ramble all night about her friends and all the fun they had partying at nightclubs. And he figured she wanted him to ask her to go clubbing, except dancing wasn't his thang. He managed to get through dinner and a very dull chick flick.

When they got back to her house, he kissed her at the front door. She rubbed him in all the right places and invited him in. They sat on her couch and kissed until he was hard as a rock. She made all the moves, even placing his hand between her legs. So he decided to oblige her and grant her wish. While they sat on the couch, he thought he heard a faint buzzing noise.

"Is that your phone ringing?"

"It's just some girlfriends being nosy. I'll talk to them tomorrow. Right now, I want to see what you're packing in those jeans."

She rose off the couch and started walking toward her bedroom, "You coming?"

Royce patted his wallet and smiled, pulling his shirt over his head as he walked. He knew she had a subtle body. She often wore revealing clothes to work like she was advertising. When he walked into her bedroom, she was down to her bra and panties. She lay back on her bed, beckoning him.

"I'll let you do the honor of removing everything else," Jamie said, trying to sound sexy.

Royce was glad he hadn't worn his usual boots. Slipping off his shoes, he was out of his jeans in mere seconds. Removing the condom from his wallet, he laid it next to the bed. His hard cock was throbbing in his boxers, and she was licking her lips. There was nothing better than a little foreplay before a good pounding. He stroked his hand across his hard member and joined her on the bed. Starting at her ankles, he kissed his way up. Spreading her thighs, he teased her with his mouth. He'd barely touched her and could smell that she was ready. She was either desperate or wanton.

Jamie stared at his massive chest and his rippled abs. She reached out and hissed. "Oh, wow! I didn't know you were hiding all this under that shirt."

Jamie leaned her head forward, looking at the bulge protruding in his boxers. She didn't care about foreplay. She wanted him, and she wanted him now. Wanting and needing him to hurry, because her phone had been buzzing, but it wasn't any girlfriends. She was sick and tired of her current boyfriend, wanting a new one. And by the looks of Royce, he was going to be it.

Her fingers had been crossed when they returned to her house, and Jeremy wasn't parked outside. She'd ignored his calls all evening and glanced over his text when she escaped to the bathroom. He'd left some stupid messages. Jeremy never took her to the movies or out to eat. He only wanted to sit on her couch and eat her cooking, the cheap bastard.

Extending her arm, Jamie reached for his shorts, but he was too busy trying to make her wet with foreplay. Damn, she was already there as soon as she saw his torso walking into her bedroom. She rubbed his chest, starting to plead.

"Oh, please, I want to see you. I'm ready for you," she begged. Unhooking her bra, she pushed at her panties.

Royce hadn't ever seen a woman who didn't like to be played with and teased. He hadn't displeased a woman after getting some lessons from a cougar that he dated during his construction days. Because of his inexperience, there had only been two women before meeting her. And he hated it when her job moved her to another state. She'd taught him well on how to pleasure a woman.

Royce was snaking his big body up so he could sample her big brown nipples. He had one in his mouth and kneading and squeezing on the other one. She let out a loud moan and finally was able to grab his manhood on the outside of his boxers.

"Oh, I want this." She had a hold of the rim of his boxers, sliding her hand inside.

There was a loud banging on a door coming from the front of the house.

"Is someone at your door?" he asked, standing on his knees on the bed.

"I don't hear anything. Come on, give me what I want," she whispered.

The banging got louder, and now someone was shouting out Jamie's name. Royce heard it clear as day. It was a man.

"Do you have a husband, a boyfriend?" He jumped off the bed, grabbing his pants. He didn't have time to put one leg in when he heard a crash. And then he heard a man screaming inside the house.

"Is there another way out of here? I'm not jumping out of any damn windows." He slid his feet into his shoes. "I can't believe this shit," he mumbled to himself.

She jumped off the bed, pointing and saying there was a door to a bathroom.

"I'm not hiding in a damn bathroom to get killed."

"There's another door leading to the hall and the kitchen. You can go out the back door. I'm sorry. I didn't think he would break my door down."

Royce held his pants and ran through the bathroom door and into another hallway. Finding the kitchen, he quickly unlocked the bolt. The chill of the night wrapped around his chest. Damn! He'd left his shirt, oh well, he sure as hell wasn't going back for it. Running between the next houses, he pulled on his jeans. Peeping around the house, he made sure no one was outside looking for him. It wasn't that he was afraid of a confrontation, but he was scared of a gun, and what if the man was packing. Hell, this was Detroit.

It was late and close to midnight. Royce's bike was parked across the street under a streetlamp. And he didn't dare crank it. Whoever had busted into Jamie's house would hear it. He sure as hell didn't want the asshole to try and trash his bike or shoot him in the back. He'd worked too hard for his used BMW 1300 S. Walking to the corner, he crossed the street, running back toward his bike in the shadows. Standing next to a tree a few feet away, he looked toward Jamie's house. It looked like every light in the house was on, and he still heard some muffled arguing, which meant she was still alive. He didn't see any movement in front of the house. So he ran the few steps to his bike.

Knocking the kickstand back, he put the bike in neutral and pushed it down the street and around the corner. He opened up the saddlebag and pulled a jacket out, and put it on. Afterward, he cranked up his bike and headed home.

Royce looked her square in her face, and she turned away, heading to the office. Emptying the last of the trash cans, he put the bags next to the back door. He wondered why she was here so early and doubted that she was his replacement for the morning shift. After looking at the clock again, and decided that whoever was his replacement was late.

Strolling to the register, he pulled the schedule out of a small drawer. According to the rooster, Shanna was supposed to be his replacement. Dropping his head, he did something he didn't want to do. He knocked on the door of the office.

"Come in."

"Have you heard from Shanna? She's supposed to be at work." He asked as politely as possible.

"I didn't sleep with you last night. You could try speaking first." She responded snidely.

Royce exhaled. "Good morning!" then he reiterated his original question.

"Yes, I heard from Shanna. She's not coming in. You have to stay and work."

"No, I'm not. I've been here all night. I'm tired and sleepy, and I promised to do something for . . . help a neighbor out with a problem."

"Well, you don't think I'm going to go out there and run a cash register, do you? You can stay and work for two more hours, or you can clock out and not come back at all!"

Royce felt steam coming from his ears. He couldn't believe she was turning into a number one bitch. She'd been extremely apologetic with him when she called him two days later trying to explain, and he wasn't having any of it. Then she had the nerve to ask if they could go to his place next time. Hell no, and he let her know that there would never be a next time. Then she dared to try and sabotage his job. She found an excuse to cut his hours.

Boy, was he glad that he wasn't the type of guy to spend every dime he had. He lived in a garage apartment behind the kindest old lady. The one-bedroom place came with a small living room and a kitchenette. Out of the sheer generosity of a sweet dear lady, he'd obtained the rental. It was during his construction days, and he'd been working across the street. It was their lunch break, and he was eating his packed lunch. He noticed an elderly lady having problems with a lawnmower in her yard. After chewing his last bite, he jumped up, running across the street. The other men sitting with him thought it was funny and laughed at the lady.

"Excuse me, ma'am. Do you need some help?"

"If I could get this old mower to crank, I wouldn't need any help."

"Let me take a look."

Royce wasn't a certified mechanic, but he knew that her mower had seen some better days. Pulling on the cord, it didn't make any sounds. He checked to see if there were gas and a few more vital things so that the lawnmower would run. The last thing he did was to take a look at the spark plug. It was old and corroded.

"Sorry, ma'am, but you need a new spark plug. How about when I get off work today, I'll come back to fix this right up for you. I'll even mow your yard."

"I can mow my *own* yard, young man," she said rather feisty.

"I would hate it if you passed out in this heat, mowing your yard. Please allow me. There's no charge."

He extended his hand. "Royce Hawthorne. I'll be back, I promise," he said with a brilliant smile. The woman made him think of his grandmother.

Royce made Mrs. Regina Jones a happy lady. Just as he promised, he returned with a spark plug and mowed her yard. When Royce finished, she invited him in for some ice-cold lemonade. He refused to come inside all sweaty, so they sat on the porch and talked for a couple of hours. Visiting with Mrs. Jones made him miss his parents and grandparents. It reminded him to call his mother, whom he hadn't spoken to the last two weeks. While they talked, Royce told her he noticed some loose shudders hanging on her house. He offered to fix them for her. She beamed at him, asking if he was sure. Royce nodded and gave her the smile that his mother loved so much.

Initially, Mrs. Jones was suspicious when he approached her earlier. The young man was mean-looking and scary. She thought he was a gang member with his tattoos on bulging muscles. Then after sitting and talking with him, she could tell that he had a good upbringing. She noticed that he had a slight accent, and eventually, she asked him where he was born. He said he was from Louisiana, telling her that his mother was a law clerk, and his father owned a body shop. And that he grew up tinkering with cars and motors. That was how he ended up in Detroit.

Royce finished off his third glass of lemonade and said his goodbyes. He promised that he would return over the weekend. After a couple of weekends and some evenings after work, they had become the best of friends. That was when she asked him where he was living, knowing that he was working odd jobs. He mumbled that he lived in Black Bottom in a run-down apartment building.

Ms. J got out of her chair, asking him to follow her. When they reached the backyard, she asked him if he wanted to move into the small apartment over her garage. Royce looked at the steps that led up, but he was afraid they wouldn't hold his weight. She told him there was a tall ladder inside the garage that he could use to look inside. Royce retrieved the ladder and extended it upward. He climbed up, peeping in a filthy window and cupping his hands around his eyes to get a good view. It was perfect for him.

"How much are you asking for rent, Ms. J?"

"For you, I will only charge $400 a month if you don't mind helping me around the house."

"I'll take it."

"Of course, you'll have to clean it up and fix the stairs first."

Royce shook her hand, his mind envisioning what all he needed to do. He knew where there was a lot of scrap wood. And there was no way he could get wood back and forth on his bike. Maybe the foreman would let him borrow one of the pickup trucks.

The following week, Royce showed up at the house with a large pile of lumber, figuring that having more would be better. Royce worked every day after work until it was too dark to see. He was excited about the small apartment. And he was just as excited about having a more secure place for his bike, considering that he could never leave his bike outside his apartment now. Cars, motorcycles, and bicycles often came up missing in his neighborhood. He was paying a storage fee a few blocks away, just to park his bike safely every night.

It took him a little more than two weeks to get the apartment ready. Giving the insides a new paint job, and a few other problems, like the bathroom. The bathroom needed everything, including a new sink and toilet. Between his construction experience and his dad, he learned how to do some simple household repairs. Not to mention, he'd called his dad multiple times during the repair work.

Royce thought about the money he had in the bank. He wondered how long he could live off it until he found another job. It wouldn't be the first time he was without employment because he didn't know if he could stomach being treated like crap by Jamie. First, he thought about calling the home office, but then he'd have to explain why she treated him like crap. They might fire him on the spot. Exasperated, he walked out of the office, slamming the door. Royce kept his mouth closed for the next two hours.

When the store was empty, he'd stare at the office door like it could explode, killing Jamie inside. He knew she was watching him on the security cameras. He did his best to make sure she knew exactly how he was feeling at the moment. After the first hour had passed, he had an epiphany. It had been a blessing in disguise that her-so-call boyfriend showed up when he did. He was even more grateful that he didn't have sex with her.

Royce was glad to be heading home. He'd called Ms. J and told her that he had to work over, and he'd help her as soon as he got off work. Even though he was tired, he drove her to Lowe's in her car, an older model Buick. She wanted some gardening supplies. He loaded up several bags of potting soil, weighing forty pounds each. Ms. J wanted to grow some vegetables in one of those raised garden beds. He helped her pick out the model she wanted and said he'd assemble it for her. Smiling, she told him she'd come back in a couple of days to get the vegetables to plant. She assured him she could manage that feat on her own.

On the drive back to the house, Ms. J told him some of the same old stories he'd heard several times before. He acknowledged her like he was hearing them for the first time. She was such a sweet person who'd lost her husband years ago. And she'd never had any children of her own, and he loved her like a grandmother. His parents had been ecstatic when he told them about her, and he'd moved to a much safer place. That was almost four years ago. She'd rescued him from the slums.

Royce unloaded the car and put all the supplies in the backyard. Telling her that he would get a little sleep, and then he'd build the garden bed. Climbing the stairs slowly, he was trying to decide if he would shower first or after he woke up. He didn't know how he was still on his feet. He'd worked all night, then two extra hours. And to top it off, he spent another two hours going to Lowe's. His feet took him straight to his bed, sitting down, he keeled over.

Waking up to yelling and banging, Royce rolled over, glancing at the clock. He estimated that he'd only been sleeping for a mere four hours. Stumbling to the window, he peeped out, wondering who was making so much noise. Then he spotted Ms. J. She had all the material for the garden bed scattered in different piles, and she was kicking some boards fussing.

Royce shuffled into his bathroom to throw some water on his face. He made his way down the stairs and stood behind her with his hands on his hips. It took her a few minutes to realize there was a massive shadow at her back. She turned quickly with a look on her face that meant she knew she was in trouble.

"Ms. J, didn't I tell you I would work on this after I had some sleep? What are you doing?"

"I felt so bad for keeping you from sleeping this morning." She put her own hands on her hips in defiance. "I was trying to help, but some pieces are missing, and I can't find the receipt. Can you make sure you don't have it?"

Royce didn't think he had the receipt, yet he pulled his wallet from his pants to appease Ms. J. He pulled every piece of paper he saw, opening all the tiny hidden spaces. He paused when he pulled the folded lottery tickets from between the folds. A fleeting thought popped into his head, and he shook it.

"Nah, I would never be that lucky," he said to himself.

Royce confirmed his suspicions and told Ms. J that he didn't have the receipt. Asking her if she checked all the bags, she nodded yes. He asked her if she checked the car, her head dropped, and she tucked in her lips. Ms. J rushed inside the house to get her car keys. She returned, waving the receipt. Royce said to give him about thirty minutes, and he'd return the kit to Lowe's.

Dragging his tired body back into his apartment, he sat on his bed. Pulling the tickets from his wallet again, he turned them over in his hands, like the method was going to give him the answers he sought. He didn't have a computer or internet. He was a simple guy living a simple life. His phone was even simple, it was a flip phone, and he had a pay-as-you-go plan. His best friend at the moment was a little old lady. There wasn't even a girlfriend in his life, but that was his choice. He'd tried dating, but all the women seem to be shallow. They were more impressed with his body and muscles than him as a person.

So when he felt a need for company, he'd hang out at a bar or a pool hall. There were always horny women there looking for a good time. He didn't have any problems letting women abuse his body. As long as it was at their place or a hotel, he never took anyone back to his apartment. He wasn't ever going to disrespect Ms. J.

Royce took a shower, changed clothes, and took the incomplete kit back to Lowe's, and exchanged it. When he returned home, he threw the heavy box over his shoulder and hauled it upstairs. It was the only way there was a guarantee that Ms. J wouldn't open it. When he returned her keys to her, she had a mean look on her face.

"Tomorrow, you get your garden bed. You have been a bad girl today." He kissed her on the cheek and winked. "Love you, Ms. J."

She smiled at his retreating back. She loved this young man as if he were her son. "Love you too, son."

Royce went back to his apartment after wasting a couple more hours again. He needed more sleep because he had to be back to work tonight. And he wanted to check his tickets, just in case. Royce fell asleep and dreamed he was a millionaire, buying a big house and filling it with cars and motorcycles. In the next image, he saw himself sitting on a private plane, drinking champagne. Then he was sitting in a hot tub surrounded by beautiful women. His dreams took him to beautiful islands with crystal clear blue waters, and beautiful women surrounded him. These were exotic places only fantasized by poor people.

Royce was brought out of his fantasy by the ringing of his alarm clock. Angrily, he kicked at the sheets; he was upset because he was about to have sex with several beautiful women. He rolled over, looking around him at his meager dwelling. "Oh well, a guy can dream, can't he?" He said out loud, getting out of bed.

Pulling into the parking lot at work, he parked in his usual spot where he could see his bike. The gas station wasn't in the best part of town. For some reason, he was apprehensive about going to work. He didn't know why he was feeling different. Was something terrible going to happen tonight? Oh God, he hoped the store wasn't going to be robbed! Was he having a premonition?

Chapter Two

$\mathcal{R}$oyce strolled in the door, eyeing all the customers and looking around like he was looking for someone with the word robber tattooed on their forehead. Nothing seemed to be out of place, and there was the usual chatter coming from behind the register. He nodded at the other clerk and headed to the back to clock in.

Pushing the door open slowly, he peered around the door into an empty room like he was expecting a gang of robbers wearing ski masks, waving guns in the air. He exhaled. "Man, get yourself together," he whispered to himself. Boy, this is going to be one long night, he thought to himself.

After clocking in, he went to the manager's office to get his cash register tray. He checked his tray to make sure everything was correct. After his Starbuck fiasco, he made a point of double-checking everything. He wished that he could have found out who stole the money and how they stole it.

Royce was finally left to run the store alone. He caught up on his other duties quickly each time the store was empty. Somewhere around 4 a.m., a customer came in and purchased tons of junk food. Royce thought the guy was probably high, considering his bloodshot red eyes. The customer paid for his purchases and walked out the door. But then, he stopped outside the door and started pacing, talking to himself. Royce watched him closely; maybe this was it, he was signaling to someone. Royce slid his hand under the counter, positioning his hand right next to the silent alarm button. If someone walked in wielding a gun, he would hit the button. The guy walked up and down the sidewalk in front of the store.

The inside of the store was so quiet that Royce could hear the clock ticking on the wall and the motors churning on the soda fountain machines. He heard every noise individually. His breathing became hard and heavy, along with the sound of his heartbeat. Was he dreaming, reliving an Alfred Hitchcock movie, or was he in the Twilight Zone? Time slowed down, and the man continued pacing on the sidewalk. He was moving in slow motion too. Royce saw his arms flapping in the wind, still holding the bag with all his junk food.

Then he stopped at the front door and ripped it open. He moved in slow motion to the register. His mouth was moving, but Royce couldn't hear anything the man was saying. His hand was hovering below the button.

"Hey . . . hey man, did you hear me? I need some lottery tickets."

"What!" Royce asked,

"I said I need some lottery tickets. What's wrong with you? You must be higher than me." He said, looking at Royce strangely.

Royce shook his head to clear his crazy thoughts. "I'm sorry, sir, how many do you need?" He exhaled slowly.

"I need $10 worth."

"You do know that they are $2 each?"

"Yeah, yeah, yeah, just give me the tickets. If I go home without them damn tickets, my old lady will go upside my head. I knew I forgot something when I walked out of here a few minutes ago."

After the customer left, Royce got a bottle of water and drank it in one gulp. He would be so glad when this night was over. Maybe he was having a bad night because he didn't sleep well. But that customer did make him remember that he needed to check his tickets. Soon, the store was empty again, and he still had three hours to go. He pulled the tickets out of his wallet and pushed the buttons on the lottery machine. After sliding each ticket in the slot, and then the last one, a message popped up, *"Jackpot Winner."* He stared at the computer. What does Jackpot winner mean? He'd never played the lottery before, thinking it was all a sham. Perhaps, he'd won a few thousand dollars. He'd paid people from the register for small amounts. So how could he find out how much he'd won?

There was a computer in the office he could check there. He looked out the window, and the parking lot was empty. Rushing to the office, he left the door propped open and punched the lottery website into the toolbar. Looking over the screen, it was too busy for him. After he found the Lottery icon, he clicked on it. He needed to find the numbers for the date on his ticket to determine the Jackpot's worth. He tried to breathe slowly, but he was too excited. He'd never won anything in his life, his short life of twenty-six years.

The bell went off on the door. Damn! Jumping up from the computer, he ran out front. He'd since forgotten about his earlier paranoid feeling. Now he was antsy for the customer to leave the store. Royce stood at the register bouncing from foot to foot. The customer was taking forever, walking up and down the chip and cookie aisle twice. He walked by the coolers full of sodas, beer, and water. The customer walked up and down each aisle, slowly, and the customers' mentality was killing Royce. The guy walked for another ten minutes before coming to the register with a pint of ice cream.

"Is this all, sir?" Royce asked, slightly annoyed.

"Yes, my wife is pregnant." He announced bubbly. "Why do pregnant women want the craziest foods in the middle of the night?"

"I don't know. I don't have a wife or a pregnant anything." Royce told him, passing him his bag. This time he tried to be more polite, and he included a smile. "You have a good morning, sir."

"Thank you, young man. You too!"

Royce waited until the man drove out of the parking lot. He hoped he hadn't forgotten something as well. Rushing back into the office, he scanned over the screen, searching, and reading fast. Finally, he found what he was looking for. He slid his finger down the screen to the same date as his ticket and then slid it across to the computer screen to the amount. Royce looked at the numbers twice and jumped, practically falling out of the chair.

"No way!" He said out loud.

He sat back in the chair again like it was going to bite him. Leaning in closer to the computer, he mimicked his movement again. There was a small ribbon across the screen next to his winning numbers. It read unclaimed.

"No fucking way. I don't believe this. I think I won the lottery." He said to the four walls.

He became afraid, almost too scared to touch his ticket. His chest started pounding, and then the bell on the door rang again. Grabbing his ticket off the desk, he stuffed it in his pocket, rushing back to the front. A couple of people had come into the store. One guy wanted to pay for some gas, and another one was at the coffee pot.

"Hey, how old is this coffee?"

"It's probably been there most of the night. I'll fix a new pot right away."

Royce went about his duties as if he were a robot. It was getting close to the morning rush time. A few more customers were coming into the store. The lottery website was still up on the computer, and he wanted to shut it down before the morning manager came in. He wasn't about to tell anybody that he was a lottery winner. The customers walked around, so he ran back to the office and closed out of the website. Pulling the ticket from his pocket, he stuffed it back into his wallet.

He still needed more information because he didn't know what to do to claim his money. Standing at the register, he was in a daze. Oh no, he had to call his parents, he had to tell Ms. J. His brain started going in different directions. He wanted to go to so many places, do so many things, buy his parents a new house, and help Ms. J.

"Excuse me . . . excuse me, can I pay for my stuff?" A customer was yelling at him.

"Sorry, yes, ma'am." He nodded. "Okay, okay . . . okay, stop thinking about the ticket. You've got another hour to go." He said to himself.

"Who are you talking to, young man?" A customer asked.

"No one," Royce responded.

Royce was glad to see his replacement walk in the door. The waiting felt like the longest hour of his life. The morning manager walked in five minutes later.

"Did everything go okay last night, Royce?" The manager asked.

"Everything was perfect."

Royce took his register tray to the back and counted it down, making sure his numbers were balanced. This moment might be his last night working at a gas station.

He jumped on his motorcycle and headed home in a daze. Dropping down on his small couch, he looked at the ticket, flipped it over, and started reading the back, where there were instructions on how to claim a prize. One of the instructions said to sign the ticket immediately.

Looking around for a pen, he realized he didn't have one in his apartment. He could go downstairs and ask Ms. J for one, or he could go to the store and buy one. He was ruptured between leaving the unsigned ticket at home or putting it back in his wallet. What if something happened to him on the way to the store? What if he had an accident on his bike and someone stole his ticket at a hospital? He didn't know what to do. It sounded quiet at Ms. J's house; she could still be asleep, and he didn't want to wake her up.

Royce decided to sit for a little while until he thought she was up. Falling off the too-small couch jarred him awake, and he couldn't believe he'd fallen asleep. Glancing at his watch, it was past noon, he'd slept almost five hours. Rushing to the bathroom, he washed his face, picked his ticket off the floor, and finished reading the instructions. The instructions told him he had to go to the central lottery office to claim his prize.

There was a phone number listed, and taking a deep breath, he dialed the number. Listening to the automated machine, he pressed the number to claim a prize.

A pleasant voice answered. "Hello, Michigan Lottery Office, how can I help you?"

"I . . . I think I won the lottery," he stammered out.

"This sounds like wonderful news. Have you signed your ticket?"

"No, I don't have a pen. I'm going to borrow one in a few minutes."

"Okay, sir. It's important that you sign your ticket before coming into the office. Do you know the address of our central office?"

"No, ma'am, I don't."

"Then, I think you need to go borrow that pen to can write down the address." She smiled into the phone.

"Yes, ma'am. I'll be right back. Oh, can you hold on?"

"Yes, sir, I'll be here when you get back."

Royce ran down his steps, jumping and missing several. Running around to the front of the house, he rang the doorbell. He bounced up and down, waiting, hearing Ms. J yelling, asking who was at the door.

"It's me . . . it's Roy."

She opened the door, speaking and smiling. Royce spoke back and asked if she had a pen he could borrow. She told him to come in while she dug in her purse. Royce was trying so hard not to ask her to hurry. He wanted to surprise her later when everything was confirmed. After finding a pen in her purse, she scratched it across a piece of paper to make sure it worked. She was scratching slowly and telling him how ink pens never worked when you needed them to. Grabbing the pen, he kissed her on the cheek and ran out of the house.

He made it back up his stairs in record time, and he was also out of breath when he got back on the phone. The lady asked him a few more questions, and he answered them. She asked him to be sure to bring his identification and the signed ticket. And then she gave him the address and some directions. Royce told her he would see her soon.

It took him an hour to get to the lottery office, Royce felt like every car on the highway was out to get him. A receptionist greeted him, and he explained that he had spoken to Ms. Jenkins, and she was expecting him. The receptionist smiled and pushed a button on her phone. She spoke softly into the phone then told Royce someone would come and get him.

Instead of one person, three people arrived and shook his hand, and escorted him to the back. He was taken to a large office and asked to sit at the table. The older gentleman asked him for the lottery ticket and his identifications and offered him a beverage. Royce handed them over very nervously.

He said, "No, thank you," and that he was too nervous to drink anything.

The older gentleman sat at a computer and punched in some numbers. He slid the ticket in a slot connected to his computer, verifying the ticket.

"Congratulations, Mr. Hawthorne, you're a winner."

More than excited that he was sitting down because Royce thought he was going to faint. There were so many questions, but before he could ask his first question, the other gentleman spoke up. Extending his hand, he identified himself as a financial adviser and passed Royce a folder. He opened another one and laid it on top of the table, explaining the process of claiming the prize and his options. All this was so overwhelming. Maybe he should talk to his parents and get their advice before making any decisions. He asked the adviser if he could speak to someone before he made his choice, and he was granted his request.

Stepping outside the building, he called his mom. When she answered, he asked her if she was sitting down. She shook her head before opening her mouth to tell him yes. Immediately, she asked if something was wrong or if he was hurt? He answered no, and that nothing was wrong, and he wasn't hurt.

He exhaled and blurted it out. "I won the lottery, Mom."

"What lottery? Roy, what are you talking about?"

"I'm a millionaire mom, a multi-millionaire."

"You're what? Stop playing on the phone, boy."

"I'm serious, mom. I need your help. I don't know what to do. I have to make all these decisions. I need you and dad. Can you and Dad come to Detroit?"

"When do you want us to come?"

"Today, tomorrow . . . can you hold on for a minute, Mom?"

Royce ran back into the building. He told the adviser that he wanted his parents, but they live in Louisiana. Would it be possible if he could pay for their travel? The adviser told him they could advance him a cashier's check for a substantial amount. He could deposit it in the bank today and pay for his parents some first-class tickets. Royce wanted to shout. He ran into the hallway this time.

"Mom, I will book tickets for you and dad for the first flights out of Shreveport tomorrow. Start packing and call dad."

"Honey, I have to work tomorrow."

"Mom, you will never have to work again unless you want to. Call in sick for tomorrow. I'll get you guys open tickets. Mom, I love you. I'll call you back later with the details."

Royce closed his flip phone and walked back into the office with his head held high. He'd won over three hundred million dollars. Now, he was a hundredth-multi-millionaire if that was a real word. Sitting down at the table, he asked what he needed to do right now. He'd have his final decisions for them tomorrow.

Chapter Three

$\mathcal{R}$oyce sat at the table again, this time with his parents. He signed documents and more documents. When he finished, they presented him with one of those giant signs that look like a check. He took the picture with both his parents standing by his side. His parents had advised him to hire an attorney and financial adviser. Millions of dollars was a lot of money for a young man. They didn't think he would waste it because they'd raised him to be sensible. He'd shown a lot of responsibility since moving so far from home, they only wanted him to continue. The financial adviser had given him a list of choices. Royce told his parents that he didn't want to make that decision in just a day. He said tonight they would celebrate.

Cranking up the SUV he'd rented, he wanted them to meet Ms. J, the only other significant person that mattered. He parked the SUV in the garage next to his motorcycle. They walked around to the front of the house, and he rang the doorbell. Ms. J peeped out the curtain opening it quickly, smiling when she saw Royce.

"Good afternoon, son, are you coming to tell me that I'm getting my garden bed today."

"Oh, yeah, I almost forgot about that. I have some people that I want you to meet first."

She ushered them into the house and closed the door.

"Ms. J, I want you to meet my parents."

Extending her hands, the elderly lady said, "I'm Regina Jones. It's so nice to meet you in person finally."

"Adam Hawthorne, and this is my wife, Samantha. We want to thank you for watching out for our son. He talks about you on every phone call." Samantha didn't want to shake her hand. She grabbed her in a hug.

"It didn't take me long to figure out that he had some kind and loving parents. You have an exceptionally wonderful son. I wish there were more young men like him." She pointed to the sofa. "Please sit down and make yourselves comfortable. I'll get us something to drink."

"She makes the best lemonade, dad," Royce said, smiling.

Regina returned to the living room with a tray. Royce jumped up to take it from her, sitting it on the coffee table, and poured four glasses.

"Ms. J, I have a surprise to tell you. I won the lottery, and that's why my parents are here. I wanted them to be with me and to meet you."

Regina was speechless. She stared at him and his parents, who were smiling and shaking their heads.

"We're going out to celebrate tonight, and I want you to come with us. Please say you'll come. You have taken me in and treated me like I was a part of your family. You're a part of my family now."

Royce got up from his seat, sat next to Ms. J, and gave her the biggest hug. Finally, she agreed to go out with the family. He'd do anything in the world for her. He was going to do just that and more. Now it was his turn to take care of her right along with his parents.

"Okay, we're going to a fancy restaurant tonight," Royce announced to the group.

"Roy, we didn't bring clothes for a fancy restaurant." Samantha blurted out.

"Good, we can all go shopping, right after dad helps me with a garden bed." He gave his dad a sweet smile . . . "I promised."

Royce showed his parents his tiny apartment. His mother smiled when she saw how clean it was, even the bathroom. Royce and his dad spent the next hour putting together the garden bed while the ladies sat in the shade, drinking more lemonade. Working together to build the garden bed was right up his dad's alley. He enjoyed working with his hands and doing the project with his son. The ladies chatted about what Regina was planning to grow in her little garden.

While they worked, Royce asked his dad what he wanted. He wanted to know if he and his mom wanted to travel or buy a new house and new cars. His dad started fussing because he didn't want him spending a ton of money on them.

Royce grunted. "Dad, you have got to be kidding. I have so much money, and if you don't tell me what you want, I'll just go and do it anyway."

"How about we discuss it later after you meet with an adviser? I want you to learn how to invest your money, not waste it."

"Okay, but I want us to take a family vacation. And I want to invite Ms. J. She's never been outside of Detroit."

"That will be up to her. But I think she loves you as much as we do, son."

After they finished the garden bed, Royce took a quick shower, and his dad cleaned up the house. Ms. J offered them a spare room after they said they were getting a hotel room.

They all climbed in the rented SUV, loaded with a navigation system. Royce searched for the nearest mall. He parked outside the Macy's, sending the ladies to the women's department to shop for elegant dresses.

Royce grabbed his dad's arm and headed to the men's department. "Come on, dad, we need suits."

Royce stopped at the designer rack, looking over the fancy suits. The last time he was ever dressed up was the day he graduated high school. A salesman approached him and asked if they needed some help, and he responded, shaking his head yes, telling the sales guy they both wanted suits. The salesman asked a couple of questions that Royce had no answers to.

The salesman looked him up and down, motioning for them to follow him. They needed to be measured. Adam told the salesman that he knew his measurements. The salesman had Royce stand on a short block in front of a set of mirrors. Retrieving a measuring tape, he began measuring all the usual places. He wrote some notes on a pad as well as said them out loud.

The salesman asked if there was a particle color he wanted. Royce didn't want to look like he was going to a funeral. He said gray, expensive, and nothing from a sale rack. The salesman brought some swatches with various colors of gray. Royce picked a couple of choices, and the salesman said he would see which ones were available in his size. He looked over at his dad when he walked out of a dressing room wearing a tan plaid three-piece suit.

Royce whistled. "Dad, you look amazing in that suit. I think it's perfect."

"I think it cost too much."

"Don't go there with me, dad."

"The pants are a little long. Maybe your mother can hem them."

"Excuse me, sir, but we can take care of that for you here." The salesman interjected.

"Okay, great then," Adam replied!

Royce tried on a couple of different suits before settling on a Jones New York gray striped suit. His pants also needed altering. The salesman said they could have both their pants ready in an hour. Royce took care of their bill before he and his dad went looking for the ladies. He found them standing next to a register. A saleswoman was hanging up the dresses to bag them. Royce looked at his mom, then the dresses.

"Mom, why do those dresses look like you're going to church? No, we are celebrating. You should see what dad is wearing tonight. Excuse me, ma'am. You can put those dresses back. They need party dresses, appropriate for their ages, of course."

The saleswoman led them to a different section, pulling out several beautiful dresses. Samantha tried on a champagne-colored metallic dress with a matching jacket. Royce shook his head, "yes," as well as his dad. Now it was time to dress Ms. J. She told him she wasn't wearing any of that shiny stuff. They eventually found her a navy dress with a matching jacket. Now it was time to find matching shoes.

They spent over an hour in the women's department, so Royce went back to the men's department to see if their suits were ready. The salesman was smiling and greeted him by name when he reached the register. Passing him two suit bags and his card, the salesman said their shoes were in the bag's pockets, and that he'd be happy to help him with any future purchases.

Royce nodded and thanked him. "So this is what it feels like to have money," he thought to himself.

As they rode down the escalator, Royce noticed the perfume section. But his mother was looking at the counter where professionals were applying makeup.

"Hey, mom, why don't you and Ms. J go and get dolled up. I'll ask the saleswoman to bring you some perfume samples." He wanted the two most important women in his life treated like royalty.

While the ladies were getting make-overs, he went in search of a cell phone store. It was time for an upgrade. He'd seen plenty of people playing on their smartphones. Now he could afford one with all the extras. His mom had an older model iPhone, and he asked his dad which model she had. Royce remembered seeing a newer model advertised on TV. He stood in front of the iPhone section and looked at the latest models. Touching the screen, he looked at all the apps and got excited like a kid in a candy store. Beckoning for the guy behind the counter, he asked him many questions about the phones and all the amenities. The salesman explained everything about the phones. Finally, Royce selected his phone with all the bells and whistles.

"Which one do you want, Dad?"

"Roy, I . . ."

"Dad, pick one, or I'll pick it for you. Do you think mom would like the newest model with a larger screen?" He asked, smiling and enjoying the fact that he was money worry-free.

"I'm sure she'll want the newest model. She likes larger screens, especially if it's bigger than the plus model."

"Tell me about the family plan. How many phones can I get?" Royce asked the salesman.

The guy answered all his questions and set up a phone for Royce with a new cell number. Royce didn't have many contacts on his old phone. There were a few people he didn't care to hear from anymore, especially since he was about to start a new life.

Royce told his dad that he'd be back with the ladies after depositing their clothes in the truck. Royce returned with a lady on each arm. The guy had a variety of brand-new phones displayed on the countertop, per Royce's instructions. Adam was playing with his new iPhone when they arrived.

"Adam, do you have a new phone?" Samantha asked.

"Yep!" he said, grinning.

"Okay, mom, which one do you want?" He turned to Ms. J., "You get to pick one too."

"Son, I don't know how to use one of those blasted things," Regina said in her feisty tone.

"I'll teach you. I get worried about you when you leave the house in that old car. I need you to be able to call for help if you ever need to." He wanted to buy her a new car, but that was a surprise for another day.

Everybody left the store with brand new phones. Adam and Samantha had all the information from their old phones transferred to their new phones. Royce said he could do the transfers manually, taking pics of everybody with his new phone and adding them to the contact page. He did the same with Ms. J's phone. Next, he added his parent's numbers into Ms. J's phone just in case. Now, it was time to go and get dressed for their evening out.

Royce wanted to impress his family with the evening at a grand restaurant and an excellent view. He'd called the restaurant as soon as he knew his parents were coming to town. The restaurant occupied two floors at the top and it was every tourist and local's dream view. He'd admired the building from afar many times after working construction jobs in the area.

He drove with ease into downtown and all the traffic. His parents noticed the tall buildings, pointing them out, while they were driving. Royce gave them a little history, telling them it was the tallest building in Michigan, and it was built as a part of seven connected skyscrapers. Excitedly, he told them the building was the world headquarters for General Motors, about the 73-story hotel, two twenty-one-story office towers, and a five-story Wintergarden atrium. He said the place was so big that it needed its own zip code. The locals called it the *Ren Cen*, which was short for Renaissance Center. They were even more surprised when he drove up to valet parking for the building.

He was ecstatic in the elevator during the ride to the top of the building, 700 feet in the air. Royce approached the hostess podium and announced his name for the reservations. They were escorted to a table by the window. When making the reservation, he specifically asked for a view of the Detroit River and Canada. His mother stood at the window and gasped, holding her hand over her mouth.

Royce stood behind her, towering. "Isn't it beautiful?"

"It's amazing, Roy. I can't believe I'm standing here looking at another country." Samantha told the whole table.

Adam stood and held the chair out for his wife. Regina made several of the same comments about the view, considering that she'd never been in this building before. After taking one last look at their surroundings, they all sat and gave the waiter their drink order. Royce wasn't much of a drinker other than a beer, but he ordered a bottle of Dom Pérignon for the table. When the waiter delivered the bottle, Royce asked his dad to do the honor of taking the first sample.

"I've never tasted real champagne before."

"Well, this will be the first of many things for our family, dad."

Adam accepted the drink from the waiter and sipped. "Taste good to me." He nodded to the waiter. The waiter smiled and filled all their glasses.

Royce made the first toast. "To my family, may we embark on new journeys and enjoy the rest of our new lives."

There were cheers all around the table. Just as the celebration was dying, another waiter showed up and took everyone's orders. Royce encouraged everyone to try a juicy wagyu steak with a side of lobster from the reserved menu. He only wished that they couldn't see the prices, but tonight was not about money, it was about how many zeroes were in front of the decimal, for him.

Royce enjoyed his parent's company for two more days. He promised he'd come home and visit as soon as he handled his business. His parents were gone, and it was time to make some serious decisions. Making a trip to an Apple store, he bought a top-of-the-line laptop. There was a basic cable package at his apartment, but he needed to invest in some internet. He had a lot of work to do, and he needed it.

Royce conversed with Ms. J about adding the internet to her account. He would gladly pay for the whole thing and suggested that she add more channels or movie stations, whatever she wanted. He sat with her while she called the company. By the time they got off the phone, they'd upgraded her package. The cable company gave her an appointment for the next morning. They informed her that they'd bring all the necessary equipment to install the internet and Wi-Fi.

Now, Royce wanted to have a sincere conversation with Ms. J, he felt that she was worried about him. The first thing he did was to tell her that he wasn't moving any time soon. Just because there was a lot of money in his bank account didn't mean that he needed to run out and buy some big fancy house. Royce said that he didn't want money to change him, and the elderly lady smiled with tears in her eyes.

And then he dropped a bomb, informing her that they were going car shopping. It was time for a new car, but Ms. J being herself, protested. Royce on the other hand did his usual grunt and asked her if she was ready to go to Lowe's for the rest of her garden supplies, and that made her smile. He was still driving the rented SUV, trying to make up his mind if he wanted that one or a different model. It would be helpful, especially when it rained because he would never give up his motorcycle. But now, he could afford his dream, a Harley. It reminded him of how he and his cousin, Chase would pretend that they were riding one.

Chapter Four

*R*oyce spent the next few weeks meeting with his new attorney and his financial adviser. He'd done some research until he found a firm with a good reputation that he liked.

Just as he promised, Royce took a trip home to visit his parents and told them about the firm and his adviser. Royce gave his parents a folder with all his private information, saying they were his official beneficiary, in case something ever happens to him.

They talked about planning a nice family vacation. Royce wanted to know where in the world they wanted to go. His mom had always wanted to go to Hawaii, and his dad said he wanted to just be with his family.

"I guess we're going to Hawaii. Mom, I'll let you organize the vacation. Just book it as soon as possible." Royce said, laying two black American Express cards on the coffee table, embossed with their names.

His mom gasped. "Roy, this isn't necessary."

"Yes, it is. I love you both." Royce stood up to leave almost teary-eyed.

"Besides, you'll need it to make reservations. Hey, I'll be back later. I want to ride around town and see what's changed."

Royce jumped in his rented SUV, and drove around Shreveport, noticing all the changes. Passing by his old high school, it looked the same. The neighborhoods looked the same, and the only thing different here was him. He didn't even have any old friends to look up, although there were a few cousins spread out and only one that he'd been close to. They'd lost contact when he moved away. Maybe he should ask his mom the whereabouts of Chase. It had been his uncle's idea for them to join scouts together. The only other people he'd hung out with regularly had been the guys in his scout troop. And that was when he saw them once a week and on their weekend camping trips. He was sitting at a light when he heard a familiar sound.

Looking in the rearview mirror, he saw some guys on bikes coming up behind him. There were six of them, all on Suzuki's. He huffed! Boy, did he wish he had his motorcycle? Damn! Why not just go and buy one and leave it at his parent's house? He wondered where the bikers were hanging out. The light changed, and he followed the guys and girls. There were two girls pushing bikes, sexy. They rode out toward the lake to Ford Park.

Royce pulled into the park where a lot of people were hanging out. Some were using the small grills, and most were sitting around chatting. He heard loud music coming from some souped-up cars. This scene was his kind of crowd, at least now it was. It was Saturday and still early enough. Picking up his phone, he slid his finger across the screen, opened the google app, and searched for the motorcycle dealerships in the area.

Turning the truck around, he headed back to town. Royce drove across the river and exited on Benton Rd. He pulled into the parking lot of the Harley dealership. They weren't busy, so he hoped that getting some quick service was an option.

He walked into the showroom and saw two sales associates, who were sitting down and didn't look to be in a hurry to get up. Would he always be treated like he couldn't afford what he wanted? He wasn't dressed in a three-piece suit, but who came shopping for a motorcycle dressed that way?

Instead, he walked around the showroom, looking at the different styles of bikes. Royce didn't want a bulky bike, he wanted something sporty, and a Fat Boy, trimmed in silver, stood out from the other bikes. Then, he spotted another one with a blackout finish. His mouth formed a perfect O! Oh no; this one was so much better. Throwing his leg across it, he straddled the bike gripping the handlebars. Now, if he could only get some assistance, he wanted to take it for a test drive and looked again at the salesmen still sitting. Royce was about to give up and leave. A customer shouldn't have to ask for help. Another man walked into the showroom from the back, eating a sandwich. He saw his coworkers sitting and a customer straddling a bike. One of them made a snide comment to him.

"Yeah, Bob, like you're going to get a commission today." Both of the salesmen snickered.

Bob did his job and approached the customer. "Good afternoon, sir. Can I help you?"

"You sure can. I'd like to test drive this bike."

"We do have a similar model that you can test drive. We don't normally use the showroom model for test drives."

"Okay, show me the way."

"I'll need to get some information first. Can you follow me to my desk?"

Royce followed the young salesman and sat on the other side of his desk. He grabbed a customer information form from a stack of papers. Filling out the application, he asked Royce a series of questions. Royce passed him his driver's license when it was requested. Bob commented on his license being from Michigan. Royce said he was from Shreveport and was in town visiting his parents.

"So, you just decided to go out and buy a Harley while in town."

"I did. I was thinking of leaving it here to ride when I visit my parents."

Bob looked at his ID. "You're twenty-six?"

"Yes, that's correct."

"I'll need to run a credit check, Mr. Hawthorne."

Royce dropped his black American Express on the desk. "No problem, Bob."

Bob typed the required information into his computer. It was enough to put a big smile on his face, and he turned intentionally to the other salesmen. "Follow me, Mr. Hawthorne, for your test drive. I take it that you already ride."

"Yes, I have a Beemer at home." He didn't have to mention that it was an old, used one.

Royce test drove a different model Fat Boy. The salesman said it was a year old and for sale, but they used it for this purpose. He left the parking lot and turned out on Benton Rd. He took the exit for I-220, wanting to open it up and hear what it sounded like between his legs. Royce turned around at the first exit and returned to the dealership. Bob was standing outside, smiling when he got back.

"I'll take the showroom model, Bob."

"Right away, Mr. Hawthorne, do you need anything else?"

"Yes, a bike trailer, a helmet, and . . . why don't I just look around and see what else I want to buy today?"

Royce walked around the retail store that was attached to the dealership. He picked out a helmet, a riding suit, a new pair of boots, and a bunch of other shit he probably didn't need. He did it to piss off the other salesmen. Bob was doing his part to show off his big sale. Royce had a big grin on his face when he signed his last document.

Bob passed him a hands-free security fob, the newest security system feature on the Harley's. Royce looked out the glass window to the parking lot. His bike was gassed up and loaded on the trailer. Bob even helped him load all his accessories. When they finished, Bob passed him a business card, and they shook hands.

Royce raced back to his parents' house. His dad looked at him like he'd grown an extra head. But Royce wanted to take his new baby for a ride. He changed into his new boots, heading straight back to the park. It had been a while, and he might even get lucky and pick up a girl.

When he rolled into the park, his twin pipes were screaming. He knew his bike would get him some attention. He'd come out of his shell since high school. Although he still wasn't a party animal, he knew how to mix in a crowd. He rolled up next to several guys sitting on their bikes and took off his helmet.

"Damn, man, that is one badass bike!"

"Thanks, yours too." one of the Suzuki riders said.

"You must not be from around here?"

"I grew up here, I live in Detroit now. I'm just back in town for a few days."

"Hey man, what kind of work do you do?" The guy asked to be nosy."

"I work in the auto industry." He lied. He wasn't about to tell a bunch of strangers his real story.

Royce told them a little about life in Detroit. A group of young girls passed by, and the guys did their usual whistling and begged for them to sit on their laps, they got blown off. Royce asked the guys if this was a typical Saturday afternoon and if they were in a riding club. They shook their heads 'no,' saying they only got together on the weekends and hung out here or shot some hoops over on Lakeshore at the park.

"Hey, Roy . . . Roy!" Someone called Royce from across the park.

Royce turned on his bike looking around. Was someone calling his name? That couldn't be; he didn't know anyone out here. Must be someone else named Roy out here. He stopped looking and paid attention to the guy next to him talking.

"Roy Hawthorne, is that you, man?" He walked closer to make sure.

"Jimmy?" Royce got off his bike and towered over his old scout buddy.

"Wow, dude, I haven't seen you in years. Where you been hiding?"

"Detroit."

"What the fuck happened to you? You were shorter the last time I saw you." The guys did a man hug.

"Oh well, I guess I grew up, must've been the colder climate."

Jimmy dragged Royce away to a table littered with food, drinks, and a lot of women. Jimmy introduced Royce to the group. They chatted and got caught up on how the other's life has been in the past seven years. Royce had to reiterate his lie about work. He did tell the truth about visiting his parents.

A couple of the girls were checking him out. He was standing next to the table, talking with Jimmy.

Royce was bald and sported a goatee and mustache, with a sexy smile. He was wearing a stretch t-shirt defining his muscled chest. His arms were folded across his chest, which made his biceps bulge even more. The girls licked their lips, watching his wolf howl on the tattoo on one arm. The other arm boasted an Indian tribal choker with feathers hanging. His chestnut, tanned brown skin tone made the colors on his tattoos stand out. He wore jeans that hugged his muscled thighs, and he had a sexy gap between his legs.

The girls examined him from his head to his feet, "oh what big feet," they whispered to each other as they checked out his features. They overheard the guys talking about going to the club tonight. That was too easy, and now they knew where he'd be tonight. Each girl was working on a plan to get his attention.

Royce stayed at the park until it was almost dark. Strolling back to his bike, he heard the alarm disarm. Wow, that was a forgotten feature. He promised Jimmy he'd see him at Kokopellis downtown. In reality, he was more interested in hooking up at the club. He'd noticed the girls checking him out, and he was long overdue for some female company, as long as they weren't married or had a boyfriend.

Climbing onto his bike, Royce left the park. He walked into the house, and his mom asked him if he had a good afternoon. He said yes, and spoke of how he planned to hang out later with an old buddy from scouts that he ran into at the park. He promised his mother that he'd be careful. Even though he was an adult, his parents still worried about him. It was too early to go out, and he figured he'd have a long night, especially if he got lucky. So he headed to his old room to get a couple of hours of sleep.

When Royce woke up around eleven, he showered, trimmed his beard, and slapped some cologne to his naked pecks. He pulled on a pair of jeans freshly starched from the cleaners, and a new cream-colored button-down shirt, that stretched taut across his chest. When he finished primping, he laced up a pair of cream-colored Timberlands. Oh yeah, he was getting some booty tonight! He patted his back pocket. Now, he was ready.

Later that night, Royce rolled through downtown Shreveport. He saw a slew of bikes lined up on a sidewalk, several of which he recognized from earlier that day. There were a couple of guys sitting on their bikes smoking cigarettes. He parked his bike closer to the club, spying two police cars parked on the corner, hoping that there wasn't trouble already. But this club had a reputation for trouble, so maybe they were just here as a precaution.

Royce walked across the street. At the door were two bouncers as big as he was, one asked for his ID. After paying his entrance fee, they stamped his hand. When he walked into the enormous room, the music was loud, and the dance floor was full. Heading straight to the bar, he motioned to a bartender and asked for a beer.

Leaning against the bar, scanning the room, he saw one of the girls from the park dancing and watched her with a little interest. She'd dressed for the nightlife. His eyes followed her as she moved and glided around the dance floor with a natural rhythm. He noticed her dance partner as he watched her hips. She turned her back to him and rubbed her body against him, sensually like an invitation.

As her head bobbed to the music, she looked up, and her eyes met Royce staring at her. She continued her dance with the other man, but she smiled at him. Throwing her hips in his direction, she touched her thighs sensually, caressing them for him. She licked her lips, parting them, winking at him. Royce took a drink of his beer as he watched the show. The song ended, and she walked straight to Royce, leaving the poor guy standing on the dance floor.

"Hey, I see you finally made it. My name is Chloe, just in case you didn't remember."

"It's nice to see you again, Chloe. Can I buy you a drink?"

"I'd love one. Wow, you *really* are a gentleman. Normally, a girl has to practically beg for a drink around here."

Royce motioned to the bartender again.

"Can I get appletini, please?" Chloe yelled to the bartender. "The gang is in that back corner if you were wondering." She threw her head in the direction where she knew Jimmy was.

She grabbed her drink off the bar as Royce paid for it. He followed Chloe through the crowd. As they passed multiple tables, one table with several ladies caught Royce's attention. They were dressed nicely in sexy party dresses with sashes across their chest, which read bachelorette party. One woman was wearing a silver dress that had a sash, with the word *"Bride"* written across it. He watched them as they eyed him passing by. He was a few feet away and heard the comments.

"I wish he'd been our stripper."

"Did you see his chest?"

"Girl, I was looking at his thighs," commented another.

Royce shook his head, laughing as he continued to follow Chloe deeper into the club. He was used to women treating him like a piece of meat now, and he loved it. Reaching the table, he gave fist-bumps to the guys. Royce sat in the only empty chair, which gave him a view of the table with the bachelorette party. Chloe moved her chair, trying to get closer, while her girlfriend Kori did the same. Chloe sipped her drink, teasing her friend. Royce noticed that she didn't have a drink. He smiled in her direction and asked if she wanted a drink. Her head bobbed up and down. And since he didn't see any waitress, he asked her if she wanted the same drink as Chloe; she looked like an appletini girl. Kori responded, yes. So, Royce left the table, and the girls watched his ass as he walked away.

Chloe turned to Kori. "I saw him first. He's mine tonight."

"Whatever! Give him a chance to choose." Kori spat out.

Royce approached the bar and saw one of the bachelorettes from the bridal party. He stood next to her admiring her natural beauty. She wasn't wearing a ring, and he was looking hard. The bartender was sitting three glasses of white wine in front of her.

"Can I take care of that for you?" He asked, smiling.

"Don't you have enough women all over you?"

"So, you were checking me out?" He asked with confidence.

"In your dreams, buddy," she said with sarcasm.

"At least I know you'll be in my dreams."

She threw some money on the bar and told the bartender to keep the change. Grabbing the three glasses with two hands, she walked off. Royce watched her sway from the bar. She walked with ease in her high heel shoes. He moaned, liking what he saw. And she wasn't easy, unlike the two at the table where he was sitting. It would be easy to take one of them or both outside and bang them in the parking lot. He didn't like easy women, at least women that were that easy. Leaving his card with the bartender, thinking he might as well run a tab. He was hoping to buy a few drinks for the lady playing hard to get.

Grabbing his order, he headed back to the table and slowed down as he passed the ladies all dressed up, smiling, laughing, talking loudly with each other. They all noticed him at the same time. He inhaled, and his chest rose and fell slowly, with each step. Their mouths dropped open, and their eyes betrayed them. They were openly salivating. He stopped and smiled.

"Ladies!" he said throatily.

Royce walked with long slow strides, his taunt muscled thighs flexing in his jeans. God, he wanted to turn around and look back at their gaping mouths. Then he heard a crash. A glass had fallen to the floor behind him. He kept walking with his head in the clouds. Returning to his chair, he blocked out the sounds of the girls babbling.

Chloe and Kori both asked him to dance, and he declined, telling them that he doesn't dance. He was glad when some other men came and claimed them to the dance floor. It gave him an excellent opportunity to watch the woman he wanted. Leaning back in his chair, drinking his beer, he stared, stalked her with his eyes. He saw her each time she cut her eyes in his direction. He smiled, winked, and she would turn away quickly.

Making a decision, he drained his bottle and walked straight to their table, and stopped in front of the woman he wanted.

"Can I buy you a drink?"

All the ladies at the table gawked at their friend. They stared at her because she hadn't answered his request.

"Doll, the man is talking to you." The bride remarked. "You have to forgive my sister. She's shy."

"I'm not shy. He's with two women; why would I play his silly little game." She said to her sister like he wasn't standing there.

"I'm not with them. Those two women are friends of Jimmy's. I just met them today." He stuffed his hands in his pockets. "So, how about that drink . . . Doll?"

Doll looked at her sister and then her friends. They were giving her a look. It was a look that said . . . girl, take the drink. And anything else he's offering. She slid off her stool and headed to the bar, and he followed like a dog in heat.

Doll didn't want her friends to listen to their conversation, even though she'd later tell it to them. Spying a space at the end of the bar, she stopped. There was only room for one person to stand, so he stood behind her, almost touching. He waved to the bartender, asking for two drinks.

"Aren't your friends going to be looking for you?" She asked, turning around to face him holding her glass.

"I came alone, and I'll leave . . . alone. You come here often?"

"This isn't really my style. I only came here because of my sister."

"What is your style?"

"I don't care for clubs, especially this one. My first preference would be to go to a lounge and listen to jazz music."

"I'm not a clubber, either."

"It's something we have in common." She smirked.

"I wonder what else we have in common. I'd like to find out."

"I must be honest with you. I don't usually go for the big, bulky tattooed men either. But I do like the bald look and your beard." She said, smiling.

Royce was beginning to think it was the wine talking. He didn't usually take advantage of women, who'd had a few too many drinks. There was a sinking feeling that he wasn't getting any booty here. Damn! He liked this one. Maybe she'd give him her number.

"I'm glad you like it. Is Doll your real name?"

"No, it's Dorothy. My parents said I looked like a doll when I was a baby, so it kinda stuck."

"Well, Doll, I'm Royce. It's nice to meet you. I don't want to steal you from your party all night, can I get your number. I'd like to talk and not have to scream in your ear."

She leaned up against the bar and stared up at his tall frame. He seemed a little different than the usual bums she met. He did have an attractive physique, and she wanted to touch him. Oh No! The wine was taking over her senses.

"I don't usually give out my number to men I just met."

"I'm only in town for a few days. I'd like to see you again, perhaps over dinner."

"How about you give me your number, and I'll call you." Doll said, smiling wickedly.

Royce knew that look. It probably meant she wasn't going to call, but he gave her the number anyway. At least she added it on her phone. She didn't even comment that it was a different area code. He escorted her back to her table. As he was walking away, he heard her friends quizzing her before he was out of hearing range. Women!

After returning to his table, he continued to watch her every chance he got. Somewhere around 4 a.m., he'd had enough fun.

Saying his goodbyes, he told Jimmy he'd give him a call. He looked over at the table of women, and it was empty. He didn't see them leave, but the club had almost doubled in occupancy.

Stepping outside in the fresh night air, he had to breathe deeply. His lungs were full of unwanted smoke, his main reason for not liking clubs. He'd made it across the street to his bike when a limo showed up. That was when he saw her again. Doll was running with her friends toward the limo. She was looking down laughing, and she threw her head back, brushing her hair out of her face, looking up right into his face. He was straddling his bike. She made an O with her mouth, staring. Someone called her name and pulled her into the limo. He saw her pop up out of an open roof on the car. She blew him a kiss and disappeared.

Royce was looking down the street at the disappearing taillights. He didn't see Chloe coming across the street.

"You're leaving already? I was hoping we could get together." She was standing close with her breast in his face. Her hand was caressing his arm up and down.

"I . . . ah, don't have an extra helmet."

"It's okay. I have a car. I can follow you, or you can follow me."

Damn! He hated being horny. "I'll follow you."

Chloe pointed in the direction where her car was parked. Royce told her to get on the bike, and he'd take her to her car. Her skin-tight skirt couldn't get any shorter, although stroking her naked leg gave him some enjoyment. Dropping the kickstand, he helped her off the bike.

After he followed her to some apartments on Pines road, she told him she had a roommate. He asked, male or female? What a terrible fucking time for him to ask that question now, he wondered to himself. She answered female, and he exhaled, and she led him to her bedroom. Closing the door behind them, she turned the lock.

Chloe began tearing at his clothes. Damn! What happened to a little foreplay? It took him less than fifteen minutes to realize he'd made a colossal mistake. She had a sexy body, and the oral sex had him hard, true enough. He was trying to put on a condom, and she was trying to stop him. She told him she liked to have sex naturally and that she hated condoms. He disagreed and said no condoms, no sex. Chloe gave in to the condom rule, but it had killed the mood for him. She sucked him to get him hard again. He rolled on the condom quickly and fast. She was a wild woman all over the place. She kept trying to change positions every other minute, and he was not enjoying himself. This experience was the worst sex he'd ever had, and she kept trying to bite him and suck him like she was giving him hickeys. Who does that?

He'd had enough! So, he jumped up off her bed, feigning that he had to use the bathroom. Pulling on his jeans, he stuck his feet in his boots without tying them up. She was still lying in her bed naked when she heard her front door slam. He jogged to his motorcycle, stuffing his boxers in his pockets and buttoning his shirt. Royce jumped on his motorcycle and peeled out of the parking lot.

Chapter Five

$\mathcal{R}$oyce spent the next few days helping his dad at the auto body shop. Adam wanted to get caught up on the vehicles that he needed to finish before their vacation. Being the owner of the business didn't give an excuse for the repairs that he'd promised would be completed on time. Adam's expertise varied on vehicles from high-end cars to older models. His expertise was rewarded when he was granted a contract by a major insurance company to repair damaged cars. The remaining vehicles or any new arrivals could be completed by his trusted staff. Royce didn't have the required certifications, so it was best to clean up around the shop and straighten up the small office.

For the most part, he hung out with his dad and the other workers. Royce didn't dare go anywhere near the park in case Chloe would be there. And he turned down an invitation to hang out with Jimmy again. The following weekend, his mom wanted to go to Dallas for a shopping trip. A road trip was right up his alley to get out of town since he wasn't ready to go back to Detroit. He was still hoping Doll would give him a call, especially since he didn't know her last name.

Royce drove his rented SUV. His mother was glad to have some bonding time with her son. She wanted to know if he was thinking about his future. And for the whole three-hour ride, he had to convince her that it was on the back of his mind. But right now, he had no idea. They were nearing the Galleria mall area, and Royce was paying attention to the directions on the GPS. He pulled into the valet at the Westin. He'd made the reservations for three nights at this hotel because it was connected to the Galleria Mall. This way, his mother could shop until she dropped and not have far to go with all her shopping bags.

After checking in, Royce escorted his mother to her room and delivered her luggage. Even though the Westin was a five-star hotel with porters, he was enjoying taking care of his mother.

Samantha had shopping on the brain, and Royce didn't. So, Royce lay across the bed in his hotel suite, thinking back to the conversation with his mother. What will he do with his life? He couldn't live like a lazy person for the rest of his life. Nor did he want to go to college and get a degree. Should he buy a bunch of stock and watch his money rise and fall? Or should he just own a business that made money for him? How about owning a business and being the boss or owning a business and staying in the shadows? All of it was so overwhelming. Having money was giving him a stomach ache, or maybe he was hungry. He hadn't eaten anything since before they left for Dallas that morning.

Several hours had passed, and he wondered where his mother was, or should he wonder how many stores she hadn't visited yet. Calling his mother, he asked about dinner plans. She suggested her favorite seafood place *Pappadeaux's* whenever she came to Dallas. Samantha said she was leaving the mall with two arms full of bags. Royce told her to stay put. Leaving his room running, he'd made it to the lobby. He headed in the direction of the mall when he passed some sexy hotties in bikinis. Damn! He needed to find the swimming pool. And here he was without any swimming trunks with him. Thank God, the mall was still open for several more hours.

Reaching his mom, he took her bags and delivered them to her hotel suite next door to his. He asked her to be ready in an hour to go and eat. Royce ran back to the mall to find the closest store to buy some swim shorts and sandals. Going to the pool in boots wasn't cool.

Royce rushed through dinner with hot babes on the brain. It took them over two hours between driving across town and the hellacious Dallas traffic just for dinner. He was hoping the bikini-clad women were still hanging around the pool or a new batch. Either way, it was good for him. His mother said she was tired from her long day of shopping and was retiring to her plush bed in her hotel suite. He had different plans for going to the pool and the bar, looking for some action.

Royce changed into a t-shirt and his new swim shorts. Like a giddy schoolboy, he walked fast down the hall toward the elevator. Pushing the button, labeled pool, he whistled. Walking out into the humid air around the pool, he spotted the bar at the far end. And luck was on his side; the pool area was full of beautiful women. Several guys looked like they were also on the prowl, so he ordered a beer and looked around. The women had filled up the tables and most of the lounge chairs.

Royce spotted an empty poolside bar table. He propped up against it drinking his beer. It didn't take long before a beautiful woman in a bikini came to his table, wearing a smile. She spoke and asked if he was a basketball player, and Royce shook his head in disagreement. It was a question he'd heard a million times. She admitted to using the question as a ruse to come over and talk to him, and he returned the gesture by offering her a drink.

Royce got the attention of the bartender. He came running immediately and took their drink order.

"I'm Haley . . . Haley Lewis," she said shyly, tucking her long blonde hair behind her ear.

"Royce Hawthorne."

"Are you here for the conference, Royce?"

"No, I'm just in town for a couple of days. What kind of conference are you attending?"

"Medical, I'm a rep for a surgery equipment company. What do you do for a living?" Haley wanted to know. He looked good enough to eat, and she could use a little fun before going home. She hadn't had a one-night stand in a long time.

"I work in the auto industry in Detroit."

"I'm from Cleveland, Ohio, and we're practically neighbors."

Royce stood by the pool and talked with Haley for a long time. He met some of her co-workers and a few other people attending the conference. He had so many women surrounding him that he felt like a sheik with a harem. After another hour, Haley had her arm wrapped around Royce like she was claiming him for herself. She was a busty blonde that had an appetite for tall black guys. Royce wondered if she was playing games with him in front of her friends. She was all touchy, and feely with him. Haley rubbed her hands up and down his back sensually. Did she want him to ask her back to his room, or did she want them to go back to her room? Maybe she had a roommate. Damn!

His mother was next door to his room. Thinking seriously that he needed to reevaluate his situation the next time he traveled with his parents. He rubbed his hands down her sides and hips, being just as touchy, feely. Whatever happened, it had to be her choice, and he wanted witnesses. He didn't want some woman crying rape against him. The group was starting to thin out, and only a handful of people were still hanging around the pool. The bar at the pool was closing down for the night.

"Haley, do you want to go inside for another drink?"

"No, but we can go to my room for one."

"How about I meet you there in five minutes?"

He needed to make a pit stop. Thank God he kept some condoms in his overnight bag, and even happier she had a private room. It would have been embarrassing to ask her back to his room and try to keep her quiet, he laughed at the thought.

They left the pool area and walked to the elevators together. The doors opened, and Haley pushed the floor number fifteen, telling him her room number, while Royce pushed the number twenty-one. He pulled Haley into his arms and kissed her. She melted against him, rubbing his crotch, moaning sounds escaped both their mouths. The elevator dinged, letting them know they were at the first stop. Haley said that she couldn't wait to have that drink with him in her room. He kissed her softly and patted her on the butt, telling her he'd be right back.

Royce made quick time getting back to Haley. She answered the door, wrapped in a towel. He knew that she was a girl that knew what she wanted. Royce closed and bolted the door. Haley sat on the end of the bed. Royce pulled his shirt over his head, and he could tell by her expression that she was in awe. Pulling the towel apart slowly, it fell to the bed. He palmed her large breasts, kneading them in his hands, sliding his thumbs across her nipples. Her nipples harden from his touch. Royce put one knee on the bed and leaned toward Haley to kiss her. She fell back on the bed, smiling, scooting backward, and beckoning him with her finger to follow.

Crawling across the king-size bed, he hovered over her. He attempted to kiss her again, and this time he succeeded, sliding his tongue deep into her mouth. She entwined her tongue with his and caressed his chest with her hands down to his shorts. Slipping one hand inside his shorts, she stroked his hardness. He moaned into her mouth. Haley pushed at his shorts, trying to free the hard object that she wanted. She felt the length of him, and now she wanted to see him with her own eyes. Breaking the kiss, she tilted her head for a better view.

"Oh, yes!" She whispered.

"Are you sure you want all of this?" He boasted.

Haley nodded her head yes and pushed at his shorts. Royce stood on his knees, pushing his shorts down his thighs, so she could see everything she was about to get. She whimpered out loud, reaching for him. Royce pulled a condom packet from his pocket before taking his shorts off. He slid two fingers inside, toying with her, getting her ready, because he was ready and willing. After his last attempt with Chloe, which went *horribly* wrong, he needed this release.

Royce tore open the packet and rolled it on. They made wild raw sex for hours, and he only had to cover her mouth twice. He'd gone through three condoms, and around 5 a.m., she'd fallen asleep. Finally, he was solely satisfied. He dressed and slipped out after leaving her a tender note by her bed.

Royce returned to his suite, took a hot shower, and climbed into his bed, naked. He wasn't the type of man that wanted the whole wake-up-next-to-a-woman kind of thing. It was something that had stayed with him from his cougar experience. He fell asleep with a smile on his face.

He was brought out of a dream by someone knocking on his door and cell ringing at the same time. Who could be knocking on his damn door? The phone stopped ringing, but the knocking didn't. He thought he hung the '*do not disturb*' sign on the outside. He bumped his toe, trying to get to the door, knowing he hadn't given his room number to anyone last night. Cursing and hopping on one foot, he peeped through the hole to see who it was.

"Mom!" He said through the door. "Give me a minute." Royce grabbed a pair of shorts before he opened the door.

"Son, it's noon; you need to get up."

"Oh, Mom, I need more sleep. I was up late." He said, falling back on his bed.

"I know I heard you when you came in this morning. This might be a five-star hotel, but I hear everything. I hope to God that you're being careful and protecting yourself."

"I think I'm a little old for this conversation." He said, burying his face in a pillow.

"You are, but things are a whole lot different for you now. Do you know how many women would try and trap you because of some money?"

"You don't think I go around bragging, do you? I have a nice little fictitious story."

"Well, that's good. You have always been a level-headed person, and I want you to stay that way. What time are we leaving? I need to get a few more things for your dad for the trip to Hawaii."

"Whenever you've finished shopping, I'll just sleep until you get back. Then we can hit the road since I'm the one driving the three hours." He pulled the cover over him. "And mom, make sure the 'do not disturb sign' is hanging on the door. Love you."

Samantha exhaled and walked out of his room. She was starting to worry about her son a little. She'd been honest when she said he was sensible, but now, the stores were calling her name, and she was getting more excited about going to Hawaii.

Royce woke a couple of hours later. He was relishing on his tryst; too bad he didn't get her number. She did say she was from Cleveland. That was close enough for another hookup or two. He stretched in the bed, hoping his mother wasn't upset with him for not shopping with her. He never said he'd go shopping with her. He was only the driver.

A flashing light caught his eye, and it was the light blinking on the phone. Had his mother called his room too? He pushed the button, thinking that his mother had left a ranting message. It was from Haley, and he remembered telling her his full name. She probably called the front desk, and they transferred her call. He smiled, she thanked him for a memorable night, and she left her phone number. Grabbing the notepad and a pen, he hit the button again.

Royce got impatient waiting on his mother, so he called her to see if she was still shopping. She told him she was on the way to her room. The only thing she had to do was to pack up the last items she bought. Opening his door, he watched as she exited the elevator with her arms loaded down again. Laughing, he asked her if she bought an extra suitcase to put all the new clothes in. She smiled, nodded yes, telling him that she'd purchased a new set for her and his dad.

Royce spent another week with his parents. He needed to get back to Detroit and help Ms. J get ready for the trip. They planned to meet at LAX and fly to Hawaii together. He let his mother make all the arrangements after he made a few suggestions. They were spending a different week on three different islands. He requested villas on the beach with private pools. Samantha only complained once because of her son's request. Royce asked that they spend the first week in Hawaii, better known as the big island, the second week, Kauai, and the last week in Oahu. This trip was going to be the best three-week vacation.

Thinking long and hard, he decided to take his new bike home. He didn't trust using the open trailer for taking the bike back to Detroit. So he rented a small U-Haul, figuring that he could handle the drive alone in a couple of days.

During his drive home, he called the number that Haley left on the machine. She answered with a cheery hello, excited when she learned it was Royce. She told him she'd been thinking about him and wanted to know why he left. After making up an excuse to have an early morning meeting, he thanked her for the call and left him a number. He told her that he was on his way back to Detroit, and he wanted to see her again. He'd call her in a few days and drive to Cleveland. He didn't know how he'd get around his idiosyncrasy, so he asked if she had to work every day, and she said yes. So he thought that would be perfect because she'd leave early. He decided he'd make it a one-nighter during the week.

Chapter Six

Royce was glad to be back in Detroit. He enjoyed visiting with his parents, but he missed home. Moreover, he'd promised to help Ms. J prepare for the trip. While they were shopping for new clothes, he encouraged her to buy a swimsuit, telling of how there would be a private pool at the villas; instead, Ms. J was rather concerned about leaving her house for so long. So, Royce arranged for a security company to check on the house several times daily.

Before they left, Royce managed to escape to Cleveland for a romp with Haley, telling her he had to go out of town on business again, and he'd call her when he got back to Detroit. His plan worked perfectly, she crawled out of bed, leaving the hotel before six.

Ms. J had never been on a plane before and learned that First-Class was the way to travel. They met his parents in Los Angeles for a short layover, and then they were off to Hawaii. The ladies were impressed with the gifts of Lei's draped around their necks at the airport.

Royce had plenty of surprises waiting for them. The first was the limo that picked them up at the airport and drove them to the villa. He'd also arranged for a car service to be at their beck and call.

Since he didn't want to be tied down, he rented a Harley. He took his mother and Ms. J on short rides; Ms. J's ride was even shorter. They toured the big island and went on multiple tours and excursions. They got to see the island by helicopter and by boat. There wasn't anything that they didn't get to experience. Adam was extremely impressed when they flew over a volcano. The view and experience were phenomenal.

The ladies had their fair share of shopping trips and buying souvenirs. Ms. J was having so much fun in the pool that she bought an extra swimsuit. Samantha complained about her weight gain, even though she never slowed down. They spent a week on each island and had just as much fun.

Royce enjoyed watching all the hotties roaming the beaches, having his extra fun after hours. Usually, he waited until his parents and Ms. J had gone to bed before he roamed and met up with various women. Boy, was he glad of the motorcycle and that he could come and go as he pleased. After the weekend trip in Dallas, he said he'd never have the same type of accommodations. There were several situations where he would have preferred the privacy of the pool in the backyard. However, it worked out for the best because he always left before they woke. Thankfully, neither his parents nor Ms. J cared that he spent some time away from them to explore without them. Adam never had a problem escorting the two ladies on shopping excursions and visiting museums that he didn't care to visit.

Royce decided after this Hawaiian trip, he wanted to travel solo. He'd applied for his passport weeks ago, wanting to go somewhere with plenty of beaches and half-naked women. Being in Hawaii gave him plenty of ideas. Now he wanted to get away without having to worry about anyone but himself. And arriving home to find his passport waiting was all he needed. Royce remembered his dream of being surrounded by beautiful women and crystal blue waters. He'd passed by many travel agencies and seen posters of beautiful islands in the Caribbean. Maybe that was where he needed to go.

The Caribbean consisted of many islands and many more activities that he could count. Now he just needed to decide which islands to visit and what he wanted to do when he got there. He wasn't sure how long he'd be gone, but there was one crucial task that required his attention.

The following day he kidnapped Ms. J and drove to a car dealership. She was under the impression that he was there to purchase a vehicle, and she was dropping him off. A salesman ran to them before they could get out of her car.

"Good morning, how can I help you today?"

"My grandmother needs a new car," Royce said, smiling and winking at her.

Ms. J almost fainted. "Ah, no, you don't. I don't think so, young man."

"Don't fight me on this. Either you pick out what you want, or I'll pick one for you. I'm going out of town for a little while. And I don't want to worry about you and this jalopy."

The salesman cleared his throat. "Um, what price range are we looking at?"

Royce did his best not to give him a dirty look. "We're not looking at a price range. We're looking for whatever she wants."

"Of course, sir, we can handle that."

The salesman asked them to walk into his office first, and he explained the various types and models. Then they'd go from there. After several hours of looking through brochures, walking around the lot, and doing some test driving, Ms. J settled on an XTS sedan. There were several colors currently on the lot. Royce gave her the option of choosing one of those models or ordering a different one. Ms. J was satisfied with the car and accessories already included. Royce removed her items from her old car, and they left the lot in a brand-new silver Cadillac.

Two weeks later, Royce left the city of Detroit on a plane headed to Jamaica. After doing more extensive research and visiting a travel agent, he selected an all-inclusive resort, wanting a suite with a view and access to the beach. Royce couldn't believe his accommodations when he walked in the door. The pictures and the description didn't do it justice. There was a king-size four-poster bed that he couldn't wait to try out. The best part of the room was the walk-out patio that opened right out to the beach. He felt like he could live like this forever. He spent plenty of time swimming, drinking, and eating whenever he felt hungry. Finding female companionship was easy. Jamaica was full of single women hanging out on the beaches. He'd toured the island, taken every excursion available, and used some benefits offered by the resort. After taking a scuba diving class, he fell in love. Two weeks later, he was bored with Jamaica.

The hotel boasted of other similar properties on various islands. He asked the concierge service to book him at one of their resorts in the Caymans, and they'd labeled him with VIP status. He flew out of Jamaica the next day. The resort in the Caymans had all the same water sport activities. So he tried some new water sports. He found that he wasn't a big fan of water skiing, but he enjoyed the Jet Skis and paddleboarding. During the week, he participated in some adventure tours, where he met a woman who was on vacation with her girlfriends. The Catamaran adventure included snorkeling at a nearby island and a beach party with Reggae music. They walked along the beach instead of listening and dancing to the music. He managed to get a quickie after they found a secluded spot behind some heavy foliage and exotic flowers. For the next two days of her vacation on the island, Royce wined and dined her.

Royce was rarely without a woman when he had a need. Leaving the Caymans, he decided to island-hop, spending a night or two on different islands. Eventually, he chose the next island of St Lucia. The suite was grander than the last one. This time, there was a soak tub on his patio. From the patio, there was access to his private lagoon.

After unpacking his bags, he headed to the beach, pulled off his muscle shirt, and dropped it on a lounge chair. Royce ran out into the beautiful blue waters; he dove and swam, thinking. This trip had been fun for him, he'd done things, learned things, and experienced things that only money could buy. However, he knew he couldn't live like this forever, didn't want to live like this. It was more important that he find something meaningful to fulfill his life.

Royce came out of the water and sat on the beach. It would be dark soon, and soft lights were illuminating behind him at the resort. He watched as the sun dipped from the sky to just above the waterline. He'd never had an appreciation of how the day turned into night.

Finally, all evidence of the sun disappeared, and the sounds of the ocean seem to change. The beach was tranquil, quite different than the daytime when it was full of people and children's laughter. He rested his head against his knees, listening for the first time to the sounds of the island. Behind him were voices, music, and laughter. A couple ran along the beach. He watched them play and tease each other. Eventually, they fell to the sand kissing, and he turned away.

At this moment, life didn't seem fair. He was charming, handsome, wealthy, and *lonely*. Of all the different women he'd encountered, he never remembered their names or even faces. And now he was tired. He hated being rude, but he told the women they had to leave his room on more than one occasion. It was the only reason he hated bringing women back to his room anyway.

There were too many issues that haunted him. One was his issues of waking up with women and playing house. He was only with them for the sex. He didn't care about snuggling or sitting across from them having a cup of coffee. Another one was that he wanted someone in his life, except he wasn't ready to commit to marriage. For tonight, maybe he could settle for someone to enjoy a meal with, or perhaps a sunrise after a night of sex. Leaving the beach, he sat at a table in a small restaurant and ordered a beer. It didn't take long for him to gain some attention.

Why were women so attracted to men with muscles? It seemed that this particular restaurant was full of tables and single women. Looking around, a lot of eyes were staring at him. He didn't know if he should run or stay, but he was hungry. They looked hungry for something too, and it wasn't food, he was on their menu. Soon enough, a waitress showed up, bringing him a menu; even she was no different from the rest, all of the time taking his order, she was licking her lips. He passed, opting to run and order room service.

Damn! That was the first time he'd turned down a chance at either a harem or an orgy. It had to be a sign. Perhaps, it was time to go home. Royce spent the next three days enjoying the comforts of his suite. He swam naked in his lagoon and ventured out to watch the sunsets.

After he started eating most of his meals on his patio and appreciating having a butler, waking each morning with the smell of fresh coffee brewing, he'd eat his breakfast and drink his coffee. He fell in love with the exotic coffee. The butler served lunch and dinner, making him feel like royalty. It made him want the same thing at home. He could have a private pool in the back yard of his mansion, several employees, seeing to his every need, Nah! Unfortunately, that was not his style. He loved his small place close to Ms. J.

Royce spent four months roaming, partying, and living the wildlife. He'd gotten it all out of his system by the time he returned home. It was time for serious business. He made an appointment with his financial adviser so that they could work on a plan. Royce wanted something that would be a money-making business. He needed it to be versatile, so if he wanted to partake in running the business or hire someone to do it. His adviser had given him several options for businesses. He didn't want to own stores to sell clothes, electronics, or video games. Royce told his adviser that he preferred to sleep on it and think it over.

The next morning, Royce woke early with a craving for some warm donuts. He bet Ms. J would love some donuts to go with her coffee. He dressed and jogged downstairs, thinking that he needed to get a vehicle. The garage was big enough for two. Later! He sat on his motorcycle, trying to decide where he wanted to go. The best donut shop was across town. Cranking up his Harley, he headed that way. Parking the bike, he took off his helmet. He'd forgotten it was next door to his old job. He wanted to be nosy and see if there was anybody that he knew still working there. The only benefit of working at a coffee shop was free coffee.

When he opened the door, the aroma attacked his nostrils. God, he loved the smell of coffee. He didn't recognize anyone behind the counter, but he did recognize the same machines that he'd learned to operate. Oh, my God! This business was what he wanted. He already knew how to run this business – well, most of it. He purchased a bag of coffee since he was standing there, probably looking like a crazy person. Rushing next door, he bought some donuts.

He knew Ms. J should be up by now and hoping that she hadn't made coffee yet. Using his key, he entered through the back door and found her in the kitchen. Asking her to have a seat, he waved the bag. She'd just put water in the coffee pot, and he added the Starbucks coffee grounds. He'd sat and drank coffee with her many times. So he knew how she liked her coffee. He put the donuts on the table and poured the coffee when it was ready.

"Ms. J, I think I know what I want to do with my life."

"You mean something, besides torturing your parents and me."

"Oh, stop fussing. I talked to all of you guys several times a week while I was traveling. I'm serious this time."

"Okay, I'm listening."

"I want to open my own Starbucks."

"Is that even possible?"

"I'm going to talk to my financial adviser about it today."

Ms. J thought he was finally heading down the right road. She'd talked with his parents several times during his traveling. She had been just as worried as they had. It wasn't because he was irresponsible. They were more worried that someone would figure out that he wasn't hurting for money. People do crazy things when it comes to money.

Royce walked into his financial adviser's office and told him about Starbucks and wanted to know how to buy a franchise. He knew they made a lot of money daily. His adviser nodded and told him that places like that could take a couple of years before seeing a return on his investment. Sooner if it was in a perfect location, this information gave Royce some ideas.

That evening when Royce got home, he sat at his small table and googled all the Starbucks in the city for their current locations. He saw the location of the store, where he previously worked. It was in a small strip mall. Looking at the icons, he didn't see one located inside of any malls. He didn't remember seeing one inside the building at the Ren Cen, either. That place should be a gold mine with all the businesses there. Next, he googled the Starbucks Corporation website, he wanted to see what information he could find out on his own. He already had a good understanding of how they operated. He'd ordered supplies, and he knew how to run all the machinery.

Royce was disappointed when he found out that he couldn't purchase a franchise. So he researched all his options. Starbucks wasn't the only company that sold coffee. But one thing he knew for sure was that people loved coffee. He sighed momentarily after reading about the popular donut franchises that sold coffee; however, he never envisaged himself focusing on donuts. After doing a little more reading, he found the perfect franchise that suited his taste.

The next morning, Royce made another trip to the Ren Cen building. He examined the board that displayed fast-food restaurants as well as a couple of fancy restaurants, a shopping center, a pharmacy, a movie theatre, everything but a coffee shop. He walked around all the different buildings looking for what services they provided. There were plenty of available spaces that he saw empty, so he made notes on his phone of potential areas big enough. Scanning the board, he searched for the management office that handled the leased spaces. Finding the office, he decided to make an impromptu visit. He knew he'd need the same amount of space as a full coffee business, neither was he ready for a drive-thru yet.

Royce introduced himself to the receptionist, asking if he could speak to someone about leasing an available space. A tall attractive brown skin woman came from the back. He smiled, and she sized him up, exhaling, and barely smiled. Royce hadn't come dressed for business, he was dressed casually in jeans and a tight-fitting shirt that detailed all his muscles.

"I'm Starla O'Neil, can I help you?" She didn't make any attempt to shake his hand, he noticed.

"Yes, I'm interested in leasing an available space." He said politely.

Ms. O'Neil looked him up and down again, she smirked. She did like the look of the package, but… She started her spiel, telling him that the cheapest leases they had were portable booths. He laughed to himself, the Bitch. He opened the note app on his phone and asked about several specific space numbers. She huffed, unlocking the screen on a tablet she held in her hand. Sliding her finger across the screen, she found what she sought. Quoting the lease price, she told him that those particular spaces could be remodeled to suit any type of business. She looked him in the face and told him that a deposit of twenty thousand dollars would be required when signing the lease.

Bobbing her head, she waited on his response. It was a look that said, 'Now I'm waiting for you to embarrass yourself.'

"I'll bring my attorney so he can review the lease. I'll see you again, Ms. O'Neil."

"Sure, you will." She said sarcastically and walked off.

Royce called his attorney and told him he'd found the perfect place to open his first coffee shop, asking him to start the paperwork. His life was about to change as a businessman. And now, he was going shopping for a new wardrobe, in an attempt to look the part.

He rode his motorcycle back to the same mall as before. When he walked into the men's department at Macy's, the salesman greeted him by name and smiled at him. Somebody knew how to treat people no matter what they were wearing. He asked the salesman to fit him with five new suits. Royce spent several hours in the store, purchasing dress slacks, shirts, ties, and new shoes. He told the salesman that he'd come back the next day to pick up all his items, there wasn't a need for rush alterations.

Royce left the mall and drove straight to the Cadillac dealership, asking for Fred Dawson, the salesman that helped Ms. J. Fred was pleasant enough and sucked up pretty well after he did a background check. Excitedly, Fred greeted him by name, and he liked that. Royce said he wanted to look at the SUV Escalades. The salesman showed him the models on the lot and the different accessories available. Royce liked several features that weren't all available on one vehicle. He and the salesman sat at the desk. Royce was able to custom order the SUV and the features he wanted; it would take a few weeks before it was ready. The salesman offered Royce the use of a vehicle while he waited on his SUV. He commented that he was on his bike and would pick it up the next day. Ms. J could drop him off, and that way, he could stop at the mall afterward.

Royce was waiting on some paperwork for the franchise before he could put down the deposit. He needed to be sure he had a business to open in that spot. It took a week before he received his paperwork. Royce Hawthorne was the proud owner of a *Gourmet Coffee House* franchise. He called his attorney in excitement, and they made an appointment to go to the Ren Cen together.

Starla O'Neil didn't recognize Royce when she walked from the back office.

"Ms. O'Neil, so nice to see you again," he said sarcastically.

"Excuse me, do I know you?"

He laughed. "Yes, Royce Hawthorne, I spoke with you in person about leasing an available space. I brought my attorney to look over the paperwork while someone shows me the space I'm interested in."

Her mouth flew open, OMG! It was the *sexy* package man. She couldn't believe he'd been serious. He looked *completely* different in a suit. "Yes . . . yes, I'm sorry, I didn't recognize you in clothes . . . I mean in a suit."

She opened the tablet in her hand, trying to remember the space they discussed. This inefficiency was very unprofessional of her. She hadn't thought about the sexy package or the particular availability since he walked out.

Royce realized that she had no idea which properties they'd discussed. He opened the app on his phone and repeated three different spaces he wanted to see. The attorney asked to view the standard lease agreement while they roamed around the building, Royce wished someone else would show him around, but that didn't happen. She rushed back to her office to retrieve some keys.

They left the office, and she showed him two of the spaces he'd requested, one of which had been leased already. She informed him of some other areas, but he was only interested in the food court. And he preferred the space closer to the end. He learned that when people were searching for something, in particular, they stopped at the place closest to them. If people wanted coffee, they would have to pass him first to get to other restaurants that sold coffee. But there were a lot of people who preferred gourmet coffee.

He walked throughout the building, picturing where all the equipment would go. There was a room in the back for an office and a nice size storeroom for supplies. Ms. O'Neil reminded him that the property could be changed to suit the tenant. She had no idea what he wanted to use it for yet. Flirting with him slightly, Starla tried to coax information out of him. She didn't see a ring on his finger, but that didn't mean he didn't have a wife or a girlfriend. Royce did his best to ignore her without being rude. He already had her number, and she didn't get interested until she knew he had some money in his pocket—a gold digger. Turning in her direction, he said he was ready to sign if his attorney didn't have any lease agreement issues.

They returned to the office, and Royce conversed with his attorney. Royce signed the lease agreement twenty minutes later and handed Ms. O'Neil a cashier's check. She read over the contract; his company name was simple, Hawthorne Incorporated. She wondered if he had other businesses as well. He listed Gourmet Coffee House, aka GCH, as the business occupying the leased space.

Four months later, he opened his first coffee shop. He'd spent some time at the franchise headquarters learning how to run and operate his business. Being the owner, he trained in all aspects of the company. He wanted to keep busy, so he used the title of general manager. There was no reason he had to let his staff know his actual title. This way, he could do all the hiring and firing.

It took him a moment to get his feet wet and make his business run smoothly. He wasn't about to give up. Although he had to deal with Ms. O'Neil, who decided that GCH was the only place she wanted to get her coffee.

Chapter Seven

$\mathcal{R}$oyce stood at the front of the coffee shop, making sure that everything was running smoothly. He observed customers placing orders and the staff preparing them with precision and pleasant attitudes. He couldn't be happier with the decision to own this type of business. The business offered everything he wished for. A noise in the courtyard caught his attention, and if he hadn't looked down, he would have missed seeing a cute little girl with big beautiful eyes waddled up and wrapped her arms around his leg. She didn't reach his knee, but she looked up and said, "Da . . . ddy."

There was no doubt in his mind that this child didn't belong to him, for several obvious reasons. He'd always practiced safe sex; he looked around and didn't see any screaming mothers barreling down on him. So, he picked her up.

"Well, cutie, where is your mother?"

The little girl laid her head on his shoulder and played with his beard. He stepped outside of the GCH, looking left and right. There were quite a few people in the food court area. He realized that a mother hadn't realized her child was missing yet. He started walking, looking for any signs of a frantic mother. He could call security, but he figured the child's mother would probably show up before they got here. Maybe she got separated from her sister or a brother. He called out.

"Hello, is anybody missing a little girl?"

He only received some crazy stares and shaking of heads. People went right back to what they were doing. God, he hated to call the police. What if someone just left her, abandoned her. She was so tiny. Having no experience with children, he didn't even know how old she was. So he kept walking around the food court, hoping that a family member would recognize her. Royce called out again when he got to the other side. Still, no one came to claim the little girl. He was holding her with one arm up against his chest. She laid on him comfortably, like she knew she was safe, protected. Royce had almost completed the circle and was on his way back to his business. He heard her before he saw her. A mother was screaming. He tightened his grip on the little girl and took off, running toward the noise.

"Ma'am . . . ma'am, excuse me. Is this your little girl?" He shouted to get her to stop shrieking.

Now the whole food court was paying attention. She grabbed her from his arms, crying.

"It's okay. I found your daughter, or more like, she found me. She wandered into the coffee shop."

The little girl was hugging her mother but reaching for Royce and still calling him her version of daddy.

"Marguerite that is not your daddy, your daddy isn't with us anymore." She talked to her daughter as if she understood everything she was saying.

She turned her attention to Royce and got a good look at him. Her eyes glazed over momentarily as she raked over his physique. She blushed and stuttered. "Thank . . . thank you. I was next door filling out an application, and she got out of her stroller."

"You're looking for a job?"

"Yes." She said embarrassed, losing the half-smile she had a moment ago.

"When you've completed your other application, come to Gourmet Coffee and fill out one. I know the manager."

"Okay, I'll do that." Her smile got a little bigger.

Marguerite squirmed in her arms and tried to get to Royce. Her mother put her in the stroller, and she screamed bloody murder.

"Marguerite, please stop screaming, mommy has to fill out this paperwork."

Marguerite screamed for Royce, continuing to call him daddy. People were staring and looking at him. He felt they thought he didn't want his child. Squatting down in front of Marguerite, he called her by her name. She stopped crying and gave him the saddest look that broke his heart. He couldn't resist her big wet tears. Royce pushed on the buckles until he figured out how to get her out of the stroller. She threw her little arms around his neck.

"We'll be at the Gourmet Coffee House when you finish. I promise she's safe."

"I know." She told him honestly.

Royce and Marguerite walked back to the coffee shop. All the employees were staring at him when he walked back in, holding the little girl. He sat her on the counter and introduced her to everyone. The employees were just as smitten as he was. One of the employees asked if she was hungry. Shaking his head, he had no idea and told the employee that her mother would be there in a few minutes. Heading back to his office, he sat her in his lap. He didn't know what to do with kids. Was he supposed to talk to her? Her mother conversed with her. He wanted to know what her mother meant when she said that Marguerite's dad wasn't with them anymore. Was he dead, or did he leave? If he left, how could a man walk out on this beautiful baby?

"Marguerite, what happened to your daddy?" He whispered, asking her as if she could answer.

She wasn't paying him any attention. Marguerite was trying to grab a pen off the desk. She stretched until she grabbed it and headed straight to her mouth with it. He took the pen and put it out of her reach, telling her he didn't think she was supposed to put it in her mouth. He looked around on his desk for something she could play with, but there was nothing. Thinking about her mother, "was she looking for a job because she was now a single parent? Could he hire her now? It would be several more months before his other store was ready. He could hire her for that location, but it was way across town. Does she have transportation, or was she using public? He didn't think she could wait for months if she needed a job now." He was thinking hard when Toby knocked on his door.

"I think Marguerite's mother is looking for you."

"Bring her back here, Toby."

Toby escorted her to the office, and Royce stood like a gentleman, pointing to a chair next to his desk.

"You're the manager?" She asked, surprised.

"Yes. I am Royce Hawthorne."

"I'm . . . my name is Rosita Rodriquez, and you already met my baby Marguerite."

Royce smiled at her nervousness. He didn't know if she was just nervous about finding out he was the manager or the fact that she'd been checking him out a moment ago. Clearing his throat, he asked her about filling out an application. She nodded, in acceptance. There were so many other questions, but he didn't dare. He pulled a generic application form from a pad on his desk. Marguerite continued to squirm in his lap. Rosita said she would take her. Holding her tighter, he told her that wasn't necessary. Royce asked how old she was and found out that she would be two years old in a few months. He asked Rosita if she was hungry because she kept trying to put everything in her mouth. Rosita laughed and told him all babies do that. But they had been out most of the day. She held her head down, saying that she'd been applying for jobs all day.

"Would you mind if I give her something to eat while you fill out the application?"

"Oh no, you don't have to do that. We'll get something from McDonald's when I get finished here."

"Please, let me. You sit there and fill out that application. We'll go to Subway. Can she eat a sandwich?"

"Mr. Hawthorne, you know nothing about children, do you?"

"Nope, I don't have any children. But I think Marguerite is about to teach me. Would you like a cup of coffee?"

"She can eat the sandwich as long as it's broken into small pieces. And yes, a cup of coffee would be nice. You are a very kind man, Mr. Hawthorne."

Toby knocked on his door again. "Excuse me, Mr. H., but the wicked bi . . . witch is outside. She wants to speak to you and complain as usual."

"I'll be right out, Toby. Can you bring Ms. Rodriquez a cup of coffee, please?"

Royce exhaled. He told Rosita to complete the form, and they'd be back. Propping Marguerite against his chest, they left the office. He walked out front, and she started ranting as soon as she saw his form emerging from the back. She stopped talking when she saw that he was holding a small child in his arms.

"Ms. O'Neil, what is the problem today?"

She looked back and forth at the small child and him. "Is she yours? I didn't know you had children." She asked snidely.

And Marguerite responded just in time to call him daddy. The shocked look on her face was priceless.

"My personal life is none of your concern. Is there a problem with your order?" He asked rudely.

He hated being rude to customers. Except Starla O'Neil was a true bitch. She'd treated him like shit the first time she met him; ever since he showed up with his attorney and a fat check to lease the space, she'd been all over him. Can you say shallow?

"No, not this time, I just needed an excuse to see you. I'm still waiting for that dinner invitation."

He kissed Marguerite on her temple and hugged her tightly. God, he was glad this little girl walked into his life. Maybe now he could be done with Starla O'Neil for good.

"That's never going to happen. You have a good day Ms. O'Neil."

Royce left holding Marguerite in the crook of his arm. He felt her leaning over and looking back. He felt her hand move from his arm. Did she wave goodbye at that woman? He hoped she did. He hated using Marguerite to make Starla think he wasn't available. The woman wouldn't take no for an answer. She used every trick in the book to seek him out and abuse his employees.

Starla watched his retreating back, and his child had the nerve to wave at her. She didn't even look like him. The little girl looked interracial, maybe half-white with gray eyes. Royce's eyes were black. She must look like her mother. Perhaps, that was why he didn't like her. He preferred white women. Huh! She should have known; he didn't think black women were good enough for his money. Well, the bitch would show up one day. And she hoped she'd be around. She left, smiling devilishly behind her coffee cup.

Royce stood in line at Subway, looking at the menu board. What could a small child eat? He scanned over the kid's menu. Marguerite was so little and thin. He wondered if she was eating healthy, or if all children this age were the same size. Nah! He'd seen some fat babies before, and Rosita, looked like she could gain some weight too. He liked his women with meat on their bones. Damn! Why did he have that thought? He wanted to give her a job and help her out, but that was all. He liked his life simple and uncomplicated. Visiting Haley was always an option. Maybe he'd open a GCH in Ohio, giving him another reason to have to visit. He lost all his thoughts when the employee asked him for his order.

Looking at the menu, he ordered two different kid's meals for Marguerite, and some extra milk and juices. He figured she would have something to eat for tonight. Then he ordered a couple of sandwiches for Rosita. Maybe if he fed her, she might tell him what happened to Marguerite's dad. Too bad there wasn't a toy store in the building. Considering that he owed her something special since she helped to get rid of Starla. How was it possible that this little girl had gotten under his skin, so quickly?

Royce and Marguerite returned to his office. Rosita was still filling out the form, so he pulled the milk bottle and a sandwich from her kid pack. Sitting Marguerite on his desk, he broke a small piece of the sandwich, holding it in his hand. He didn't know if he needed to feed her or if she could feed herself. Rosita looked up and saw the confused look on his face. She told him to put it in her hand, and she would put it in her mouth.

Rosita pulled a worn-lidded cup from her bag, pouring milk into it for Marguerite. Royce noticed it had been empty and dry. The baby drank almost half the cup before pulling it away from her mouth. He repeated the steps of breaking the sandwich until she'd eaten nearly all of it. The poor baby had been hungry. He knew he had to hire Rosita.

Rosita finished the form and pushed it toward him. He passed her the other bag from Subway and told her to eat, while he looked over her application. Reading over her form, he learned that she was almost twenty-two, and she lived in Black Bottom. He recognized the street name. It was only a few blocks from his old place. She didn't have a lot of work experience, but she was a high school graduate and she completed a Medical Assistant program at a Technical College. He made a note with a question mark. Her phone number had a comment of a friend in parentheses, putting a notation there as well. She answered the criminal and drug questions with *no*. That was good, but he still had to do a background check, and she listed three references for him to verify her character.

Royce peeped down at Marguerite, who had fallen asleep in his arm. She was a beautiful baby, apparently a baby without a father. Rosita had finished her sandwich and drank a bottle of water. Royce asked her if she was ready to answer some questions for him. She looked astonished because she didn't expect him to do this today. Usually, people would tell her that they'd call her.

"Sure," she answered nervously.

"I see you completed a medical course. Why aren't you working in that field?"

"I'm deathly afraid of needles, and . . . blood. I thought I'd be helping people get in and out of beds. I don't want to have to touch needles."

Royce made a note on her application. "Is this a cell number or a landline that belongs to a friend?"

"It's a cell number. It belongs to my friend Alejandra that I live with." She was speaking low and dropping her head by the time she finished her sentence. "I don't have a phone."

"Okay." He answered and made another notation on her application.

He didn't need to ask if she had transportation, he doubted it. Now he wondered if she would have someone to watch Marguerite when she worked.

"I know this is a little unorthodox to ask, but do you have a babysitter for your daughter if you get a job?"

"Yes . . . yes, there's a woman in the neighborhood that keeps children in her home."

"I have some positions coming up. I'll be managing another store that is opening closer to your home. You could train here at this location for a few weeks. But I will need to do a background check and check your references."

"Oh, really, are you serious? You're going to give me a job?"

"Yes, Miss. It's Miss, or is it Mrs.?"

"It's Miss. I'm not married."

"Yes, Ms. Rodriquez, I will hire you if everything comes back clean, and you will have to submit to a drug test."

"No problem, I don't do drugs."

"You should hear from me in about a week. I think you should take Marguerite home while she's sleeping." He laughed.

Marguerite had gotten attached to him for some reason. She kept calling him daddy, or did she call every man daddy? And he was sure that if she weren't sleeping, she'd cause another disturbance. Royce kissed Marguerite one last time and put her in the stroller. He helped Rosita pack up her leftover food, sneaking several bottles of juice in Marguerite's baby bag. Passing her a business card, Royce reminded her to call him if she didn't hear from him in a week. He'd be busy working at the other location.

Royce put a rush request on Rosita's criminal background check. He wanted to hire her as soon as possible if her background was clean. Next, he contacted the references that she listed on her application. Surprisingly, the last person on the form had been Rosita's foster parent. Each of her contacts had only high praise for Rosita. She was a sweet and kind person. She never caused any problems, and she'd done well in school. Royce was pleased to hear of her characteristics.

Now he had to wait on the rest. He'd made several trips back and forth to the new location across town. Everything was on schedule. This location was much bigger and had a drive-thru. He knew he'd be spending more time there, and he was trusting Toby to take care of his first location since he'd been training him as an assistant manager.

The information on Rosita's criminal background check came back clean with no arrests. Royce almost became alarmed because he called the number she provided. His calls were unanswered for a couple of days and he wondered if her friend was leery of answering unknown numbers. Finally, after leaving a message that he was making a visit to her address to talk to Rosita about the job, Rosita called him within the hour. Maybe her friend was just frightened enough to give her the message.

Royce informed her that as soon as he received results from her drug screen, she could start her training. Before he continued, he asked her to call him in the next 48-hours, just in case her friend didn't answer his calls again. Using the call as an excuse, he asked about Marguerite. Rosita was more excited about starting a new job, and hopefully a new life for her and her daughter. Eagerly, she said that Marguerite was doing wonderful, but she didn't divulge the full truth.

While Royce waited on the final results for Rosita, he thought of Marguerite every day. He worked hard toward the opening of his new location. So much that every late evening when he got home, Ms. J made sure that he had a hot meal. It was funny because, in their conversations, she was still enjoying the new car smell. The joke was funny because he didn't still have that new car smell in his truck. Royce knew it was her way of saying thank you for the car.

It took almost three weeks before Rosita began her training at the coffee shop from the day her daughter attached herself to the manager. She didn't dare tell him that Marguerite cried herself to sleep every night for a week calling for her daddy. Rosita didn't know why she was calling out to a man that wasn't her father.

Rosita had been training for a week, and she hadn't seen Royce once, wanting to thank him again for giving her the opportunity. She knew it would still be a while before she was entirely on her own two feet. It was becoming unbearable to continue living at Alejandra's without a job. Now she could help to pay some bills and try and save money. Having a place of her very own was her ultimate dream. At the moment, she and Marguerite were sleeping on the couch. The apartment was small, and Alejandra had two children of her own and a boyfriend that came and went.

Royce was so busy trying to get the new location ready that he hadn't had time to go by the other store. There were a few complications that he had to tend to personally. Considering he was the owner/manager. He'd owned his first coffee shop and learned how to run it smoothly before opening another one. His primary location had done so well that he saw a return on his investment in less than one year. Now two years later, he was opening his second location and on the prowl for more.

Rosita was at the beginning of her third week of training when she saw Royce. For the first time, she was late for her shift by thirty minutes. Toby was talking to her about it when Royce walked into the office. She was explaining to Toby that Marguerite had been sick during the night and had thrown up on her uniform right before they were leaving the house. After changing, she had to take her to the babysitters and catch the bus for work. Rosita admitted that she didn't have a phone to call and let them know that she'd be late. And she promised it would never happen again. Royce didn't interfere, because Toby was doing his job of chastising the employee. When they finished, their discussion Royce spoke to both of them and asked Rosita about Marguerite. Rosita mumbled that she was fine and rushed from the room.

"How is she doing?" Royce asked.

"She is doing very well, and she catches on fast. And the wicked witch has only berated her twice."

"I was hoping she'd start getting her coffee at McDonald's." Royce joked.

"I saw what you did. You let the witch think Marguerite was your daughter, smart man."

"Apparently, it didn't work as well as I wished. It hasn't stopped that crazy woman from harassing me."

"Well, Rosita is a hard worker. I think she'll do well at the new location."

"Thanks, Toby. I hope having an extra person didn't add too much work for you."

"It was okay. I think I know why you did it. Marguerite is too cute."

Toby left Royce to do some paperwork. Damn! Was he that obvious giving Rosita a job? They were all cooing over Marguerite, except she was stuck on Royce. He hoped she was okay. Then he started to wonder if she needed to go to a doctor. She said that Marguerite was throwing up, that can't be good.

Royce stood in the doorway behind the counter. He wanted to watch Rosita interact with the customers. She always smiled when taking their orders and repeated the request before punching it into the electronic cash register. It had taken him weeks to figure out that machine. Rosita was personable and seemed to be liked by the customers. And he noticed that she always thanked them for their business. He observed her for most of the day. She went about her tasks without being told what to do. She kept the counters clean and even walked out front and wiped off the tables when she didn't have customers. He nodded his head he'd made a good decision to hire her.

Two months later, his second location was open. He'd spent a lot of time hiring new staff and training them at the new site. Because Rosita had become so efficient, he allowed her to help with additional training at the new location before the official opening. He mixed in his staff between the two locations. He was so pleased with Rosita that he was thinking hard about giving her a leadership position at the newest location.

Chapter Eight

Royce thought of Marguerite often and asked about her. He remembered Rosita saying that she had a birthday coming up the first day they met. He still wanted to do something kind for Marguerite. Rosita told him her birthday was in two weeks.

Royce wanted to surprise them both. He checked over the schedule and made sure she had a morning shift that day. He called Toby and asked him if he would close that night since the other location closed a lot earlier. That was one of the things he liked about that location. The primary Gourmet Coffee House was inside a business center. On a typical day, the manager could be home by seven unless he stayed to do paperwork. The new location, which was on a busy street, was open until 10 pm every night. He was trying to decide who he wanted to train as an assistant manager. Several employees had been working for him now for two years. He hoped Rosita planned to be around. She'd be a good one to train in a year or so. His thoughts drifted of having a small place with an all-night drive-thru in the club district because party-goers love coffee late at night.

Three days before Marguerite's birthday, Royce announced that he was taking them out for her birthday.

"Oh, Mr. Hawthorne, you don't have to do that."

"I want to do it. Anyway, I haven't seen Marguerite in a while unless you already have plans with your family."

"I don't have any family, and don't you have to work?"

"I asked Toby to close for me. I haven't had a night off in a while, so this will be good for me."

"You want to spend your one night off with a two-year-old?"

"Yes, I do. I owe Marguerite a present. By the way, what do two-year-old little girls like?"

"Dolls . . . little girls like dolls." Rosita laughed and walked out of his office. She wondered what he meant that he owed her a present.

"Dolls?" Royce exhaled.

As soon as Royce closed that night, he found the closest store that sold toys. He walked up and down the aisles until he found one with some dolls. His eyes got big because there were rows and rows of dolls, all shapes, sizes, and colors. It was overwhelming. Shopping for a doll was way out of his expertise. He found an associate and asked which doll a two-year child would want. She started asking him questions, and he didn't have any answers. She suggested buying a gift card and letting the child or the mother select one. He didn't want to buy a stupid gift card. He wanted to give her a wrapped present and watch her rip open the paper.

Remembering his childhood, he remembered how much fun it was when his parents gave him presents. Walking around, he looked for something that she would hopefully like. Royce ended up walking down an aisle with stuffed animals. He looked at some giant stuffed animals, which were too big. He was worried that Marguerite might smother herself, she was so little. Then he saw a teddy bear dressed as a princess, thinking that every little girl should get to be a princess. He had a new idea, grabbing the teddy bear, he headed to the register. Forking over his credit card, he asked the associate to gift wrap it.

On the day of the birthday party, Royce was at the store early to open up. Rosita was the first employee to arrive. She set up the machines so they could open at 6 a.m. Royce watched her through the glass window from the back. She seemed happier, and he hoped it was because she knew Marguerite would have a wonderful birthday. Rosita always had a smile at work. He wondered if she had that same smile at home after work. He didn't doubt that she was trying to be a good mother. His thoughts still wondered what happened to Marguerite's father. Rosita smiled at work, but there was sadness in her eyes.

Around midday, Rosita found Royce in the office. "Where will Marguerite be celebrating her birthday?"

"I hope she likes Chuck-E-Cheese. I heard it's the best place for children."

"She's never been there, so I don't know if she'll like it. Before I forget, I want to thank you for doing this. We were going to share a cupcake."

Royce remembered seeing his baby pictures, and his mother always let him have a cake of his own to make a mess. "Don't forget to bring your camera."

"I don't own a camera. Why?"

"I was just thinking about something from my childhood."

Royce made a mental note about his extra surprise for Marguerite and now one for Rosita. Every parent should have mementos of their children growing up.

"I'll pick you up around six."

"Can't we meet you there?"

"No, I don't want you riding a bus and walking." God knows how far she'd have to walk just to get there. "Besides, we have a stop to make before going to Chuck-E-Cheese."

"What are you up to, Mr. Hawthorne?" She didn't have a car seat and was too embarrassed to tell him. She only owned the cheap umbrella stroller. She'd never needed a car seat.

"Nothing, I just want Marguerite to have a wonderful birthday." He smiled at Rosita.

"Now, don't you have some work to do before you get off?"

Rosita walked out of his office, confused. Why was her boss so nice? She hoped he didn't want a favor in return. She was so tired of untrusting men.

The last man had left her high and dry the moment he found out she was pregnant. He threw money at her and told her to get an abortion after admitting that he had a wife and a family. An abortion was out of the question, so she quit her job and hid from him.

Rosita tried one last time after Marguerite was born. She called him and told him that he had a daughter. He was furious because he thought she'd had an abortion. Marguerite's father, whom she now referred to as *M.F.*, threatened both their lives. And the *M.F.* initials didn't mean Marguerite's father; she never wanted her daughter to hear her say, *"Mother Fucker!"* Rosita left California that same day. She bought a bus ticket for the farthest place her money would buy.

She slept on the streets for three days until she heard about a shelter for displaced women. The shelter helped women get on their feet. It was at the shelter where she heard about the school and its programs. There was a daycare at the shelter that kept Marguerite while she was at school. There, she met Alejandra. They seemed to hit it off immediately, or she was one of the few students with Mexican ancestry.

Although Rosita had grown up in California, her mother had been Mexican, and her father was African American. Her mother died from an overdose of drugs, and she never knew her father. She was ten when she went to her first foster home. Most people said that she was lucky that she only lived in three different foster homes.

After turning eighteen and graduating from high school, her foster parents said it was time to search for her first job. Rosita worked at a couple of fast-food places until she got a full-time job at a late-night diner waiting tables. She'd been working for a few months, and this was where she met Marguerite's father. He came in two or three times a week, always sitting in her section. He'd order coffee, sometimes food, and left a fat tip.

Soon he started pursuing her by telling her how beautiful she was. He'd touch her legs when she passed his table. Then one night, she was sitting alone by the back door on a break. He sat with her talking sweetly, telling her how much he liked her. It was the first time he kissed her. He baited her in slowly.

Rosita should have known better after months of him toying with her, teasing her in the back of the building. That's what you get for being naïve. He asked her to sit in his car with him. The first time he fingered her, making her climax for the first time in her life, and he masturbated while she watched.

Weeks later, he asked her for oral sex and every time she obliged, he left her fat tips. He did this for months until one night he came into the restaurant and sat in another waitress's section, making Rosita jealous. He touched her on the leg the same way. Rosita pouted all evening, but she never approached him.

When it was time for her break, she stormed out the back door. She was so upset with M.F. because he made her feel things for him. How could he just move on to the next woman, she thought he liked her? She had tears in her eyes, crying. She was crying so hard that she didn't hear him approach. He touched her face, and she opened her eyes.

"Did you miss me, Rosita? Do you want me?"

She wiped her face and looked at him. "Yes, you know I want you. I want you to touch only me."

"Then, after tonight, I will only touch you." He led her to his car, opening the door to the back seat.

Sliding in the seat next to her, he began his ritual of making her climax. He pushed his pants down his legs and rolled a condom on his erect penis. Rosita mounted him willingly, and he took her virginity. She didn't care that she never saw him outside of his late-night visits to the diner, and it never dawned on her to ask questions. The only number she had was his work number, and she rarely called him on that.

Rosita thought she was in a perfect relationship and that she was with a man that loved her very much. Until one night, some truckers came into the diner and sat in her section. They made derogatory sexual comments and rubbed their crotches in front of her. She saw him as soon as he entered the diner, telling him what they said. He sat in his booth and didn't respond to her words, and she thought he smelled like liquor.

Walking away fast, she realized he wasn't going to defend her honor. She went about her regular duties trying to ignore the truckers. They kept beckoning for her to return to their table, and she got in trouble with her boss because they complained. Unwillingly, she went back to their table. One trucker was asking how much for a good time, and another one grabbed her butt. Hitting his hand, she knocked it away. She let them know that she wasn't for sale and that she wasn't that type of girl.

That was when he walked up. The man she thought loved her. He asked the men how much money they had, and that he'd let them fuck her for the right price. Rosita ran out of the diner. How dare he try to sell her to some other men? Is that what he thought of her? She wasn't a prostitute, except she'd been accepting his money, his large tips. Hearing him calling her name, she tried to hide behind the cars. Shouting for her, he said he was sorry and that he loved her. He shouted across the parking lot that he wanted her and needed her.

Believing him, she stood so he could see her. He opened his arms for her, and stupidly she ran right into them. When she reached him, she asked him to repeat what he said. He whispered in her ear that he loved her and wanted her. Grabbing her hand, he rubbed his crotch so she could feel his hard cock.

They walked back to his car, and this time he pushed down his pants and pushed her panties to the side. He pushed her body to lean against the hood. Rosita didn't know he hadn't put on a condom until he was deep inside her. She squirmed against him, begging him to stop. He put his hand between her legs rubbing on her, exciting her, making her want him. She moaned and begged him for more.

Covering her mouth with his hand, he kept her from screaming out her release. He thrust deeper and grunted his release. He whispered in her ear that he liked fucking her without a condom. She knew then that he was drunk and holding her head down in shame. Rosita hated herself for giving in to him. She wasn't dumb enough to realize that she didn't want to get pregnant. It was an easy decision that night, and continuing the relationship was out of the question.

She'd seen enough romantic movies to know that she deserved a man who would treat her like a woman with respect. Hell, he'd never even taken her to a motel.

Rosita was glad that she hadn't seen him in weeks. He left the restaurant so fast that night that she didn't get a chance to tell him that she didn't want to see him anymore. Although she felt lonely and depressed, she wondered if this was what a broken heart felt like.

Another month went by, and he was still a no-show. Night after night, she watched and waited for him to walk in the door. One morning she woke up feeling sick to her stomach, throwing up violently. Then she thought she'd be sick all over again. She realized she hadn't had her period in over two months. Collapsing to her floor, she woke up an hour later. First, she cried, knowing that her life would never be the same.

The last time a man had been nice to her didn't end so well. She wasn't going to fall into that same trap again. She'd keep this one at arm's length. Marguerite deserved a wonderful birthday, and this day was for Marguerite.

Chapter Nine

$\mathcal{R}$osita didn't dare let him see the apartment where she lived, neither did she want him knocking at the door. So she was waiting on the sidewalk when a gray Escalade stopped next to her. Marguerite was sitting in her stroller. Her first thought was that she couldn't get in this expensive luxury vehicle; what if Marguerite threw up again. He might put them both out.

"Why are you standing outside? I would have knocked on the door." But, he'd forgotten to ask the apartment number, anyway.

"Oh, no reason, it's okay." She held her head down again.

Damn! Royce had a fleeting thought and realized that she didn't want him to see where she lived. He would respect her and not say anything else.

"Did I tell you that I used to have a place a few blocks away?" He said, trying to make her feel better.

"Really, you used to live in Black Bottom?" Her head bounced up.

He nodded. "Where is the car seat? I think small children are supposed to ride in those."

"I don't have one. We always ride the bus."

"It's okay. You can buckle Marguerite in the back seat and sit with her. Is that okay with you?"

Rosita nodded, "yes," and Royce opened the back door. Rosita took Marguerite out of the stroller, sat her in the middle, and buckled the seat belt. She sat next to her and buckled her own. Royce put the stroller in the back of the SUV after Rosita told him how to fold it. He jumped in the driver's seat and looked in the rearview mirror. Rosita was looking around the vehicle like she was scared. He saw her rubbing the leather seats. Turning his head around, he looked at Marguerite, smiling. She looked at him with her big smiling eyes.

She yelled, "Da . . . dddy."

"Hello Marguerite, you remember me?" He asked, bubbling. She did remember him. "You guys ready back there?" He asked, cranking up the truck.

Royce drove, making small talk trying to alleviate Rosita's fears. She admitted that she didn't want Marguerite to mess up his truck. He assured her that it was only a truck. If anything happened, it cleans up easily. He began wondering if Marguerite was still sick and throwing up. Rosita hadn't mentioned it, and he needed to find a way to ask without sounding nosy.

Soon, Royce pulled into the store's parking lot, and Rosita was forced to ask, "I thought we were going to Chuck-E-Cheese?"

"We are, but Marguerite needs something, and I don't know her size."

"Her size . . . what does that have to do with going to Chuck-E-Cheese?"

"Would you please stop worrying and let me have some fun on my day off."

Royce got out of the truck and opened the back door. He was glad he put the child lock on because she was yanking on the door, and he wanted to be a gentleman. Marguerite was trying to escape her seat belt, reaching for Royce and calling to him. Rosita passed her out the door to him. She'd never seen Marguerite act like this before to any person and especially a strange man. She hoped she wasn't making a big mistake by letting her daughter latch onto her boss. Rosita tried to take Marguerite and sit her in the buggy, but the little girl refused; she'd never refused her before. Marguerite tightened her grip around his neck. Royce laughed and hunched his shoulders.

"It's okay, Rosita, but we do need a buggy."

Royce led the way, stopping in front of the princess dresses. "Marguerite is going to be a princess today for her birthday." He squatted so she could touch the pretty dresses.

"Marguerite, which princess would you like to be?" He said with all the emotions he could muster. He didn't know if he would ever get this chance again, wanting her birthday magical.

Marguerite looked at him, and she looked at her mother. Rosita had tears in her eyes. Here was a stranger that wasn't even her father and making her daughter feel special. She repeated Royce's words, picking up the first dress and putting it in front of her. Marguerite shook her head from side to side. Rosita asked again with the same question.

Rosita wondered if she didn't want to be a princess. She hadn't ever seen any of these characters. The aisle displayed eleven different Disney princesses. She pulled two more dresses from the rack, and Marguerite said no for the third time. Marguerite touched Royce's arm and said, "Dog."

Rosita hadn't ever noticed the tattoo on his arm. He wore long sleeve shirts at work. She stared at a wolf howling and then noticed there was another partial tattoo on his other arm. It was the first time that she noticed his massive biceps, and she swallowed. He was squatting next to Marguerite, pointing at the other dresses. He took a costume of Pocahontas off the rack, and she squealed. She grabbed it and hugged it close to her body like it was a doll.

"I think I found what she likes. Can you check to see if it's the right size?"

Rosita talked to Marguerite and told her the dress was pretty while she distracted her, looking at the size tag. In doing this, she saw the price tag and shook her head.

"Mr. Hawthorne, this is too much. Do you know what this dress costs?

"No, I don't. It doesn't matter. Marguerite can have whatever she wants." Royce wanted her to have a dress and look like a real princess. He spotted a green dress with a tiara, pulling it from the rack, he continued. "Marguerite, don't you want two dresses? This one has a crown."

Marguerite shook her head yes and hugged it as well. Royce grinned. Rosita disagreed, but she was helpless in this situation, so she just shook her head in disagreement.

Royce looked at the dress in the buggy at the tag to see what size it was. Then he found the same green dress size and a package of accessories that went with it.

They'd walked to the end of the aisle when he saw all the Disney movies. He grabbed both the DVDs of the princesses Marguerite had chosen. He thought it was a good idea that she could watch the films.

"We don't have anything to watch a movie on, Mr. Hawthorne."

Royce stopped and looked her in the face. "Can you please not call me Mr. Hawthorne tonight? Call me Royce or Roy, but not Mr. Hawthorne. We're not at work."

Royce held Marguerite in his arms and pushed the buggy leaving Rosita staring at him from behind. He headed straight to the doll aisle. Rosita said every little girl liked dolls, and he hadn't gotten her one. She could pick out the one she wanted. He put her down on the floor so she could see all the different dolls.

Marguerite touched box after box. Royce looked at his watch. She stopped in front of a box and examined the doll by touching its face and squeezing the hand. Royce could tell that the doll was soft and half her size. There were many dolls all dressed up. Marguerite looked at her mom, and then she looked at Royce. She looked back at a couple of dolls like she was confused. Royce squatted next to her.

"Which doll do you want, Marguerite? You can have whatever you want."

Marguerite touched his face, and then she felt the face of the doll. Royce had no idea what she was doing. He wondered what such a small child could be thinking. Her skin was much lighter than her mother's, so he figured that her father must have been white. But he wasn't one to judge people, nor did he care what color her mother or father was. Marguerite was playing with a doll that was closer to his skin tone. He picked up the doll and held it up beside his face.

"Is this the doll you want? I think she is just as beautiful as you are." She smiled at him as if she understood. She reached for the doll and called him daddy again.

"Come on, sweetheart, we need to get a couple more items before we leave the store."

Now Royce was walking around, holding Marguerite while she held the box with her doll. Royce looked for the electronic section. He found a portable DVD player that Marguerite could watch her movies on and grabbed a pair of kid headphones for her.

The last stop Royce made was on the aisle with children's car seats. He didn't care about getting a ticket, but he wanted Marguerite to be safe in his vehicle. Rosita wasn't any help, so he asked an associate. The associate asked her age and made a suggestion. He explained how the seat changed to fit the child until they were older. Rosita was having fits about the money he was spending. Royce justified the purchase, saying that a ticket would cost him more than a car seat if he got stopped by the police. He grabbed the big box off the shelf and laid it across the top of the buggy.

He looked at his watch again. "Come on, or we'll be late." He said, trying to hold Marguerite, who was still holding her doll, while he pushed the buggy.

"Be late for what? I thought Chuck-E-Cheese was open until 10 p.m.

"It's a surprise. You can change Marguerite into her green dress in the truck."

Marguerite was so happy holding her doll that she didn't realize Royce put her in the buggy. He went over his mental list to make sure that he hadn't forgotten anything, and couldn't just remember anything. Shopping with a two-year-old was mentally draining. He couldn't imagine what kind of fun or drama he'd have for the rest of the night. Pushing the buggy to the register, he unloaded everything onto the conveyor belt. The cashier started scanning the items, but Marguerite wouldn't let her doll off her tiny grip. The cashier laughed and said, "No problem." Royce's phone rang, and he looked at the ID and answered it quickly. Rosita heard one side of his conversation.

"Yes . . . yes . . . yes . . . fifteen minutes." He hung up the phone.

Still trying hard to remember the list and couldn't. He saw a rack of gift cards next to the register. Rosita was probably going to have another fit. She was looking in another direction. So he grabbed a pre-set card with a $100 marked on the front and a gift card box to put it in. It would be easy to sneak it in with her other gifts.

When they reached the truck, Royce ripped open the box and slid the car seat out. He scanned the directions and buckled it onto the backseat. Rosita had been busy putting Marguerite into her new princess dress and getting her cabbage patch doll out of the box. Royce loaded all her other items in the back of the SUV.

Like a proud father, Royce walked into Chuck-E-Cheese with Marguerite in his arms. Rosita walked beside them with two wrapped gifts. Walking toward the party section, Royce spotted the rest of the group already there. Rosita recognized most of the faces.

They yelled, "Happy Birthday, Marguerite."

It was her co-workers and their children. Royce had planned a whole birthday party for Marguerite. Marguerite was bouncing in his arm, and Rosita thought she was going to cry. They had a reserved section, and it was all decorated in princess. Rosita noticed a table that was piled high with gifts as Royce put Marguerite to her feet. He took one of the presents out of her hands and added it to the pile. Rosita leaned to put the other one on the table, but Royce was quick to halt her.

"That present is for you, and you need to open it."

"What is it?" she asked, her face shrimp-like.

He laughed. *Why do people ask what was in a gift when they have it in their hands?* "Just open it. It's something that you need for tonight."

Rosita peeled the tape like it was going to bite. She hadn't received a gift since she was a little girl. She opened the package and saw a box with a camera on it.

"You bought me a camera?"

"Yes, so you can take pictures of Marguerite and watch her grow."

"Oh, Mr.—I mean, Roy, you shouldn't have."

"In a few years, when she is all grown up, you're going to look back at these pictures and smile. At least that's what my mother says." He looked over at Marguerite, who was laughing and playing with the other kids. "Let's get this open and figure out how it works. We need plenty of pictures of *our* little princess."

Rosita heard every word he said. He probably didn't realize he said "*our.*"

He sounded like he wanted to do more for her than this birthday party. She wasn't ready for that. First of all, he was her boss, too damn cute and sexy as hell. And second or was it third, she'd lost count. He'd never want a woman like her, a single mother, and a poor single mother. He could have any woman he wants. Like that woman, Ms. O'Neil from the Ren Cen. She was pretty and wore expensive clothes. Rosita pushed all her thoughts to the back of her mind. She was ready to have fun with Marguerite. Her daughter was having her first birthday party, and she noticed all the other little girls were dressed up as princesses as well. She couldn't believe that her co-workers were doing all this for her little girl.

Rosita saw a flash and noticed Royce was taking pictures. He looked like he was having more fun than Marguerite, she decided it was time she start having some fun too. The children played for an hour, and Royce hovered over Marguerite. Rosita sat with the other mothers while he supervised and tried to corral the children. He lost two children in the balls, and three got away from him in the jungle gym. The birthday package where the children got lots of coins to play games and ride the rides was supposed to save him.

Royce was glad when the pizzas arrived so he could sit down and rest. He'd been chasing kids, and it seemed like forever. Thirty minutes later, a big birthday cake was brought to the table and a small personal cake for Marguerite with a candle for her to blow out. The group sang happy birthday, and Rosita encouraged Marguerite to blow out the candle. Royce was holding down the button on the camera. He must have taken fifty pictures in a minute. He didn't want to miss her blowing out the candles.

Around 9 p.m., Marguerite had crawled up in Royce's arm and fell asleep. The birthday party was over for her. Rosita and her co-workers, who were now her friends, helped her pack up the gifts. Marguerite was having so much fun that she hadn't opened up her presents. Rosita thanked them for helping to make Marguerite's birthday special. Royce passed a sleeping Marguerite to Rosita while he loaded everything in the back of his truck.

When they got back to Rosita's place, Royce remembered how nervous she'd been when he arrived to pick them up. He volunteered to sit with Marguerite while she made several trips back and forth. Now was not the time to push the issue. He only commented that she leave the car seat in his truck. Royce hugged and kissed Marguerite one last time and passed her to her mother. He bade his goodnights to the girls and watched as they entered the building.

The next day, Rosita was off work. She and Marguerite spent the morning opening her gifts, and she played with all of them. Rosita wrote down the names of her co-workers and the presents they bought. She was confused when she found a small box, and there was no card. It was from the same store they'd visited with Roy, and she had a feeling that he'd snuck something else in. He was genuinely a good man, but she still wanted to kill him. The man was incorrigible, where it concerned her daughter.

Rosita wanted to give everyone a thank you card. She especially wanted to appreciate Mr. Hawthorne for everything he'd done. She and Marguerite walked a couple of blocks to a store where she could buy some blank cards.

While Marguerite took a nap, she wrote out all the cards. When she started writing the note for Royce, she began to cry. Why couldn't Marguerite's biological father be this loving and thoughtful? She didn't know what to say or how to say it. Eventually, she wrote, *"Thank you for making my day so special, love Marguerite."*

Rosita knocked on the door to Royce's office the next morning. He didn't look up to see who was entering after he told them to come in.

"I can't accept this gift card."

Royce continued writing on his papers. "It isn't for you."

"Then Marguerite can't accept this card." She said defiantly.

"If that's the case, then Marguerite has to come and tell me herself."

Royce grabbed one of the business cards on the desk and scribbled on the back of it. He stood from his chair, putting on a jacket, and walked across the room. After picking up a helmet from the chair, Royce stood in front of Rosita, towering over her. He was so close that she had to look up.

"I have to go to the downtown store for a couple of hours. You're in charge until I get back." He passed her the card. "This is my cell; call me if you need me or if there's a problem you can't handle."

Rosita stood, shocked and confused. She didn't move to accept the card. So, he laid it on top of the gift card and started walking out. Her eyes focused on the helmet in his hand.

"Mr. Hawthorne, wait . . . can you take some thank you cards for me? I don't know if I'll get over there any time soon." She said solemnly. She'd offended him.

"Sure, I'll deliver them." He walked out the door.

Rosita followed him out and jogged to the breakroom to get the cards out of her purse. She came out of the breakroom searching for him and looked out the front glass window. There he was, sitting astride a big motorcycle. She stepped outside and passed him the cards. He slid them inside a pocket on his jacket. She wanted to thank him verbally, but she couldn't find the words to say. He was such a mystery, and she didn't know he rode motorcycles either.

Royce sensed that she wanted to say something, except she didn't. He waited, and they stared at each other. They must have stared at each other for a couple of minutes before he exhaled and put on his helmet. Royce cranked up his bike, and Rosita jumped back on the sidewalk. He wondered if she was afraid of motorcycles.

Royce was upset with himself. He'd driven home the night of the party, and Marguerite's car seat kept popping up in his peripheral vision. It nagged at him again the next day, driving to work. He would have loved to have seen her face when she opened all her presents. They'd had so much fun running around the toy store, and it tore his heart to see such a sweet girl living in poverty. He had so much to give and wanted to share. Why didn't she want what he had to offer? On the second thought, he knew the answer without asking. It was Rosita's pride talking when she tried to give back the gift card. He'd given her his cell number intentionally, and more or less hoped she could read between the lines, hoping she'd call him if she ever needed him for anything.

Royce had almost forgotten what it felt like to have an evening off from work. And he wanted more of those, not that he had a life after work. The Midtown location needed an assistant manager. And he was seriously considering promoting Rosita to a shift team leader. Maybe if he paid her a little more money, she could move to a better neighborhood.

There was one more errand to run before going to the Ren Cen. Royce rode downtown toward the entertainment district, riding up and down several streets past the theaters and the nightclubs. The perfect location would be at a busy intersection with drive-thru access. The distraction gave him something else to think about other than the safety of Marguerite and her mother. There were several available buildings. He just didn't know if they would work. Maybe he should do this during a time when the nightlife was in full swing.

Now he had an assignment for the weekend. Rounding a corner, he headed to the Ren Cen.

Royce had the worst timing, he walked up, and there was Ms. O'Neil. Toby was straining to keep a smile on his face. She must have been berating his staff again. He couldn't hear everything Starla said, but he could tell from her body language that she was in full bitch mode. The crazy woman was running off potential customers and acting unprofessionally.

Royce motioned for Toby not to say anything, moving to stand directly behind her. He listened as she called his employees stupid and ignorant. She complained that they couldn't make a decent cup of coffee, pointing her finger at everybody to make her point. Royce was getting angrier by the second, and then she went overboard. Starla O'Neil yelled that she could have his business shut down due to incompetence. Royce was blowing hard. Her eyes bucked, and she realized that someone was standing behind her.

She started speaking before she turned around. "And whoever the hell is standing behind me . . . you need to back the fu . . . up." She turned around and came face to face with a steaming Royce.

He had a flaming fire in his eyes. "Ms. O'Neil!" He exhaled, trying to calm down and think before he spoke. "Ms. O'Neil, I suggest. No, I demand that you get your da . . . coffee somewhere else, especially since you think my staff is so incompetent." Royce pulled his phone from his pocket. He opened it to the camera. "Smile, Ms. O'Neil."

Instead of a smile, she smirked, making an ugly face. "What, smile for what?"

Royce took a picture. "I have a wonderful idea. I will print your picture and put a *big red circle* with a line drawn through it. And the caption will read *Banned from Gourmet Coffee House*. If I ever catch or hear that you are at my place of business berating my staff again, I'll file assault charges against you."

"I didn't touch your stupid employees."

Royce turned around. "Excuse me, staff, did Ms. O'Neil assault anyone here?"

"Yes, she threw hot coffee in my face," Toby interjected.

"Well, I never," she yelled and stormed off.

"And you never will," Royce shouted behind her. "Did you pay for that cup of coffee, Ms. O'Neil?"

She forgot she had it in her hand. She threw the cup to the floor and left, walking fast. All the employees started clapping. Royce stormed to the office, with Toby following. As soon as they were in the office, Royce wanted to know how long she'd been doing that. Toby told him regularly, especially since he'd been spending so much time at the other location. God, he was glad that he had sense enough never to get involved with women like that. They could be bitter, vengeful, and dangerous. He was delighted Rosita wasn't here anymore, so she wouldn't come into contact with Marguerite.

Royce sat down with Toby, and they discussed promoting a shift leader to an assistant manager for the new location. Toby wanted to know why he wouldn't train Rosita for the position. Royce said that there were employees that had worked for him longer and had more seniority. He wanted Toby's recommendation, so Toby suggested Janell. They discussed more business for an hour, and Toby noticed that Royce kept checking his phone.

"Is something wrong, you keep checking your phone?"

"No, nothing is wrong. I left Rosita in charge. I'm considering her for a shift team leader. I just think she's a little soft, and she'll have to toughen up for a leadership position."

"I agree. Oh, how was the birthday party the other night? My kids came home, telling me how much fun they had. And my wife thinks you're still cute."

"It was great. Marguerite had a blast. That reminds me Rosita sent some thank you cards for you guys. And tell your wife I said thanks." Royce passed the stack of cards to Toby, laughing.

Toby looked at the cards and saw one with Royce's name on it. He passed it back. "I think this one is for you."

Royce didn't open the card; instead, he just slipped it back into his pocket. Pulling out his phone, he showed Toby a picture of Marguerite all dressed up. It made him think of the photos he took with the camera. He wanted to ask Rosita if he could get a printed copy of Marguerite to put on his desk.

Looking at his watch again, he realized that he'd overextended his outing. Everything must be running smoothly at the other store. Rosita hadn't called his cell or the store line. He decided to get something to eat before going back since he had a long night ahead of him. Subway was calling his name.

He stood, looking at the Subway menu board. The first thing that caught his eye was the kid's menu. Everything seemed to make him think of Marguerite. She had a good meal at the party, and he even fed her some of his salad. She still looked thin, so he hoped Rosita was doing okay with her since she had a job now. He wondered if Rosita was an excellent cook, and he wanted to know more about her. Or was it the fact that he wanted to know how and why she'd been in foster care? And what happened to Marguerite's father, not that it mattered.

Royce sat in his old chair at his old desk, eating his sandwich. His thoughts were on his future, wanting more stores, wanting to build his empire. It wasn't about the money. He had more money than he could ever spend. His parents had refused to move into a new house. They only accepted the brand-new cars, and he bought all new furniture for his room. He monitored his credit card bill every month and noticed that his parents rarely used their cards.

Was Marguerite making him yearn for his own family? Damn! He wasn't ready for the whole wife thing yet. He knew for sure that he cared for a beautiful little two-year-old girl, and he'd do his best to make her happy. He wanted to buy her as many dolls as she wished to have and hear her laughter in his ears. He'd thrown her in the air and tickled her. She was music to his heart.

The office phone rang, and Royce was on it. "Gourmet coffee house, Renaissance."

"Mr. Hawthorne, I thought you were only going to be gone a couple of hours?"

"Is something wrong, Rosita?"

"Yes, we're almost out of lids for the small cups. The stock room is low on several items."

"I'll bring some lids from this store. In the meantime, why don't you start filling out an order form?"

"I don't know where they are, and I've never done that before."

"I'll be there soon, and I'll show you."

Royce went into the stockroom and saw an extra case of lids. He could borrow the whole box. Damn! He was on his bike. Now he needed to go home and get his truck. He hoped they had enough to last at least an hour. It would take that long to go home, get his vehicle, come back here, and head to the other store. He told Toby what was going on and that he'd be back. Rushing back and forth across town, it only took him a good forty-five minutes. He walked in the back door, carrying a huge box on his shoulders.

Rosita was shocked and asked him how he got that big box on a motorcycle. He shook his head and told her he didn't. Pulling out two sleeves of lids, he passed them to Rosita. Royce told Rosita as soon as she came back; he'd show her how to place orders. Royce spent the next twenty minutes explaining the process of ordering supplies. Rosita shook her head, letting him know that she understood.

"Rosita, would you like this responsibility added to your job title?"

"I . . . I don't have a job title."

Royce took a step closer, but he left plenty of space if another employee came into the room. He didn't want their conversation to look personal.

"You're a hard worker, I've noticed. And I like to reward my hard-working employees."

"Are you rewarding me because of Marguerite?"

"Marguerite doesn't work for me; you do." Was he doing this for Marguerite, Rosita, or both? "Come on to the office so I can show you how to enter the order in the computer."

"Does this mean I'm getting a title and a promotion?"

Royce didn't answer her question. Instead, he returned to his office, opening the website to order the supplies. He knew all the information, except this was a training exercise for Rosita if she showed up. Rosita showed up ten minutes later with two cups of coffee.

"Is this a bribe? You're late."

"Excuse me, *boss*, but you left me in charge, and I was working."

"Good answer, shift team leader."

Rosita screamed. "Are you serious? You want me as a shift leader?"

"Yes, but that means you'll have to open four days a week and work one midday shift."

"Where will you be if I have to open?"

"I . . . I'll be around. There are going to be a few changes. Janell is the new assistant manager, and she'll be closing."

"So, I won't see you every day?" She asked slowly.

"No, I have some other duties."

"Is the company sending you somewhere else? Is that why you're giving me a promotion before you leave?"

"I'm not leaving, and you earned your promotion. I have to do some traveling."

Royce wasn't lying about the changes and the traveling. He needed a weekend away so that Haley could relieve him of a load of stress. Opening the inventory binder, he showed Rosita all the necessary information to complete an order. Asking her to sit in the chair, he pulled up the extra chair in the office. Training her, he pointed out all the steps.

During the lesson, he asked her to order an additional case to replace the one they borrowed. The replacement was necessary because each store was responsible for its inventory. He told her to meet him in the morning, and he'd give her a set of keys and a code to the alarm.

Rosita went back out front, a happy woman. Royce was about to trust her with keys and codes. She was excited and scared at the same time. Was he going to want something in return? This circumstance was almost how she got caught up before. It started with small tips and then bigger tips. Now she was getting a promotion and a raise. If he asked her to sit in his truck, she would quit. Was that why he wanted to keep Marguerite's car seat? Would he use her as an excuse? Maybe this wasn't such a good idea. But she wasn't a gullible nineteen-year-old girl anymore. She was a grown woman, a single mother, and she was also a woman who thought she had a fine ass, sexy boss. Damn!

Chapter Ten

Royce sat at his computer, looking at some available properties downtown. Figuring that there had to be some places he didn't know were available from riding around. He scribbled the addresses down on paper to check them out when he staked out the entertainment district. For a fleeting moment, he wished he had someone to take along and talk to for company.

But he was like a superhero. He had a secret identity; he was the CEO of Hawthorne, Incorporated, where everyone around him thought he was the General Manager of two properties. How long could he keep up the pretense? Changing his title to the regional manager after he acquired more locations was an option.

Eventually, he'd have to spill the beans. He just didn't want his employees to treat him differently. Rosita already thought he was so far above her in status. She would probably laugh if she knew he lived in a garage apartment. He was still the same simple man that moved there six years ago. The only difference was the millions of dollars in the bank now.

Royce remembered that he needed to ask Rosita about the camera before she left, so he went looking for her. The evening shift team leader told him that she'd left already to catch the bus. Royce stared out the window, and it was pouring heavily and she would have to walk two blocks to the bus stop. He ran out the back and jumped in his truck, drove half a block before seeing her standing on the sidewalk under a small ledge.

Pulling the truck up on the sidewalk, Royce rolled down the window. "Jump in. I'll take you home."

Rosita's thoughts returned. He wanted her to get into his vehicle. She heard him call to her again. Damn, Rosita looked up at the sky. It didn't look like the rain was going to stop any time soon, and she needed to pick up Marguerite, another ten-minute walk to her place, without an umbrella. Damn! She decided she was getting in the truck for Marguerite.

"Do you rescue all your employees from the rain?"

"I think you're the only one without a car. But I would gladly help any of my staff. All they have to do is ask."

"Thank you, Mr. Hawthorne, for picking me up. Do you mind making one more stop? I have to pick up Marguerite."

"No problem. I came looking for you to ask if you looked at the pictures on the camera. I wanted to beg for a printed copy of Marguerite."

"I don't know how to operate it. I can bring it to you when you drop me off."

Royce followed the directions given to him and pulled up to a run-down house a few blocks from her apartment. She ran in to get Marguerite. Royce wished he had an umbrella in his truck, but he didn't. He opened the back door so she could jump in. Marguerite was giggling, and Rosita strapped her in her seat. For the first time, she was glad it was here. Marguerite knew exactly where she was and called out to Royce.

Royce turned in his seat, "Hey, Marguerite!" He had the biggest grin on his face. Marguerite was reaching for him. "I'll give you a big hug in a few minutes."

When they reached the apartment, Rosita said she'd go into the house and get the camera. She took Marguerite out of her car seat so she could sit with Royce for a few minutes. Marguerite stood on her legs, twisting the steering wheel like she was driving. The radio was on, and she danced and jumped up and down. Rosita ran back to the truck with the camera in her pocket, jumping in the front seat.

Royce sat Marguerite on the console in the middle. He turned the camera on and showed Rosita how to advance the pictures on the screen. She was laughing so hard by the time she finished looking at all the pictures. Marguerite made a mess eating her miniature cake, and someone else used the camera to take pictures of her mashing cake on Royce's face and her mother's clothes. Royce liked the sound of her laugh. They talked about the photographs, as Royce looked at them slowly. Rosita offered the camera to him to have the pictures he wanted to be printed. He asked her if she wanted a set printed. She shook her head, yes, and reached for Marguerite so they could go to the house. Marguerite jumped back in Royce's lap, yelling, "No," yelling daddy again.

"Marguerite, we have to go. Mr. Hawthorne has to go back to work."

"No . . . da . . . ddy." Marguerite wrapped her arms around his neck.

"I could drive around until she falls asleep, or we can go get something to eat. I haven't eaten since this morning."

"Mr. Hawthorne, I don't think that would be a good idea, either of them."

"I understand. I'll see you in the morning."

"Come on, Marguerite. Let's go and play with your toys and your doll."

Marguerite looked at Royce with sad eyes. She didn't want to leave him, but she wanted to play with her doll. It was as if she understood her dilemma. Marguerite hugged his neck, and he hugged her tight and kissed her on the forehead.

"Bye, Marguerite." He didn't know when he'd see her again. It didn't sound like he'd see her anytime soon.

Rosita held her close and ran out into the rain. Royce watched them until they disappeared into the building. After returning to work, Royce opened the safe and grabbed two extra sets of keys.

He made a folder for Rosita, which included a list of her duties and the duties of the ordering process. In the folder, he attached the instructions on the alarm system. On a separate note, he wrote down her alarm code. Each person had a unique alarm code, more like a security feature. Next, he made a similar folder for Janell. She was starting her managerial duties tomorrow as well.

Royce decided to hang around for the rest of the week to ensure the closing process worked smoothly. Looking over the employees' work schedule, he wanted to make sure there were some male employees in the early mornings and for the late shift. He pulled a folder from the filing cabinet, and it was full of applications. So he reviewed them to decide if he was ready to hire more people. He was mainly looking for some college students that were looking for part-time jobs.

Rosita had been working in her new role for almost three weeks. She'd only seen Royce a few times her first week. He returned her camera and gave her a bag with a set of printed photos and an album to put them in. She looked through the pictures twice. There weren't any pictures of him or the photo of Marguerite smashing the cake on his face. She knew she saw them on the camera, and now, all the images had been erased when she got the camera back. He'd been MIA for two whole weeks. Was he avoiding her because she rejected his invitation, or had it genuinely been a friendly gesture? He didn't act differently toward her that first week, although he'd mentioned that he would be busy.

Meanwhile, Royce was working with a Real Estate agent, they found a small building for sale downtown. It was on a corner, and the side parking lot would be perfect for a drive-thru. The building sat a half block from two different nightclubs and one block from a theater. The front was a huge glass window where he could build a high bar, and the customers could look out. There was room enough for six or seven tables. It wasn't necessary for more than that at this location.

Royce had plans of advertising on some bus stop benches nearby. There were even a few other businesses that might benefit from his late-night coffee shop a few blocks away. He'd give it a shot, and if it didn't work out, he could move the location. It would be chilly soon, and that was when it would do more business. He hired some contractors to get started.

Now it was his turn at some relaxation. He called Haley and said he could get away from work for a couple of days. He booked his favorite room at the Westin on the club level with a view of Lake Erie. Royce drove to Cleveland, enjoying the time to clear his head and think about rolling around a big bed with Haley. He liked this arrangement, except sometimes, he wished he could see her more. This trip had more than one advantage for him. His Real Estate agent emailed him some properties to look at while he was in town. If he opened a couple of stores here, he'd have a reason to see Haley more. Although he couldn't tell her that either, and keep his identity a secret. It's been working for him so far. Starla O'Neil was the very reason he didn't want anyone to know. And he was sure there were a lot more like her. He knew he'd meet the right woman someday, and she'd want him for him and not his money.

Royce checked into the hotel and texted Haley his room number. He opened the curtains to let the sunshine in, and he watched some activity on the Lake. Too bad this room wasn't like the one in Dallas where the bed faced an open window. He could enjoy making love to Haley with this view in the background. Retrieving his laptop from his bag, he opened it on the desk. He could get a little work done before Haley arrived.

Toby and the managers were the only people he notified that he was going out of town for a couple of days. Janell had instructions to call Toby for any emergencies. Toby was proving to be an outstanding manager. If his empire grew too big for him to handle, he knew he could rely on Toby.

Royce opened his email and looked over the properties and maps to show their locations. He wanted to use the same concept of a coffee shop downtown in the middle of nightclubs, bars, and entertainment. Maybe if they weren't too tired tonight, they could walk around downtown. Either way, there was always tomorrow night. He had a strong feeling they wouldn't be leaving the hotel tonight. Royce was looking at all the different signs of nightlife in Cleveland when he heard a knock at his door. He knew who that was, so he closed his computer.

"Hey, handsome."

"Hey sexy, do you know how much I've missed you." Royce picked her up with one arm kissing her and closing the door.

"I do now, and you have too many clothes on."

Royce and Haley made a trail of clothes. Royce released all his pent-up frustrations and cleared his body and mind of work.

Although he still had his hang-up of waking up with a woman next to him. He'd slept a couple of hours and got out of bed. His body was so used to being up at the crack of dawn to open up his business. He was sitting at the desk on his computer when his cell rang. It was next to the bed, and he ran to get it so it wouldn't wake up Haley – too late!

"Who is calling you this early?" She mumbled.

Royce answered his phone. "Hello."

"I'm sorry to call you so early, Mr. Hawthorne, but the main coffee maker isn't working. Something is wrong, and it's making a funny noise."

"Rosita . . . Janell should have told you that I was out of town."

"Royce, get off the phone and come back to bed," Haley murmured in the background.

"No, she didn't," Rosita answered.

"You need to call Toby. He'll know what to do."

"I'm . . . I'm sorry for . . . waking you, Mr. Hawthorne."

"It's okay. Bye, Rosita."

Rosita laid the phone down on the cradle. Why was she feeling a pang of jealousy? She heard the woman in the background. Does he have a girlfriend? He didn't act like he had one with the way he worked. And he asked her and Marguerite to go and eat with him. Guys with girlfriends or wives didn't usually do that. He didn't sound like he was asleep, and the woman was begging for him to come back to bed.

A mental picture of his muscled arms hovered in her head, and she wondered what the rest of him looked like. She could see a small outline of his chest under his shirt. He never wore tight-fitting shirts at work. And she'd only seen him in a pair of jeans once, and that was for Marguerite's party. If she hadn't been so nervous that night, she might have paid more attention to how fine he was. She bet he had rock-hard abs and muscled thighs like those men in the magazines. She exhaled. Oh well! Some other woman was playing with his body right now, and she had work to do. Looking up at the list of names and numbers, she called Toby.

Haley looked at the clock. It wasn't even six yet, and Royce didn't look nor sound sleepy. She could tell he'd been out of bed for a while. His side of the bed was cold. He did the same thing every time they'd been together, at least here in Cleveland. Their first time in Dallas, he'd left her alone in bed with a note. At least he called her. The man didn't give an appearance of an auto industry worker, he sounded more like a boss, who drove an expensive vehicle, and stayed at expensive hotels--she wondered what he did for a living. At one point, she thought he was married because he never invited her to come to Detroit. She noticed that he didn't wear a ring or have any ring tan lines. The paradox was still debatable. He was such a mystery and also the best lover she'd ever had.

Royce opened a security program and saw Rosita sitting at his desk, staring at the phone. She looked like she'd lost something. Had she heard Haley through the phone? He wondered what she was thinking about so hard. She hadn't moved in five minutes, and she looked confused and sad. He saw her exhale, dejected like she was coming out of a trance.

Finally, she looked up at the board and picked up the phone, guessing that she dialed Toby. He'd call him later to make sure the problem got fixed. Looking over the top of the laptop at Haley, she was watching him with curious eyes. He logged off the computer and closed it, returning to the bed.

"Do you have problems sleeping?" She asked.

"No, I don't."

"Then why do I wake up alone every time I'm with you?"

"I'm an early riser. I'm used to being at work extremely early. So when I wake up, I get out of bed. It's not you, I promise." He pulled her closer for a kiss, caressing her breast. "How can I make it up to you?"

"You can start here." She pointed to her mouth. "And finish here." She put his hand between her legs.

"Um, I think I can handle that," Royce said before covering her mouth with his.

Royce stayed in bed until his stomach growled, and then he suggested that they shower and grab something to eat. He wanted her to show him around downtown during the daytime, and then he'd find something to do later tonight. His previous trips had different motives than this one.

It was way past breakfast, so they found a restaurant within walking distance of the hotel and ate lunch. Royce drilled Haley about places to go and things to do downtown. They talked about some nightclubs, and there were some comedy clubs. That piqued his interest. Comedy clubs were always a good hangout for late-night people. He asked her if she liked comedy, and she nodded yes, chewing her food.

He opened his phone and searched for the comedy club. It was too far to walk, but they could do a cab, or he could drive and take a look around at the same time. He thought about looking at the properties in his email to know if they were close to the clubs.

Royce was so caught up in his thoughts that he didn't hear Haley talking to him. She eventually tapped him on the arm. Royce apologized and said he was thinking about work. It reminded him that he needed to call Toby. Even though Rosita or Toby never called to say there was a worse problem. It would make him feel better if he knew for sure. He excused himself, telling Haley that he needed to make a call. Strolling away from the table, he wondered if he should call Toby or Rosita. He decided to call Rosita since she was the shift team leader and in charge.

"Good afternoon, *Gourmet Coffee House*, Midtown, how can I help you today?"

"Hello, Rosita."

"Hel . . . lo, Mr. Hawthorne."

"I'm checking to make sure that everything is okay."

"Yes sir, I spoke with Toby, and he told me how to reset the machine. I . . . I'm really sorry for disturbing you this morning."

"It wasn't your fault. Janell should have informed the shift leaders that I was out of town."

"I don't want to get anyone in trouble."

"You're not getting anyone in trouble, Rosita. You just need to remember the protocol because one day, you may be a manager. Now how is Marguerite?" He asked, changing the subject from work, so she'd stop panicking.

"She's good and still enjoying all her new toys," she answered bubbly. "She . . . she asks about you . . . every day. I don't know why she thinks you're her father. She's never seen her father." Rosita admitted solemnly like she was talking to herself. "I'm so sorry. Mr. Hawthorne, is there something else? I need to get back to work."

"No, Rosita, that's all . . ." He opened his mouth to ask her a question.

Rosita held the phone to her ear, hearing the hesitation in his voice. She knew he was still there. Did he want to see Marguerite again?

"Mr. Hawthorne, would you like to take Marguerite for some ice cream or something when you get back? I think she'd like that."

"Yes, yes, I would if you don't mind."

"No, I don't mind. Bye, Mr. Hawthorne."

Rosita hung up the phone. She didn't dare tell him that Marguerite was calling for him until she cried herself to sleep. Why was her daughter so desperate for a father that she picked her own? She didn't know if she was making it better or worse by letting Marguerite spend time with him. But how could it be any worse than it was now?

The phone rang in the office again, and they wanted to speak to the owner of Hawthorne Incorporated. Rosita repeated what he said to herself. She didn't know anything about an owner. She responded that Mr. Hawthorne was out of the office and asked if they wanted to leave a message. The man said yes, and Rosita scrounged around on the desk, looking for a pen. She asked the gentleman to hold on while she got a pen. Opening a drawer looking for a pen, something glossy caught her attention. She stared at some printed pictures until she remembered there was someone on the phone. She kept digging until she found a pen to use. The gentleman left a message to call him about some real estate property. Rosita wrote down all his information and plopped down in the chair.

She looked through the pictures. It was the same pictures she had and some she didn't. There were several pictures of Royce holding Marguerite while she was smiling and laughing. She saw the photo of Marguerite smashing the cake on his face, and he looked happy about it. Just like a real father would. They were looking at each other with genuine affection. If a stranger saw these pictures, they'd swear that he was her father, except she looked nothing like him. She had the misfortune of having her father's eyes and half his skin color. Rosita loved her daughter but hated her daughter's father.

At the bottom of the pile, she found a CD with photos printed on it. Ignoring the CD, she looked again at the pictures of Royce and Marguerite. She'd put all her photos in the album that he'd bought for her. Because of him, Marguerite had had the best birthday, and she'd have pictures to look at forever. So why or how could it hurt to let him spend a little time with Marguerite?

Tapping the red button on his phone, he turned it off, smiling. Rosita was going to let him spend some time with Marguerite. He wondered if she liked animals, he could take her to the Aquarium or look for some other fun places little children want to go.

Royce made his way back to the table, asking Haley if she was ready to go. He was ready to do some exploring. They walked back to the hotel, and Royce retrieved his SUV. They rode around, and Haley pointed out some fun and exciting places in Cleveland. Royce tried to look interested in some of the sites. In actuality, he was only interested in available buildings to open more Gourmet coffee locations. He asked specifically about some of the nightclubs.

Haley got the impression that he wanted to take her dancing. She'd love to show him off to some of her girlfriends. Immediately, she started telling him about the most popular clubs. Then she asked him if he wanted to go out dancing tonight. He didn't dance, and he didn't want to tell her that, either. Royce smiled and suggested they go to a comedy club after dinner. He needed to make her forget about going to a club.

The next afternoon, Royce drove home thinking about the properties. He needed to rethink mixing business with pleasure. He thoroughly enjoyed Haley's company in the bed. But she wasn't the type of person to help him scout out some potential property. And after seriously thinking about it, he didn't want to expand into Ohio. Haley might get the wrong idea and feel the relationship was becoming committed. He needed to concentrate on Michigan. There were so many other cities nearby that he hadn't had a chance to check out. Hopefully, he'd hear from the real estate agent soon.

Royce spent the next two days at his newest location downtown. It was still a couple of months from being ready. He started marketing by advertising on the bus stop benches around all the nightclubs and theaters. Since most of the clubs closed at 2 a.m., he'd try the hours of 6 p.m. until 4 a.m. The theaters started much earlier than the clubs, and he knew from experience that standing outside in the cold in a line wasn't any fun. Most people thought that a cup of coffee would sober them up after drinking for hours. And then again, some people just weren't ready to go home. Being in the building with the construction company, he noticed quite a few people were taking notice. He hoped this business was going to be as successful as his other two.

Royce walked into the Midtown GCH around 7 a.m. The drive-thru was full, as well as the lobby. He stood at the back of the line and watched his staff work like a well-oiled machine. Rosita was wearing headphones for the drive-thru and repeating the customers' orders with precision. She was good at this. He remembered his beginning days, and it had been rough. It was a wonder he didn't get fired for all the orders he messed up. He noticed several customers would walk up to the register and not even give an order. The cashier would grab a cup, write a name on it, and punch information into the cash register. Less than five minutes later, that customer was walking out smiling, must be regulars. He'd seen enough, so he headed to the office.

Royce sat at his desk and saw that he had several messages. He read them and saw that the real estate agent had called the office instead of his cell. Damn! Now he had to wait an hour before he could call him.

Royce pulled the folders and started looking over each day's reports. He was satisfied that his two assistant managers were doing a good job, so were the shift team leaders. He needed to set up all the reports on this computer. If he wanted to take on more properties, he wouldn't have time to come and sit and read these every few days. The reports could be accessed from his laptop anywhere.

All his managerial staff at the Ren Cen was already putting their reports on the computer. He'd have a meeting with the team about it. What he needed was for his IT people to set up a network between all his properties. The only reason he hadn't done it was because he wanted to keep his secret as long as possible. When he did that, he'd need a central office. Was he ready for office life yet? He'd have to be if he wanted to grow his empire.

Royce was in his own little world when Rosita knocked on the door. "Hey, we're glad your back. How . . . how was your trip? She asked with a pretty shy smile.

"Unproductive."

"Sorry to hear that. That sounds like you have to go back soon."

He looked at Rosita, and his thoughts of giving up on that project jumped out. "No, I don't have to go back any time soon. Not there anyway. I might have to go to some other places."

"I see, so you'll be doing a lot of traveling for the company?"

"Hopefully, most of them will be day trips. And by the looks of it around here, I'm not needed."

Rosita rushed forward and touched his arm. "Oh, Mr. Hawthorne, I need you. I mean, we need you; all the staff needs you." She dropped her hand and stepped back. Shaking her head, she hadn't meant to touch him.

Royce looked down at his desk before he spoke. "I wish you would call me Royce or Roy."

She hunched her shoulders and swallowed. "I'm sorry I can't do that, Mr. Hawthorne. You're my boss, and I have to show you that respect." She looked down. "Even if you care for Marguerite the way you do. I want you to know that I appreciate everything you've done for us." She wanted to let him know she saw the pictures, but she didn't want him to think that she had been snooping.

"I have to get back out front. I just wanted to let you know that we're glad to have you back." Rosita turned and rushed out of the office.

Royce stared at the closed door. He shook his head, pondering what bad things happened in her life. She doesn't think that she deserves happiness. Is that why she has sad eyes? He wondered what her story was and why Marguerite hadn't ever seen her father. Maybe he doesn't know he has a daughter. Perhaps, she was raped? She seemed timid around him, or was it around all men? Did an old boss possibly rape her? He pulled a folder from his filing cabinet and reread over her application. He'd been so concerned about Marguerite that he never checked out her previous work history. She worked at a diner as a waitress and a couple of fast-food restaurants in Los Angeles, California. Was she a runaway? She wasn't a minor when she had Marguerite. So being a runaway doesn't count anymore. And the lady he spoke with from her foster home didn't mention that she was a runaway. Rosita was a big mystery. Perhaps, it was time to take *them* on an outing.

Royce looked at the work schedule to see when her next off day was. Rosita had left for the day when Royce went looking for her. He looked at the board with all the staff's contact numbers and the same information for Rosita, her friends' cell was on it. He decided that he'd ask her tomorrow about picking up Marguerite on her off day. Royce wondered why she hadn't gotten a phone. She'd been working now for a few months and received a raise with her promotion. Cell phones were cheap. God, he'd lived with a flip phone for years. Was she having more money issues? He thought that giving her a raise would get her out of the current situation she was in. He wished she'd let him help her and Marguerite.

The following day, Royce and Rosita settled on a time that he'd pick up Marguerite. He was learning a lot about Rosita, especially that she didn't want him knocking on the door. Just as he guessed, she was there waiting on the curb. When he got out of the truck, Marguerite screamed and ran into his outstretched arms. He picked her up, throwing her in the air and catching her, she squealed. He hugged her, kissing her on the temple.

"Hey, Marguerite, I have missed you. Have you been a good girl for your mother?"

Marguerite shook her head no, called him her version of daddy, and started crying, big crocodile tears.

"Ah, baby girl, don't cry." He looked at Rosita and asked frantically, "What's wrong? Did somebody do something to her?"

Rosita's shoulders dropped. "No, I just didn't want to tell you that she cries every night for you. I thought she'd forget about you and stop."

He stepped closer to Rosita. "How long has she been doing this?"

She exhaled and held her head down. "Since the last time she saw you."

"You mean the night I asked to take both of you out to eat? That's been over three weeks." Royce huffed.

Royce wasn't mad at Rosita. He just wished she'd told him what was going on. What was he supposed to say? He wasn't her real father, and he had no right to interfere. Holding Marguerite close to his chest, he couldn't imagine how she was feeling, crying herself to sleep every night because of him.

"I was just taking Marguerite to the Aquarium. Do you want to come with us?"

"No, you two have fun."

"Are you sure? I bet Marguerite would love to have her mother with her too."

"I'm sure."

"I brought you something. It's not much; it was just an old phone that you can have. I need to be able to call you when we get back."

Royce passed Rosita a cell phone from his pocket. He grabbed her hand and pressed it on her palm. She was reluctant to accept it but needed a way for him to call her so he wouldn't knock on the door. She closed her hand, deciding that she'd give it back when he returned. And this didn't look like an old phone. She knew better than anyone that gifts came with a price. Initially, she thought he was using Marguerite to get to her. But after seeing those pictures, it was proof that he cared for Marguerite and she heard a woman in the background. He wasn't interested in her at all.

Royce buckled Marguerite in her seat, and they were off. They spent a couple of hours at the aquarium, and then he took her to get something to eat. He picked a place where they had kid-friendly food, remembering that she liked pizza and subway sandwiches. This time she ate chicken nuggets, and he helped her eat some mac-ncheese. Marguerite sat in a high chair at the restaurant like a big girl. He thought about Rosita and wondered what she would eat. Royce wasn't sure what kind of foods she liked to eat, so he ordered a couple of different items.

He called the phone, telling Rosita that they'd be arriving in about fifteen minutes. She was waiting outside when he drove up. Marguerite was in a good mood when he took her out of her car seat, especially when he passed her a big stuffed fish from the aquarium. He gave her a big hug and a kiss on her cheek, telling her to be good for her mother. Royce passed Rosita a big to-go bag from the restaurant.

"We brought you dinner."

"You didn't have to do that. Thanks," Rosita said shyly.

"Marguerite and I wanted to do it."

Rosita passed him the phone back. "Thanks for letting me use this phone."

"No, that is for you to keep. And anyway, Marguerite and I have another date next week if it's okay with you."

"Then you bring it back next week."

"No, I want you to keep it. I want you to call me if Marguerite cries for me again. She might go to sleep if she hears my voice. Please keep it." He wanted to console her because she was looking at him with those sad eyes. "My number is programmed in it, under Royce, not Mr. Hawthorne." He started walking back to his truck. "See you tomorrow, Rosita." He blew a kiss to Marguerite, and she laughed.

Once a week, he took Marguerite on an outing, and every time he asked Rosita to accompany them. She refused. It was getting closer to the opening of his new location. He knew his evenings and nights were going to be busy. He didn't want to cancel his weekly date with Marguerite. And he often asked Rosita if she'd been crying anymore. So his visiting and a few late-night calls had helped.

Chapter Eleven

$\mathcal{R}$oyce's new location opened with success. Employees were staked out at the clubs, passing out discount coupons for the first couple of weeks. He was a lot busier on the weekends than weekdays; however, he accounted for that, so he worked with a small crew on weekdays. They did enough to get by, and he still managed to spend some time with Marguerite even though it was early afternoon dates. Royce took her for ice cream or sometimes just to a playground. He had to confess to Rosita that he was managing another location and couldn't spend long evenings with Marguerite. He reminded her to call him if she cried out at night. Several times, on their evening dates, Marguerite passed out in her seat on their ride home. He'd taken her shopping for more dolls and toys until Rosita fussed and said she didn't have anywhere to keep any more toys. Royce promised to stop shopping, but that made him wonder what kind of accommodations she had.

Royce popped in and out of his other locations. They all still needed to know that he was the general manager. Finally, he got around to having an IT tech build his network. The security program was set up on his laptop to monitor all his locations from anywhere.

Next, he hired a company to back-up data and the security cameras at each location. He felt he was lucky that he hadn't had any theft issues.

Royce had his usual weekly date with Marguerite and this time they enjoyed ice cream at the park. Afterward, he headed to his newest location downtown. He'd been open for three months and hadn't hired any managerial staff. It was still his responsibility to open and close. He only felt comfortable recently to leave for a couple of hours here and there. He had thoughts of shifting a few employees around and bringing an experienced employee as the opening shift leader. There were a couple of choices from the Ren Cen, and those were his oldest employees. Most importantly, he needed a break.

He was sitting in the office when one of his staff knocked, telling him a guy out front wanted to fill out an application. Royce passed him the forms, and he disappeared back through the door. Twenty minutes later, he returned with the filled-out form and informed Royce that the guy wanted to speak to him if he was available. Royce agreed, saying he would like a minute. He looked over the application, and the name jumped out, *Frederick Shuman*. The name sounded familiar but continued to read. Then he saw his previous employment had been at a Starbucks. It looked like Freddie had quite a few jobs in retail. His reasons for leaving each of them were lame. He always wondered if Freddie had been the one to set him up. But he had no proof. He'd talk to him.

Royce walked out front and saw Freddie sitting at the high bar drinking a cup of coffee. Several customers were seated at other tables. He didn't want him to know that he remembered him.

"Frederick Shuman." He called out.

Freddie turned, and his eyes grew. Oh yeah, he remembered who he was.

"Oh, wow! Royce . . . Royce Hawthorne, is that you, man?"

"Yes, it is." He shook his hand. "Freddie, right?"

"You remember me? Wow, you finally made a big-time manager, huh?"

"Yes, I did. Starbucks isn't the only place that sells coffee."

"I thought you got fired. At least that was what I heard. Somebody said you stole a shit load of money."

"I've never stolen anything in my life." He spat out. How dare this punk assume he stole money?

"Well, that's good to hear because if you didn't know it, that Cindy chick quit a few days later. She was probably the one who did it."

Royce shook his head, wondering if that was indeed the case. "So, you're looking for a job?"

"I'm looking for something part-time. I . . . I'm in school."

Royce looked at his application, and it didn't mention he was in school. "Come on back to my office, and we'll talk."

Royce sat down with Freddie and went over his application. He asked questions about his previous employers and wanted to know why he left the other Starbucks. Freddie told him that the manager didn't like him and kept giving him all the worst shifts. He said he had more seniority, and he didn't deserve to work like that. Royce made some notations on his application, asking more questions. Freddie had a few valid reasons for leaving his other jobs. Several times he said he got a better job making more money. Royce needed more help on the weekends for the late shift. There wasn't a valid reason to not hire Freddie, so he said he'd check out his references and his previous employment before he made a decision.

Two weeks later, Royce hired Freddie. He needed someone familiar with the equipment, and all his references had checked out. Each previous employer said he was a hard worker and was upset to see him leave. Royce wanted to know if they'd experienced any theft problems, but he couldn't ask that question. So maybe Cindy had been the thief.

Freddie turned out to be valuable. He volunteered to work all the late shifts and help Royce close every weekend. Royce tried to keep his weekly dates with Marguerite, except they were getting shorter and shorter.

Between keeping up with tons of paperwork and handling three businesses' work was starting to take a toll on him. He was considering putting off building his empire. He'd been talking with the real estate agent on finding him some property in Grand Rapids and Lansing, Michigan. There were some prime location spots in both cities. But he needed to decide quickly because he wasn't the only person interested in the properties. Royce wanted more drive-thru coffee shops, they were the most profitable. He needed to make a day trip, but he needed a reliable person to open the new downtown location; he would be back before closing.

Looking on the network, he checked the other locations' schedules, and there was only one available person, Rosita. He wondered if she'd help him on her day off. There was only one way to find out.

Royce called Rosita's cell number because she'd left work for the day. He asked her for the favor and promised her double pay for that day. Gladly, she accepted his offer; she needed the extra money anyways.

Rosita hadn't been able to save any money. Her supposed friend, Alejandra, was charging her extra rent to continue living there. She said Rosita owed her back pay when she let her live with her before she got a job. Rosita had been furious when the $100 gift card Royce had given Marguerite had come up missing. She'd planned to buy Marguerite some clothes with that money. But how was she ever going to get away from this situation?

Alejandra had noticed all the extra toys that Marguerite was accumulating. She'd also seen Marguerite leave with Royce. Alejandra insinuated that she could sleep with her new boss for more money, but that was never going to happen. That was the reason why she asked Royce to stop buying stuff for Marguerite.

The next day, Royce picked up Rosita from work and took her to the new location. He led her into the office, and the first thing she noticed was a picture of Marguerite on his desk. After getting a grand tour of his smallest business, Royce introduced her to the staff on duty, advising them that she would be their boss the next afternoon. He gave her a set of keys and issued her a code to the alarm. She was familiar with the opening process because she did the same job every morning at the Midtown location.

Royce told her about an additional employee that she'd be working with, Freddie. And he told the rest of his employees to hold down the fort until he got back. When they were done at the office, he drove Rosita to pick up Marguerite, and before she could refuse, he drove straight to a restaurant. Rosita gave him a dirty look when he took Marguerite out of her seat.

The restaurant was small, and they served Mexican. Marguerite loved the quesadillas because she could hold them in her hand and eat them. Royce enjoyed the spicy salsa with chips. He asked for a double order of hot tamales and kept a stare at Rosita while the waitress waited for her order. After a few seconds of staring back, she huffed and ordered a single of the same.

"Why are you looking at me so mean? You have to eat too." He joked.

The thought had hit him as he was waiting for her to come back to the truck with Marguerite. It had been a few days since he'd seen Marguerite, so why not utilize this opportunity. If he'd asked her to eat with them, she would have refused. He didn't know why she did that? But he was also afraid to ask.

"I don't need you to take care of me. I appreciate that you take good care of Marguerite. She is gaining weight and bursting out of her clothes because of you." She shook a chip at him. "Thank you for kidnapping me and forcing me to eat dinner with the two of you." She smiled when she finished her sentence.

Marguerite sat in her high chair, chewing on a chip that Royce had given her. She was looking from one to the other as they talked. Calling out to Royce in her daddy version, she wasn't used to being ignored. It was always just the two of them. She patted him on the arm and grunted, stretching for her cup of water.

"Marguerite, what did I tell you? You have to ask for what you want. I don't understand baby grunts. Do you want your water? Then ask for it." He held up the cup, "Water."

Marguerite tightened her lip. He sat the cup back on the table and turned to Rosita. Her mouth dropped open, is this how he was treating her daughter when they were together? Marguerite grunted again because she couldn't reach the cup; she looked up at Royce like she was going to cry.

"You know the rules, young lady. You can say it, "Water."

"Wat . . . r," she said barely.

"Good girl." He kissed her on the temple and passed her the cup.

"You are so good with her. No wonder she likes you so much. Mr . . . I mean Roy, why don't you have a family? You look like you'd be a good father." She looked away and grabbed her glass. "I'm sorry I shouldn't have asked such a personal question?"

He looked at Rosita, she was trying to smile, but it didn't reach her eyes. They were still sad.

"I ah, work a lot. And I'm rarely home enough, and who wants a husband that's never home."

"Well, it should be a woman that knows you work hard to provide for your family."

He swallowed before he spoke. "Rosita, what about you, tell me where your family is?" He asked softly.

"I don't have any family. My mother died of an overdose when I was ten, and I never knew my father." She looked at him, waiting on him to look disgusted, he didn't.

He touched her hand that was next to him. "Oh, Rosita, I'm so sorry. I didn't mean to pry."

"I owed you an answer. You answered something personal." She turned up her lips in a small smile and dropped it.

Royce was still speechless, and his hand was covering hers. She didn't attempt to pull it away. He didn't look at her like she was the scum of the earth. That had been the way everyone treated her when they found out she lived in a foster home. She'd been teased her whole life during school. A server showed up with their food, and Royce moved his hand. They ate their food and didn't talk of any family anymore.

When they were done, Royce dropped them off at home after kissing and hugging Marguerite. Rosita watched the exchange between them, and she wondered how long he would play his game of daddy with her daughter. She didn't want Marguerite hurt.

Royce looked at Rosita with a different set of eyes. He knew now why her eyes were sad. Marguerite was the only family that she had, and he'd invaded their space. No wonder she didn't tell him about her crying every night. He wished there was something he could do to guarantee that he wouldn't hurt her little girl. That was the last thing he wanted to do. She craved the attention of a father figure, and right now, he was it, and he wasn't going anywhere, anytime soon. He'd be there for her as long as she wanted him. If anyone got hurt, it would be him.

Early the next morning, Royce got on the road and left Detroit. He had a lot to do in the few hours he had available. His first appointment was at 10 a.m. in Lansing, and then there were several properties to look at in Grand Rapids. The locations in Lansing were more than adequate, and he fell in love with three spots in Grand Rapids. These purchases would be his biggest challenge.

Two of the properties in Grand Rapids could be potential locations with a drive-thru. Both of them were at busy intersections. His favorite was near a hospital with several medical clinics. He met with the real estate agent and found out several other prospects were looking at his two favorite places. He could lease the properties or buy them. If he bought them and it didn't work out, he could turn around and sell them.

Royce sat in a restaurant discussing his options with the real estate agent. He wished he had more time to think about it for at least a week. He'd read over the paperwork and details about the properties. His first question was how and why the property was even available. The agent informed him that the bank repossessed the property, and the owner was arrested for tax evasion. Royce made a quick decision, he was buying. Afterward, the real estate agent smiled and told him that the property was a steal. The properties were worth way more than he was getting them at.

"Let's go to the office and the bank," Royce said, rubbing his hands together.

Calling his attorney, Royce said he was faxing him some paperwork, and he needed a rush job. He gave him two hours. In the meantime, he and the real estate agent went back to the office. The real estate agent had his secretary print up all the necessary documents that he needed to sign. The remaining paperwork could be handled via mail.

It was late when Royce left Grand Rapids, and he had a two-and-a-half-hour drive back to Detroit. He parked and rushed into the coffee shop. A couple of customers were sitting at the tables, and Rosita was nowhere in sight, and neither was Freddie. He went to the office; she wasn't there either.

Passing by the storage room, he heard voices. Freddie was asking questions about him and how long he'd been a manager. Rosita answered and told him she had no idea. Freddie wanted to know how long she'd worked for him and where she worked, and then had the nerve to ask if she was dating the boss or just doing the wild thing. Freddie filled her head with tales, saying that all the women at Starbucks wanted him, they thought he was the shit. He said that he'd bet that Royce slept with all of them.

Freddie wanted to know if she would be coming back to work at this location any time soon. He bragged about how much money he had and wanted to take her out on a date, but she declined.

Was he hitting on Rosita? Now he was pissed off, or was he jealous? And he never disrespected any of the women he worked with, but he did sleep with one of them. Royce called Rosita's name, and she came out of the storeroom alone.

"Hey, sorry, I'm so late. Are you ready to go?"

"Yes, and I need to pick up Marguerite from the babysitter."

"Freddie, I'll be right back," Royce said into the storeroom, letting him know that he knew he was there. Passing through the front, Royce told the employees the same thing.

As soon as she buckled in, she started talking. "I guess you heard the conversation."

"I heard enough."

"You know that guy is a jerk, don't you? He thinks he's God's gift to women. All he did was brag all night. I think he's jealous of you."

"What gave you that impression?"

"All the questions he asked about you, and the things that he said. He sounded jealous, that's all. So how was your day?"

"Today was productive. I was going to ask if you wanted to work over here again. But I don't want you working this late, away from Marguerite."

"I would only work if you're working; if you need me. I don't think Freddie would hit on me if you're around."

"Don't worry about Freddie. I'll take care of him," Royce said rather harshly.

Royce hugged and kissed a sleeping Marguerite, she smelled like smoke. Was the babysitter smoking around the children? Royce was already in a foul mood because of Freddie. He asked Rosita if Marguerite had smelled like cigarette smoke before, and she shook her head, 'yes'. She'd asked the sitter about it, and she said that it was one of her relatives that came to visit. Royce commented on finding a new sitter for Marguerite. Rosita said she couldn't afford one of those fancy daycare centers.

"Rosita, please let me help you."

"No, I can't accept that kind of help. You're not her father! And who's to say that you'll be tired of Marguerite soon. Your job is already taking more and more of your time. We don't need your help." Rosita held Marguerite tight and ran into her building.

Why was she being so stubborn? He knows he had no reason to interfere with their lives. Damn! He felt helpless.

Royce thought it was best to keep himself busy in his work. He couldn't handle running all the GCH's by himself. It was time to hire a management team. He'd started the process for three new locations in Grand Rapids and two locations in Lansing, Michigan.

Two weeks later, he called Rosita's number to set up a day to pick up Marguerite, and she didn't answer. He looked on the computer for her schedule. She was off work for the next two days, so that means he couldn't reach her at the store. The following day, he called her phone, and it went to a generic message. He left a message, asking her to call him, but she didn't.

Now, he was worried. Was Rosita upset with him? He hadn't spoken with her since the night she told him they didn't need him. He thought that giving her some space would calm her down.

Apparently, giving her two weeks of space wasn't the answer. She was the most stubborn woman. And he wasn't in a position that he could force her to let him help. It wasn't just Marguerite that he wants to help, he wants to help both of them.

Early the following day, he showed up at GCH Midtown, walked in, and headed straight to the office. Rosita saw him when he came in the door, and he didn't look happy. Well, she wasn't in a good mood either. Marguerite had started crying again at night; she barely got any sleep, and her friend had been complaining bitterly, so much it caused a huge fight.

Rosita didn't know how much longer she could live there, and neither does she have the money to move out either. It was crazy that she'd been working for about nine months and giving most of her money to pay bills. The rest of her income was spent on some food, they barely got to eat.

What else could she do? A shelter was an option, or suck it up and let Royce help her, but at what cost. She wasn't going to be any man's fuck doll ever again. He cared about Marguerite, not her.

Royce saw the phone he gave Rosita on the desk. Is that the reason why she hadn't called him back? She didn't get his messages because she didn't have the phone. He sat in the office for an hour, waiting on her to come to him. So far, she was a no-show. He didn't want to make a scene at work, because he felt this issue was more personal than work-related. Royce didn't want his employees to get the wrong impression--they weren't in a relationship, but if they argued at work, it would look like it. He still needed to talk to her.

Royce walked out front, standing in the door, staring, watching, and looking extremely intimidating. Rosita did her best to ignore him. He only made the other employees nervous. The employees looked around like something was wrong, so they started cleaning, sweeping, emptying clean trash cans, and straightening up like the store was a mess. Royce stood in the door, filling it and brooding. Rosita was the only person who wasn't intimidated or nervous. He didn't scare her, and she had a feeling that his attitude was directed at her. As soon as she took care of the last person in the drive-thru, she passed the headphones to another person.

Walking across the room to the door, she folded her arms across her chest. "You need to stop looking like a grizzly bear. You're upsetting everyone." She spat and gritted her teeth.

"I wouldn't have to look like anything if you'd stop ignoring me." He replied in a low tone he was sure only she could hear, his chest rising and falling.

She gave him a dirty look before she put her hand on the door. "Can we do this in the office, please?"

Royce huffed and followed Rosita.

Rosita closed the door and started first. "What is wrong with you? Is your girlfriend keeping you up all night?"

"I don't have a girlfriend. Why haven't you returned my calls?" He picked up the phone he gave her. "Why is this phone on the desk?"

"Because it's your phone, *Mr. Hawthorne.*"

"You're back to calling me that again. It's your phone . . . no, it's Marguerite's phone. I called you so I could pick her up, and you haven't returned my messages."

"I . . . I don't think that's a good idea anymore." She crossed her arms and held her head up.

"Are you kidding me? What are you going to do when she starts crying again?"

Rosita looked away. She didn't want to look him in his face.

"She's already doing it, isn't she?" He said a little too loud.

Rosita wouldn't look at him. Royce put both his hands on her shoulders, turning her around. She had tears in her eyes.

He pulled her into an embrace. "Rosita . . . please let me help you and Marguerite."

She pushed him away. "Don't touch me!"

Royce released her quickly and backed up. "I'm sorry, Rosita."

He turned and left the office. Rosita wiped the tears from her face. She waited a few minutes before she left the office. She went back out front, and there was no sign of Royce; he'd left.

Chapter Twelve

Royce didn't know what else he could do. He'd upset Rosita, and now he'd touched her inappropriately. She could file sexual harassment charges against him. He called his attorney and asked if his insurance covered harassment charges. His first question was what happened, who did he touch? What did he say? Were there any witnesses? All the crazy questions an attorney would ask. Royce didn't want to go into any details, nor did he want to talk about his relationship with Marguerite. He reminded his attorney that no one knew that he was the owner. So he wasn't worried that someone might try and sue him for millions.

Royce stayed away from the store and only communicated with his assistant managers. He was mostly concerned that Rosita would quit. After two weeks, he noticed that she was still turning in her reports on the computer.

Royce spent a lot of time at the location downtown. It was quiet during the day, and he could get a lot of work done on his newest projects. He advertised in several newspapers and on some websites that he was looking for experienced managers. He needed to hire a district manager that would travel to oversee his out-of-town properties. The general managers would be responsible for hiring the staff for those properties. It was also time to hire a manager for his downtown location. He was tired of staying up all night.

Toby was his first choice of district manager, and Janell, the general manager for the Midtown location. Royce asked Toby and Janell to meet with him downtown. He met with them individually, and he told Toby that he was considering him for a promotion. Toby wanted to know why and asked where he was going. Royce asked Toby if he could keep a secret. Toby nodded. Royce revealed his secret identity to Toby, telling him that he had too many properties to manage. Toby was astounded. Royce thanked Toby for being a loyal employee. He knew Toby had a family, and yet he asked him if he ever thought about a traveling job.

Royce offered him the DM position, saying the job might entail a few overnight stays, but not that many. All of the cities were within driving distance. Toby asked if he could discuss it with his wife before he gave him an answer. Royce thought that was a good idea. Next, he met with Janell and offered her a promotion. She asked some of the same questions. His answers to her were a little different, telling her that he was taking an office job with the company. She'd still be reporting to him indirectly.

Quickly, the news traveled that Janell was taking over as the GM of the Midtown location. Rosita hadn't seen or heard from Royce in weeks. At first, she wondered if he'd gotten in trouble because of her. Was he being fired or transferred? She contemplated whether someone overheard their conversation or heard her yelling that he touched her. His touch didn't mean anything sexual. She knew his touch was only to console her because of Marguerite. So why did she yell at him? Why was she so afraid to let him be kind to her? She heard him say that he wanted to help *her* and *Marguerite*, but how could he help her? She'd looked at his number a hundred times and thought of calling to apologize, but at the moment, she felt like an ass. He'd never said or done anything inappropriately. He probably didn't want anything to do with her anymore, and now Marguerite was the one suffering, and it was all her fault.

Royce wanted a man to take over as manager of the downtown location. He thought it might be too dangerous for a female to be closing so late or early. However, you look at it. Freddie was proving to be valuable except for the fact that he hit on Rosita. He'd questioned Freddie about the conversation between him and Rosita. Freddie said he was just curious. Royce wanted to tell him to stay away from Rosita, but he couldn't without it looking damaging. So he brought up the fact that a female employee could cry harassment from unwanted attention.

Had Freddie done the same to the other female employees? With that type of manners, Freddie wasn't showing exemplary management skills. Royce didn't want that type of employee as a team leader, even if no one had reported him. Royce still had a bad vibe about Freddie; he seemed sneaky, especially after he heard his conversation with Rosita.

Royce never had a set schedule where he did anything at the same time. He preferred being unpredictable. He sat in the office doing paperwork, comparing his receipts week by week. It was noticeable when more activities were going on downtown. Usually, his earnings totaled up higher when the theaters had performances on weekends. He was getting plenty of club business but noticed several amounts were different in total receipts over various busy weekends.

The last weekend of the month was approaching. Three theaters were running shows all day on Saturday and Sunday. Royce decided to try something different. And he wondered if it would draw more business during the daytime. Scheduling enough staff to cover all the shifts, he came in early and opened up. They had a steady run of customers. He knew he would have a long day. So he decided to go home and get a few hours of sleep.

Returning to work, Royce felt refreshed and rejuvenated. He printed tickets from the cash registers and thinned out the cash. It was getting late, and he didn't like the registers to have too much money. Doing a quick count, he put the money in a locked money bag, writing his figures on a notepad. He'd balance everything after the weekend. Leaving the bag on his desk, he went out front to help.

They were extremely busy from midnight until they closed at 4 a.m. Royce had his staff count down their drawers and totaled up their receipts. He added all the credit card tickets, cash in the money bag, and locked it in the vault. After a few hours of sleep, he'd be right back. The next day, Royce followed the same routine of working and going home for a nap. They had a busier day than night. At least on Sundays, they closed at midnight.

Monday came, and Royce was there at his usual time. He wanted to use the quiet time to total up everything from the weekend. Sitting at his desk, he counted up all the cash and added up the credit card tickets. Looking at his notepad, he added that total to his numbers, and the money didn't add up. He compared the printed tickets from the registers to the credit card receipts, and they all added up. The cash was two grand short.

Turning on his computer, he typed in the security program, selecting the downtown location. He started looking at the video from Friday afternoon and hit pause on Saturday. The camera feed froze, and he switched to the other camera. He saw when Freddie walked into the office and typed onto a mini-tablet: *did that fool hack into his system?* Freddie didn't know that there were two cameras, and the other camera was independent of his security system.

Royce saw Freddie take a small key from his pocket, unlock the money bag, and count out a thousand dollars. Royce was beyond pissed; his suspicions were accurate. Even more stunned, he watched Freddie do the same thing on Sunday. Royce wondered just how long Freddie had been stealing. This was the first time a considerable sum had gone missing from the money bag, so he must have been taking small amounts in other ways.

Royce called the police, explaining what he found on his video surveillance. An hour later, two detectives showed up, and Royce showed them what he discovered. He also talked about his other suspicions, and the officers requested access to all his videos. They needed as much evidence against him to make the charges stick and his jail time increase. Freddie was on the schedule to work that afternoon. The detectives were in plain clothes when Freddie bounced into work later that evening. He walked in, smiling and speaking at everyone, just like every other day. He went through the door leading to the back to clock in, and the detectives followed.

"Frederick Shuman, you are under arrest for grand theft," the officer said from the door.

"What . . . what are you talking about? I haven't stolen anything. I . . . I just got to work."

One of the officers handcuffed Freddie while the other officer read him his rights, as they led him to the office. Royce was there sitting at his desk. The officer sat Freddie in a chair, and Royce turned the monitor around, and then Freddie saw himself counting out money from the bag. He dropped his head. He was so busted.

"How did you do that? I know I turned off the camera," he said, mumbling.

"Apparently, you didn't turn them all off. Get him out of my sight," Royce told the officers.

The next day, Royce received a call from the detective. Freddie admitted to stealing the money bag keys years ago from a previous job. He'd take small amounts of money and then quit before he was caught. The officers checked all the footage from his surveillance cameras and found out that Freddie had been giving away free coffee. He pretended to ring up the customers' orders and pocket the money. Now, Royce knew that Freddie had stolen the money years ago, causing him to get fired. He was glad that he hadn't gotten arrested. The DM must have believed his story, or there wasn't enough proof.

Royce was wound up so tight; he needed a distraction. As soon as a manager was hired for the downtown location, he wanted to take a trip to Ohio. Royce knew he needed to visit the Midtown location. There were some personal items he'd left in the office. He had to do it early since he needed to be back downtown. Moreover, he wanted to see Rosita in person. He'd seen her on the cameras at work. It almost looked like she'd lost weight, and her sad eyes were worse. Rosita didn't admit that Marguerite had been crying the last time they talked, but her tears told him all he needed to know weeks ago, so he hoped she had stopped crying by now.

Walking into the GCH Midtown, all eyes were on Royce. He found the one set of eyes he sought, and they stared at each other. Rosita was the first to turn away. Several of the employees congratulated him on his promotion. At least they thought he'd received a promotion within the company. He thanked them and headed to the office. Looking in the storage room, he found a small box for his items. He'd forgotten his pictures were still here and packed them first.

Opening another drawer, he saw the cell phone. It was still here, which meant it was a message that she didn't need or want his help. He closed the drawer and sat at the desk for a while, hoping she'd come into the office. Scaring the staff again wasn't an option. After an hour had passed, he knew she wasn't coming. Picking up his box, he wanted to walk out the front door without looking back; that didn't happen.

An employee stopped him. "Mr. Hawthorne, are you moving away? Are you moving out of town?"

"No, I'm not going anywhere. I'll always be here. If anyone needs me, *I'm just a phone call away.*"

He said these words to his employees, but they were meant for the one person who wasn't even looking at him. She had her back turned and her head down. They all wished him well and success. Sitting in his truck, he stared at the tinted glass. Rosita knew he couldn't see her, but she could see him. She noticed when he leaned his head against the steering wheel. Why had she been a coward? Why was she the only one that hadn't said anything? Had he left because of her?

His words were ringing in her ears, *"I'm just a phone call away."* She rushed to the office; the pictures were gone. Snatching open the other drawer, she saw the cell phone staring back at her. She picked it up and listened to the last voicemail message he'd left her. He said that he was worried about her . . . *her*. Royce didn't say he was worried about Marguerite. He'd begged her to call him and let him know that she was okay. At least she knew she could hear his voice sometimes. Leaving the office, she stuffed the phone in her pocket.

As Rosita walked to the front, she worried about Marguerite. She was missing Royce terribly. Her poor baby barely ate and cried herself to sleep, holding her doll and a stuffed fish. Later that night, Rosita cried as she rocked Marguerite, who did her nightly ritual of crying herself to sleep.

Anyways, life goes on for Royce; he decided to open the downtown location earlier in the daytime on weekdays. There was a courthouse a few blocks away and some law offices. So he advertised his new hours, and business was relatively steady. He'd hired one of the staff as a shift team leader that could open up in the mornings. He still hadn't gotten around to hiring a full-time manager. For some reason, he didn't want to go home at a decent hour, preferring to stay up. It tore at him, wondering if Marguerite was crying. He couldn't sleep thinking about her.

Several weeks after he'd collected his personal items from the Midtown location, he still couldn't get Marguerite off his mind. So he buried himself in his work. Royce was working his usual late-night shift downtown when his cell rang after 11 p.m. The ID displayed Rosita's name. He answered the call and heard screaming; Marguerite was screaming so loud, it was scary. Rosita was shouting as well, and there was more shouting in the background.

"Hello . . . hello Rosita, what's wrong?" He shouted into the phone.

"Roy, Help me! She's going to hurt Marguerite!" Rosita was shouting into the phone.

"I'm on my way." Royce held the phone and didn't hang it up.

Royce ran out front and told his staff that he had an emergency, and he'd be back, he hoped. Driving like a crazy man across town, he ran red lights and stop signs. The phone had gone dead, and he tried calling back, but it went to voicemail. He wondered if he needed to call the police and have them meet him there. Instead, he kept driving, trying to focus on the road and traffic. Something was terribly wrong; Rosita had never called him this late at night. Fuck the police! He might be killing somebody anyway if they hurt Marguerite or Rosita.

It took him almost thirty minutes to get there; stomping on the brakes, he jumped out. Looking up, he didn't know where to go. He'd never been to the actual apartment. The building was only three stories, so he'd take his chances. He ran into the building, listening until he heard a loud noise. He ran toward the direction of the sound, climbing the stairs. The closer he got, the louder the screams. One of those screams was from Marguerite.

Stopping at the apartment, he beat on the door calling Rosita's name. All he heard was more shouting, and no one was answering the door. Twisting the knob, he found it locked. So he kicked it, and the door crashed open. Running into the apartment, he found Rosita up against a wall holding a screaming Marguerite, and a woman was shouting and waving her arms. She was yelling at Marguerite to shut up, saying she was sick and tired of hearing her scream every night.

"Hey, that's enough!" Royce roared. "Rosita, come here."

Rosita rushed to him, and he held her in his arms. She was crying, and so was Marguerite. Marguerite was trying to crawl up around his neck, calling to her daddy.

"What the hell is going on here? Why are you screaming at a child? Are you fucking crazy?" He was beyond pissed. "Rosita, get your stuff, get all your stuff. I'm taking you and Marguerite away from here."

Rosita gathered her belongings, stuffing everything into two large trash bags and a cardboard box of toys. She snatched a pillow and a blanket off the couch. That was when Royce realized where she and Marguerite were sleeping--he became even more furious. She grabbed Marguerite's doll and her stuffed fish, adding them to the box. Royce held Marguerite in one arm and the two trash bags. He nodded for Rosita to go in front of him.

"Hey, who's gonna pay for my door?" Alejandra shouted, running toward them.

"You better be glad that's the only thing I broke. I've never hit a woman before in my life. But lady, you better back up." Royce said with fire in his eyes.

Rosita held the box and ran down the stairs. Royce opened the rear door, waving his foot under the bumper and putting the bags inside. He buckled Marguerite in her seat, and Rosita gave her the doll.

"I have nowhere to go. Alejandra will never let me come back now." Rosita cried.

"You are never going back there. You've been sleeping on a couch, for God's sake."

"So, where am I supposed to go? I can't afford an apartment. I don't have enough money to get my own. And a hotel would take all that I have."

"You're coming with me."

"I . . . I can't, I won't come to your house. Roy, I'm not going to be your . . ."

"You're not going to be my what? I would never take advantage of you. I'm taking you and Marguerite someplace safe. I'm taking you somewhere that you and Marguerite can sleep in a bed. Would you *please* let me help you?"

"I have to work tomorrow, and Marguerite has to go to the sitters."

"She's not going back there either. I'll keep Marguerite in the morning, and we'll figure something out."

Royce pulled his phone from his pocket and made a call. "Hey, Ms. J., I'm sorry to call so late, but I need your help. No . . . I'm okay. I'm bringing you some guests. I'll explain when I get there."

Forty minutes later, Royce knocked on Ms. J's front door, carrying a sleeping Marguerite. Royce introduced Rosita to Ms. J., and he smiled and told her that this was Marguerite.

Ms. J rubbed her tiny face. "Royce, she's beautiful. Bring her back here and lay her down."

Ms. J. showed them to an empty bedroom, and Royce put her in the bed. Ms. J. showed Rosita to a room next door, which was connected by a bathroom. She asked Rosita if she wanted anything, food, water, and Rosita shook her head 'no'. She was mentally exhausted. Royce told her he had to get back to work. He suggested that she get some sleep, and he'd take her to work in the morning. Closing the door, he followed Ms. J. back to the living room.

Ms. J. knew about Marguerite, and Royce told her briefly about the situation. He also said to her that Rosita didn't know anything about his personal life. She thought he was just a manager, and Ms. J nodded her head, she understood. Rosita heard part of their conversation and didn't know what he meant about his personal life. He didn't have one. The man was a workaholic. She heard him returning with her bags and all the stuff they'd left in the truck. He knocked on her door, and she told him to come in.

He sat her bags on the floor by the bed. "Are you okay?"

"Not really. Why are you doing this?"

He chuckled softly, "Because I care, and once upon a time, someone helped me."

"Who is she? Is she your grandmother?"

"No, she's not. She is someone who I care about as well."

"Roy, do you live here?"

"No, I don't live in this house. I live nearby. You and Marguerite are safe, and no one is going to hurt you ever again. Not if I can help it. Now get some sleep, and I'll see you in the morning."

Royce wanted to hold her and tell her everything would be okay, but he didn't want to touch her. He stopped at the other room and peeped at Marguerite. She was so tiny in that big bed. He was worried that she'd roll out and fall on the floor. Grabbing several pillows from around the room, he positioned them on the floor around the bed.

He kissed her goodnight and whispered in her ear. "Love you, Marguerite."

It was around two in the morning before he went back to work. Royce had gone to the store shopping for groceries, buying all kinds of juices for kids, healthy snacks, cereals and milk, and anything else he thought they'd want. Rosita could go shopping in a couple of days because by the looks of things, the two bags that he took in the house, they didn't have much. He remembered hearing her comment that Marguerite needed more clothes. Ms. J had already volunteered to babysit Marguerite.

Royce was sitting in the kitchen when Rosita walked in. She was startled because it was 5 a.m., and he was sitting there in some gym shorts and a muscle shirt. Wow! She'd never seen this much of him before, looking at both his thick muscled arms and his other tattoo. She'd never seen anything so beautiful. It had rich, vibrant colors. It was some sort of band with feathers hanging from it. It looked like an American Indian design. He looked up, and she could tell that he looked tired.

"Have you been awake all night?"

"Pretty much, I just closed up at four."

"Oh, Mr . . . Roy, I'm so sorry this is my fault."

"Rosita, it's okay. I'll get some sleep. Are you ready to go?"

"Marguerite, what about Marguerite?" She asked frantically.

"Go kiss your daughter goodbye. You'll see her after work."

"She'll be afraid when she wakes up around a stranger."

"I'll be the first face she sees when she wakes up. I promise."

As he drove, Royce assured her that Marguerite was in good hands and that he didn't want her to worry all day about her. Rosita gave him a weak smile, nodding and saying that she would try. Rosita had no idea how this new situation would play out, but for now, she and Marguerite were safe. Royce dropped off Rosita and waited until she'd entered the building. Returning to the house, he sat in an overstuffed chair next to the bed. He woke up when he felt someone crawling on him. Opening his eyes, it was Marguerite.

"Daddy," she said and crawled into his lap.

Ms. J found them both sleeping in the chair. She shook Royce and told him to lie down in the other room.

When Royce woke, he jumped up, looking for Marguerite, and ran from the room. He found Marguerite and Ms. J sitting at the table. Marguerite was eating a grilled cheese sandwich. Royce exhaled. Marguerite squirmed to get out of Ms. J's lap. She ran to Royce, wanting him to pick her up, yelling daddy, and hugged his neck.

"She found me several hours ago, yelling pee, pee, and potty. Royce, why are you playing daddy to this little girl?"

"I already told you the whole story."

"So why haven't you brought her around before? That woman will use you until she meets some other man, and you'll never see Marguerite again."

"Don't you think I've thought about that, and that's the reason I haven't brought her around? It's bad enough that she stole my heart. I didn't want her to steal yours too."

"You can't go around picking up every stray in the street." Ms. J said.

"Yeah, like you picked me up and treated me like family. I love this little girl, and I'll do everything in my power to take care of her until . . . that happens." Royce stood up, looking at Marguerite. "She needs some clothes. I'm going to change so *we* can go shopping. I don't know how to buy clothes for little girls. And I want you to fatten her up." Royce tried to put her down, but she was holding on tight.

"Marguerite, I have to change clothes. I'll be right back, okay. I want you to stay with Ms. J."

"No!" It had become Marguerite's favorite word.

"Baby girl, we are not going to fight about this. I'm not taking you home with me." He looked at Ms. J for help.

"Marguerite, why don't you show me your doll, where is she?" Ms. J asked in a soft voice.

Marguerite turned in circles. She wasn't sure where to go. Regina grabbed her hand, talking softly and leading her to the room where she slept, while Royce sneaked out the back door.

During the drive, Royce asked Ms. J if Rosita and Marguerite could stay with her for a while. Rosita admitted that she didn't have the money to rent an apartment yet, and she wasn't going to let him pay for it. And then he asked if he could fix up the room for Marguerite. Royce was concerned about the bed being too big for her. Ms. J suggested he get a toddler bed. They were smaller, close to the floor, and usually had rails. Royce liked the sound of that.

They walked into the store, and Royce put Marguerite in the buggy. They started in the clothes section, and he asked Ms. J to get her everything she needed. Royce pointed out several cute outfits that he liked and paid attention to the sizes she was picking out. Marguerite had pretty black silky hair, and he wanted her fitted with lots of little girly stuff. Looking at his watch, he needed to hurry so he could fix up her room before picking up Rosita from work.

Royce sent Rosita a text, telling her that Marguerite was doing fantastic, and she was with him, but he didn't tell her that they were shopping. Next, he cruised down the aisle with the children's beds. He saw the perfect one, it was pink, and it had a canopy over it. Ms. J nodded her approval as she picked out the bedding. After he grabbed a cart to load the bed, he remembered that he saw Marguerite sitting on Ms. J's lap. Next, he grabbed a high chair. It looked high-tech, and he'd figure it out later. This one was versatile, where the tray was removable, and she could sit at the big table.

They were ready until Marguerite yelled, doll. He rushed to the doll section, took her out of the buggy, and told her to pick whatever she wanted. Ms. J suggested some educational toys, considering that she was a retired school teacher. Royce sent her to accomplice that feat because he had no idea what a two-year-old could learn. He smiled when he spotted the rack of movies again, grabbing several that Marguerite didn't have. He wanted to sit on the couch and hold her while she watched a movie. Marguerite was trying to run and hold one box, and at the same time, she was dragging another doll behind her. Royce thought it was the cutest scene.

Royce picked her up, laughing. She squealed with laughter. That was the only sound he wanted to hear from her. He didn't want ever to hear her crying for him again. It was a sound that no parent should have to hear from a child. Her piercing screams had hurt him, and he wasn't even her parent. Royce put the doll she was dragging on top of the boxes.

"We have to get home. I have some work to do before your mommy gets there."

Royce yelled for Ms. J. She came around a corner, pushing the other overloaded buggy. She'd added some books and other electronic stuff that Royce had never seen before in his life.

Royce rushed to the house. He let Ms. J take care of Marguerite while he hurried and transformed the room. He put the toddler bed together in record time. Ms. J folded all the clothes, putting them in an empty dresser in the room, and hung the other clothes. Royce carried the old bed in parts to the garage storage room. Finishing off the room, he put Marguerite's newest dolls in her bed. He left Marguerite alone with Ms. J while he picked up Rosita. He'd dressed for work because he was doing a quick drop-off after he kissed Marguerite bye.

Rosita had a worried look on her face when he picked her up. He smiled and reassured her that everything would be okay. They talked about work during the drive back. Rosita was worried that he hadn't gotten enough rest, and now he was off to work again. He was going to work a little later than usual, but it was okay. He'd talked to his staff, and they were handling the store.

Royce pulled his SUV into the garage, and Rosita noticed two motorcycles. One of them looked like the one she saw him on before. There was a car there, also. She still had sleep in her eyes that morning, and she hadn't paid attention. He unlocked the back door with a key and called Marguerite's name.

Marguerite came running into the kitchen, looking at her mother and Royce. She didn't know who to run to first. Rosita scooped her up, kissing her. Her beautiful daughter smelled clean, wearing new clothes. She was around her mother's neck and reaching for Royce. He stood slightly behind Rosita and leaned in to tickle Marguerite on the neck with his beard. She laughed and hunched her shoulders to keep him away from her neck. Rosita liked the sound of her laughter, and she also felt Royce's presence. He didn't touch her, but she knew how close he was. She felt his massive chest expand across her whole back. It made her feel protected.

Royce kissed Marguerite on her head and told Rosita he would see her in the morning, telling her to call him if she needed to. He looked at her profile for a few seconds, and an urge to kiss her in the same spot he'd kissed Marguerite overwhelmed him. A kiss that said I would protect you too, but he didn't. He walked out the door feeling a huge weight lift off his shoulders.

He'd been at work for two hours before his cell rang, and Rosita started teasing. "Roy, what did you and Marguerite do today?"

"Nothing," he answered quickly.

"I've never heard of a bedroom fairy."

"Neither have I."

"So you must be a fairy Godfather," Rosita retorted.

"I like the sound of that. Can I get it in writing?"

"Yeah, sure, I'll do that first thing in the morning. I wish you would stop spoiling Marguerite. I can't ever repay you for all that you've done for us."

"That's what a fairy Godfather is for."

Royce laughed and asked Rosita to please not picture him in a pair of wings, and she laughed along with him. He was glad to hear her laugh; it was way better than seeing her cry like she had the other night. Rosita wished him a good night and that she'd see him in the morning.

Royce kept up his routine for another two weeks. Marguerite was adjusting and had even started to fill out. Ms. J had her on a routine of study time, playtime, and nap time. Rosita and Ms. J would cook dinners together, and sometimes Royce would come and eat with them. Those were his favorite times, sitting around the table, eating dinner together. Marguerite was asking for what she wanted and not grunting. Ms. J or Rosita would read to her every night. A few times, she called for daddy, but she never cried, especially when Rosita placed a short call so Marguerite could hear his voice.

Rosita still wondered where he lived. Every morning he was sitting at the table waiting for her. She told him she could ride the bus, and he flat out said *No*, that he didn't want her catching the bus that early to go across town.

On Saturday afternoon, Royce showed up to work downtown. His employees told him they'd been busy all day, the theaters were running multiple shows. Royce liked it when it was busy because it made his night go by faster. He dreaded having to come to work. Rosita was off, and they'd taken Marguerite to the park. They were even planning a big dinner. However, by the looks of the steady customers, he might not be able to sneak away. He was expecting another employee any minute now. Royce looked at the clock, and he was late. Two minutes later, the phone rang, and his employee was calling in sick. Damn!

He needed more help, and Rosita was off tomorrow. Perhaps she would come and help him. She answered his call and agreed to work with him; at least Freddie wasn't there anymore. Too bad she didn't know how to drive. He told her to get ready, and he'd pick her up. Rosita told Ms. J what was going on, and she told her not to worry about Marguerite.

Royce tried not to break any more traffic laws, especially after he rushed across town to save Marguerite and Rosita. He'd gotten some traffic pictures in the mail. He paid the fines, and he didn't care one bit. Immediately when Rosita arrived, she went right to work. It was so busy that it took all of them to get the customers their orders promptly.

4 a.m. came so fast that Rosita never realized it was so late. Everyone worked quickly to finish the closing process. Soon, they left the store, and Royce asked Rosita if she wanted to grab some breakfast as neither of them had had time for dinner. Everybody was tired of muffins, donuts, and cookies. She consented to the idea, and so they rode to a 24-hour pancake house, where they ordered water and orange juice with the breakfast special and talked.

"You know Roy. I don't know anything about you. When Freddie asked me all those questions, I didn't have any answers for him."

"What do you want to know?"

"Whatever you want to share," she told him.

Royce wanted to know more about her, so he figured if he talked, then maybe she would. He said that he was from Louisiana and that he was an only child who moved to Detroit right out of high school. She wanted to know how long he'd worked for Starbucks. A small laugh escaped before he told her he'd worked there for about three years. She repeated what Freddie had told her about him. He explained that Freddie didn't know that he took a job at another coffee company. Well, part of his story was true. He wanted to tell her more, but he wasn't ready to do that yet.

She asked about Ms. J. With a big smile on his face, he told her how they met, and it was because of her that he was able to move out of Black Bottom. Her curiosity was still piqued, so she began thinking that he stayed in a house on the same street or nearby. He would never tell her, no matter how many times she asked. They started talking about Marguerite and how much she'd improved, she was talking much better.

"You remember when you teased about me being Marguerite's fairy Godfather."

"Yes," she laughed and flapped her arms like wings.

"How do you feel about me being that for real? It's the only guarantee I can give you that I would protect her. I don't want you to think that I would ever tire of her. I love her as if she were my child."

Rosita gasped. "Are you serious? I was mad and upset when I said you would tire of her. It was never about the daycare, it was more about my pride. You've been nothing but generous since you met us. I didn't know how to be humble and let you help us. I'm so sorry. I know how you feel about my daughter. I saw the pictures in your desk drawer that you didn't give me a copy of." She put her hands in her lap and looked down. She wanted to say more but didn't. "You've been her fairy Godfather since the day you found her, or should I say the day she found you."

"I don't mind signing my name on a piece of paper to prove it. She will never want for anything, even if you . . . even when the situation changes," he said softly.

"What about when you have your own family?"

"You mean if I ever have my own family. If that happens, *she* or my family will have to accept Marguerite even if I have to lie and say she's mine."

"That is going to be a hard lie to pull off." Rosita was already feeling sorry for whoever *she* might be. Maybe *she* was the woman she heard in the background a few months ago.

"Yeah, I know, you think I should buy some gray contacts?"

They both laughed. Royce asked her if she'd finished eating. She nodded yes, saying she was full. Rosita knew he was telling the truth about everything he said.

"We should take Marguerite some pancakes, she loves pancakes," Royce said like Rosita didn't know that.

Royce unlocked the back door and let them into the house. They walked together to Marguerite's room. The bed was so low that Royce had to get on his knees to kiss Marguerite. Then he bumped his head on the canopy getting up. Rosita was standing at the door, holding her sides laughing.

"Oh, you think that's funny." Royce rushed to the door lifting Rosita and tickling her sides. She laughed louder.

Royce whispered. "Shh, you're going to wake her up."

A memory flashed before him, and he put her back on the floor. Her eyes were sparkling, with no signs of sadness. He smiled, giving her his mother's favorite smile.

"You . . . better get some sleep. Marguerite will be up soon." Royce stepped around her and was gone.

Rosita's smile dropped; they were having a good time. Then she remembered that she had yelled at him for touching her. She'd enjoyed their playing together; he tickles and plays with Marguerite every day. She wanted to be tickled too.

Chapter Thirteen

$\mathscr{R}$oyce climbed the stairs to his apartment, sat on his small couch, and placed his head in his hands, confused. Was he falling for a woman who was such a mystery? Rosita was living with a past that haunted her, and he doesn't care about that past. She was the one that was letting it get in the way of *her* happiness. He'd known her now for almost a year, and in that year, he'd learned nothing new other than she still needed someone to protect her.

He felt wealthy in more ways than one. He'd grown up with two loving parents, a family that loved him, and a happy childhood that he didn't appreciate until this very moment. Rosita only had Marguerite. Marguerite had him; does Rosita need him too? Royce took a hot shower and climbed into his bed.

During the following week, Royce poured over dozens of applicants. He'd interviewed several people, and none fit what he needed, or they had stipulations- he'd keep looking. Toby agreed to be his new district manager, and as soon as he found the right manager for the downtown location, Toby and he needed to make a trip to the headquarters. Toby needed to get some extra training, which means they'd be away for several days.

Royce wanted his new team to make the final decisions in the hiring process for the new Lansing and Grand Rapids locations. They would decide together on hiring the managers, and Royce needed to make another quick trip back to both cities. He thought about going two different days when Rosita was off, and she could work downtown until he got back. He knew he wouldn't be as late as before, thinking that she could ride the bus, take a taxi, or Ms. J could drop her off.

Royce downloaded more applications from an online website, wondering if he'd ever find the right person. He wasn't about to settle for anything, he'd been working too hard. It took another week and a few more interviews for him to finally find an applicant to fill the manager job for the downtown location. Since Toby was now the DM, Royce scheduled a second interview before he named him manager. Now that everything was about to fall into place, it was time to find an office.

He wanted enough space with a few offices, a conference room, and a file room. Damn! Did they need a secretary or one of those administrative assistants? Thank goodness the network was backed up in the clouds. He'd be ready to officially open Hawthorne Incorporated after he opened the next five locations. Toby was working at the Ren Cen, and he'd work from the downtown location for the time being.

For the next three weeks, Royce worked diligently to get the new manager up to speed. Between the three of them, they selected two staffers and promoted them to supervisory positions. Toby continued his GM position at the Ren Cen until the new locations were ready to open, but he was already considering who would replace Toby.

Royce had a conversation with Rosita and asked her not to discuss her residence with any of the staff. He didn't want any of them to get the wrong idea. She needed to be in a position for promotion, and he didn't want it to look like favoritism. Rosita assured him that she'd never talked about her personal life with any of them before. It wasn't a secret that Royce had taken a particular interest in Marguerite ever since her birthday party. But she was so sweet and cute it was like she was the job mascot. Rosita's co-workers were often bringing her something for Marguerite.

Royce was more excited about having his evenings and nights free. He could spend time with Marguerite again and Rosita if she wanted to tag along. Royce didn't tell Rosita that he'd hired a manager; instead, he wanted to surprise them with an evening out.

After picking up Rosita from work, they went into the house as usual. Royce hugged and kissed Marguerite. She wanted to show him a book with some pictures in it, so he sat on the couch with her in his lap. Rosita watched them from a doorway, they had a special bond that was unbelievable. It was the type of father-daughter relationship that every mother wished for their child. Marguerite pointed to the pictures and told him what each object was.

"Oh, Marguerite, that's awesome. I'm so proud of you." Royce whispered into her ear and tickled her neck with his beard. She giggled, and he sat her on the couch.

"Bye, daddy."

"See you soon, baby girl." He kissed her on top of the head.

Royce got off the couch and saw Rosita standing behind them. She had such a happy look on her face. Royce stopped right in front of her. She had to tilt her head back, inhaling his cologne.

"What are you so happy about?" he asked.

"It makes me happy to watch the two of you together."

"Why?"

"You're a natural." She commented, honestly.

"I just give her the attention she deserves," he said emotionally like it had extra meaning. "Are you planning on wearing your work clothes all night?"

"No, I'm going to change. Why?"

"Nothing. See ya."

He lingered, looking at her features, she had a beautiful smile and a perfect nose. Marguerite may have her father's eyes, but she had her mother's beauty. Royce wanted to touch her face. Instead, he turned slowly back toward the couch. Marguerite was standing on the couch, watching them, smiling. It was like she could read his thoughts, so he stepped around Rosita and left.

First, Rosita kissed her daughter, who was jumping up and down on the couch, and then she was scolded for jumping on the furniture. Lastly, she sent her to play with her toys in her room. She liked the sound of that, her room. She didn't think she'd ever get out of that situation with Alejandra. It wasn't hers, but Ms. J had made them feel so welcome. Finally, she was in a position to save money, and soon she and Marguerite could afford an apartment.

Rosita went to her room and fell back across the bed, touching her cheeks to see if they were burning. She closed her eyes and inhaled. His cologne burned in her nostrils. Had she been blushing when he stood over her? He'd been so close that she thought he was going to touch her. What a fool she'd been to yell at him. She didn't know how to fix it.

She wanted to yell, "You can touch me now. I want you to touch me. I want . . . you to tickle me again." She could touch him, but she was scared. What if he didn't want her that way? She just happened to be the mother of a little girl that he loved, how strange.

It was starting to get chilly outside, and she was cold-natured. Rosita found some comfortable jogging pants and a sweatshirt. Putting her hair up in a ponytail, she headed to the kitchen. She almost screamed when she saw Royce sitting at the table, wearing a pair of jeans and a tight shirt that displayed his muscled pecs.

"Why do you look like you've seen a ghost?"

"Roy, what are you doing here? I thought you went back to work."

"I finally found a replacement, so no more . . . late . . . nights for me, unless there's an emergency. Right now, I want to take *you* and Marguerite out for dinner."

"You want to take me out?"

"Yes, why should Marguerite and I have all the fun? And besides, it's getting embarrassing to keep asking women to take Marguerite to the bathroom. Do you know how many women ask for my phone number?"

"You're kidding?" she asked, laughing.

"No, I'm not kidding. They look at my hand and make comments about me not being married."

"Wow! Women have no respect for a man out with his daughter. I mean . . . you know what I mean."

"How about you go and change . . . if you want. I think you look cute in your baggy . . . pants."

Marguerite came running around the corner. "I'm dressed, daddy."

"See, even Marguerite dresses better than I do," she laughed.

Royce laughed louder. Marguerite had on two of everything, all mismatched. Poor baby tried to dress herself. After Royce picked her up and kissed her on the cheek, they all stop laughing. Rosita took her from Royce's arms, telling him they'd be back shortly.

Marguerite came running first, this time appropriately dressed. She had on jeans and a new pair of kids Timberlands, hers were pink, and they matched her shirt. She ran to Royce on the couch, putting her foot next to his to show that they had matching shoes, except his boots weren't pink. Rosita came around the corner dressed in a pair of jeans and a sweater, minus a pair of Timberlands.

"Roy, you do know that she's a little girl, and you can't dress her up as a boy."

"I know she's a girl, and all her boots are girl boots. She has to dress like her . . . Godfather. She loves it."

"I know she does, but does she need them in every color?"

"What's wrong with that? I have them in every color. I wish you'd let me buy you a pair or two. They have pink in your size."

"I think . . . no, I know you paid too much for Marguerite's. I don't need a pair of pink boots that cost that much money."

"Okay, so you don't get pink. Let's go. I'm taking my *family* out to dinner."

Rosita almost choked when he said, family. He didn't stutter or slur, he said, "*his* family."

Royce pulled up to an expensive steak house with valet parking. The valet ran and opened the door. Royce held Marguerite in his arms and strolled through the door. Rosita looked around at the décor and other people. They wore either fancy clothes or business suits, only a few dressed casually. For a moment, she wanted to ask Royce that they leave. They were waiting to be seated after Royce announced the name on the reservation.

He noticed Rosita's apprehension. "What's wrong?"

She whispered. "Most of these people are all dressed up, and we're wearing jeans."

"They don't care what you're wearing. They just like to know that your credit card is going to clear. Why, do you want to dress up?"

"I don't have anything like what they're wearing."

The hostess announced that their table was ready and asked them to follow her. Royce's first thought was that Rosita would be beautiful, all dressed up. They were seated at an elegant table. Royce sat Marguerite in the high chair they provided. She was already grabbing at stuff on the table.

"Marguerite, stop touching stuff," Rosita said nervously.

"Rosita, it's just dishes."

"Roy, this stuff looks expensive, and I don't want her to break anything."

"And if she does, I'll pay for it. Now, let's enjoy a wonderful meal. I want the biggest steak on the menu and a lobster. Would you like a lobster? Marguerite can have one too."

"I've never eaten lobster."

"They're good. I ate plenty of them when I was in Hawaii."

"You've been to Hawaii."

"Yes, with my parents, it was a family vacation."

"You didn't tell me about that."

"You asked about me, not where I've been."

"True, but I would love to hear about where you've been. I grew up in Los Angeles. I never went anywhere other than coming to Detroit."

She was finally talking, and he wanted her to say more without him asking. He told her all about his vacation to Hawaii, minus his sexual encounters. He divulged his roaming around a few islands in the Caribbean, again minus a few details. She wanted to know how long he roamed. Pausing, he confessed that he traveled for over three months.

"Your parents must be rich."

"No, my parents aren't rich. Ah . . . I think our food is here," Royce looked up into the face of their waiter.

Royce managed to make her forget, focusing his attention on feeding Marguerite some of his salad. The server sat a platter with an enormous dressed lobster in front of her. Rosita had one too, and she didn't know where to start. Marguerite wanted to play with it like a toy. At least she wasn't afraid of it. Royce pulled the meat from the tail and cut it into bite-size pieces. Rosita watched him and did the same thing to her lobster.

Royce cut into his steak and moaned from the first bite. He ate a few more bites and watched Marguerite eat so she wouldn't put too much food in her mouth. He'd become a pro at taking care of Marguerite, and he quickly noticed that Rosita was enjoying her food.

His primal instinct kicked in, so he cut a piece of his steak and angled his fork at Rosita's mouth. She looked at him then at the fork. After a second or two, she opened her mouth, and he closed the distance with the fork. She closed her lips around the meat and the fork. Royce pulled the fork out slowly and watched her chew.

"Mmm, that's tasty," she remarked.

Rosita bent her head, looked at her plate, and cut another piece of her food. Royce put an empty fork in his mouth and pulled it slowly like he had eaten a piece of meat. He tasted her on the fork, if only she'd let him touch her. Turning, he checked on Marguerite before he cut into his steak again. This time, he put a small piece in front of her. Marguerite was content, Rosita was content, and he was on edge. They got through dinner and dessert, and Marguerite didn't break anything.

Royce and Rosita were quiet for the ride home. Marguerite kept up enough chatter for the three of them. When they got back to the house, Royce sat on the couch while Rosita got Marguerite ready for bed. He was deep in thought, wanting to dress Rosita in elegant clothes and take her to expensive restaurants. He wanted to watch her experience a sunset on a beach. She was so much like him, plain and simple. She appreciated things, little things, and she didn't feel the need to show off.

Marguerite woke him up from his daydream. She jumped in his lap, dressed in her pajamas. He asked her if she wanted him to read, and she yelled, "movie." He told her to pick a movie. She ran to her collection of Disney movies and gave the case to Royce. He opened the case and inserted *The Princess and the Frog*. He liked this movie too. The characters talked about his home state of Louisiana. Marguerite jumped up and down, excited. Royce sat back in his spot on the couch, as Rosita emerged from her room wearing baggy pants and a sweatshirt. Most women would either be still dressed or redressed into something sexy.

The movie started, and Marguerite jumped back in her spot on his lap. The movie had been playing for about forty-five minutes, and everybody had gotten comfortable. Marguerite was lying in the crook of Royce's arm and the arm of the couch. Royce was slouched down with his shoes off. Rosita was propped up on the other end with a blanket across her legs.

Ms. J passed through the living room on her way to the kitchen. She spotted the trio all asleep on the couch, and the credits were rolling from the movie, it was a perfect Kodak moment. Tiptoeing back to her room, she got her phone. She loved her phone after she learned how to use the blasted thing. Ms. J took several pictures, saying that she'd send them to Royce later. She made her way to the kitchen with a big grin on her face.

Royce was the first to wake up after hearing some noise in the kitchen. He rolled his neck because of his uncomfortable position. He knew Marguerite was lying on his right arm, and she was now dead sleep. And something was resting against his left side. He looked over at a sleeping Rosita. She had curled up against him under the thin blanket. He sighed at his pretend family, and here he was, stuck in the middle.

Ms. J showed up and saw that he was up, and he mouthed for her to get Marguerite. He moved slowly so he wouldn't wake Rosita, easing her down on the couch. First, he deposited Marguerite in her bed and kissed her goodnight. And then he went back to the living room and looked down at Rosita. She had an angelic look about her as she slept. He thought about taking a picture and teasing her later, telling her that she was snoring, or he just wanted a picture of her. He had the other pictures of her at Marguerite's birthday party, but that was a long time ago. That was when she was sad, she didn't have those sad eyes anymore. He pulled out his phone, snapped a picture, slid it back in his pocket, and then he shook her slightly.

"Rosita, wake up and go to bed . . . Rosita."

She mumbled and curled into a ball under the blanket. He tried to wake her again. Damn! He went to her room and pulled the covers back. Picking her up off the couch, she snuggled close to his chest, just like Marguerite. He laid her down carefully in her bed and pulled the covers over her.

He kissed her on the top of her head, "Goodnight, Rosita."

Royce thought about Rosita his whole short trip home. He wanted her to have what Marguerite had, someone to love her. He knew it would take time; she was opening up slowly. Hopefully, she'd come to trust him enough to let him in. Now, he had a new plan, could he just secretly date her without her knowing it?

Chapter Fourteen

Royce was sitting in his usual spot at the table when Rosita walked into the kitchen. She didn't want to look at him because she was embarrassed after waking during the night. The last thing she remembered was being on the couch watching a movie with Marguerite and Royce. She had a strong suspicion, and now, she was mortified?

"Good morning, Rosita."

"Morning," She spoke softly.

Royce wondered if she remembered snuggling against him last night, and now she was acting shy. They headed to the truck, and he opened her door for her. During the ride, he told her that he had to make a trip out of town. She asked how long he'd be gone. Immediately, she thought of the woman's voice she heard in the background from a previous trip. He said it was only a day trip, and he told her where he was going and that Toby was going with him. Slowly, he wanted to give her bits and pieces of his business life. He revealed that the visit involved some new property. It disturbed her a little that he would have to spend a lot of time out of town. Did that also mean that he'd be working late nights or spending nights out of town?

On the way to work, he pulled into a restaurant and drove toward the drive-thru. Royce started telling her about this small place and the breakfast burritos they sold. He planned to get some burritos and take them back to the house for Marguerite. Turning in his seat, he asked her how many she wanted because he would eat his at GCH with a good cup of coffee. She smirked because there was plenty of coffee at the house. So why was he eating there? She cut her eyes at him and told him she'd eat a couple. He laughed and said he could eat five or six by himself, and that Marguerite could eat two.

"Is that why she's getting so fat? I can barely pick her up."

"Then, I need to feed you more steak and lobster."

She blushed, thinking about him feeding her a bite of his steak. She didn't comment on his remark.

"Would you like to take a trip?" He asked off the top of his head.

"You mean a business trip . . . with you?"

"No, I mean . . . let's take Marguerite somewhere fun before it gets cold. She enjoyed the Aquarium, and I want to take her to a zoo or an amusement park. You girls could share a room, of course."

"Of course . . . yes, we would share a room . . . with Marguerite. I mean, I will share a room with Marguerite," Rosita was stumbling.

Her insides turned to jelly. He wanted to take them both on a trip. Should she do this? Why was he so kind? He loved Marguerite. She knew he needed her to take Marguerite to the bathroom, and it might be inappropriate to take her away alone. A man who wasn't her father alone with a little girl was extremely inappropriate.

"Sure, Marguerite would love that."

"Okay, I'll find us a fun place to go to."

He already knew where he wanted to go, and he crossed his fingers that it wouldn't cause a problem. Rosita's job application said she'd worked in Los Angeles, and she said she'd never been anywhere else.

Royce planned two-day trips. Each day, he took Rosita to work, and Ms. J and Marguerite picked her up from work. The second-day trip surprised Rosita when he walked into the house dressed in a suit.

"Wow! You clean up nicely."

"Why, thank you, ma'am. Maybe I can get you to dress up for me one day."

"Yeah, sure, can you see me in a party dress?" She pointed to her comfortable baggy pants.

He made quick strides with his long legs and stopped directly in front of her, she had to look up again.

"Yes, I can imagine you in a party dress." He lifted her hair. "With your hair, all pinned up, and diamonds are dangling from your ears. Would you like a diamond necklace to go with those earrings?" He spoke to her softly.

Rosita closed her eyes and saw herself all beautiful, just as he described. She whispered and parted her lips, "Yes, I would."

Dropping her hair, he caressed her face. "You can have anything you want if you believe you deserve it."

Royce wanted to kiss her lips; her eyes were still closed. God! She was beautiful and natural. Her face was free of makeup. Rosita opened her eyes and saw something in his face that she'd never seen before.

She dropped her head and stepped back, "I don't live in a Disney movie where the girl always gets her Prince Charming." She walked off, calling for Marguerite.

"Yes, you do. You deserve a happily ever after," Royce said to an empty room.

Royce sent out a mass email to all his employees, announcing Toby's promotion. He asked that all senior management report directly to him about all matters. They were to start following their new chain of command immediately. He'd also done something a little sneaky, and he didn't want any of his employees to know that he and Rosita would be out of town together. He wasn't surprised when he got a call from Toby.

"Hey, boss, you got something to tell me?"

"No, why do you ask?"

"I happen to see a list of vacation requests waiting for my approval, except one. I would have approved that one for you."

"It's not what you think. I wanted to take Marguerite somewhere, and I couldn't very well take a two-year-old little girl that is not my daughter out of town. I would appreciate it if this stays between the two of us."

"No problem, your secret is safe with me," Toby said and smiled as he hung up the phone.

Toby knew Royce for a few years now and saw that he was a kind person. Royce hired him and gave him a chance. But what surprised him more was when he'd confided in him, and now Toby considered him a true friend. Who would have thought the man was fucking rich? He felt deep down that he deserved to find someone that made him happy. He'd seen some changes in him since Marguerite had come into his life. It wasn't a surprise that he would start to feel something for her mother.

Royce was making big plans for their get-a-away. He needed some vital information, and he didn't know how to ask without revealing his surprise. He was just going to have to ask.

Royce picked up Rosita from work. She climbed into the SUV and started talking. "Guess what happened to me at work today?"

"What happened?" He asked panicky, thinking something terrible.

"Janell called me in the office and told me my vacation request was approved. First off, I didn't remember requesting a vacation. Second, I didn't know I got paid vacation time, and third I didn't know it had to be requested on the computer. So what can you tell me about all this vacation stuff?"

Royce laughed, "You crack me up. Okay, first answer . . . it pays to know the right people. Second . . . your boss should have informed you that you qualify for paid vacation time when you were promoted. And third . . . is part of the second answer."

"What are you talking about? You're my boss. You were the boss that promoted me."

"Okay, so I forgot to tell you everything. Let me ask you this? Is your ID current?"

"Yes, it is. You know I don't have a driver's license."

"Okay . . ." He exhaled. "Do you have something or some kind of . . . paperwork?" He paused again. "Do you have Marguerite's birth certificate handy?" he asked quickly.

"Why do you want to know about Marguerite's birth certificate?" Her voice went up one octave.

"Because you're going to need it for our vacation," He cringed and leaned against the driver's side door.

"What does a birth certificate have to do with a vacation?"

"The vacation involves an airplane ride. Marguerite will need some type of identification, and you have to prove that you're her mother."

"Oh . . . I've never been on an airplane." Rosita was stunned, and she knew whenever Marguerite was involved, there weren't many choices where Royce was concerned.

"Good, you can have the window seat."

Royce looked at her, and she wasn't mad. She was smiling. He imagined her in a two-piece bikini. Damn! He couldn't tell her where they were going, so he couldn't ask her to pack one. Pack! When he brought them to the house, their clothes had been in two trash bags.

"When we get home, let's pick up Marguerite and go do a little shopping."

"I don't know what to pack."

"The only thing I can say is to pack for warm weather."

Rosita's mind ran in circles. Where was he taking them? Were they going to Hawaii? Nah! This trip was really for Marguerite. She would have to wait and see.

The following week Royce loaded their luggage in the back of his SUV and headed to the airport. He sat comfortably in a chair with Marguerite in his lap while they waited to board. Rosita sat, looking around, absorbing all the activity around them. Royce had packed a backpack with Marguerite's entertainment and a couple of books. She also thought it was strange that he grabbed Marguerite's car seat, saying they needed it for the plane and the rental. When the announcements came over the speaker, Royce slung his laptop bag across his shoulder and grabbed the car seat and the small bag while Rosita held Marguerite. They boarded the plane and sat in the front section. Rosita got the window seat, and Marguerite sat in the middle. They were in their seats and served beverages.

"Roy, are we in first class?"

"Yes, nothing but the best for my *two* favorite girls."

Rosita mouthed, "*Two.*"

Royce nodded and held up two fingers. He rechecked Marguerite's seat belt as a distraction, asking her if she was scared.

"No, daddy, I'm not scared."

Royce told her if she got scared to let him know. He explained that after the plane leveled off, she could watch one of her movies, or there might be something on her personal TV screen. Marguerite drank her juice and ate the warm cookie the flight attendant had given her. Rosita now knew where they were going. She didn't think she would ever step a foot back in California, but they were going to San Diego and not Los Angeles, a place she never wanted to see again. She didn't want to ever run into Marguerite's father.

They were driving down the streets of San Diego, and Rosita was just as excited as Marguerite. During the flight, Royce told her that they were going to the San Diego Zoo and Sea World. It would take more than one day to see everything, so he purchased a multi-day package. He wanted to surprise Marguerite with adventures at Sea World.

Royce followed the directions on the GPS in the rented SUV. He turned and drove down a street, which led to their hotel. The building loomed before them.

"Roy, this place looks like a castle; it's beautiful."

"I booked a two-bedroom suite. I hope that's okay. I can change it to two rooms if you want?"

"It sounds nice. Marguerite and I have our bedroom, and you have yours." Rosita exhaled slowly. She'd spent many evenings sitting on the couch with him but never slept mere feet away. It sounded like a small apartment.

They checked in at the front desk, and Royce held Marguerite in his arms as usual. The desk clerk went over their arrangements. She commented that they provided baby-sitting services if needed.

Royce told her quickly, "She goes where we go, but thanks."

Rosita heard him, and he sounded more protective than she did. She saw him pull out his credit card and slide it across the counter. The desk clerk's voice changed. It was Mr. Hawthorne this and Mr. Hawthorne that. She sounded like she was sucking up and treating him like royalty. They were returning to the SUV because their accommodations were around the other side of the building.

"Roy, what did you say to that woman at the desk?"

"I didn't say anything. What are you talking about?"

"She started treating you like you were the prince of Egypt."

He gave her his funny laugh again. "I told you they only care if your credit card works."

Royce opened the door to their suite. He put Marguerite on the floor, and she took off running. Royce knew that one of the rooms had two beds, and the other had a king-size bed. He wanted Rosita to choose which room she preferred. She walked around the room in awe and told him the place was larger than the apartment she'd lived in, where she slept on the couch.

Royce opened the drapes and moaned at the bay's view, calling Marguerite so she could see. He and Marguerite were staring out the window when he heard Rosita rolling luggage.

Rushing across the room to help, Rosita said she wasn't helpless and could roll a suitcase or two. Throwing his hands up, he surrendered, but he wanted to see which room she'd chosen so he could move his things to the other one. Royce found her in the room with the two beds. He wanted to remind her about Marguerite falling out of the big bed if she slept alone, but didn't.

Royce rolled his luggage to the room with the king bed. They were spending a week in San Diego, so he unpacked his luggage, putting his clothes in the closet and the drawers. There were multiple doors in his room. One of the doors led to the other bedroom, and the other led to the living room. He'd closed the door between the bedrooms, thinking about locking it. Instead, he kept it unlocked for Marguerite. She was already making herself at home. He was putting some things in the bathroom when he heard little feet for the third time.

Marguerite was well aware of that door. He also knew he would have to lock his bathroom door anytime he was in there. He'd finished unpacking and was lying across his bed. Marguerite was jumping up and down on his bed. Rosita walked around the suite to his other door, which was propped open. She fussed at Marguerite for jumping on the bed and at Royce for letting her.

"She's having fun. Leave her alone."

"You know, if we shared a child, you and I would argue about discipline. You can't keep letting her get away with murder."

Royce smiled. He liked the sound of that, them sharing a child. He had a long way to go before any of that could happen.

"I would never condone murder." He laughed.

"What are we doing today?" she asked, smiling.

"Well, since you girls didn't know where we were going, we need to go shopping for swimwear. I want to take Marguerite to the pool. We can relax today and start our adventures tomorrow."

"I don't know how to swim."

"You don't have to swim, but I'm sure you look good in a bikini."

"No bikini for me. I'll let you look at the other women in bikinis."

"I don't want to look at the other women."

"Oh!" Rosita was momentarily speechless. "I don't feel comfortable dressing like that."

"I was teasing. You can wear whatever you want, okay."

Rosita dropped her head and blushed. She was still stuck on the fact that he wanted to look at her and not the other women. They climbed back into the SUV, and Royce searched for a mall or a department store on the GPS. He'd driven a couple of miles when he spotted a beach and swim shop. He pulled into the parking lot, and Marguerite was excited looking at the inflatable toys.

Royce sent Rosita to find a swimsuit while he searched for what he needed for Marguerite. He searched for a float suit in the children's section, finding a cute dark blue polka-dotted one. The next thing he dropped in the buggy was a wet suit and a one-piece swimsuit. He thought about finding a place where she could take swim lessons when they got back home or teach her.

Strolling around the store, Marguerite rode anxiously in the buggy, and he grabbed three beach towels and some water shoes for him and Marguerite. He didn't know what size Rosita's shoes were. She wouldn't tell him, and he knew why. She was afraid he'd buy her a bunch of boots. He passed a rack loaded with beach bags; they needed one of these, so he grabbed one of them too.

Royce and Marguerite headed to the women's section looking for Rosita. She had a couple of suits in her hand and standing in front of a mirror. She was holding them up against her body.

"Did you try on anything?" Royce asked, coming up behind her.

"No."

"You can try them on and model for us."

Rosita looked at the buggy, which was full of stuff. Royce stood in a defiant stance, folding his arms across his chest. Even Marguerite mimicked him by trying to cross hers. Rosita dropped her shoulders and gave in. Grabbing a couple more swimsuits that she'd admired, she headed into the dressing room. She tried on the first suit and looked at herself in the mirror behind her curtain. She didn't think she looked beautiful; she looked plain. Her breasts were average; she had a tiny waist and barely a hint of some hips. Why would he want to look at her when there would be plenty of women with a lot more to offer? She had on a one-piece, and the color was hideous against her skin. Shaking her head, she wasn't going out there in this. Quickly, she changed into another one and walked out of the dressing room.

"That is cute. Do you like that one?"

She didn't see a change in his face, which meant he didn't like it. He was being a kind man, and in actuality, she wanted him to have a reason to watch her. She'd grabbed a bikini off the rack only because she was curious.

"I have more to try on before I make a final decision."

Rosita returned to the dressing room. She tried on three suits for him to view. He still had the same reaction. She tried on another one-piece, it was a navy and white swim dress with a low-cut V in the front, and the back opened to the top of her butt. She could swear the skirt barely covered her butt cheeks. She walked out and immediately saw a difference in his face. He twirled his finger for her to turn around. She did as he asked and blushed.

"I like that one," he said with a big smile on his face.

It was written all over his face that he liked it. Rosita also knew he wanted to see her in a bikini. "I have one more before I choose."

She bounced back to the dressing room, hanging the one-piece on a hook, *her I'm going to keep this one hook*. Looking in the mirror one last time, she exhaled and walked out. The suit was a mixture of purple and black. The top was a two-layered tankini with a wrap that covered the bottoms. She walked closer, and he had a small smile. Strolling even closer, she started untying the sides of the matching wrap. She was about three steps away from him when she pulled it off. His eyes roamed from the top to her exposed midriff down to her thighs.

"Wow! Is that for me?" He whispered.

"You like this one better?"

"I want you comfortable." He bucked his eyes. "But yes, I like that one too. I think you should get both of them. Who knows, we might go to a different place with beautiful beaches?"

Rosita swallowed. "Okay."

Rosita returned quickly back to the dressing room. That wasn't the reaction she was expecting. She felt he would like it but to comment on another trip with her to a beach was breathtaking. Quickly, she changed back into her clothes and put the bikini and wrap back on the hanger. She hung it next to the one-piece. That was when she noticed the price tags, and her mouth dropped open. The suits were too expensive, and she couldn't get both of them. The one-piece would be enough, or she could look again, and this time she'd look at the prices first. She put all the swimsuits in one hand, leaving the dressing room.

"Rosita, you need to pick out a pair of swim shoes and make sure you want this beach bag. You can pick a different one if you don't like this one.

"Ah . . . I think I want to look at more swimsuits."

"Why, I like the two you chose."

"I just do."

Royce crooked his finger at her, seeing the suits mixed with the other ones. He held out his hands for the pile. Rosita shook her head, no.

"So, you're going to act like Marguerite; she hasn't told me '*no*' all day. Give them to me, or I'm going to chase you down and take them."

Rosita took two steps backward. "I don't want them. I don't like them."

"Liar," he said with a smile.

Rosita took another step, and Royce pounced. He picked her up with one arm and grabbed the swimsuits with his other hand. He hooked them on the nearest rack and took the two he wanted. He still held Rosita next to his body.

"Are you going to behave, or do I have to hold you like this until we finish shopping?"

Rosita was breathing hard, not because he was hurting her, but because she felt the strength in his arm and the hardness of his chest.

He was holding her like a ragdoll. She could have wrapped her legs around his waist, but she didn't.

"I'll . . . behave," she whispered throatily.

Royce slid her down the length of his body to the floor. He kept his arm around her waist as they walked back to the buggy and a laughing Marguerite.

"Daddy . . . mommy . . . funny."

"Oh, you think that was funny that he picked your mommy up?" She kissed Marguerite.

Right now, she knew how Marguerite felt in his arms, warm and protected. She'd watched her daughter hold him around his neck, lying on his broad shoulders. And now, she wanted the same.

Royce dropped the suits in the buggy and strolled back to the section of water shoes. He reminded Rosita about the beach bag, and she looked at the ugliest bag she'd ever seen. She grabbed her size of shoes and took the bag out of the buggy, asking him where he found it. Royce pointed behind him, saying he didn't remember. He passed them while walking. They walked around the large store until they found the beach bags again. This time Rosita selected a straw-covered bag she liked.

When they returned to the room, they all changed into their swimwear and headed to the pool area. Rosita was impressed with the fact the Royce had shopped for all the necessities. He even snuck a cover-up in the buggy for her. She hadn't thought about that, and she would have felt naked walking around the hotel in just a swimsuit. Marguerite was wearing one as well. Royce had on a pair of swim shorts and a t-shirt, considering that he knew where they were going and was prepared. Rosita pointed out a couple of free lounge chairs, and Royce shook his head and pointed at an area of cabanas.

"We have VIP status," Royce showed his platinum room key to a hotel employee standing next to an empty cabana. Sitting the bag on a small table, he removed Marguerite's cover-up. Royce pulled his t-shirt off and dropped it on one of the lounge chairs.

"Are you coming with us?"

Rosita dropped down on the other chair, staring. She couldn't speak, she nodded her head no. She tried to tell him she wanted to take pictures of the two of them in the water first. Royce was bewildered for a moment. Then he remembered that she'd never seen his bare chest before. The look on her face was a reaction that he'd become accustomed to too many times. He was astounded sometimes because even after his construction days, he was still massive like he worked out at a gym every day. Well, she might as well get used to it.

Royce picked up Marguerite and walked out of the cabana. He threw her up in the air and caught her. She squealed with laughter. He walked to some steps and descended slowly into the water so he wouldn't frighten her. When her feet touched the water, she tried to climb higher. He assured her that he wouldn't let anything happen to her, holding her tightly, close to his body. After a moment, she adjusted to the water, and Royce let her float in the water alone, holding her hands. Marguerite giggled and kicked her feet.

Rosita recovered from her shock. She sat breathing hard when he walked away, carrying Marguerite. Why in the world was this fine ass sexy man single? Something had to be wrong with him. He was too perfect and the kindest person she'd ever met. She was already familiar with his mannerisms. He was generous with Marguerite, and now he included her in everything they did. The man spent money like it was nothing. Her swimsuits cost over a hundred dollars each, and Marguerite had more stuff in the buggy than anybody. He only had a beach towel and swim shoes for himself. And what happened to the woman in the background? Had she been his girlfriend? Oh no, she hoped they hadn't broken up because of her and Marguerite.

Digging the camera out of the bag, she found the two of them playing in the water. She snapped some pictures of them splashing around in the water. Royce threw Marguerite in the air, and he let her drop into the water. Rosita rushed to the other side of the pool. Where was her baby? He was going to let her baby drown. It was seconds that seemed like hours, and Marguerite popped out of the water, spitting and laughing. She was yelling for him to do it again. Royce looked up to see Rosita out of breath, she looked scared.

"You okay?"

"I thought you were drowning my baby."

"Sorry, but she loves the water. She's not afraid. I want to teach her how to swim when we get back home. I can teach you too."

Rosita shook her head no.

Royce patted the side of the pool. "Sit down and wet your feet."

"I don't want to get the camera wet."

"It's not a problem. That reminds me I forgot to get a waterproof camera at the store."

"Why do you need a waterproof camera?"

"Do you trust me? Do you trust me to keep *our* little girl safe?"

"*Our?*" He shocked her again. She took a deep breath. "Yes, I do."

"I booked some special water activities for Marguerite, and I reserved the VIP tours for all of us. There are encounters with dolphins, sea otters, sea lions, and even sloths. I'll be with her. I'll protect her with my life. That's why I'm playing with her in the water to make sure she won't be afraid. I even booked the family adventure tour. I hope you don't mind, but I had to lie and say she was three. She's tall for her age."

Rosita laughed as she sat on the side of the pool, dangling her feet. She watched them play and splash. Royce put Marguerite on his back and told her to hold his neck, she did, tightly. He swam the length of the pool several times, making short dives under the water, taking Marguerite with him. Rosita was amazed and snapped so many pictures she couldn't count. Royce swam back to where she was sitting.

"Come into the water with us. You can stand in the shallow end. Are you going to let Marguerite outdo you?"

Royce pointed to the stairs and told her that they would meet her there. He and Marguerite left with her on his back. Rosita took the camera back to the cabana. Slowly and slightly scared, she stepped into the water. It was cool at first, but she kept walking with her eyes on Royce and her daughter. The skirt on her one-piece rose in the water as she descended. Royce's breath caught in his throat, meeting her at the bottom of the steps and reaching for her hand for the final step. He pulled her close. She looked up at him and waved her hands in the water.

Marguerite broke their trance with her chatter. Her suit made her bob up and down in the water. Royce grabbed both her hands and pulled her forward and told her to kick her feet. He showed her how to hold her breath and told her to wet her face. Marguerite put her face in the water and pulled it out quickly. They had been playing by splashing water on each other.

"Marguerite, splash your mommy." Marguerite hit at the water. It didn't do any damage. "Like this, Marguerite." He cupped his hands together and hit the water, making a big splash that covered her face and hair.

Rosita yelped, spitting out water. She tried to do the same but didn't have the big splash as he did. Royce asked the cabana boy to take a few pictures of his family playing in the pool. They played in the pool for another couple of hours until Marguerite announced that she was hungry.

Rosita knew pool time was over, so they went back to the room to shower and change. Royce reminded Rosita to keep her room key handy and charge it to the room if she needed anything. They ate dinner at one of the restaurants located inside the hotel. There would be plenty of time to venture around the city.

Chapter Fifteen

They spent the first couple of days at Sea World. It took that long to see and do all the activities. Marguerite begged to ride in a stroller that looked like a miniature Shamu. They did everything that Royce promised. Rosita stood in the background and took pictures of all the interactions with the animals. She'd never seen Marguerite so excited, and she wasn't scared of anything.

The third morning, Royce woke when he heard Marguerite crying. He snatched open the door separating the two bedrooms. Marguerite was sitting in the bed alone. Royce heard the shower running in the bathroom and exhaled. He sat down, holding Marguerite telling her that her mommy was only in the bathroom. Rosita thought she heard Marguerite crying and came running out of the bathroom wet and wrapped in a towel. It was Royce's turn to stare. She saw him sitting on the bed topless, wearing pajama pants, the very bed where she slept. The sexy man was in her bed. She had to shake herself to keep from thinking about what she was fantasizing about at the moment.

He was the first to speak. "I'm sorry to intrude. I heard Marguerite crying." He picked her up and headed to his room. "We'll be next door." He closed the door softly.

Royce sat on his bed and lay back, bringing Marguerite with him. She curled up next to his chest and fell back asleep. He closed his eyes because he wanted to keep the current image burned on the back of his eyelids. If she had been any other woman, he'd have thrown her on the bed and made love to her. It was crazy because he saw more skin in her swimsuit, but she was dripping wet and her damp hair curled around her neck and shoulders. It was erotic. He had to stop thinking dirty thoughts. Marguerite was lying next to him but wishing it was her mother.

Rosita found them holding each other after she'd finished her shower and dressed. In her mind, this was a Kodak moment. But she didn't want it on the camera. This photo was one of those private pictures for her phone. Who couldn't appreciate the cuteness of them sleeping?

Rosita let them sleep. They'd been out late both days and falling asleep as soon as they returned to the room. Marguerite had been too tired to watch a movie or read a book. She fell asleep in her car seat both evenings. Royce was treating them like royalty. Marguerite had so much stuff that she wondered how they were getting her stuffed animals home. Her little girl had a stuffed killer whale that was as big as her bed. And she was sure that Royce wasn't finished spoiling her.

Royce woke up first and found Rosita sitting at the table drinking a cup of coffee. "Good morning."

"Did you sleep okay with Marguerite sprawled all over you?"

"She is so light I barely knew she was there."

"Would you like a cup of coffee? I didn't realize that hotels stocked Starbucks in their suites."

"Sure," he answered. He didn't doubt it because of the prices they charged. It was a five-star hotel.

They'd sat and had coffee before in the morning, but this was more intimate and pleasurable. It felt different for both of them. He put on a t-shirt when he got out of bed. He didn't need to be bare-chested to impress Rosita as he did with other women. Royce asked her if she was having a good time. She nodded yes and expressed a brilliant smile. They sat and talked about nothing in particular. They were on vacation and not in a hurry to leave the hotel.

They heard Marguerite when she slid out of bed and landed on her feet. They were expecting her to show up in the living room. Instead, there was a tiny voice calling for mommy.

"Bathroom," they said at the same time.

Rosita went to her room, and the bathroom was empty. She walked through the connecting door and found Marguerite in Royce's bathroom.

"Marguerite, you are supposed to use the other bathroom."

Marguerite looked at her mother like, I own all this, and I can go wherever I want. Rosita used the opportunity to look around, and she noticed all his toiletries lined up neatly on the vanity. Rosita picked up a bottle of cologne and opened the top, inhaling. Now, she knew what cologne he wore if she wanted to get him a gift. She touched a couple more items like they were gold, wondering if he was a neat freak. Her bathroom had stuff everywhere, hairbrushes, combs, barrettes, and tons of things you need for little girls and their hair. Marguerite let her know that she'd finished. Rosita held her at the sink and helped her wash her hands. She lectured that it was always important to wash your hands when you finish using the bathroom. Marguerite left the bathroom and ran, looking for Royce.

She held up her hands. "Clean, daddy . . . smell."

Royce smelled her hands. "Good girl."

Rosita was getting her coffee cup off the table and witnessed the exchange. "What are you two doing?"

"When we'd be out alone, and I had to ask a strange woman to take her to the bathroom, I would always tell her to wash her hands. And when she came out . . . yes, I would be standing by the door. I would tell her to let me smell her hands."

"Okay, you are such a wonderful Godfather. Do you know how many times I've seen mothers or women with little girls, and they don't wash their hands, just nasty."

"I've witnessed the same in the men's room. Let's go get some breakfast and head to the zoo."

They spent the whole day at the zoo. This time Marguerite wanted to ride on Royce's shoulders. Rosita teased her, telling her she was taller than the giraffes. They ate ice cream, hot dogs, and plenty of other junk food all day. Royce suggested that they order room service when they returned to the hotel. He wanted to take his shoes off and not move. Marguerite was the only one not worn out. After they ate dinner, Marguerite wanted to watch a movie, and Royce pulled out his laptop.

"Are you working?" Rosita asked sharply.

"I'm just checking emails. I'm waiting on some material from Grand Rapids. If there was an emergency, Toby would call me."

"Toby? Does he know we're together?"

"Yes, he does. He's the only one that knows. He's not going to say anything to anyone." Royce turned in his chair to face her. "It's not that I want to keep secrets. I don't want you to have problems at work." He exhaled and looked her in the eye. "I don't want anyone thinking you're having sex with the boss for favors. I'm not that kind of man."

She smiled. "I know that . . . I mean, I know you're not the kind of man to use a woman. You have always treated me with kindness and respect. And I have only seen you treat all your staff with respect."

Rosita got off the couch and looked down at Marguerite. She was lying against a giant stuffed animal on the floor. Rosita sat in a chair next to Royce, looking down at her hands before she spoke.

"I ah . . . I originally thought you were using Marguerite to get to me. I thought you wanted to use me. After a while, I realized that you weren't interested in me. And that morning, I called you when you were out of town, I heard the woman in the background."

Royce always felt that she heard, and now she was sad again. He lifted her face by her chin. "Rosita, I would never use you. And that woman you heard in the background was a . . . friend. She was never a girlfriend. I haven't seen her since, and I have no desire to see her again." He wanted to say so much, but she wasn't ready for that yet. "I will always respect you."

"Thanks, I appreciate that."

She heard every word he said. The only thing he didn't say was that he was interested in her. Yeah, he flirted about the swimsuits, and he teased her that night about the diamonds. But that didn't mean he had feelings for her. And respecting her *meant* that he wouldn't touch her. At least he wouldn't touch the places she wanted him to touch. She smiled and left the table, sitting on the couch, and watched the movie Marguerite had chosen. Rosita wondered, why all the Disney movies involved a poor helpless girl who needed rescuing by Prince Charming to live happily ever after.

Royce wanted the next day to be relaxing. They'd been busy for three days straight. He wanted to surprise Rosita with a spa day while he and Marguerite swam, hung out, and did some exploring. Marguerite had fallen asleep on the floor, and Rosita was sleeping on the couch. He spent more time on the computer than he thought. That was the last time he'd do that.

Marguerite was already dressed in pajamas, so he picked her up and put her in the same bed where he found her crying. She was sharing a bed with her mother. He pulled the covers back before he went to wake Rosita. He shook Rosita like before, and again she didn't wake up. She looked like she was cold. He saw her shiver. Slipping his arm under her gently, he scooped her into his arms. He put her in the bed and pulled the cover over both of them. She shivered again. Royce lay next to her on top of the covers.

He put his arm around her and whispered. "I am interested in you." He played with a few strands of her hair.

Eventually, he heard her breathing even out and she sighed in her sleep like she'd warmed up. He kissed her on the top of her head and got out of the bed, walking around to the other side, he kissed Marguerite.

"Good night, princesses."

Returning to the living room, he turned everything off and went to bed. Royce lay in his bed, thinking about the woman in the next room. He did his best to make her understand that he didn't want another woman. He couldn't say it outright. It wasn't time. He wanted her to know that her past didn't matter to him. She had to deal with her issues and insecurities before they could have a future. Apparently, she'd been used, one more thing he learned. Was it an old boss, Marguerite's father, or they were the same person?

Royce woke to small hands pushing on his chest.

"Daddy potty…daddy, daddy."

Royce blinked several times until he comprehended that Marguerite was telling him she needed to use the bathroom.

"Where's your mama?" He asked. Marguerite pointed at the door.

Royce jumped up worried that something might be wrong. He snatched the door open wider and rushed into the room. Rosita was breathing and sound asleep. He exhaled and rushed back to Marguerite. Damn! He opened his bathroom door, and she went to the bathroom; he stayed outside.

She yelled, "I'm finished."

He peeped around the door and asked if she pulled up her clothes. She was standing at the sink with her arms in the air. He picked her up, turned on the water, and gave her some soap. When she finished washing her hands, he helped to dry them. She could go to the bathroom by herself. She just wanted someone to know where she was and to help her wash her hands, so smart. Marguerite ran back into the room and climbed on his bed.

He whispered. "Marguerite, this is not your bed. Your bed is in the other room."

She fell back on the pillow and covered her head.

"You're going to be difficult, aren't you? Okay . . . okay, I'll let you sleep here this time." Royce lay on top of the covers next to Marguerite. They both fell back asleep.

Rosita woke the next morning and found Marguerite's side of the bed empty. She almost panicked, but she had a sneaky suspicion of where her daughter was. The door was partially open, and she knew why. Peeping inside, she saw both of them. She'd had the strangest dream and knew it was Royce that put her in the bed, just like last time. But this time, she dreamed that he held her and talked to her, except she didn't remember what he said.

Rosita went and made her usual cup of coffee. She was so used to getting up at the crack of dawn. Old habits are hard to break, even on vacations. She couldn't believe that she was actually on her first vacation and getting paid. And Royce wouldn't let her spend a penny of her own money. She opened the curtains, looking out at the bay. There were some beautiful boats or ships. She was puzzled because she didn't know the difference.

"Would you like to go for a ride on one of those?"

She yelped. "Roy, you scared me."

"Sorry, I didn't mean to."

"Can you stop putting me to bed like I'm Marguerite?"

"I like putting you to bed. Did you know you snore?"

"I do not."

Royce laughed. "How would you know, you're fast asleep?"

She scrunched her nose at him. "I just know. Would you like some coffee? You can come and watch the boats with me."

"I would prefer to watch a sunset with you sitting on a deck from one of those boats."

Her heart fell to the floor. Why was he making her feel this way? Why was he making her feel so special if he didn't have any feelings for her? When this vacation was over, they would go home and back to the way they used to be, only friends. They were two people that loved the same little girl. She was doing this for Marguerite.

"Yes, that sounds nice. I think Marguerite would love a boat ride."

Rosita went into the small kitchen and made his coffee. She didn't want to make more of the conversation than was necessary. He couldn't possibly want a woman like her. Returning to the living room, she wore a smile. They sat in the window and watched the activity on the water. Both of them admired and commented on all the various sizes and styles of boats.

They heard Marguerite moving about, and Royce told the story of how she ended up in his bed. Rosita laughed and asked if he helped her in the bathroom. Royce shivered, shaking his head a big no. He stood outside the door like a coward. She only needed help with washing her hands.

Getting up the nerve, Royce asked Rosita if she had a comfortable sundress or something. She shook her head, yes. Clapping his hands, he told her to get dressed. She asked if Marguerite needed something special as well. He shook his head and said, no, she doesn't. They ate breakfast, and afterward, Royce hooked his arm through Rosita's and led her away. He had Marguerite in his other arm. She wanted to know where they were going, and he wouldn't tell her. They walked to a different part of the hotel, turning down a hall toward a big arch that read SPA.

He walked up to the desk. "Excuse me, ma'am, I think you have a reservation for Ms. Rosita Rodriquez," Royce asked.

"Yes, we do, right this way, ma'am." The clerk said.

"What . . . what is this?"

"Enjoy yourself, and don't worry about us. We'll be just fine." He tilted her chin and gave her a beautiful smile and a quick peck on the lips.

Rosita followed the clerk and looked back at Royce and Marguerite, who waved. She didn't know what to expect. She'd never been to a spa.

Later that evening, after many hours of being pampered, she returned to the room on cloud nine. She'd gotten massages, body wraps, and facials, she'd been treated to the hair salon, and she got a mani-pedi. Sticking out her fingers and toes, she showed off her freshly painted nails. She told Royce all about her day. Excitedly, she asked him if he knew that they did couples massages. He said he knew, but it was her day.

When she calmed down, she wanted to know what he and Marguerite had done all day. He said they went swimming and exploring, and he'd arranged for a boat ride for them the next evening. As part of the package, they'd get dinner and spend quality time onboard. Tonight, they were headed to the beach for a bonfire. He asked if she would wear her bikini the next evening.

Rosita hunched her shoulders, "Maybe."

Getting off the couch, he told her he'd be right back.

"Close your eyes," he said softly from behind her.

He opened a box and removed the contents. Rosita felt him over her head, and then something cold touched her chest. Immediately, she touched it with her hand and opened her eyes. She looked down, and he'd put a necklace on her with an Amethyst stone surrounded by tiny diamonds.

"Oh, Roy, this is beautiful."

"I thought it would match your bikini."

"Thank you, I love it," She jumped up from the couch and hugged him. He held her longer than necessary, kissing her temple before releasing her.

"I'm glad you like it. Would you like to see the one Marguerite is going to wear with her suit?"

"You didn't?"

"It's small. It's not as large as your stone. The lady said it was her birthstone."

"How did you know this was my birthstone?"

"You never told me when your birthday was. I liked it because it matched your suit. I'm glad to know that." He lifted the stone on her necklace. "Would you like a party at Chuck-E-Cheese for your birthday?" He laughed.

"No, I want it on top of a mountain," she said.

"Okay, be careful what you wish for."

After dinner and a bonfire, Royce announced to Marguerite that she was getting a story from a book, no movie tonight. They got comfortable on the couch, and he read to her, eventually noticing her yawning and eyelids drooping. He read softer and softer until her head fell back. She fought sleep hard. Closing the book, he laid it on the couch, and then he put her to bed.

"Good night, princess." He kissed her on the top of her head.

When he returned to the living room, Rosita was still curled up on the end of the couch, partially covered with a blanket. He'd asked the maid to leave an extra blanket, just for her. He scooped her up off the couch.

"I'm not asleep, and didn't I tell you to stop putting me to bed."

"Maybe I like holding you while you sleep."

"Why . . . would you want to do that?"

He sat on the couch, still holding her in his arms. "Because you can't protest, and you're so cute when you're sleeping."

She scrambled to get off his lap, sitting on the couch next to him.

"See . . . protesting."

"This is not protesting. This is . . . I'm not asleep, and . . . I can walk and get in my bed."

"You take all the fun out. Do you want to watch some TV or a Disney movie?"

"We can see what's on TV. I'm burnt out on Disney movies." She was tired of everybody else getting their happy ending.

"You have to share the blanket." He teased.

"It's not big enough for two people to spread out on this couch."

He arched an eyebrow, turned on the TV, and found the guide. Rosita picked a chick-flick. He lay down and patted the couch in front of him. He'd fallen in love with this wide couch. She pointed at herself, and then she pointed to the couch. He nodded and patted the couch again. She thought about it for a minute. They were fully dressed, so it couldn't hurt to lay and watch TV. Cautiously, she lay down next to him, and he positioned the blanket around them. Royce wrapped his arm around her waist to keep her close. She scooted her butt closer to him for warmth. They fell asleep before the movie was over.

Rosita opened her eyes, thinking that she was dreaming.

"Good morning, Sunshine," Royce spoke.

She wasn't dreaming. Royce's strong arms held her against his body, and his legs trapped her.

"Do you know how beautiful you are when you're sleeping?"

She opened her mouth to speak, and all she could do was shake her head and mouthed the word, "no."

She'd spent the night wrapped in his arms. She'd slept with a man, literally. He was watching her, and she sighed, bending her head to his chest.

"What's wrong? It's a little late to be shy."

"Nothing is wrong, and yeah . . . I'm a little shy. I've . . . never woke up wrapped in a man's arms before.

"You want to know a secret? Neither have I." He laughed. "You were supposed to laugh at my joke. But seriously, I've never woken up with a woman wrapped in my arms either. I'm glad you were my first." He bent his head and kissed her softly.

"Mommy . . . daddy!" Marguerite ran into the room and jumped on the couch. She dove right on top of them.

"Good morning, baby girl," Royce said after grunting.

"Potty."

"Mommy, it's your turn." he kissed her again before he turned her loose.

Rosita grabbed Marguerite's hand and led her to their bathroom. Standing in her bathroom, she touched her lips, sighing. Was she still dreaming? This wasn't happening to her.

Exhaling, Royce rolled over on his back on the couch. He couldn't help himself, wishing that he could pretend to be asleep. She'd turned over and faced him, and it woke him. He watched her, studied every inch of her face, her lips. He hadn't wanted to kiss her yet. But her soft, luscious lips were right there. He wanted to know if she tasted as sweet as her lips looked. Thank God for little children.

Royce went to his room and locked all the doors. He wanted to take a hot shower without steaming up the bathroom and walk around naked. This situation was new to him. He was so used to being alone. Now, he was trapped with a little girl who owned the place and a woman he wanted to wrap his naked body around. How did parents ever have any fun after children? He'd never dated a woman with a child before. This friendship/relationship was going to be a challenge. Royce finished his shower and walked into his room to get his clothes. He heard someone twisting the doorknob, and he knew who that was. Maybe if he didn't answer, she would go away. He still needed to shave and trim his beard. Putting his clothes on the bed, he went back into his bathroom. He heard the tapping on the other door leading to the living room and a small voice.

"Daddy . . . daddy."

His challenge was already undergoing a test. He stood at the door. "Marguerite, I'll be out in a few minutes. I'm getting dressed."

"Daddy, open . . . daddy." She started to cry.

"Shit!" He whispered to himself.

Royce grabbed some shorts and put them on. He opened the door, and Marguerite was sitting by the door with a wet face.

"Ah, baby girl, don't cry. What's the matter?"

She didn't answer. Instead, she poked out her lip and stretched out her arms, wanting him to pick her up. Royce shook his head and told her she was spoiled rotten. Opening the door all the way, he took her to the bathroom with him. Marguerite got to sit on the vanity, and he teased her with his electric shaver, making her giggle. He was almost finished trimming his beard when he looked at a corner in the mirror and saw they had an audience. He didn't know how long Rosita had been there watching them. She was wearing a sundress, a pair of sandals, and her necklace. He smiled at her and finished his grooming.

Rosita had been in her bathroom, getting dressed. She'd combed Marguerite's hair and dressed her first. She heard Royce in his room, figuring that he was getting dressed as well. And saw Marguerite twisting on his door and realized it was locked again. Rosita didn't know what he had planned for today other than the boat ride for the evening. Whatever it was, she wanted to be beautiful, she wanted to feel beautiful, remembering how he'd held her hair up and teased her about diamonds. With her hair pinned up, she left a few tendrils touching her shoulder. She didn't have any diamond earrings, but she was wearing a beautiful necklace. No one had ever given her a gift so extravagant before. She wanted to please him, wanted him to kiss her again. Did she want too much? But what she wondered was . . . She wondered if he would have kissed her longer, deeper, if Marguerite hadn't shown up.

Standing in the door, Rosita realized that Marguerite had invaded his dressing. His clothes were lying on the bed, and he was shirtless. Her eyes roamed up and down. She could stare at his body forever. Staying in the background, she didn't think he wanted everyone in the bathroom while he shaved. Why was she jealous that Marguerite had the best seat in the room? He finished trimming, washed his face, and cleaned up the sink. Picking Marguerite up off the vanity, they walked back into his room until he was standing in front of Rosita.

"I like your hair," Royce said

He picked up the gem with two fingers. It hung right above her mounds, brushing her skin with his touch. They stared into each other's eyes. She had beautiful brown eyes, and Rosita thought his deep dark eyes sparkled.

He spoke, never breaking eye contact. "I thought we could get some breakfast and explore the city today."

"Oh yeah, explore—that's what I want to do," she said, her breathing a little heavy, having a deeper meaning. And it had nothing to do with the city.

Marguerite touched her mother's face. "Mommy . . . juice."

Rosita broke the stare and looked at Marguerite. "Sure, baby, let's get you some juice." She took Marguerite from Royce's arm and didn't look at his face.

Lowering her head, she walked out of his room. Royce closed the door, locking it. He exhaled and touched his forehead to the door. His current situation was going to be harder than he thought. Why did he have to ruin it by kissing her? Now he wanted to kiss her, hold her, and wake up with her wrapped in his arms forever. Damn!

Royce rushed around his room, getting dressed. Was he caught up in the moment because of a vacation? He needed to change his frame of mind. Was he caught up because they were spending so much time together? Maybe it was because of the proximity, and it felt more intimate. He hadn't felt like this at home, and they'd spent time on a couch together watching movies with Marguerite. What was wrong with him?

They drove around the city looking at the sites and visited a museum which was an Aircraft Carrier. The next stop was Seaport Village, with lots of restaurants and shops. Rosita warned Royce not to buy Marguerite any more junk. On the way back to the hotel, he spotted a billboard that advertised something called LEGOLAND. He remembered playing with Legos. He'd search for it on the computer when they got back to the room. They only had one more day of vacation. Oh well, they might as well go out with a bang. He would have loved to take his princess to Disney, but that was too close to Los Angeles. He had a better idea.

"Rosita, what do you think about taking Marguerite to Disney for her third birthday?"

Rosita's eyes grew large, and she had a scared look on her face. Her breathing was erratic. She was trembling and squeezing her hands together.

"Hey . . . Florida . . . we can take her to Florida."

Royce pulled over to the side of the street. He jumped out of his seat and ran around the truck. He'd never seen a look of terror before on her face. She was afraid to go back to Los Angeles. He pulled her into his arms and rubbed her back.

"I would never let anyone hurt you. I don't know what you're afraid of, and I'm sorry I didn't say Florida first. I'm so sorry." He pulled away so he could see her face. She had tears in her eyes. He wiped her tears away, "I could kill whoever hurt you," he said fiercely.

Rosita laid her head against his shoulder. Why couldn't she have found him years ago?

"Mommy!" Marguerite called out.

"Mommy is okay, sweetheart. Daddy won't let anyone ever hurt her again."

"Do you want to go back to the hotel?" he asked softly.

"No, I'm okay now. I'm sorry if I upset you."

"You didn't upset me. I have a feeling that Los Angeles is a problem for you."

He touched her chin and kissed her softly again. He wanted to tell her that they could talk about it later, except he dropped it. If she ever wanted to talk about it, he'd listen. Right now, he would protect her the best way he knew how.

Rosita wiped her face. "I'm okay. Let's . . . get some ice cream for Marguerite."

She heard him refer to himself as daddy to Marguerite. She'd never heard him do that before. He allowed her to call him that, and he'd never tried to stop her. Did he do that to make her feel better?

They drove until he found an ice cream parlor before heading back to the hotel to get ready for the evening activity.

Chapter Sixteen

$\mathcal{R}$oyce dressed in his swim clothes, and Rosita wore her bikini under a sundress. Marguerite was in her swimsuit and covered with a little dress. Rosita had no idea what this trip entailed because Royce had secrets. They left the hotel and headed to a marina. Royce looked around until he found the pier that he sought. Removing Marguerite from around his neck and holding Rosita's hand, they boarded a grand yacht. Rosita saw a few other people walking around. They were welcomed aboard and shown to a cabin. Royce told Rosita that they could leave their stuff in the cabin. She grabbed the camera from the bag before he closed the door. Leaving the cabin, they returned to the deck with several lounge chairs and a hot tub.

Royce straddled a lounge chair and patted the seat in front of him. Rosita sat in front of him while Marguerite ran circles around the chair. Their steward introduced himself as Andre and offered them drinks. Royce took two glasses from his tray and passed one to Rosita.

"Cheers," he said, slightly touching her glass with his.

He took a sip of his drink and moaned. Rosita was looking at him, wondering what he was thinking. He motioned for her to drink.

She took a small sip since she wasn't much of a drinker. "This is good. What is it?"

"Champagne."

While she'd been at the Spa, he and Marguerite went exploring. He'd inquired at the concierge's desk about a dinner cruise. This unique cruise was top of the line. It wasn't cheap, and it came with a private deck and a cabin. There were only four couples on board besides the crew. The cruise included a three-hour visit to a secluded island, where they'd serve dinner. The yacht would sail away at sunset and return to the harbor. He wanted the cabin, especially for Marguerite, if she fell asleep. Hopefully, he planned to relax in the hot tub and watch the sunset holding Rosita in his arms.

Rosita was concerned about Marguerite running around. She didn't want her bothering the other people, the other people she hadn't seen since they boarded.

"She can't bother anyone on this deck but us. We're on a private deck. You will only see a waiter or two," he said and smiled.

"Roy, what have you done? This must have cost a fortune."

"I got a raise, a big raise, and a bonus with my last promotion."

"And you're going to spend it all in one week."

"You and Marguerite are worth it and more. Would you stop worrying about money?"

"Roy, I'm not blind. I know this trip is costing a lot of money. You don't need to impress me."

"I know that I don't need to impress you. I've known that since the first time I saw you in baggy pants. This trip is because you deserve it. You and Marguerite both deserve to be treated like princesses. Now finish your champagne and enjoy our cruise."

Marguerite climbed on the lounge chair, trying to drink from her mother's glass. Rosita said no, that she couldn't drink the adult drink. Royce asked her if she was thirsty and if she wanted water or juice. Marguerite wanted her mother's pretty glass. He told her she could have some juice. Royce left to take care of it, remembering that he'd seen a phone. Lifting the receiver, he heard a voice calling him by name. He was thoroughly impressed, asking if his daughter could have some juice in a plastic champagne glass. The voice on the other end said that someone would be there right away. Royce returned to his seat on the lounger. Five minutes later, Andre showed up with apple juice in a plastic champagne glass. He carried it on the same tray and bent down to pass it to her.

"Ms. Marguerite, I think this is for you."

Excitedly, she accepted the glass.

"I have a gift for you too," Andre said, sitting a small box in front of her.

The box was imprinted with the words *'treasure chest'* across the top. Rosita opened the box and began taking everything out. There was a coloring book, a box of crayons, and a small book. The candy looked like gold coins and fake jewelry that lined the bottom.

Rosita smiled and glanced back at Royce, he had nothing to do with that. Royce had no idea that they spoiled children. When he made the reservation, the questions were how many were in his party and everybody's name. Royce answered his daughter, who was almost three, and he used the word girlfriend for Rosita. He didn't think it was nice to say the mother of his daughter. Rosita was helping Marguerite color in her book. They all sat together on the lounge chair. A voice came over the loudspeaker, announcing they'd be at the island shortly.

"An island, I thought we were only cruising?" Rosita asked.

"Surprise! We get to play on a secluded beach, swim, play or relax, doing nothing. We'll be served dinner on the island."

"Are you serious?"

"There's more, you'll have to wait and see," Royce said excitedly.

"Do we need anything from the cabin?"

"Yes, I'll get Marguerite's swim stuff and we can bring our camera. They have everything else we'll need."

Andre showed up, telling them it was time to go. He announced that he'd be their steward on the island, directing them down some stairs where the other couples were waiting. A tender was bobbing in the water at the back of the yacht. They watched and waited as others climbed aboard and left. When it was their turn, Royce's group and another couple stepped into the small craft.

As they neared the shore, Royce saw huts spread out along the beach. Each hut had a pier, and water toys moored. In the background, he saw a large building. The tender pulled up to the pier, and the other couple got out with their steward.

Marguerite squealed, pointing. Royce was almost shocked when he saw the waterslide and trampoline anchored in shallow water. The boat took them to the next pier. The steward got out first and reached for Marguerite, who was holding onto Royce tight. She shook her head, no. Royce told Andre he had her. He held Marguerite and stepped onto the pier, which was level to the boat. Rosita was a little scared. She didn't like the tender and thought they drove entirely too fast. Royce stood on the pier, and he and the steward helped Rosita out. She hobbled onto the pier; with Royce's arm around her waist, they followed the steward to the hut. They soon passed cushioned loungers on the beach with small tables, covered by giant umbrellas.

Andre opened the front door to reveal a Caribbean-style room with wicker furniture. In one corner was a table set for three, two chairs, and one high chair. Andre opened another door which led to a bedroom and bath. He offered beverages and told them that everything was for their use. The steward disappeared toward the back.

Rosita's mouth dropped open. "I can't believe this place. It's so beautiful."

"Yes, it is. What do you want to do first? I want to ride the Jet Ski's."

"I don't know. You know I don't swim."

"That is why you wear a life jacket. They are a lot of fun once you get the hang of it."

Royce thought Rosita looked a little frightened, so he suggested playing on the waterslide and trampoline first. Hopefully, that would calm her nerves enough to enjoy all the water toys fully. The steward returned with some cold refreshing drinks. Royce said they would take the drinks outside to the beach. Excitedly, they removed their outer clothing, and Marguerite was dressed in her float suit before heading out.

After thirty minutes, Rosita had jumped and slid long enough. Marguerite loved sliding into the water and bobbing up like a fish, but the jet skis seemed to be calling to her. And she didn't know if she'd ever get the chance to ride one again.

"Roy, can we play on the Jet Ski's now?"

"Sure, I was waiting for you to ask. Let's go."

Royce asked her to dress Marguerite in her wet suit. He didn't want the water to sting her, and she was riding with him. Royce asked the steward for life jackets for all of them. Even though he was a good swimmer, he knew he had to wear one as well. There was a safety mechanism on the jacket that connected with the skis. Royce assured her that she would enjoy this adventure, and she caved because of his smile. He buckled and tightened Rosita's vest. Sitting on the ski, he helped her to sit in front of him. The steward stood on the pier with Marguerite and took pictures while he gave Rosita a lesson. It only took her about fifteen minutes, and she felt comfortable enough to do it on her own.

Royce climbed on the other ski, and the steward passed him a reluctant Marguerite. He sat her in front of him and promised her that he'd protect her. They played in the water with the Jet Ski's until Royce saw Andre waving for them to come in. Rosita had had so much fun that she didn't want to get off now.

Rosita zoomed around, screaming, *"I have got to get one of these."*

She liked it when Royce rode next to her ski. He faced her, leaning over, and gave her a quick kiss. She almost fell off, trying to sit up straight. By the time they finished, Marguerite was attempting to drive. Royce never sped with her on the ski, they bobbed along slowly. Marguerite enjoyed it when he did circles on the ski, screaming with laughter.

Andre was waiting on the pier to receive them, and he grabbed Marguerite when Royce passed her off the ski. Then Royce helped Rosita off hers. They stood on the pier facing each other.

"Did you enjoy that?" he asked, smiling.

"Yes, it was the most exciting thing I've ever done in my life."

"There's more of that to come." He kissed her on the nose.

They followed Andre back to the hut, and Marguerite ran the whole way. Andre told them there were robes in the bedroom for everyone. Rosita peeled Marguerite's wet suit off, and her swimsuit was only damp. The girls used the bathroom and washed their faces.

Rosita emerged from the bathroom while Royce was standing in the bedroom dressed in a thick robe, holding one for her. She turned her back to him, and he helped her into it, turning her around to face him. Pulling the robe around her damp body, he tightened the belt. He looked at her with admiration, wanting to kiss her and not stop. She had that sexy wet look again, even though she wore a ponytail. Marguerite jumped in between them. He picked her up and stood her on the bed, dressing her in the small robe, and tightened the belt just like he did for her mother.

"I think our dinner is ready. Let's eat," Royce announced, putting Marguerite back on the floor. He walked out of the bedroom behind them and glanced back at the bed. "If only."

Andre was standing next to the table with flicking candles burning. Royce picked up Marguerite and put her in the high chair. Andre held a chair for Rosita and pushed it forward when she sat. He laid a napkin across her lap, and he did the same for Royce. Marguerite got a bib with a picture of a lobster on it.

"Oh, I need a picture of that." Rosita chuckled.

Andre said he'd take care of that. He served their first course of lobster bisque. Royce and Rosita took turns feeding her the soup. When she finished, Royce thought Marguerite was about to lick her bowl. Next, Andre served a small arugula salad with crabmeat. Marguerite did better than her mother with the salad. Rosita was impressed, knowing Royce had been making her eat salads since her birthday party. Andre cleared away their dishes and pushed a cart from the back. He had a platter for each person displaying a giant lobster, a cup of steaming drawn butter, and filet mignon. Andre took care of the adults first, and then he cut up the food in tiny bites for Marguerite.

Using a spoon, Andre drizzled butter across her lobster. You would have thought that Marguerite was the queen because of the attention Andre was giving her. Royce and Rosita were able to eat while Andre took care of Marguerite. Royce cleaned his plate and asked if he could have a second. Andre nodded and removed his platter. He returned moments later with another steaming lobster.

Rosita looked at him and mouthed, "Greedy."

"I'm a big man. You should know that one lobster isn't going to fill me up."

"Ms. Rosita, would you like another lobster as well?" Andre asked.

"You have more?" She looked at Marguerite, and she was finishing her food. And then she looked at Royce, who was dipping a large piece in his butter.

"I'll help you eat it," Royce said between another bite.

"Okay. You only live once, right?"

Andre removed her platter and returned quickly. Rosita ate most of it, sharing a few bites with Marguerite. Royce ended up finishing it for her.

"Oh my God, I hope he doesn't serve us any dessert. I don't think I can eat another bite." Rosita said, rubbing her stomach.

Andre refilled their glasses, and Marguerite thought she was a big girl drinking her juice from a champagne glass. Andre cleared the table and placed dessert plates in front of them.

"This better not be what I think it is," Rosita said, dropping her head.

Andre pushed another cart out next to the table and removed a lid from a small sizzling grill.

Rosita looked at freshly sliced pineapples. "Oh no, that smells so good."

Royce laughed and held up his plate. He'd had some grilled pineapples in Hawaii, and he knew it was delicious. Andre put several pieces on his plate. Rosita held up one finger. Andre obliged and also put one on a plate for Marguerite. He cut it into bite-size pieces, holding onto her plate for a moment to let it cool off. Rosita asked for it so she could double-check it. She blew on it and tasted it to make sure it was cool enough. She set the plate in front of Marguerite, and she grabbed a piece with her fingers.

Andre had a cooled piece set aside for Marguerite if she wanted more. Rosita finished hers and begged for another, while Royce ate the most and now sat pushed back from the table.

Andre said he needed to clear the table and that they could retire to the lounge chairs on the beach. Royce picked up Marguerite, and they walked out, still wrapped in their robes.

Royce stretched out in a chair, putting Marguerite in the middle of them. They lay and listened to the water crashing ashore. Royce had thoughts of lying at the edge of the beach, holding Rosita while the water splashed at their feet. Except he was too full to move, and he didn't want Marguerite playing in the water.

The sky was changing, and Royce knew they'd be heading back to the yacht for their grand finale. Soon, the sound of an engine was heard. Andre came out of the hut a few minutes later, carrying Marguerite's swim clothes and their camera. He told them they could wear the robes back to the yacht. They saw when the boat picked up their neighbors first and came for them. Royce looked around the area, figuring there had to be people working in the large building. That was too much work for one person. He looked over at Rosita and saw that Marguerite had fallen asleep. The baby was a real trooper.

Royce carried a sleeping Marguerite to the cabin and tucked her in the bed. He left the door open in case she woke up and joined Rosita on the deck. She was sitting in the lounge chair.

"Join me," he said, standing next to her with his hand extended.

Strolling to the hot tub, he removed his robe. Royce untied her belt and slid the robe off her shoulders, letting it drop to the deck floor. He stepped in the tub and scooped her up so fast, she squealed. He lowered them down into the warm bubbly water.

"I had a really good time today," she told him.

"So did I. Life is so much better when you have someone to share it with." He kissed her, hoping she knew how he felt.

He held Rosita and kissed her softly and passionately. After a minute, he broke the kiss, not wanting to push his luck. The last thing he wanted was for her to think that he wanted to use her. He didn't want to take advantage of their romantic evening, even though he wanted to. Damn! Sex in a hot tub was hotter than the water, he thought from a flashback. He turned her around so her back rested on his chest.

"Watch." He pointed to the horizon.

They looked into the red sun looming in the distance, and the lower it descended, it turned bright orange. The full sun changed its shape as it disappeared into the depths of the horizon. It seemed to fall off the face of the earth and turn their world into darkness. The dim lights around them that had been barely visible shined brighter and made the shadows dance. Rosita was in awe of what she'd just seen. She knew the sun rose and set every day, but to watch it in its glory and the ripples of water below the sinking sun reflecting was . . . she didn't have a word for it. It gave her a new appreciation for the sun that warmed the earth.

She couldn't believe that she just experienced this with the most extraordinary man. Watching the sunset was an experience that she would cherish forever. Turning around, she looked at him.

"Oh my God, that was so beautiful. I think I want to cry."

"Oh, please don't cry."

"I'm not going to cry." She turned back to face the darkness with wet eyelids.

"Good. I don't like it when you cry."

"I . . . I guess that you've seen this beautiful sight before?" She muttered softly, saying it like a question. She wanted to know . . . or did she want to know how many others he'd done this with?

"I've never been on a sunset cruise before. Truthfully, I was sitting on a beach in the Caribbean . . . alone . . . trying to figure out what I wanted to do with my life. I often found myself sitting on the beaches at sunset every evening." He said quickly without any hesitation. "This is a special evening for both of us."

"What do you mean . . . do with your life? You have a good job, and you're so . . . everything."

"There was a time when I needed to make some changes in my life. I wasn't always . . . so everything." He laughed at her words. "Let's just say that I settled down, and it made me the man that I am now."

"So you haven't always been charming and sweeping little girls off their feet." She turned back around to face him.

"I have always been charming, and *your little girl swept me off my feet*." He smiled and kissed her again.

They heard someone clearing a throat behind them. "Ah, excuse me, I was checking on Marguerite, and she was just waking up," Andre said behind them.

Royce stood up in the hot tub, and Andre delivered Marguerite to him.

"Daddy!" She stretched her arms to him.

"Thank you, Andre, I appreciate you checking on her."

"Water . . . daddy."

"No, baby girl, this water is too hot for you, and I think your mother should change your clothes. We're all going to change clothes. Okay."

He'd enjoyed his hot tub time alone with Rosita. It was a different experience for him. Usually, his time with women only involved sex. Being with Rosita made him more protective and caring. The last thing he wanted to do was act like the man who used her. They'd be arriving back at the harbor soon, so Royce sent the girls to the cabin to change clothes. They were sitting on the deck in the lounge chair when they had another visitor.

"Excuse me, Mr. Hawthorne, Ms. Rodriguez," he bowed down. "And you must be Ms. Marguerite, he said shaking hands with everyone. "I'm the captain, and I'd like to invite you on a tour of our bridge."

"We'd love to," Royce said.

Royce picked up Marguerite, and they followed the captain. They enjoyed the grand tour, and the captain spoiled Marguerite with more gifts.

Royce and his family spent the last thirty minutes admiring the view from their deck. The closer they got to the marina, the more boats and ships they saw. Marguerite jumped up and down with excitement. Royce had a feeling that since she'd had a late nap, she would be up for a while.

When they reached the suite, Marguerite ran around like she was high on sugar. Damn, Treasure Chest! Royce searched for information about LEGOLAND for their last day of vacation. It was a thirty-minute drive on the outskirts of San Diego. LEGOLAND was more of an amusement park. And just like before, he purchased the VIP package. He keyed the information into his phone, so he could put it in the GPS in the morning.

There had been another sign next to it advertising Mexico. It gave him another grand idea of taking his family out of the country. Deep in thought, he was tempted to check his email. Toby hadn't called, which was a good thing. But he was getting impatient about the project in Grand Rapids. Perhaps, he was trying to do too much at one time. It was too late to think about that now. Too much money had changed hands. He was content with his current three stores, and they'd surpassed his goals. Rosita walked into the living room after putting Marguerite's bedclothes on.

"Are you working?"

Royce logged off and closed the lid, "No ma'am," He jumped up from the table and ran to the couch. "Marguerite, are we watching a movie tonight?" He yawned.

Marguerite shook her head yes, flipping through the CD book that Royce bought her to put her movies in for traveling. She pointed at the movie she wanted, and Royce put it in the DVD player. Squatting down on the floor, she propped up on one of her large stuffed animals. Rosita stood in front of Royce with her hands on her hips.

"Roy, how are we getting all this *stuff* back to Detroit?" She pointed at the numerous stuffed animals littering the floor. "I'm not getting on an airplane with a six-foot stuffed killer whale."

"I already talked with someone here at the hotel. They've arranged to ship them for us since they have this problem all the time. When we get back to the room tomorrow, all this will be on the way to Detroit."

"For a minute, I thought you were buying the big guy his own seat."

"You know that might be cheaper . . . I'm just playing. Don't give me that look."

"Which look is that?"

"The one you gave me when I bought it."

"Actually, I thought you'd lost your mind."

"But it's perfect for her room. It's like a small couch. She can sit on it or lay on it and watch her movies."

"Her TV is bigger than mine."

"You could have had a bigger TV. She needed 3-D, and that was the smallest size.

"I didn't want a TV, you forced me."

He pulled her down on the couch into his lap, "Stop fussing at me. I'm new at this daddy stuff."

He tried to lie down and pull her with him. Rosita told him that she was sleeping in her bed. He poked his lip out, pouting. She left him on the couch and went to her room, leaving him to babysit. Royce was sleepy, but he didn't want to leave Marguerite up alone. He grabbed a coke from the fridge, hoping some caffeine helped, coffee would be too much. Royce nodded for another thirty minutes before realizing that Marguerite had fallen asleep. He picked her up and put her in the bed with her mother, kissing both gently before leaving the room.

Standing in the door for a moment, he watched them sleep. "Goodnight, my princesses."

Royce woke the next morning with a warm figure lying next to him. Her tiny arm stretched across his chest, and he kissed the top of her head before easing out of bed. He wondered if life with these two would always be so joyous. After washing his face, he listened to the quietness of the suite, wondering if Rosita was still asleep. He stepped into the living room, and she was sitting in a chair, staring out the window.

Rosita felt him when he walked into the room. She sipped her coffee as she stared out the window at the water and the boats. She'd been up so long that she watched a layer of fog dance above the water and dissipate. Her thoughts were on the previous night, their memorable afternoon at the island, the patience he'd had teaching her how to operate the Jet Ski, taking care of Marguerite, and letting her enjoy the fun with them. And their time alone in the hot tub was magical. Is this what love felt like? She thought she'd been in love before, only to realize too late that it was one-sided. And she realized that no man had ever loved her. Was all this going to change when they got back home? He'd made no attempts to touch her other than an enjoyable kiss or two. Does he want to touch her? Why didn't he want to touch or make love to her?

"Good morning, sunshine," Royce said as he blocked her view and gave her a chaste kiss.

"Good morning. Would you like some coffee?"

"I'll get it. I don't want you thinking that you have to fix my coffee. I want to be able to fix you a cup sometimes."

"Sorry, my inner clock didn't turn off because of vacation," Rosita said.

"I'm sure I'll get my chance soon enough."

Royce fixed his coffee and joined her to stare out the window at their gorgeous view. Rosita made a joke and asked him what he'd done to her daughter. Marguerite never left her bed at Ms. J's to get in the bed with her. He hunched his shoulders, sighing, having thoughts of waking to a different warm body next to him.

He reminded her to pile all the stuffed animals on the couch, and someone would collect them after they left. They had two cups of coffee before they attempted to get ready for their last adventure.

Chapter Seventeen

$\mathscr{R}$oyce leaned back in his seat on the airplane, watching Rosita play with Marguerite and her coloring book. He was the happiest man, more than he'd been in a long time. How could he approach the subject with Rosita?

Presently, he'd called it secretly dating her, and he didn't want to hide their relationship anymore; that's if it was a relationship. It was bound to come out to his employees soon. He'd never gotten involved with a member of his staff, and in his eyes, this didn't look right. What if it didn't work out? Would she quit and take Marguerite away, and he'd never see either of them again? She'd run from the last man that hurt her.

A couple of days after they'd returned, Royce hooked the camera to the TV in the living room, so they could watch the pictures from their vacation. It was indisputable that they'd had a good time. Royce was excited to see all the photos from the island. Andre had taken plenty of them, even capturing the kiss on the Jet Skis. Ms. J loved seeing Marguerite having fun. Royce thought it was the first of many memories for them. They quickly fell back into their routine of work. Royce managed to take Rosita on a couple of dress-up dates without Marguerite.

Two weeks after they returned, Royce ran into a snag of a problem with the projects in Grand Rapids. Two of his new businesses were operating in Lansing. Unfortunately, he had to make trips every day for a week, dropping Rosita off at work and coming back late at night. Marguerite would already be asleep. He'd kiss her goodnight and sit in her room, worried that she'd cry for him. Rosita often sat with him on her whale of a couch, and they'd talk. Each night she made him leave to go home and get some sleep. She still didn't know where he lived, even asking him why he wouldn't just stay in Grand Rapids instead of driving back every night. He told her that he couldn't sleep without seeing and kissing his two princesses.

It had been a year now, and Marguerite's third birthday was coming up. He'd told Rosita that he wanted to take them to Florida. He was also tired of hiding the fact that they were an item, minus the sex. It was time to let the cat out of the bag, taking Marguerite with him to pick up Rosita. Royce walked into the building with Marguerite wrapped around his neck. Most of them hadn't seen Marguerite in a while. She'd grown taller and filled out. He kissed her on the temple and put her on the floor.

"Go find your mother, princess."

A few had a shocked look on their face at the intimacy of his words. Rosita showed up with a clipboard in her hands.

"Ah, you're early," she whispered.

Royce pulled her close and kissed her in front of all the employees. "I need to talk to Janell about our vacation next month." He said out loud enough for all to hear.

He left her standing on the floor, mouth open and eyes wide, as he disappeared through the door leading to the back office. After finding Janell in the office, he told her he was putting in a vacation request for Rosita and that he would approve it.

"Boss, what took you so long?" She asked with a big smile.

"What are you talking about?"

"All of us aren't blind. I knew it was going to happen sooner or later. Rosita's a very nice woman, and I'm happy for both of you."

"Thank you, Janell. It took me a while too. I didn't want her co-workers to think she was getting favoritism."

"Rosita is one of the hardest workers I have. I'm just waiting on the next bomb."

"What . . . what bomb?"

Janell pushed him out of her office. Royce walked back out front and found Marguerite sitting at a table eating a muffin and drinking juice.

Marguerite held up her container. "Want some juice, daddy?"

"No, baby girl, you need all your juice so you can grow big and strong. I'll have some coffee." Royce walked around the counter to the machine.

"Can I help you, sir? Customers aren't supposed to be back here."

Royce looked into a young face that he hadn't seen before. "That is a true statement, young lady, but I . . . I'm the regional manager. You must be new?"

"Yes, sir, I started a few weeks ago. I work with Rosita." She was smiling and checking him out. He forgot he was wearing one of his tight stretch shirts.

"So, you open with my girlfriend?" He talked and fixed his coffee.

"Your girlfriend, sir," she swallowed and repeated, losing her big smile.

"Yes, my girlfriend." He couldn't believe he'd said the girlfriend word out loud in front of his staff. He'd already implied it. But he didn't like the way the new employee was checking him out so blatantly.

Rosita emerged from the back, holding her purse.

"Are you ready, sweetheart?" He asked with a brilliant smile, and he was facing his employees. "Come on, baby girl, let's go home." He picked up Marguerite from the table.

Royce walked out of the front door and opened the truck door for Rosita. Putting Marguerite in her seat and strapping her in. Rosita was looking at him like he'd grown another head. He turned in his seat and smiled, asking her if she wanted another kiss; they were all watching.

"No, you have already ruined me. Now I won't get any respect. My co-workers will think I've been banging the boss."

"Excuse me, you'll get your respect, or I'll fire their ass. And anyway, you haven't banged the boss. You want me to go and tell them."

"Oh my God, I would be mortified. Just drive!" Rosita demanded.

"Because you haven't banged the boss or that I'd be telling them you haven't banged the boss?"

"What?"

"Mortified?"

"Take me home. I'm not talking to you anymore today."

Rosita laughed at him, but she didn't think it was funny. She wanted to know why the boss hadn't made any attempts to bang her. But, she was too afraid to ask. And she preferred that he'd take her to his place instead of a restaurant or a movie when Ms. J babysat Marguerite. She knew without a doubt that he'd never do anything inappropriate under Ms. J's roof. Rosita had indicated to Royce that she'd saved up enough money to get an apartment. She wanted to get something close to work and try and find a daycare in the area.

Royce was adamant that Marguerite wasn't going to daycare. Ms. J was teaching her and taking excellent care of her. Next, he played on her sympathy that it would hurt Ms. J if she took Marguerite away. He even gave her puppy dog eyes. Rosita argued that she couldn't continue to live off Ms. J forever. What she didn't know was that Royce was taking care of that too, even though Ms. J put up a huge fight about the money.

Royce himself was confused. He didn't want her to leave, yet he wasn't ready to move forward.

Royce and Rosita planned their trip to Florida. Royce had been researching the website, and he liked the hotels located within the parks. He'd picked one with the same type of accommodations as before, a two-bedroom suite. Rosita was having fits because this time, she was looking at the prices. The crazy man selected the most expensive resort in the park. Royce said they needed the large suite so they could have two bathrooms. He didn't want to intrude on the girls and their bathroom time. He commented that he liked having the living room so Marguerite could enjoy her movies.

The best part about this particular suite was that it came with a full kitchen and a balcony. Royce kissed Rosita, saying he wanted to drink coffee with her on the balcony. Those extra amenities were the last thing on her mind. Again, she argued that a room with two beds was enough. She had thoughts of sleeping with him again, and a bed was better than a couch. She wanted to snuggle the same way they did at Ms. J's, but with fewer clothes.

Rosita gave in to his plans because fighting him was a lost battle when it came to anything concerning Marguerite. Royce showed her the information online about the Magic Bands. They were used to accessing their room and all the rides at the parks. He was waiting for them to be delivered any day.

One evening, they were sitting on the couch when he asked her if she was bringing the sexy swimsuit. Rosita teased him, saying no. There were no beaches where they were going, and she was saving it for a beach. Royce had a devious look; oh yeah, she'd be wearing it for her birthday.

Royce and his family flew to Orlando, Florida. They were spending a week at Disney World. Royce outdid himself again. Instead of a six-foot animal, he purchased a miniature Cinderella castle and had it shipped directly home. He and Rosita spent quality time sitting on the balcony having coffee, snuggling, and kissing on the couch. Royce never attempted anything beyond that.

Rosita was getting frustrated after day three, wanting to know why. One night after Marguerite had gone to sleep, she tiptoed into Royce's room. It was dark, but she saw his silhouette lying in bed. Rosita wanted to touch him, but she didn't want to be rejected either. She wanted to know what it would feel like to lie next to him naked, feel his lips on her breast, her body. Rosita hadn't been with a man since she learned she was pregnant with Marguerite. Royce made her feel warm and hot when he kissed her. She wanted to burn from his touch. Why wouldn't he talk to her and tell her why? He'd announced to his staff that she was his girlfriend. She didn't feel like a girlfriend. After a few moments, she exhaled softly and turned to leave.

"Rosita."

"I . . . I thought you were asleep."

"I've been watching you. What's wrong?"

"Nothing."

Most men knew that when a woman says nothing, it's something. And he knew her nothing sounded like his shy Rosita. She wanted something, or she wanted to know something. It didn't take a brain surgeon to figure it out, and he needed to reassure her that he wanted her more than anything. If she knew just how much he wanted her at this very moment, she might run back to her room screaming.

He patted the bed and sat up, "Come here."

Rosita sat down on the bed and looked down. Royce turned her face toward him.

"Do you want to talk about something?" He asked softly.

"No."

"I think you do. Are you wondering why I'm not acting like a typical man? You probably think that I don't want you."

"I don't know what to think," she sighed.

Royce put his arm around her waist and pulled her closer, kissing her softly. She leaned into his bare chest, and he opened his mouth wider, exploring her mouth with his tongue. He pulled her tongue into his mouth and caressed it. She whimpered into his mouth. Oh no! Maybe this was a bad idea. But it was more important that she know that he wanted her. He slid his hand down her body and pushed her to lie on top of him. Gripping her butt, he pressed her hard into his swollen manhood.

"Rosita, I do want you. I want our first time to be special. I don't want to whisper," he said, whispering. "I don't want Marguerite in the next room, and I don't want to have to worry that she'll wander in or cry at a locked door." Royce paused, thinking of his words. "I don't want to have sex with you. I want to make love to you. I need you to wait until we're both ready. Can you wait for me?"

"Yes, I can wait. I thought you didn't want me. I thought I wasn't the type of woman you like. You've never touched me."

"This is why I haven't touched you." He pressed her to his body again. "You deserve more than just sex. If I touch you, I won't be able to stop. I want to make you mine in more ways than you know." He kissed her again softly, "Will you sleep with me?"

"Yes, I'd love that."

Royce slid her body back to the bed, telling her that she couldn't stay there. She lay partially on his shoulder and chest, pulling the blanket up covering her. He remained under the sheet, pulling her close and wrapping an arm around her. He kissed the palm of her hand and placed it over his heart.

"Rosita, are you on birth control?"

"No, I didn't see a need for that extra expense, considering I didn't have a boyfriend or haven't been with a man in a long time. Why?"

"I was just asking." He knew that had to change if they were going to be in a relationship. He'd never been with a woman without wearing protection. But he seriously doubted Rosita was the type of woman to try and trap him.

It was a slow beginning for them. They continued sleeping together in the same bed. Marguerite continued to find her way to the bed during the night. Royce woke to a princess on each side. Twice he woke before Rosita and brought her coffee in bed. Of course, it came with a price, a kiss.

After they returned from Florida, Royce called his mother and told her that he thought he'd found the woman of his dreams. He wanted them to meet her and a beautiful little girl, who started calling him daddy since the first day she saw him. He hadn't told his mother about Marguerite before now because he didn't want her thinking that it was a set-up or mislead.

The Christmas holidays were coming up, and they were going to Louisiana. The only thing he shared with his mother was that Rosita thought he was the regional manager for GCH.

The next month, they flew to Shreveport, Ms. J included. Royce didn't want to leave her home alone, and this wasn't her first time visiting Louisiana. She was a part of the family now. He was the son she never had, and she treated Marguerite like she was her grandchild.

Royce's parents fell in love with Marguerite, just like he knew they would. A stranger would have thought she was at least five. She didn't talk like a three-year-old, and she'd experienced so much since coming into Royce's life. He'd taught her how to swim and signed her up for dance and ballet classes. She was reading books above her age level. Royce praised Ms. J to his parents because she was the reason that Marguerite was so far along in reading.

Samantha, Rosita, and Ms. J spent the day Christmas shopping. It was the first time, in a long time, since a child had been in the house for Christmas, and Samantha wanted to spoil Marguerite on

Christmas day. Samantha liked Rosita immediately because Rosita was frugal in her shopping. She never grabbed the most expensive items. Samantha liked her even better when they stood at the check-out counter, and Rosita waved a bank card at Samantha and said she had to use it while they were in town. Rosita disagreed because she had a job and her own money? Royce told her that he didn't want to look bad in front of his parents. Rosita told Samantha that she fussed at Royce constantly about spending too much money on Marguerite and shoes. Samantha laughed when Rosita told her that several times, she made him take stuff back to the store.

Ms. J added her sentiments about Royce being generous, and sometimes he acted like he was the elder when it came to shopping for the house. She didn't want to say too much because Rosita didn't know that Royce had taken extra responsibilities and expenses at the house. He told Ms. J that he didn't want them to be a burden on her.

Samantha noticed that Rosita wasn't wearing any expensive jewelry other than her necklace. She wasn't wearing designer clothes, only a designer purse. Samantha commented on her purse and found out that it was a gift from Royce as well as the necklace. In Samantha's eyes, Rosita didn't act like a gold digger. Samantha learned of their vacations recently and that Rosita had protested. Samantha wondered if she'd change when she found out the truth about her son, that he was a multi-millionaire.

Christmas day came and went. Marguerite had the most presents under the tree. Royce shrugged his shoulders, saying they'd ship her toys home. He wanted to buy more gifts for Rosita, but she would have had a fit. Her birthday was coming up, and he'd spoil her then.

After eating a huge feast for Christmas and leftovers, Royce wanted to take Rosita out to one of the hot spots in town. They went to the Oyster Bar, where Royce ordered a dozen oysters on the half-shell. She ordered some fried shrimp. He told her that this was one of his favorite restaurants, and he ate there every time he'd been home, which had been a while. He'd managed to come home a few times in the last few years over a weekend or two.

It was a pleasant day, so they sat on the outside patio. Royce enjoyed his oysters, and Rosita said she wasn't going to kiss him after eating those slimy things, but he stole a kiss anyway.

Royce was enjoying a beer and waiting on another order. He heard someone calling his name. It was a woman, and he looked up.

"Ah . . . hello there, Royce, I thought that was you. Long time no see," she said seductively.

"Hello, Doll, you're the stranger."

"It was good to see you again." She walked off, smiling.

"Was that an old girlfriend?" Rosita teased.

"Nope, she was just a girl I met at a club a while back."

"You must have made quite an impression for her to remember you."

"Yeah, well, I was trying pretty hard. I was lonely at the time."

"You, lonely! I can't believe that you have ever been lonely."

Royce laughed at her comment. "You want to know a secret," he whispered, and she nodded. "I didn't always look like this. I was a virgin when I left home and moved to Detroit."

"I don't know if I believe you," she said with disbelief written over her face.

"I'm serious. I can show you pictures at my mom's house. I was skinny, shorter, and after my growth spurt, several years of working construction did this." He flexed his muscles and leaned over, giving her a quick kiss.

"Oh yes, I want to see those pictures."

After they finished eating, Royce drove around town, showing her the sites of his hometown. Too bad he hadn't left his motorcycle here. This would be a perfect day to ride. He still hadn't taken Rosita for a ride. Now he had a reason to buy a sidecar so he could take Marguerite for a ride.

On New Year's Eve, Marguerite and Rosita experienced the first time playing with fireworks. Marguerite showed no signs of fear and held the sparklers with Royce's help and twirled it in the air. She laughed and giggled for hours. It was a full family activity, even the adults shot off a few bottle rockets, all but Ms. J, who sat and watched. Instead of going out for the evening, Royce enjoyed relaxing with Rosita on the back patio in front of the fire pit. At midnight, they toasted with champagne and a kiss.

The next day he left Rosita at home with his mother, and Ms. J preparing another big meal for New Year's Day. He wanted to hang out at the garage with his dad, wanting his opinion. They were sitting in his office. Royce asked his dad how he knew that his mom was the one he wanted to marry. Adam answered that he couldn't explain exactly. He just knew that she was the woman he wanted to be with forever.

Royce didn't want to tell his dad that he had issues spending nights and waking up with women; all women except Rosita – he wanted to wake up with her. He'd felt it for the first time when they slept together on the couch. And now they were sleeping together at his parent's house with Marguerite in the middle. Often, he'd laid down with her at Ms. J's but never spent a whole night. He felt that would be disrespectful. One of these days, he planned to take her to his little place. The only reason she didn't know about it now was that the stairs were on the other side of the garage. And most of his windows were still blacked out because of his graveyard shift work.

Royce admitted to his dad that he didn't know what to do about Rosita. He didn't know if he was ready for a serious commitment. His dad asked him if he loved her. Royce cocked his head, looking across the room. He knew he wanted to protect her. He'd never said the words, *"I love you,"* to her, nor had she said them to him. Maybe neither one of them was ready. He knew he couldn't sleep without seeing and kissing her. He almost killed himself driving back from Grand Rapids like a maniac. Was that love? He'd told her that he wanted their first time to be special, but special like what?

"Dad, I haven't had sex with Rosita. I told her that I wanted us to wait. Does that mean I love her?"

"Son, I don't know what else it could mean. Young people today don't know the meaning of the word "wait," especially when it comes to sex. It is rather noticeable how you feel for Marguerite. Do you love the mother as much as you love the daughter? That's the question you need to answer, and then you'll know."

His dad looked down and laughed. "I'm glad to hear about the non-sex part because I had to calm your mother down when you called and said you were bringing a young lady and her daughter home."

"I sent her pictures of Marguerite."

"I know . . . I saw them."

"Does mom have a problem with us staying at the house? I could get a hotel."

"No, son, your mother is okay. You never brought a girl home before."

"I never had anyone I wanted to bring home before."

"She knows that too."

Royce spent the rest of the afternoon at his dad's shop, tinkering. He got back to the house, greasy and dirty. Marguerite ran to him, and he had to hold her back. Royce rushed to his old room, the one he was sharing with Rosita and Marguerite. He took a hot shower and came out wrapped in a towel. Rosita was sitting on the side of the bed, holding a cold drink for him.

"How did you know I was thirsty?" He pulled her to her feet.

"I've been around you long enough to be a mind reader," she said softly as they held hands.

Then Royce's cell rang by the bed.

"Someone has been calling you," Rosita commented.

Royce looked at the caller ID. It was a 318 area code and a number he didn't recognize. "Hello."

"Hey, stranger, it's me again," the sexy voice said.

"Who is this?"

"It's me . . . its Doll. I took a chance to see if you still had the same number. I'm sorry it took me so long to call."

"Well, sorry about that, Doll, you called extremely too late. I'm unavailable. Bye, Doll."

Royce hung up his phone, and Rosita was watching him with a look. It was an unusual look that spoke loudly.

"Sweetie, I didn't know she still had my phone number. I swear."

"You're unavailable? I'm your girlfriend to all your employees, and unavailable to some woman you say that you met at a club a long time ago. What am I to your parents? Am I just Marguerite's mother?" Rosita tried to step around him to leave the room.

"I don't have to explain my personal life to some woman on the phone. You know who you are to me. And my parents . . . you're my girlfriend. I have never brought anyone home to meet my parents. I . . . Don't you know how I feel about you?"

"No, *Royce*, I don't know how you feel about *me*." She moved from his touch and put space between them. "I don't know what this . . . is." She ran from the room.

Royce dropped down on the bed like a hole had been punched through his heart. He wanted to make her feel special. He was trying to treat her special. Someone had used her for sex. Hell, he'd used women for sex too, actually he'd used plenty, and he didn't want to use her for sex. She doesn't deserve that type of treatment. Why couldn't she see that? Why couldn't she see that if he touched her now, he'd be doing the same thing the other man did. He couldn't say that he loved her. He wasn't going to say it and not mean every word of it. Considering that he'd never said "I love you" to any woman other than his family. Royce had a sinking feeling. He didn't know if he was capable of loving a woman that strongly.

Their last two days in Louisiana were strained. His mom talked about his cousin Chase who had a daughter. His daughter was a few years older than Marguerite. Samantha said that he was still having a rough time adjusting to the death of his wife. She told Royce that he should call his cousin and check on him. Royce didn't think that was a good idea, not right now. He was in the middle of his own problems.

Royce and Rosita pretended in front of his parents. He didn't know if they'd recover. Rosita wanted the whole full bang of a relationship. Royce didn't want to hurt her any more than she'd been hurt already.

A few days later, Adam and Samantha saw them off at the airport. They hugged and kissed Marguerite and told her they'd come to visit. Royce thought it was to spoil her more than he did.

While they were biding farewells, Samantha pulled Rosita to the side, "I don't know what's wrong, and I don't want to be an interfering type of mother. Royce is different, and I know he cares for you and Marguerite. He doesn't know how to express that; just give him a little time."

"Mrs. Hawthorne, no disrespect, but he has loved Marguerite for over a year and cared about me for a few months. How much time does he need? I know he's a wonderful, kind, and loving man. Do you know how it feels to watch a man love your daughter and just care about the mother?" She hugged her tight and kissed her cheek, "It was so nice to meet you, and thank you for caring enough to talk to me." Rosita concluded.

"You can call me and talk to me anytime. We want you and Marguerite to be a part of our family."

Rosita nodded her head slowly and walked toward Royce, who was holding Marguerite and waiting with Ms. J. Royce, wondering about the conversation Rosita was so deep in with his mother.

Rosita glanced up, and he saw the sadness in her eyes. Rosita turned and waved goodbye to Samantha and Adam, doubting that she'd ever see them again. Maybe it was time for her to get on her own two feet. She didn't want to be dependent on Royce any longer. Why was he making her wait, wait for what? His mother wanted her and Marguerite to be a part of their family. That was a joke, she wasn't having sex with her son, and she sure as hell wasn't getting a ring.

"What was all that about?" Royce asked

"Girl talk," she said and walked past him.

The small group checked in for their flight inside the Shreveport terminal. It was a small airport and a small plane that would take them to Atlanta, before heading to Detroit. When they boarded, Rosita sat next to Ms. J and left the other seat so Marguerite could sit next to Royce. Rosita knew it was a short flight and pulled out the tablet that she received as a Christmas present from Royce. Since she didn't have romance in her life, she selected a romance novel to read. At least someone would have a happily ever after.

When they arrived in Atlanta, they had a long walk to their terminal and gate. Royce took this into account and asked for assistance so Ms. J didn't have to run or walk fast. He arranged for a cart to take them to their terminal. The small plane only served drinks and snacks, and Marguerite said she was hungry. They found a restaurant that everyone agreed upon and ate. Rosita picked at her food; she wasn't really hungry. After eating, they had a couple of hours to wait for their flight, so they hung out in the Sky Club. Rosita stayed and read a magazine. Marguerite wanted to roam around, or she wanted to beg for something, and Royce would continue to spoil her. Ms. J sat across from her, reading her "O" magazine. Rosita wasn't paying attention when a man sat in the seat next to her.

"Hi there," The stranger said, speaking.

Rosita looked up from her magazine, "Hello." She turned back to reading.

"Are you from the area or passing through?"

She never looked up, "Passing through."

"Where are you going? It would be nice if we're going to the same place."

"Excuse me! Are you hitting on me?"

"Why not? A beautiful woman like you, sitting here all alone, you look like you could use some company."

"Well, for your information. I'm not alone." She said with a smile.

Royce walked into the Sky Club just in time to see Rosita smiling and talking to a man in his seat. He walked a little faster than he needed to.

"Excuse me, but you're in my seat."

"Hey man, I see plenty of empty seats around here." He looked way up at a tall man holding a little girl. "Oh, you're with her. Well, I didn't see a ring on her finger, so I assumed that she didn't belong to anyone." He stood up and faced Royce.

"Well, she belongs to me," Royce said, putting Marguerite on the floor, and she jumped in her mother's lap, showing her a bag of goodies.

"Cute kid! If she belonged to me, I wouldn't leave someone so beautiful alone and looking lonely." He winked at Rosita before he walked off.

"Who was that guy, and why were you smiling at him?"

"I have no idea who he was. He sat next to me and started talking. Why do you sound so jealous? Do you have a problem with me talking to another man?"

"I . . . I was concerned that he was bothering you. You can talk to whoever you want." Royce dropped down in his seat.

Was he jealous? Hell yeah, he was upset when he saw the man sitting next to Rosita, and she was smiling at him. She didn't belong to him. He'd done nothing to claim her. Taking her places and spending money on her didn't mean that she belonged to him. There was only one way to fix this problem.

Chapter Eighteen

It was late in the evening when they returned to Detroit. Royce brought the luggage in while Ms. J walked in and out of all the rooms; this was her ritual every time she returned home. Royce thought that it was time to have an alarm system installed in the house. Rosita bathed Marguerite and got her ready for bed. Royce stopped Ms. J in the kitchen.

"Can you watch Marguerite for a little while? I need to take Rosita somewhere . . . to talk."

"Ah, son, I hope you aren't about to do something stupid. This better not be about that jerk in the airport. I saw and heard everything. She wasn't paying him any attention, and she had already told him that she was with someone."

"It's not about that, Ms. J. I've been . . . I'm not the boyfriend she needs. She needs someone who will love her."

"And you think that you don't love her?"

"I don't know. I can't tell her, and she needs to hear the words. She's been hurt, and I'm making it worse. I want her to know that she has options. That's all." Royce exhaled and paused before he spoke. "I've been keeping her for myself until I was ready. I'm not ready, and I don't know when I will be."

"Then, you take the chance of losing both of them."

"I know. No one knows that better than I do."

Royce sat on the couch, holding his head in his hands. Marguerite bounced in the room, squatting on the floor looking up at him.

"Daddy, why do you look sad? Do you miss grandma and papa?"

"Who are you talking about?"

"You know, your mommy and daddy. They said I should call them grandma and papa."

"I'm not sad anymore. You're here to give me a big kiss, goodnight."

"Are you going to read me a story?"

Royce answered yes and asked Marguerite to get a book, which he'd read to her in bed. Royce hadn't seen Rosita since they returned to the house. Was she avoiding him? Royce read to Marguerite and thought about what he wanted to say to Rosita. It took thirty minutes before Marguerite drifted off to sleep. Royce sat and watched her for another ten. He didn't want to lose her or Rosita, nor did he want to lie to Rosita anymore. Not that he'd been lying about their relationship. He wanted her, wanted to protect her, and he cared deeply for her. He just didn't know if he loved her. It was time to meet the sun and take the heat. He went in search of Rosita, knocking on her door.

"Come in." She answered faintly.

Rosita was lying across her bed in the dark. She'd wondered if she'd see him before he left the house. He'd been quiet for the whole flight home. Was he that upset with her for talking to the stranger at the airport? She battled between the facts that he claimed her when another man was involved. Yet he hadn't truly claimed her as a woman, his woman.

What was she going to do? She'd never been in this situation before and thinking back to the conversation with his mother. She heard Marguerite talking to him. Did everybody else know something that she didn't? Why would his parents tell Marguerite to call them grandma and papa? Like they knew she and Royce would be together. Why should she be the last one to know? Had he taken her home for their approval? Did she pass? According to the conversation between her and his mother, she did. So how long was she supposed to wait? Everybody wanted her to wait.

"Did I wake you?"

"No, I wasn't asleep."

"Come and go somewhere with me."

"I'm not dressed to go anywhere."

"You don't need to change for where we're going."

Royce held out his hand for her, and she took it. They crept through the house and out the back door. She walked with Royce across the yard and around the garage. He opened a tall wooden gate, and behind it was a set of steps. When they reached the top, he unlocked a door, and they stepped in.

He turned on a light. "Welcome to my home."

"This is where you live? You've been living here all this time. Are you embarrassed to be living over a garage?"

Royce sat on the couch and patted the spot next to him. "No, I'm not embarrassed. I'm a simple man that lives a simple life. I've never in the six years that I've lived here brought a woman to this apartment."

"Why are you telling me this? Why did you bring *me* here?"

"I'm trying to show you . . . help you to understand me. I don't know what to do with you. I've never been in a committed relationship before." He dropped his head. "I . . . I've only used women for my own needs. I can't do that to you even if it means that I'll lose you and Marguerite. You deserve to be happy and have a real boyfriend."

"Roy, why does it sound like you're breaking up with me?"

"I'm giving you some space to decide what's best for you and Marguerite."

"I don't want to lose you, Roy."

"Come on . . . let's go back to the house."

Royce didn't acknowledge her comment. He was determined to fix this problem that he'd created. And right after her birthday, he would make some changes. First, he'd help her to get an apartment. Maybe he'd buy her a house. Whatever happened, he wanted them to be safe. He would always help her with Marguerite until she . . . He couldn't begin to think of Marguerite calling another man, 'daddy.'

They walked in silence to the house. Royce followed her inside. He said he was going to kiss Marguerite good night. Rosita knew he'd kissed her after he read to her. She heard him call her his princess. She had one more day off before returning to work and a terrible feeling that he wouldn't be sitting at the table in the morning. Rosita stood in the doorway, staring at him. He sat in the chair, watching Marguerite sleep. She thought that the chair should have a hole in it by now. He spent many nights sitting in that chair, just watching her sleep. Looking up at Rosita, he recognized her sad eyes.

Rosita didn't speak out loud. She only mouthed the words, "Sleep with me."

Royce rose from the chair slowly. Rosita leaned against the door frame watching him. He stopped right in front of her and tilted her chin up, staring like he was studying her face, memorizing it. Rosita wrapped her arms around his neck, and he picked her up off the floor, wrapping her legs around his waist. Walking with her in his arms, he never strayed from her face. He couldn't believe that he didn't love this woman. She made him feel different, act differently. What was wrong with him? She kissed him first, palming his head and deepened the kiss, opening her mouth and making him open up to her. Her tongue searched his mouth, dancing around it slowly sensually. He wrapped his arms around her tighter, squeezing her body into his own. They kissed soft, they kissed hard, and they made love to each other's mouths. Neither could breathe, and their chest hurt from kissing and lack of oxygen. Neither could let go either. Their chests were heaving hard and heavy.

Royce felt his knees brushing the bed and bent down slowly while Rosita clung to him tightly. Lowering them to the bed, he never broke their kiss. He felt for the bed with one hand and knew when Rosita's back rested on it. Using his arms, he braced his body to keep from crushing her. She was still wrapped tightly around his waist. He wanted to unravel her legs, but he liked how she made him feel alive and wanted. It was a different kind of want than he'd experienced with other women. With them, it was pure sex. There was no care or affection, and definitely, no love involved. He was hard with a need, yet he didn't feel a need to satisfy his sexual hunger. He wanted something else, and he was so confused.

Rosita knew this might be her last chance. It wasn't like she was trying to seduce him, she wanted to savor this moment. He wasn't going to change his mind, not after confessing that he'd used women for his own sexual pleasures. She also knew that he wasn't the type of man to threaten a woman or disown a child. He may have used women, but he was nothing like Marguerite's father. Royce was honest with her. He could have used her too, and he didn't. He had a heart that hadn't ever suffered a break. According to him, he'd never shown affection of the heart. But she knew for a fact that he loved Marguerite from the moment she swept him off his feet. But she was also a child. Royce didn't know if he was capable of loving a woman because he never tried.

Rosita whispered into his mouth between a kiss. "Touch me," She kissed him again. "Just once, please." She disentangled her legs and stretched them out on the bed.

Royce was using both his arms braced on the bed above her.

She mouthed, "Please."

He rested his forehead against hers and closed his eyes. He'd wanted to touch her so many times. Right now, he had to get his breathing under control. She was breathing hard, and her breasts were heaving . . . up and down, he could feel them. Opening his eyes, he swallowed hard, gathering his thoughts. Slowly, Royce moved one hand to touch her breast. Rosita closed her eyes. She covered his hand with her own and squeezed her breast. Closing his eyes again, he exhaled, kneading her breast on his own. He exhaled with each squeeze like he was fighting with himself. He toyed with her nipple through her shirt and bra.

Rosita wanted to scream. She'd gone untouched by a man in almost four years. Desperately, she wanted to feel his warm hand against her skin. Calmly she slid her shirt up, stopping when it was right at the base of her bra. She covered his hand again and slid it under her shirt. His warm hand was on her mound. She whimpered. He didn't move or squeeze, his hand frozen in place. He stared into her eyes with a pained look on his face. She needed more, just a little bit. Pulling her bra to the side, she slid his hand quickly.

"Oh my, you don't know how good that feels," she whispered.

He wasn't sure, but he thought he saw a tear fall down the side of her face. Her breast felt so good in his hand. Moving his hand slowly, he wanted to feel all of it. He encircled it with his palm, rubbing his thumb across her nipple, and she jerked under his touch.

"Rosita . . . don't scream. I want to taste you," He fought to say the words.

Royce pushed her shirt higher and bent his head, licking her nipple, drawing it into his mouth. He moaned, and Rosita whimpered and jerked. Royce sucked hard and kneaded her breast, opening his mouth to suck on as much would fit. He licked the nipple with her breast, deep in his mouth. His whole body hardened like a statue. He froze and quickly jumped up off the bed, he had to stop. Enjoying what she was offering wasn't about him. He didn't care about himself, and it wasn't fair to entice her and leave her wanting more than he was willing to give.

"Oh, Roy, I'm so sorry. I shouldn't have asked you to do that. Please don't leave, don't reject me." She started to cry.

Royce rushed back to the bed. "I'm not rejecting you."

He lay down next to her and rocked her in his arms. He whispered that it was his fault. And that he should never have tasted her.

"I have to confess that you taste delightful."

Rosita laughed, happy that at least she was in his arms. Royce held her until she fell asleep. Rosita woke alone, and the house was still quiet. She rolled over in her bed to the other side. His scent was on the pillow, the sheets. Or was his scent burned in her nostrils? She moped around the house, cleaning and putting away their things from the trip. She did her best, trying not to think of Royce, which was hard to do. His presence was there even if he wasn't. She pictured him sitting on the couch, at the table in the kitchen, and in the chair in Marguerite's room. The chair he spent a lot of time watching or reading. She hadn't seen him all day.

She had to know, running out the back door to the garage. His SUV was gone. Blindly, she walked back into the house and sat at the kitchen table. Ms. J strolled into the kitchen and asked if she was hungry.

"Ms. J, he's gone."

"Ah baby, he'll be back. He always does."

Rosita folded her arms on the table and buried her head. "Not this time," she said to herself.

She helped Ms. J with dinner and eventually got Marguerite ready for bed. She sat in his chair and read her a story. Marguerite didn't ask where he was or if he was coming home. She was the only one not bothered by his disappearance. Rosita closed the book and kissed her goodnight after she'd fallen asleep. She lay in her bed, thinking that she'd see him in the morning.

Royce kissed Rosita after she'd fallen asleep and eased out of bed. Getting down on his knees next to Marguerite's bed, he caressed her soft hair. Royce teared up, telling her that he had to go away for a while, and he loved her very much. Royce stroked her hair, saying that she'd see him soon and that he'd try and talk to her every day. He begged her not to cry for him. Royce kissed her one last time and left the house, going home to pack a bag.

Rosita got up the next morning and dressed for work. The house was quiet, and she listened for any sounds coming from the kitchen. She didn't know why he never made any noise. He always sat quietly at the table, waiting for her. She exhaled deeply, leaving her room to face him in the kitchen. Stepping through the door, she stared at an empty chair. She looked around the room frantically like he was going to appear. She could see every corner, every cabinet, and he was nowhere visible. There was a note propped up on the table with her name on it. It was his handwriting. She read the message in disbelief. He'd arranged for a driver to take her to and from work. He told her that he had to tend to some business out of town.

Running to the front door, she snatched it open. A man was standing there next to a car, and he waved to her. She acknowledged him, saying she'd be right back. Slowly she closed the door, standing there frozen, wanting to scream. How could he do this to her? Numbly, she walked back to the kitchen. She stuffed the note in her purse and left the house. The man, Jerrold, spoke as she approached the car, and he held the door for her. He dropped her off at the back entrance, just like Royce had done many mornings. He waited until she was inside before he got back in the car and was gone.

Rosita worked as if she were a robot going about her duties like a second skin. She didn't know how she got through the day and was especially glad that no one asked about her vacation. It wasn't a secret anymore that she was dating the boss or had been dating the boss. She didn't know how she should react if someone asked about him, although no one asked. Good!

Hopefully, she wouldn't have to explain anything any time soon. The end of her shift came, and she walked out the back door.

Jerrold was standing by the car. His head nodded as he held the door open. He didn't talk, he just drove. The car stopped in front of the house, and he opened the door for her to exit. And again, he waited for her to enter the house before he got back in the car. Rosita went about her daily routine at home as well. She wanted to ask Ms. J if she'd heard from Royce, but she didn't. She could call him, except she was a coward.

Jerrold continued to pick her up and drop her off daily. He even knew her days off. She hadn't heard from Royce now in a week. Marguerite didn't even seem to be upset about not seeing him every day.

Rosita was getting Marguerite ready for bed and pulled some clean clothes from her dresser. She saw a MacBook on her dresser.

"Marguerite, did Roy visit you and leave his computer?"

"No mama, daddy said it was my computer. I talk to him every day."

"You've been talking to him on the computer?"

"Yes, and sometimes he reads to me.

Rosita didn't ask her any more questions. At least it was good to know that he was okay. No wonder she wasn't asking or crying for him. He'd been communicating with Marguerite. So why couldn't he talk to her? This was ridiculous. At least Marguerite wasn't suffering.

Royce knew he had a company to run, and he needed to keep busy. He spent some time at the Ren Cen with Toby, and they talked about opening the central office. Royce wanted something close to downtown. Toby suggested that he lease an office in the Ren Cen building. Royce didn't want to deal with Starla O'Neil. Instead, he looked at some other available properties around the downtown area first. They were doable, just not the ambiance he wanted. He wanted something with a nice view, something that spoke confident, impressive. He wished he could ask Rosita for her opinion. For once, he didn't want simple; he wanted complex.

Damn Starla O'Neil, it would be something else to rub in her face. He didn't feel like wearing a suit. She didn't deserve that kind of respect, besides he had nothing to prove. His money was the same, whether he was in a suit or a pair of jeans. Royce strolled into the management office and asked the receptionist for Starla. He didn't give a name, and he stood with his back to the door that she would come barging through, like a crazy person. Starla was her usual bitchy self when she burst through the door.

"Amy, who is it so important that I have to stop what I'm doing to come to the front."

Royce turned around. "Good morning Ms. O'Neil."

"Oh, it's you."

"That doesn't sound professional," Royce said snidely.

"What do you want? I haven't been back to your stupid coffee shop."

"Why? Did someone tell you they saw your banned picture hanging at the entrance?"

"You wouldn't dare."

"Don't try me; I can still put up your picture. Now I am veritably here on an important matter. I need to lease an office."

She rolled her eyes, "Follow me."

They sat in her office, and she showed him some hard copy photos of various styles of suites. Royce rattled off his demands, wanting something with at least four or five separate offices, a conference room, a file room, and a break room. He wanted the two larger offices to have views of the Detroit River. She was glad to smirk and tell him that the request would be expensive. He asked her if he needed to conduct his business with one of her superiors. It wasn't her job to criticize and suggest what he couldn't afford.

For the first time, she apologized for being unprofessional. After tapping some information into her tablet, she grabbed a set of master keys. She showed him several offices, and he was torn between two. He stood in the window looking out at the river and noticed the sun high in the sky to his left. The window faced west.

"I'll take this one."

"I didn't tell you the lease amount yet."

"I don't care what the amount is."

Royce followed her back to her office and signed the lease agreement, requesting the key. Starla argued that the office would need a fresh clean before he could move in. He nodded to signify he understood; however, he still wanted a key. She opened a cabinet and passed him one key, saying he'd get the others after the cleaning.

As soon as he finished his business with the management office, he went in search of Toby. Sitting across from Toby, he announced that they now had an official office. Toby was glad to hear that he'd chosen an office in the Ren Cen. They shared a laugh talking about *Ms. Bitch*. Royce said the office wouldn't be ready for a week, and they could take that time to prepare.

Royce didn't have anything pressing, so he went back to his new office. He didn't want to go back to his lonely hotel. He'd chatted with Marguerite earlier that morning, wondering if Rosita knew about their chats yet. She hadn't called him to complain, say hello, or say, "*I hate your guts,*" nothing. He wished Rosita would lash out at him. He'd been a coward leaving before she woke, arranging for the driver, and visiting Marguerite while she was at work.

Ms. J had torn him a new one. She did it to make him feel guilty. He was feeling guilty all on his own, and he didn't need her to remind him. He missed Rosita too so much. He almost canceled all the arrangements he'd made for her birthday, one she didn't know about yet. Would she even go with him after all this?

He needed to know if he could stay away. Although it wasn't fair when you sneak into someone's room in the middle of the night and watch them sleep, that wasn't staying away.

Opening the blinds, he sat on the floor. He watched the sun descend, and for the first time in his life, he shed a tear for a woman. If this was love, then why couldn't he say the words? Did he want her to say it first? He sat on the floor in darkness for another hour.

Rosita was feeling so distraught after two weeks and nothing from Royce. She was beginning to hate him for leaving her. And he wasn't spending all his time out of town either. He was making visits to Marguerite during the day while she worked, and she had a suspicion that he was making late-night visits. Especially after finding new dolls in the bed that hadn't been there when she put her to bed. Was he coming into her room as well? Why? Why? Why?

Should she settle for a man that didn't love her or couldn't love her? Which was it? She wasn't ever going to be in a one-sided relationship again. She didn't have enough love for two people.

Rosita was in the storeroom making out an order for next week's delivery. She heard Janell calling her name.

"Rosita."

"Hey, Janell, what's up?" Rosita asked, annoyed that her thoughts had been interrupted, which was indeed a good thing.

"Girl, I was just wondering where you're off to on your next vacation."

"What next vacation?"

"You're one lucky girl. I wish I had a man to whisk me off to parts unknown."

"Janell, what are you talking about?"

"Your ten-day vacation, I was wondering where you're going this time."

"My birthday is in two weeks," she said mostly to herself and thinking out loud.

"Cool, happy early birthday. It's been on the calendar for over a month. I hadn't seen you in a while, and I almost forgot to ask you about it."

"Well, I doubt I'll be going anywhere." She mumbled to herself. "Thanks for the heads up, Janell."

Rosita wanted to throw the clipboard across the room. He'd probably forgotten about her birthday. Oh well, she could spend it with Marguerite at home. Then again, she couldn't afford to take off for ten days without pay.

At the moment, she wanted to kill Royce. Rushing into the office, she asked Janell if she could cancel the vacation, telling her that she didn't have enough paid time. Janell looked at her and asked twice if she was sure that she wanted to cancel. Rosita nodded, and Janell said she'd put the cancellation in the computer.

It took two days before Royce saw the cancellation of Rosita's vacation. He called Janell and asked her why she canceled it. Janell said that Rosita requested the cancellation because she didn't have enough time. Royce told Janell to reactivate the vacation request, and he would take care of Rosita.

Royce knew he had to face Rosita eventually, her birthday was coming up, and he'd made a lot of plans. He was looking for a piece offering and made a late-night visit to the store, again. Was he buying dolls for Marguerite because he felt guilty, yes? But this time, he was looking for something for Rosita. He walked up and down all the aisles hoping something would jump out at him. Eventually, he ended up on the aisle of stuffed animals. She wasn't the teddy bear kind of girl. He ambled, scanning all the rows. Stopping short, he saw an orange stuffed pillow with rays of sunshine sprouting. He headed to the register with one single item.

He crept into the house quietly, stopping in Marguerite's room first, and sat in his chair. She was asleep, holding the first doll he'd bought her. Why that doll? Was she missing him at night, reading to her, and watching movies with her? He knew he was missing his whole family. After watching her for a few more minutes, he made his way to Rosita's room. He stood at the door, intending to leave the pillow on her bed. She was tossing and turning and talking, like she was having a nightmare. Royce sat on her bed and shook her; she didn't respond. He didn't want to scare her. So he lay down next to her and wrapped his arms around her. She was crying in her sleep.

"Oh, baby, please don't cry," he whispered. "I'm so sorry if I've hurt you. Please forgive me."

He caressed her hair and rocked her in his arms. She turned in his arms to face him. Mumbling, she never opened her eyes.

"Why don't you love me? I've never been loved. No one has ever loved . . ." she murmured in her sleep, and tears rolled down her face. "I love you, Roy. Why can't you love me?"

He felt like a monster, rocking her softly, apologizing. He felt her breathing slowing down, and she wasn't talking in her sleep anymore. She was cradled in his arms, sleeping like a baby. He'd made things worse, and now she probably hated him.

Rosita woke when her alarm sounded. She'd had the strangest dream, dreaming that she slept in Royce's arms. He held her and rocked and soothed her. Except her bed was empty or was it. She saw something strange on the other side of her bed. It was a pillow of the sun. He had been here; he was thinking of her. She hurried to get ready for work. Jerrold was always on time. Rosita grabbed her keys and her purse and headed to the front door. She opened the door, and Jerrold wasn't waiting for her. Glancing at her watch, she wasn't early. He'd been waiting for her for over three weeks every morning. She pulled her note from Royce that she'd been carrying around in her purse. There was no number to call, nothing, only his message. She turned when she heard a male voice clear his throat behind her.

"Good morning, sunshine."

Rosita was momentarily speechless. He was here in the flesh. She didn't know what to say. They stared at each other. "I thought I dreamt that you were here last night."

"You weren't dreaming."

"Roy, why are you here?" She asked, puzzled.

"I want to know why you canceled your vacation."

"Are you kidding me? I haven't seen or heard from you in weeks, and all you're worried about is some vacation time." She remarked angrily.

"I over rid your cancellation. I just wanted you to know."

"What makes you think that I'll go anywhere with you."

"Tell me why you were crying in your sleep." Royce made slow steps toward her.

"I don't know what you're talking about. I wasn't crying in my sleep."

"You talked in your sleep. You said you love me. Is that true?"

Royce was distracting her while he slowly stepped toward her. He had no idea what he was going to do when he got to her. Their eyes locked onto each other. He wanted to be close when he got his answer. She had a bad shy habit of whispering.

"Rosita, do you love me?"

Rosita looked down at his shoes. He was close enough to reach out and touch her. She didn't want to tell him. She didn't want another one-sided relationship. Even if she admitted it to him, that didn't mean he wouldn't leave her again. Even if she told him, it didn't mean that he loved her back.

"Rosita, you don't have to give me an answer. Can you do me one favor? Please celebrate your birthday with me?" He wanted to touch her to kiss her. What he needed was her forgiveness.

"Why should I do you any favors?"

"Because I owe you this birthday present, I need to do this for you, for us."

"Is this one of your guilt presents like all the ones you've been leaving for Marguerite in the middle of the night?"

"I do feel guilty for not being here for her. I'm not going to stay away from her anymore, I swear, other than when you and I go out of town *alone*." He held her hands and stared into her eyes.

Royce couldn't say the words, but he knew deep down that it wouldn't be because he was using her if he made love to her.

"Alone? What about Marguerite? I've never . . ."

"Ms. J is going to take care of Marguerite. You don't have to worry about her. You can chat with her on the computer whenever you want."

"Really! Like the way that you've been chatting with her?"

"She told you about that?"

"What did you expect? I found a laptop in her room. She is three years old and owns an Apple computer." She gave him that look again. "Where are you planning on taking me for my birthday?"

"How about we talk about it in the truck, I'm here to take you to work."

"Where's Jerrold?" She asked sarcastically.

Royce gave her a serious face and said he fired him, saying he was the only man that would drive his *girlfriend* around town. He apologized for hurting her, and if she forgave him, he'd spend every waking day and moment making it up to her.

Royce wanted her to bring that sexy bikini. He couldn't request that she pack it. Damn! He didn't want her to know that a beach was involved with her surprise. And he didn't want to go digging through her personal belongings. What were his choices? He could buy her another one once they arrived at their destination, but she'd have a fit. He'd have to figure something out.

Rosita grilled him the entire ride about the destination, asking him at least a hundred times. He pulled into the back parking lot of the Midtown location, and yes, she was a little late. The other staff was already there and waiting. He jumped out and ran around to her door. She was still fussing, but he was so glad to hear the laughter in her voice.

"I have no idea what to pack."

He pulled her into his arms. "What if I told you nothing, only the clothes on your back?"

She looked directly into his smiling, devious face. "I would think you'd lost your mind. Can you give me just a hint, please?"

"I think you should open the business, or your boss will be upset with you."

"I'm with the boss, and the boss made me late."

"I'm not talking about me. I'm talking about Janell." He winked. "Now, go to work, and I'll see you later."

Royce left her, going straight to the hotel to check out. From now on, he'd spend his days and nights with his whole family. Now he just had to figure out a way to love Rosita and make sure she knew how he felt. First, he was taking his family out to dinner tonight. All dressed up.

Royce knew the next two weeks would be busy. He needed to have everything ready to open his office before he left town and prepare for his vacation in Hawaii with Rosita.

Chapter Nineteen

Royce thought he'd planned the perfect birthday for Rosita. They arrived the day before her birthday. He'd rented a Chateau with beachfront property on the island of Maui. The house came with a hot tub in the backyard, surrounded by trees and heavy brush. It was extremely private. He wanted everything to be perfect. On this vacation, she would positively become his girlfriend and his lover. She thought that he didn't care about her because he wouldn't have sex with her. He'd done his fair share of using women to satisfy his primal male hunger. She was different, and he'd never wanted to use her. He wanted… He was still unsure of what he wanted from Rosita.

They'd been traveling for most of the day and arrived in the afternoon. Since Rosita had a fear of Los Angeles, he'd found a route through Chicago. After arriving in Maui, they picked up the rented SUV and he plugged in the rental office's information. Once he'd secured the keys, their next stop was at the chateau. Rosita loved it immediately.

"I can't believe you did all this for me, for my birthday."

"Yes, you deserve to have a special day just like Marguerite, except you get the premium package."

They inspected the house, which had two bedrooms and a modern kitchen. A spacious living room, except the couch, wasn't wide enough for them to snuggle. They walked down to the beach. Royce didn't think they'd get a good sunset from this beach, but it was lovely. Next, they checked out the hot tub. Royce had strong desires to test it out.

Afterward, they drove to a nearby restaurant for dinner and stopped at the store for some necessities for the house. When they returned to the house, they unpacked, and Royce suggested that they get some sleep. Her birthday surprise meant leaving very early in the morning. He slept with Rosita in his arms until the alarm went off on his phone.

"Wake up, sleepyhead, it's time to go."

Rosita blinked, opening her eyes, "It's still dark outside. I want to go back to sleep."

"You can sleep in the truck." He helped the sleepy woman get dressed, and she never noticed the mask he slipped on her face.

Rosita had drifted back to sleep, and he carried her out to the truck and put her into the back seat. Covering her with a blanket, he put a pillow under her head and put the middle seat belt around her waist. He'd already stashed her other surprises in the back. It was funny the ruse he used to make the purchase.

Royce drove for over an hour before reaching the Haleakala Visitor Center. When he reached the peak, there were a lot of vehicles. The area was a popular spot, just like he'd read during his research. He was glad that he left early enough to get a parking spot. She was going to love it. There were people set up with big expensive cameras and some people with small regular cameras. He forgot to bring the camera. Damn! It was almost time for the show, so he woke Rosita.

Royce stood behind Rosita and pulled the mask from her face.

Rosita looked around and noticed all the vehicles and a few headlights illuminating the parking lot. "Where are we?"

Royce pointed. "Just watch." He spoke softly into her ear just above a whisper.

They stood on top of a mountain peak and watched the sun appear from the depths. The earth was basked in a sea of orange before the sun ascended. There were waves and waves of red and yellow, barely touching the earth's surface. The glowing colors danced just for them. The forewarning of the rays was evidence that the sun was approaching. It rose slowly like spiked flames rising from the depths of hell.

Rosita couldn't believe that she was so captivated by the rising sun and enamored by one man, this man. Royce stood behind her, holding her in an embrace. She loved him, wishing that he felt the same way about her. She didn't realize she was crying. Her breathing was erratic, and she was shaking.

Royce felt her shaking and thought she was cold until he felt water dripping onto his arm. When he turned her around, something broke inside him. He cupped her face and wiped at her tears with his thumbs. He kissed her, tasting her tears.

"Oh, Rosita, *I love you so much*," he whispered into her mouth, kissing her and picking her up. She wrapped her legs around his waist. His arms tightened around her back.

"Don't cry, baby . . . please don't cry." He heard his own words ringing in his ears. He'd said it out loud. "Oh, my God! Rosita, *I love you . . . I love you!*" He shouted to the rising sun and everybody around them.

"*Marry me!*" he said. "*I want to make love to you . . . I want to make love to you as my wife.*" He palmed her face and kissed her.

"What?" She asked, stunned.

"Marry me . . . today. No tomorrow. Women need more than one day," he said excitedly.

He'd just demanded a woman to marry him. His mother would kill him for being insensitive. He had to ask appropriately. Rosita deserved a better proposal than that. Untangling her legs, he stood her to the ground. He got down on one knee and held one of her hands.

"Rosita Rodriquez, would you do me the honor of becoming my wife and a real father to Marguerite?"

Rosita looked around, and no one was watching the rising sun. They were all looking at them. She looked down at Royce and knew he was serious. He didn't just *say* that he loved her. It was real, and now he was asking her to marry him.

"Yes . . . yes, I'll marry you!"

People shouted around them, and several were taking pictures. He picked her up again, spinning, and kissing her softly and passionately. Royce held her, kissing her as the sun continued to rise higher in the sky. He had to stop kissing his bride-to-be because so many people were congratulating them. Three people asked for his email address to send him pictures of his proposal. Thanking them profusely, he gave them the information.

Rosita was still in his arms. Opening the back of the truck, he sat her inside. Almost forgetting the real reason that they were on the mountain, he unpacked the box. Inside were two cupcakes, one with a candle.

He lit the candle. "Happy Birthday, Rosita! I hope you like your party on top of a mountain. Now make a wish and blow out the candle."

Rosita closed her eyes and puckered. She couldn't believe that he remembered what she'd said even though she'd been joking at the time. But this was way more than she could have ever imagined. She couldn't believe that she almost refused to come on this trip.

She opened her eyes. "What if my wish came true already?"

"Baby, I'm sure there is one more thing in the world that you could wish for."

Rosita closed her eyes again, and a few seconds later, she blew out the candle. Her eyes followed the rising sun that was dancing up toward the clouds. She couldn't believe that he'd done all this just for her. He'd set this up even before he proclaimed his love. She had a feeling that he already loved her. No one would go to all this trouble for someone they only cared for. So far, they'd shared a sunrise and a sunset. She wondered what was going to happen every day in between.

Rosita's mood changed; she needed to tell him about her past, about Marguerite's father. He might change his mind about marrying her when he found out the truth. He deserved to know, or she'd hate herself. She dropped her head in shame.

"I need to tell you about my past. You might not want to marry me."

He lifted her chin so he could see her face. "Baby, there is nothing that you could tell me to keep me from loving you as much as I do right now. We can talk about it later. Right now, I want to watch this beautiful scenery with my fiancée."

He picked up his cupcake and took a bite. He kissed her with icing on his lips, but Rosita still had a faraway look.

"Eat your cupcake before I do a Marguerite on you." He joked.

He chewed his cupcake, smiling at her. Rosita gave him a small smile and bit into her cupcake. Royce draped an arm around her shoulder and pulled her into his chest. He had no idea what she wanted to talk about or how bad it was. It didn't matter. They'd deal with it together.

All he knew was his heart cracked wide open when he realized that she was crying. Her crying words rang in his ears. *"Why don't you love me? I've never been loved."* He knew at that moment that he did love her and had loved her for a long time. The words burst out from deep within his soul. This moment was what his heart needed all along. His heart wanted the most memorable moment, especially knowing that he'd make love to her as his wife. It would never be just sex between them. It would always be love. They watched the sun until it was high in the sky.

"Hey, we better go. We have a wedding to plan, and we have to call Marguerite, Ms. J, and my parents!"

He jumped from the back of the SUV and lifted Rosita out. He cradled her in his arms and opened her door, sitting her on the front seat. He kissed her softly. She still had a sad look on her face.

"Rosita, I love you, and that is all that matters. I don't care what happened in your past or what happened between you and

Marguerite's father. She is *our* daughter. As far as Marguerite is concerned, I am her *daddy,* and I always will be."

Rosita palmed his face, "I love you, and I can't wait to be your wife."

"You don't know how good it feels to hear you say that." He gave her a quick kiss and ran around the truck.

Royce rushed back to the chateau so that they could make a call home first. Ms. J was so happy to hear the fantastic news. They talked with Marguerite for a little while and told her they'd chat with her on the computer later. There was a lot of work to do. First, they needed to know how to get a license. Together, they sat searching the website.

Rosita dropped her head to the table because she didn't travel with a birth certificate. Her state ID wasn't valid to obtain a marriage license. Royce smiled and gave her a quick kiss. God must be smiling on them because he'd used their Passports checking in at the airport. He pointed to the screen; it was an identification option.

Next, they looked for places to get married. A venue popped up, displaying a sunset wedding on a beach. They both saw it at the same time. Royce started reading all the amenities associated with a wedding package. He called the venue, but they were already booked. The lady on the phone gave him several options. She told him about several hotels on the island of Oahu that performed sunset weddings. Royce started making phone calls, and he soon found one hotel that had an opening. Speaking with the coordinator, he reserved the wedding package, which included hair and make-up service. It included all the wedding necessities. He wanted Rosita to have the works.

Oh no! They were alone. What if she needed some help? He told her to keep reading, and he jumped up from the table. Royce went into the next room and made a call, returning to the table, smiling.

He asked Rosita to pack because they were going to a different island for a couple of days. They had shopping to do. He wanted her to have the wedding of a princess. After searching for the local airline, he booked two tickets to Oahu.

When they arrived at the airport, he felt insensitive. He'd asked this beautiful woman to marry him and now they were rushing off to another island. After they arrived at their gate, he sat down and pulled her into his lap. He kissed her, snuggling her neck, and telling her how much he loved her. Picking up her hand, he kissed her wrist, examining her left hand. He wanted to buy her a big beautiful diamond. Shortly thereafter, they boarded the plane and were treated like royalty for the short forty-five minute flight.

They arrived at their resort two hours later. Royce suggested they grab a bite to eat first. Afterward, they sought out the wedding coordinator and introduced themselves. She gave them the information on where to go and obtain the license, asking them how long they'd been engaged. They looked at each other, and Royce looked at his watch. "About six hours," he said, adding that it had been spontaneous. Laughing, she said that that wasn't the record. The coordinator gave them a list of local jewelers, wedding dress shops, and tuxedo rentals. She asked how many were part of the wedding party.

Rosita answered, "Two."

Royce answered, "Four."

"Four?"

"Yes, Mom and Dad are on the way. I wanted you to have some help getting ready. I hope that's okay."

She kissed him. "I think it's perfect. I would love for your mother to help me."

"My mom? She's going to be your mother too."

Rosita smiled at the idea of Samantha as her mother-in-law. They left the coordinator's office to obtain the license. Their next stop would be the jeweler. Royce was ready for Rosita to put up a fight. The time wasn't right to tell her everything. But right now, he wanted her to have the largest diamond her hand could hold. Immediately, a salesman greeted them, walking in the door. Royce gave him their names and told the associate that they were looking for wedding rings.

The salesman escorted them across the room and seated them in front of a glass case. The first question he asked was what style of cut. Rosita looked at Royce, having no idea. He clutched her hand and brought it up to his lips.

"Can you show us the different styles of cuts?" Royce asked, holding her hand tightly.

The sales associate placed a tray in front of them. It displayed all the styles of cuts labeled. Royce did a double-take. He knew which cut he wanted her to have. But he figured a joint decision was also a choice. Rosita looked at all the stones, and she felt when Royce's body language changed. And she knew why. Their eyes must have seen it at the same time. She hadn't ever believed in fairy tales, but her Prince Charming was sitting next to her. He'd already been in her life. She pointed to the stone.

"Princess, I'd like a princess cut stone."

"Okay, Ms. Rodriquez, that's a beautiful choice."

"I wholeheartedly agree with that choice, my Princess, Royce said, smiling.

The salesman removed the tray and retrieved two trays displaying wedding sets. He pulled a large ring with lots of circles from behind the counter.

"We need to find your correct size now, Ms. Rodriquez."

The salesman tried on a couple before he found her correct size. Rosita scanned the rings, touching them with her finger. They were all so beautiful. The trays were set up from single stones to multi bands with lots of diamonds. Royce watched her linger on the tray with the single stones and plain bands. He picked it up and passed it to the associate.

"We don't want anything on this one."

Rosita wanted to murder him again. Royce had rented a house in Hawaii for ten days. Now they'd flown to a different island, and he'd booked a hotel suite there. She saw the prices on the website for the wedding package. And she still needed a dress. The man was spending a fortune. She figured he was blowing through all his savings and maxing out his credit cards.

"Roy, I like simple."

"So do I, but today you're getting a big beautiful diamond. I want you to show me which one a princess, my princess would want."

He pushed the remaining tray in front of her. She picked up a couple of rings, turned them over, and slid them on her finger, repeating the process. Finally, she picked up a white gold cluster double framed bridal set in three pieces, and the ring had three-tiered levels. The top had six princess-cut stones all set together, and the tiers were squared. She slid it on her finger and held it up.

"Aweee . . . this is beautiful."

"I love it," Royce whispered into her ear.

Rosita slid the ring off her finger, trying to see the tag holding the bands together. Royce grabbed it, kissing her. He knew she was trying to look at the price. Instead of the cost, he had a different question for the sales associate.

"How many carats?" He wanted her to have a ring with plenty of bragging rights.

The associate turned the ring over and looked at the tag. "It has a total of eight carats, sir. Is that . . . enough?" He'd been working long enough never to judge clients and what they could afford.

"We'll take it. My fiancée loves it."

"Now, sir, are you ready to look at some men bands?"

Royce selected a white gold band with two diamonds on top. The sales associate made sure he had both rings in stock, and they were being cleaned and polished. Royce pulled out his wallet and passed him his black American Express card. The sales associate brought him their rings displayed in ornate boxes. Royce separated the rings and slid two parts onto her ring finger.

"Now, you are officially engaged." He lifted her hand and kissed her finger.

Rosita stared at the ring like she was going to wake up from a dream. Excitedly, they left the jewelry store, strolling down the sidewalk, holding hands. There was a bridal shop and a tuxedo rental store located in the same strip mall. Royce stopped on the sidewalk in front of the bridal shop. He asked her if she was ready to search for the perfect dress. She shook her head, unsure, and said she wanted his approval. He suggested that it was something she and her future mother-in-law could do together.

"Besides, I heard it was bad luck for the groom to see the wedding dress before the wedding."

"Well, do you have anything, in particular, you want to see in a dress—a specific color, a style?"

"Color? I thought all the wedding dresses were white."

"Well, virgins are supposed to wear white, and I'm not a virgin."

"I want you in white. You're my virgin bride."

They stood in the window and looked at the dresses displayed. Something captured his attention about a dress. It gave him an idea. Rosita stared at her hand longer than looking at the dresses. Royce knew she was happy, and he too. To kill some additional time, they strolled along the street, looking in multiple store windows.

Royce's cell rang; it was his parents. They'd landed at the airport and would meet them at the hotel. Royce thought his mother would kill him after telling them to spare no expense and get to Oahu as soon as possible. They chartered a private plane out of Dallas, Texas. Luckily, they were able to catch a flight out of Shreveport heading to Dallas, which was only a forty-five-minute flight. Even though it was late in the morning when he called, they began moving in fast motion. While Samantha packed for both of them, Adam made phone calls and booked flights. Samantha was excited, knowing that the flight from Dallas to Oahu was less than eight hours, and they were assured that they could relax in comfort for the long flight. They were going to need all the rest they could get because as soon as their feet hit the ground, they'd be running.

It was almost time for his parent's arrival, so they headed to the waiting car. Royce had hired a driver since they'd only be on the island for a few days. They were waiting in the lobby when the taxi pulled up. Royce was holding Rosita around the waist, watching them get out of the car.

Samantha shrieked when the doors opened, and she saw them, leaving Adam on the curb and rushing to them. She was in the middle, hugging both of them and getting kisses on both her cheeks. Royce would have sworn he saw tears in his mother's eyes. Adam dropped the bags he was carrying at the desk and joined them. He hugged Rosita first and kissed her on the cheek. And then he looked at his son with love in his eyes. They hugged each other.

"I'm so proud of you, son. I think you made a wonderful choice."

"Thanks, Dad. I'm glad you guys could make it."

"Son, we wouldn't miss this for the world."

"That makes two of us," His mother chimed in, even though they were tired from probably making the quickest trip to Hawaii in history. She turned to Rosita. "Do you have a ring?"

"Yes, we just left the jewelry store, and we made a stop by a bridal shop and a tuxedo shop before you called."

"Oh no, did he see your dress?"

"No ma'am, I was hoping you'd help me pick out one in the morning."

"Oh, Rosita, I would love to. Since you guys won't see each other until the wedding anyway."

"What?" Royce and Rosita said at the same time.

"Sorry, son, it looks like it's a two-man bachelor party tonight."

"Mom, you mean after breakfast, I won't see Rosita until the wedding."

"No, son . . . you won't see Rosita after tonight . . . let's say bedtime."

"So . . . what you're saying is that I'm sleeping somewhere else tonight."

"You can sleep in the room with your father. I don't trust you. I'll be staying with Rosita."

Royce protested, saying that his dad snored. Rosita laughed and told him that he snored too. She said it was a cute soft snore.

"It's not fair. At least mom has her own room." He pouted.

He'd reserved a two-bedroom suite. So Rosita would have a separate room to get dressed. Now his mother would be using it.

Adam laughed on his way back to the desk to check in. Royce dropped his head in defeat and followed. The clerk at the desk changed his parent's suite from one king bed to two queen beds. Royce had done one important thing: make sure that his parent's suite wasn't next door to his. He requested that it be another floor, at the other end of the hall, or the other side of the building.

Royce and Rosita headed to their suite to gather Royce's things. She teased him and said it would only be for one night. He didn't have to take everything. Unlocking the door, he threw her over his shoulder, strolling through the suite, and tossed her onto the king-size bed. Sliding his hand under the pillow, he pulled out a small box.

"I was going to give this to you later tonight."

"I wasn't expecting more gifts. I thought the trip was my gift."

She looked at the rectangular box and pulled the ribbon. Lifting the lid, she gasped. "Oh my God, Roy, this is beautiful and too much."

"Do you like it?"

"I love it. But how did you know that I needed a new watch?" She stared at the silver watch with a black face surrounded by diamonds.

"I didn't. It matches mine, and I wanted us with matching Seiko's."

Royce pounced onto the bed and hovered over her. She reached up and caressed his face, tracing her finger along his beard line and across his lip. He recognized the look on her face and the sparkle in her eyes. Sliding her hands down his chest, she extended both her arms to his sides.

Rosita roamed, grazed, and caressed, and she'd never touched him like this and pulled him down closer. Royce lowered himself to brace on his elbows. She could touch him now and not be worried about rejection. He would be all hers in one more day. The knowledge of knowing that he loved her, encouraged her to caress his back and slide her hands lower, moving them slowly and sensually. His breathing was getting heavier and heavier. Royce enjoyed letting her explore his body. Rosita slid her hands until she rubbed them across his taut butt.

"Ah, I've wanted to touch your butt for a long time. You have a nice ass." She laughed, squeezing his butt, and pulled him down closer, wanting to know if her touch affected him. Her legs wrapped around his waist instinctively. Oh yeah, he wanted her. She felt him.

"Why are you tempting me when you know mom and dad are on the way?"

"I wanted to know what I'm getting on my wedding night."

"Oh, our wedding night, I like the sound of that."

Royce kissed her on the lips and down her neck. He kissed her exposed mounds peeking out of her low-cut blouse. Rosita moaned from his kisses and ground her hips against him. Yanking on her blouse and pulling one side of her bra down, he licked her nipple. She jerked and ground into him harder. He pulled and sucked on her nipple, moaning with her nipple in his mouth. The moment was too good to be true, but they were interrupted by a loud knock at the door.

"Damn, my mother is a smart woman. And because of what you did to me . . ." He looked down between them. "You have to open the door."

Rosita jumped out of bed, fixing her clothes. Running to the door, she opened it with a smile. She invited them in and pointed to the other room where Samantha's things would go. She and Samantha sat in the living room while Adam rolled her luggage to the next room. Royce showed up a few minutes later with Rosita's small pink bag.

He gave her a look and mouthed, "Don't say a word."

She laughed at him because he only had a large suitcase, whereas she had a large and small bag. He sat it by the door. She'd left the bedroom so fast that she left her present still in the box. Royce slid it on her wrist and snapped it closed. And then, he offered beverages while he told his parents about the wedding plans. He was excited to tell them about the sunset wedding package he'd reserved.

Rosita touched Samantha's arm at the table. "Ms. Hawthorne…"

"You might as well call me, mom."

"Ok . . . Mom, would you be my Matron of Honor?"

"I would love to, honey!"

"I guess that makes you the best man, dad?"

Adam nodded his head, "I'd be honored."

Royce told them about the hired car, and they could share it. The girls could go shopping for dresses, and he and his dad would visit the tuxedo store. Royce told them that in an hour, they were attending a Luau to celebrate Rosita's birthday. Adam and Samantha wished her a happy birthday. Royce spoiled it by telling them that was the reason they were initially in Hawaii. He mentioned that they had a chateau on Maui. Royce didn't tell the whole story to his parents on the phone when he told them to charter a plane and get to Hawaii.

Royce wanted to get his mother alone so he could give her his suggestion on the type of dress that would accommodate a special gift he had in store for Rosita. As they walked down the hotel's corridor, he told her that he needed to talk to her. Immediately, she thought that something was wrong. He reassured her that all was well with him and Rosita. They passed through the lobby heading out to the beach for the Luau.

A man passed Royce and looked at him strangely, and then he yelled congratulations. Adam asked Royce if he knew the guy, and he shook his head no and said he'd never seen him before in his life.

He had his arm around Rosita's shoulder as they walked. She gave him a look and told him that they still needed to talk. He assured her that they'd talk about it later.

The Luau consisted of lots of food and entertainment. Royce spotted their wedding coordinator, and she waved for them. She was standing next to some benches on the front row.

"I was hoping I'd see you here. Would you and your wedding party join me in the VIP section?"

"Thank you, we'd like that," Royce told her.

Royce introduced his parents to the coordinator. They took their front-row seats and waited for the show to begin. A waitress stopped in front of them with a tray of fruity-looking drinks with cute tiny umbrellas, and everybody grabbed a glass. Royce had seen these shows before when he'd been on vacation with his parents. He thought Rosita would enjoy it for her birthday. The show was spectacular with the dancers and their costumes. Rosita shrieked when the guy started twirling fire on the sticks.

The highlight of their evening was when dancers pulled Rosita and Royce onto the stage. The women danced circles around him while the men did the same to Rosita. They performed a Hawaiian-style wedding ceremony. Instead of rings, their wrists were bound with palm tree leaves and lei draped around their heads and necks. It was so beautiful that Samantha had water in her eyes. She hoped she didn't cry at the real wedding.

While they ate, Royce managed to speak to his mother for a few minutes. He told his mother what kind of suggestion to make on his behalf. His dress requirement had something to do with a wedding gift. They'd discussed something special that she was supposed to bring from home. Samantha assured him she'd packed it in her luggage.

The evening came to a halt, the midnight hour was approaching, so Samantha told Royce to escort Rosita to her room and kiss her good night. They entered the suite and sat on the couch, not touching.

"I feel like I'm in high school and afraid to be caught by my girlfriend's father." Royce jested.

"I never had an experience like that. Growing up in foster care made you a leper, so boyfriends were never on my itinerary."

Royce pulled her over to straddle his legs. "Let them catch us. What can they do, forbid us to get married?"

He wrapped his arms around her back and kissed his bride-to-be. He heard his parents coming in the door, considering that his mother took his room key. Rosita attempted to move from his lap.

"Oh no, you don't. Mom said I could kiss you good night."

Royce kissed, tickled, and whispered sweet nothings until his mother said it was time to go. She said brides need their beauty sleep. He kissed her one last time at the door.

"Good night, Rosita Rodriquez. I love you."

"I love you too, Royce Hawthorne."

Rosita closed the door and leaned up against it, dis-believing this was happening to her. Okay, so now, she wanted to watch a Disney movie. And that thought made her glad that, even more since they'd chatted with Marguerite before they went to the Luau. Marguerite wanted to know why grandma and papa were there, and she wasn't. Marguerite had no idea what they were telling her about a wedding. Royce was going to surprise Rosita and let them watch the ceremony. He planned to set up the laptop and FaceTime Marguerite and Ms. J. It was the only way they could be a part of this special day.

Rosita lay in the big bed, thinking about her big day. She tried hard to go to sleep, except her past issues kept nagging at her. It was after one o'clock. She wanted to . . . no, she needed him to know before she'd let him make a mistake. He might come to resent her, thinking that she should have told him a long time ago. She sent him a text.

Rosita: Roy, I can't sleep. I have to talk to you *now*. I can't let you make a mistake.

Royce woke from his phone, pinging next to his head. He'd just dozed off to sleep, being too excited and knowing that he was about to marry the perfect woman for him. He couldn't be happier, knowing that Marguerite came as a package deal. He peeped at the phone and sat straight up in the bed.

Royce: Sweetie, you are worrying about nothing. I love you, and that is all that matters.

Rosita: I will not marry you with this hanging over my head.

Royce knew his mother would kill him if she found him in that room. If Rosita wanted to talk, they needed privacy. And he didn't need his parents thinking anything terrible about Rosita if they knew about her past.

Royce: Come out the patio door to the beach. I'm on my way.

Royce rushed to jump into some shorts. He was so concerned about Rosita that he didn't put on a shirt and ran the whole way. Their room was on the other end of this big-ass hotel. He wasn't sure which room was theirs from the outside. It was dark except for the lighting of the outside wall lamps. Royce called her name above a whisper and didn't hear anything or see anyone. There were only faint sounds in the background. Calling out to her again, he saw some movement ahead of him. She was on the patio waving to him. He rushed to her, almost out of breath, scooping her over the railing.

"Let's walk." Royce led them toward the beach. He spotted a dune, and they sat on it facing the ocean. "I'm sorry for being insensitive. I didn't know this was bothering you enough to cancel our wedding."

"Roy, I just need you to know . . . what happened." Rosita was whispering by the time she finished her sentence.

Royce wrapped his arm around her and told her he was ready to listen. Rosita started her story, telling him how Marguerite's father baited her with tips and how their affair started. Tears were rolling down her face by the time she told him about the truckers, and he offered to sell her to them. Royce pulled her into his lap and rocked her. He felt like he was in kill mode. She finished her story, telling him that he threatened to kill her and Marguerite after discovering she didn't get an abortion. That was when she fled out of Los Angeles.

She even told him about living on the streets with Marguerite as a newborn.

Royce asked, "What's the bastard's name?"

Rosita wouldn't tell him, and it wasn't on Marguerite's birth certificate. Rubbing her arms, he said it wasn't her fault that she got caught up with the wrong man. They sat on the beach until 4 a.m., holding each other.

Rosita had fallen asleep in his arms. She wasn't ever going to have to worry about Marguerite's father because he would protect both of them forever. He stood with his fiancée in his arms and walked back to the patio, hoping he remembered which one was the right one. Too bad he couldn't tuck her in bed, but the door needed locking from the inside. He woke her up and put her across the rail. She kissed him and whispered that she loved him so much and would see him on the beach at sunset.

Rosita crawled into her bed, feeling better because she'd gotten all of it off her chest. She'd told him the whole dreaded story, and he didn't flinch a bit. It truly didn't matter to him, and he loved her and Marguerite. He had plenty of room in his *heart for two.*

Chapter Twenty

$\mathscr{R}$osita and Samantha left after eating breakfast served in the suite. Samantha wanted to do everything possible, so the bride and groom wouldn't run into each other. The driver dropped them off at the bridal shop. Samantha crossed her fingers that they could accomplish everything in a few hours.

They had to select a wedding dress and get it altered if needed. Samantha knew that she also had to find a dress, and both of them needed shoes. Shoes? Beach wedding! Barefoot, flats, or Sandals? They were glad that there was a whole section of beach-style wedding dresses and accessories. Rosita searched through the dresses and picked out several that she liked. Samantha advised her to start trying them on.

While she was in the dressing room, Samantha browsed the racks looking for a dress. She looked for something simple yet gorgeous. No one is supposed to upstage the bride. After she found the perfect dress, an A-line knee-length chiffon, she needed to pick a color. It would do perfectly as the Matron of Honor/Mother of the groom outfit.

Rosita tried on three dresses before she had any idea of what she wanted. She tried on several long dresses until she decided that she wanted something shorter. With the assistant's help, she tried on a short dress with upper body lace that extended down the sleeves.

Nah! Neither one of them thought it was her style after she tried it on.

Samantha felt it was time for her to intervene. She suggested something strapless. They went back to the racks to start over.

Royce slept way past breakfast time. He'd been thinking about Rosita and couldn't get back to sleep. When he rolled out of bed, Royce found his dad sitting in the living room area watching TV. He'd dressed, eaten breakfast, and was ready to leave. Royce gave him a crazy look and told him to give him twenty minutes.

"It's not my wedding day, son." He laughed.

Royce emerged from the bedroom, all clean and dressed. Thirty minutes later, a taxi dropped them off at the tuxedo rental shop. Royce and Adam sat with a consultant and picked out their suits. The consultant suggested that Adam wear a colored vest to match the matron's dress, of which he had no idea what color that was.

Adam made a quick call to Samantha, asking what color he was supposed to wear. The consultant flipped through a set of swatches and showed him the color he requested. After the men were taped and measured, the consultant said it would cost a little extra for the rush job, but they were used to it. Their tuxedos would be ready in two hours.

Royce mentally checked that off his list. Now it was time to head back to the jewelry store. His mother had mentioned that a bride needed something new, something old, something borrowed, and something blue. She had the old and borrowed items, and he was on his own for the new and the blue.

Although he'd spent a week on this beautiful island before, he never imagined the extras, the behind-the-scenes that so many people took for granted. Never in his wild imagination would he guess that he'd be getting married in such splendor. The islanders prepared for everything and knew how to assemble a memorable event.

For the first time, he appreciated the serenity and the décor of the jewelry store. The store matched the warmth and beauty of the island. Maybe, it was because he'd been nervous the day before, and wanted more than anything to please Rosita. The salesman had been pleasant and knew just the right words to please them. Rosita wore the biggest smile he'd ever seen on her face when he slid the engagement ring onto her finger.

As soon as he entered the jewelry store, the salesman from the previous day spotted him walking in the door. They shook hands, and Royce gave him an idea of what he wanted. They walked to a different section of the store, and he pointed out some items. Royce didn't like any of them. He wanted his bride dressed as a princess about to be crowned. Perusing around the store, looking in all the cases, he hoped something would catch his eye. He exhaled, disappointed, and looked toward the exit, thinking he could check out another jewelry store. On the wall was a poster of a partially nude woman wearing precisely what he wanted.

Royce pointed and exclaimed loudly. "That is what I want, that is what I'm looking for. Please tell me you have it."

"No, sir, Mr. Hawthorne, it's at another location. Let me make a call." The salesman left, rushing to the back of the store.

Royce walked around the store while he waited. He still needed something blue. Why would a woman wear something blue with a white dress and nothing else is blue? He called his mother for ideas. She said it was symbolic and usually worn under the clothing. He was standing next to a case of pins with charms hanging from them. He asked his mother if a pin was acceptable. She told him yes. Hanging up the phone, he scanned, looking for something blue. Choosing something blue was a tough decision. So far, he didn't like anything he saw. It was a bunch of colorful balls and different stuff to add to the pin. He didn't know if she'd like any of this stuff. And thinking that he should have let his mother find something blue, but it was too late. Rosita and his mom were back at the hotel, pampering at the Salon. Damn! He asked his dad to help him find something. Adam was looking in a different case.

"Hey, son, what about this locket, sorry but it's not blue."

Royce wanted to see it anyway. It was a locket in the shape of a heart. He loved the locket, but that wasn't helping his blue situation.

The salesman came running from the back. "Mr. Hawthorne, our downtown store has the necklace in their vault. You would have to go there to see it." He said, almost out of breath.

"Excuse me, but do you have these little hearts in blue?" Adam asked.

"No, sir, they are only available in silver and gold. They hold a picture. You could put a blue picture in the frame."

Royce repeated his words, "a blue picture." He opened his phone and scanned his pictures until he found what he was looking for.

"A picture like this," he said, smiling, turning the phone around.

"Yes, but we don't do the pictures here. You can probably get one printed at a photo shop."

"Great, I'll take a pin and this heart in silver." He pointed to his chosen items.

The salesman gave him the address of the other store when he rang up his items. Royce and Adam raced across town. They entered the store, greeted by name. The salesman asked them to accompany him to a back office. The necklace was in a vault. It was too expensive to be displayed. They were seated at a table while the manager retrieved the necklace. He returned a few minutes later with an armed guard at his back. He sat a black box on the table and opened it. Royce and Adam both gasped.

"Oh, yes, I'll take it." The necklace came with a matching pair of dangling earrings. It was perfect.

"Sir, you didn't ask the price."

"No, I didn't," Royce pulled his wallet out of his pocket and slapped his black American Express card on the table. "I don't have all day. I'm getting married in a few hours. The necklace stays. You can leave your security guard." He said rather smugly, picking up the case, and admiring the necklace.

"Yes, sir, Mr. Hawthorne."

The salesman slid the card off the table slowly. He was aware that the customer had just spent a fortune the day before on wedding rings. So he didn't doubt he could afford the necklace. He was more upset that he wasn't getting the commission. After the payment had been taken care of, Royce left the jewelry store.

Royce spotted a place that did photos a half-block away when they were riding. Since the jeweler said the necklace and earrings needed polishing, he could run his other errand. It was a short walk to the photo store, so there was no need for a taxi. Royce asked the clerk if she could print the picture that would fit in the locket. She answered, 'yes.' Royce wanted to clap and do a happy dance right here in the store, instead he pumped his fist in the air, mouthing, 'Yes'! He was excited that everything was fitting into place.

He looked at his watch. They still had three hours before the wedding. He started to sweat. Was he getting nervous? Royce walked around the store nervously, waiting on the picture, and the photo clerk had offered to insert it into the frame. He stood at the register with a six-pack of cold beer. Damn, he needed a drink. He eyed something extra he could use some more of, asking the clerk for a box of condoms.

Royce and Adam made it back to the hotel after picking up the jewelry and stopping to get their tuxedos. He was down to two hours. Now he needed to deliver a package to his mother for the bride. Calling his mother, he said he was dropping off the items for Rosita. Samantha said she'd meet him at the door. She opened the door with a small crack, and he passed her the two items he'd purchased. She'd been the creative one and prepared three boxes that were all marked. Lastly, he handed her one bottle of beer.

"This is for my bride. Tell her that I love her and that her Prince awaits her on the beach." He kissed his mother on the cheek. "I love you, mom."

"I love you too, son."

Rosita was standing at the door in her room and heard him for herself. She'd drink her beer and honor him. She had a feeling he was drinking more than one. Her hands began to shake, and she was getting jittery by the minute. The coordinator had visited them at the Salon and gave them the final details. They were to get dressed, and they'd be escorted to the beach to an enclosed cabana, where they'd wait until it was time.

Royce returned to his room and leisurely drank one beer. He took another shower and trimmed his beard. He had a flashback of Marguerite sitting on the vanity and Rosita standing in the background. She'd never be in the background again. When he left the bathroom, he called Ms. J to see if they were ready. He wished Marguerite could be there with them as part of their wedding. But they needed this time to be alone. He was serious when he told her that he didn't want to whisper, and he didn't want Marguerite tapping on a door to get in. Tonight was their night, and he planned to take his time and make love to his wife. He didn't want anything or anyone to interfere. She needed this as much as he did.

It was almost time to meet his bride on the beach. Royce finished dressing and packed the remainder of his things. He wouldn't be coming back to this room. Thankfully, his dad was dropping off the pink bag. Royce and Adam made their way to the beach. He'd asked the coordinator for a small table where he can set up the laptop.

Rosita put on her undergarments and smiled. She hoped Royce liked what she'd be wearing underneath her dress. The saleswoman told her it was the latest in wedding lingerie.

Samantha helped her into her dress and zipped up the back. She told her how beautiful she was, but something was missing. Quickly, she retrieved the four boxes, lining them up on the bed so Rosita could see them. Each box was labeled. She opened a box labeled *something old*, picking up a beautifully ornate silver antique brooch.

"This was my mother's and before that, her mother's. I'd be honored if you'd wear it and pass it down to your daughter. You are my only daughter." She pinned the brooch along the waistline of the dress.

Next, she opened the box, labeled *something blue*. She picked up the charm pin with a dangling heart. Rosita thought it was strange because it wasn't blue. Samantha opened it to reveal a picture of Marguerite in a fancy blue dress. Rosita was speechless. She recognized the photo as one that Royce had on his phone. They'd dressed up one evening for dinner, and he'd taken his family to an exclusive restaurant at the Renaissance Center. Samantha added the pin to the inside of her dress directly over her heart, per Royce's instructions.

Samantha thought it best to give her *something borrowed* next. Right about now, both of them needed this. Rosita was tearing up, and Samantha didn't want her fresh make-up to ruin. She opened the box and passed her a beautiful lady's handkerchief. Rosita dabbed at the corner of her eyes.

The last box was black, sleek, and velvety smooth. Samantha asked her to close her eyes and turned her around toward the mirror. She opened the box and carefully picked up an intricately looped necklace of pure diamonds. She wasn't even sure what the shape was. Each section linked at both ends, and they looped, connecting all the way around to the closing clasp. She'd never seen anything so beautiful and unique. Her son had done an excellent job of picking out the necklace. Samantha draped it around her neck and secured the clamp.

Rosita felt something cold, large, and heavy against her skin. She touched it before opening her eyes, tracing it with one finger. Slowly, she opened her eyes, and the glare of the diamonds almost blinded her.

"This is the most beautiful thing I've ever seen in my life. This has to be one of those borrowed necklaces like in that movie "Pretty Woman." Rosita said in awe.

"You will have to ask your husband," Samantha said, already knowing that it wasn't. She pulled the earrings from the box. "You better put these on, the escorts will be here any minute."

Samantha helped her into her sandals and, lastly, added her floral headband. Rosita had asked the stylist to pin up her hair. The headband was beaded with tiny diamonds that draped and framed her face. Samantha was glad she'd talked her out of getting a choker that matched the headpiece. Rosita was a beautiful bride.

There was a knock at the door. It was time to go. Samantha opened the door, and two large men were standing there. The escorts wore Hawaiian costumes, similar to the ones at the Luau. The men were shirtless with boned necklaces and wore grass skirts. The ancient-looking tattoos adorning their arms and chest were beautiful. One was holding a wrap draped across his arm. "Are you the bride?" he asked smiling.

"Oh no, not me, this is the bride." Samantha opened the door wider to introduce the bride.

"Wow! You are one beautiful bride, ma'am."

He held open the white cape. Rosita turned around and slid her arms into the cloak. The escort lifted a wide hood to cover her head. Samantha stepped in next to her, and they left, walking down the long hallway and through the lobby. One of the men asked Rosita to keep her head down so she couldn't see anything. They received lots of stares and quite a few verbal "awes." They crossed through another building and then outside through a backdoor into a cabana.

She wished she could sneak and take a peek at the beach. Her two huge escorts were outside and blocking the entrance. She was extremely nervous. Boy, she needed another beer. There was a chair, but she paced inside the tent. Samantha asked if she was nervous. Rosita nodded and answered yes. She didn't have her watch on, so she didn't know what time it was. Her soon-to-be mother-in-law was cool as a cucumber, but she wasn't the one about to get married.

The front of the Cabana opened, and the escort beckoned for Samantha. She kissed Rosita on the cheek before she walked out. Rosita took one last look at her lavender dress and the beautiful orchid she held in her hand.

Rosita thought she was about to faint. When the flap opened again, they would find her passed out on the floor, okay the sand. She took deep breaths and rubbed her hand across the heart inside her dress. She wished there was a mirror so she could look at her necklace again. This evening was magical, and she truly felt like a princess in one of Marguerite's Disney movies. The flap opened again, and the escort draped her in the cloak.

Walking out of the tent with two escorts at her sides, she barely felt them touching her arms, leading her. She held her fresh orchid bouquet under the wrap. They stopped her from walking and slowly removed the cloak. Rosita looked up and stared into the eyes of Royce.

Royce looked at her and thought she was a goddess in her white strapless dress, short in the front and hanging low with a train touching the ground in the back. She was more than a princess. She was his queen and worthy of the world he was about to introduce her to.

"Wow!" She read the word as it escaped his lips.

He was a mere thirty feet away. Rosita had to walk down an aisle of sand adorned with flowers and lit torches. Soft music started to play, and this was her cue. Her feet moved, taking her to him, her eyes never breaking contact with the man, her Prince Charming.

Royce and Rosita faced each other while the ordained minister stood on the other side of an arch. Beautiful fresh flowers surrounded them, Samantha stood to her side, and Adam stood next to Royce. Rosita thought she heard Marguerite's voice in the distance, but that couldn't be, she was home in Detroit with Ms. J. She couldn't take her eyes off Royce and repeated the words asked by the minister. She was living a dream, a fantasy. Royce repeated his words, and they could see the sun dropping slowly in the background. Neither could turn to appreciate the setting sun at the moment. They only had eyes for each other.

The minister asked for the rings, which Samantha and Adam passed pleasantly. He blessed them and asked them one at a time to slide on the ring after the oath. His last words were what Royce had been waiting to hear.

"I now pronounce you, man and wife. You may kiss your bride."

"You are so beautiful." He whispered as his lips covered hers.

Royce kissed her longer than necessary. He heard his father clearing his throat, and he unlocked his lips from his wife. They turned and faced the torched aisle. The minister announced the couple.

"I now present Mr. and Mrs. Royce Edward Hawthorne." There was a small audience on the beach, clapping.

"Mommy . . . daddy!" Marguerite yelled from the computer.

Rosita turned to her side. "Oh my! Marguerite, Ms. J." She rushed over to the computer with tears and dropped down to her knees in the sand. She looked at Marguerite, who was all dressed up like a flower girl. Marguerite had white silk petals in her hands and threw them into the air.

"Oh my, baby, did you see mommy get married?"

"Oh yes, mommy, you are so pretty. Can I come with you and Daddy?"

"We'll be home in a few days, baby girl. We love you," Royce said, leaning over Rosita and kissing the top of her head. They said their goodbyes and closed the computer.

Royce lifted Rosita from her knees, telling her that the photographer wanted to take some pictures before the sun completely set. They posed for pictures and went inside the Cabana to sign the marriage license. The table held a cake and champagne glasses. The package came with sparkling cider, and Royce changed it to a bottle of Dom. They ate a slice of cake and toasted for the photographer. Royce was ready for this party to be over. He was ready for the next party. The sun had set.

"Mother, can I have my room key now?"

Samantha opened her purse and pulled out the card. Royce picked up his wife, wrapping her legs around his waist, kissing her again. He was walking out of the Cabana.

"Son, where are you going? This is your wedding reception."

"Sorry, guys, we have a private party waiting for us in our suite," Royce said to his parents. He whispered in her ear. "I want to make love to my wife, my beautiful virgin bride."

Chapter Twenty-One

$\mathcal{R}$oyce walked out, holding Rosita. He walked through the lobby of the hotel and received a lot of cheers. When he reached their room, he opened the door and carried his wife across the threshold.

He deposited her on the bed and started to undress. Rosita told him he had to help her out of her dress. So he took off her sandals and threw them across the room. He finished taking off his shirt, shoes, and pants, crawling to her, wearing only his underwear. She was still in her dress.

Royce hovered over her kissing her lips. He toyed with her tongue and kneaded one of her breasts. He deepened the kiss, and Rosita started roaming with her hands. She explored his chest as before, rubbing both her hands, touching every muscle, every crevice. She shuddered from his kisses and his touch. He kissed her lips and made a trail down her neck, stopping to trace his fingers around her necklace. There were no words to describe how he felt the moment he saw her standing there; he'd been envisioning this moment with his wife. Kissing her chest right below the necklace, he used his tongue to make a trail to her mounds. He liked how they protruded out of the dress, kissing every inch that was exposed.

Royce took the time to examine her dress, touching her around the waist. He touched the brooch and slid his hand slowly down to her thigh. The dress lay across her legs above the knees. He moved

261

to one side of her and used both hands to slide the soft dress up, caressing her legs as he pushed the dress upward. Rosita watched him with anticipation. She was breathing heavier. She had no idea what he was going to do, thinking that he'd undress her and then play with her.

He'd pushed the dress up above her thighs, scanning the length of her naked legs and back up. His eyes rested on a pair of white laced bikini panties. He felt his breathing catching, and he traced a finger along the rim of her panties and slid a finger underneath. He lifted the edge and pulled them toward her thighs. She lifted her hips to help him. The panties were dropped on the floor next to the bed in his pile of clothes.

Royce moved between her legs and slid his hands back up her thighs, spreading her legs with his hands. His only thought was that he had to slow down and get his bride ready for him. He was so ready to claim his woman. He crawled upward, scraping his hardened penis along her legs, thighs, pelvis, and stomach, making her hiss. He kissed her with soft wet kisses. She was nervous, and he noticed.

"You didn't tell me your middle name was Edward," she said, trying to shake her nervousness.

"There's a lot about me that you're going to learn very soon," he said and kissed her again.

"Aren't you going to help me out of my dress?"

"Yes . . . eventually," he said throatily.

He kissed her to silence her and slid his hand between her legs. He caressed her softly, rubbing his fingers around her clit and mound. She jerked from his touch, moaning slightly in his mouth. Slowly, he slid one finger inside and backed out again. He toyed with her canal, sliding a finger then adding two. She was responding to his touch, grinding into his hand and whimpering. He knew he had to loosen her up. She was tight. The last thing he wanted to do was hurt her. He wanted her to enjoy her wedding night, not regard it as painful. She'd told him that she hadn't been with a man since she got pregnant with Marguerite.

Royce inched backward, moving lower. He kissed her thighs and nipped and licked until he reached his prize. Sliding his tongue across her clit, she lurched up off the bed, sensitive.

"Mmm," he moaned, draping his arms across her thighs to hold her down. He sucked and nipped on her while she expressed her pleasure.

"Oh, yes, baby. I want you to scream."

He kissed and sucked on her clit, making her writhe. Sliding a finger inside her, he thrust into her canal as far as his finger would go. He thrust faster with his finger and licked her clit faster. She was close, and he wanted her good and wet. He needed her to climax and relax her tight muscles. The faster he licked, the more she thrashed on the bed. He encouraged her between sucking and licking.

"Oh yes, come for me, baby. Just let go."

Royce was so hard and turned on, but he would never hurt her. He sped up his assault of licking and thrusting, now with two of his fingers. She was about to explode; he felt her whole body tighten and started to shake. She screamed and called out his name. He kissed her wet mound while she continued to shudder.

Rosita was trying to catch her breath while her heart was jumping out of her chest, and Royce was moving on the bed. She couldn't speak. How could she when she could barely catch a breath? She'd never experienced such an orgasm nor had she ever been licked to death. Lifting her head from the pillow, she watched him remove his underwear. Her eyes expanded; he was hard and stretched to full length. Oh my . . . Was she going to be able to handle all that? He was rolling on a condom. She wanted to know why because they were married now.

He positioned himself between her legs. Rubbing her wetness onto his tip, he rubbed and stroked the condom to lube it. He smiled at her as she watched him.

She whispered, "My dress."

"I know. I want to make love to my wife in her wedding dress and naked wearing that necklace."

He'd distracted her by talking, pushing, feeling her expand, and opening for him. God, she was tight. He pushed harder, and she gasped.

He stopped moving. "Did I hurt you?"

She shook her head no, so he slid out and back in slowly. He worked a slow rhythm in and out so she could adjust to him. Slowly, she began to move her hips and meet his thrust. He was leaning over her, rocking back and forth, moaning. Royce moved deeper with each slow thrust. He leaned down and kissed her lips, telling her how much he loved her. She expressed her love by wrapping her legs around his waist and raising her hips off the bed.

"I won't break. You can make love to your wife a little faster."

Royce didn't need her to tell him twice. He moved a little faster and deeper. Rosita closed her eyes and let the waves of ecstasy roll over her. She gripped the sheets with her hands as she felt each blow to the depths of her soul. She hooked her ankles and held on for dear life. He plunged deeper and faster. Rosita noticed beads of sweat forming on his chest. She didn't know how much longer he was going to hold out. He'd been ready long before she was. They both needed this.

He was grunting and grinding, and his head was leaning and dropping forward. Looking into her eyes, they were full of love and passion for him. He saw his face reflecting in her big brown eyes. God, he loved this woman. And right now, he wanted her to scream again for him; he wanted her to scream all night.

Rising onto his knees, bringing her hanging body off the bed, he grabbed her legs and untangled them, putting them on his shoulders. He held and lifted her off the bed, and she squirmed in his hands. He was hitting her at a different angle, and he saw it in her face.

Her breathing changed; likewise his. He stroked her with long slow strokes, enjoying the way she made him feel. His body was powerful and full of energy. He could do this all night, slow or fast. The look on her face was pure passion as he stroked her slow and steady, in and out, feeling her tighten around him.

Royce stroked her faster, watching her body change. Oh, how he was going to enjoy learning her body. She called out softly, moaning her pleasure. He pulled her legs off his shoulders and planted her feet on the bed with her knees bent, spreading her legs wider. Royce plunged deep and hard, causing her to whimper louder.

"Oh, yes," he said out loud, feeling the repercussions.

Royce watched his own sex sliding in and out as his hips thrust faster and deeper. He wanted to hear her scream first; he was so close and could feel her body tightening, getting stiff. His brain was screaming faster, faster . . . or was it Rosita yelling? He was so lost he didn't know where the sounds were coming from. He heard his name and a loud, growling sound. His head fell back, looking toward the ceiling, and he gripped her hips and squeezed. When his hands loosened their grip, he was gasping for air. He looked down at Rosita, and her body had contorted. Her head was on the bed, and the rest of her body arched up in the air. Oh my God, what had he done? Slowly her body floated back down to the bed, and she was breathing. He bent over her, touching her face, trying to talk.

"Rosita," He called softly. "Are . . . are you . . . okay? I hope I didn't hurt you."

"No, but if you don't get me . . . out of this dress, I'm going to die."

"As soon as I can move." His arms were locked so he wouldn't crush her.

His breathing slowed, and he inhaled sharply for more air. "My God . . . woman, what did you do to me?"

"Me? I'm the innocent one here."

Royce felt it when he went limp and rose slowly to his knees. He grabbed the condom that was slipping. "I'll be right back," he said, stumbling to the bathroom.

Rosita rolled over onto her stomach.

"Where's the zipper?" He asked.

"It's on the back."

"Can you stand up?" He helped her to stand next to the bed.

Rosita stood on wobbly legs while he fumbled with the zipper. He finally managed to get the dress unzipped. It dropped and pooled at her feet. He was standing behind her, admiring her naked ass. She turned around so he could see her wedding lingerie corset.

"You were supposed to take off my dress and admire this." She put her hands on her hips.

"Oh, baby, I'm already admiring it. You can wear them for round two if you like."

"Round two?"

Royce held up two fingers and mouthed "two" right before sliding those two fingers between her legs. It was a good thing that she was bottomless, and he was ready for another round. He picked her up and tossed her in the middle of the bed. Rosita squealed, and he pounced. She had questions, and he had more sex on the brain.

He toyed with her clit, stroking her with his fingers, and kissed her, exploring her mouth with his tongue. She caressed his body, moving her hands along his ribcage. Her fingers were grazing each muscle, skimming his chest, probing every groove. She felt him growing, hardening between her legs, and she wanted to inch her body toward him; she wanted to feel him inside her again. He'd made her want more. Hell, he wanted more too.

Her nipples were calling to him. He'd dreamed of those nipples ever since the first sample. Pulling her bodice down so he could see them again and squeezed them together. Rolling his tongue across his lips, he felt like the cat that was about to consume the canary. He licked each nipple and sucked them like he was a newborn baby. Rosita showed him how much she enjoyed his sucking and licking. She stretched her hands, wanting to touch him. She trapped him between her legs, and he was lying half on her stomach, having his own fun.

"I want to touch you," she said.

"Oh no, you're dangerous. I might explode in your hands. I prefer to explode deep inside of you."

"Why did you put on a condom?" She asked shyly and a little embarrassed.

"Baby, I don't want anyone to think I married you because you were pregnant. We have plenty of time to give Marguerite brothers and sisters; besides, there are so many things I want us to do." First, she needed a visit to a gynecologist. He wanted his wife without having to worry about condoms.

Royce grabbed another condom off the nightstand next to the bed, rolled it on, and buried himself deep in his wife again. He kissed her breast and licked her nipples, stroking her while he sucked and licked. Rosita thoroughly welcomed her new pleasures. Her husband was definitely worth the wait. Royce was enjoying learning about his wife's body and watching her face glow. He stretched out above her with his arms and hands underneath, gripping her butt, plunging deep, giving her his full length. She whimpered with pleasure with each thrust, wrapping her arms around his back and digging her nails into his flesh. He was tall enough to kiss her and stroke her like this. He liked this angle. He could feel her pulse around him as he thrust faster, gripping her tighter to his body.

Rosita made him feel ways that he'd never felt with other women. He knew how to pleasure a woman, but she was different. He didn't doubt some women exaggerated an orgasm. Rosita was real. Her sounds, body language, and the fact that she was inexperienced almost made her a virgin. She was shy and a little embarrassed when she orgasmed, almost afraid of what she was feeling. He wanted to experience many more orgasms with her. It was so new and fresh for both of them.

Royce gripped his wife and thrust faster and deeper. She whimpered into his ear as he kissed her neck and ear, sucking on her lobe. She thrust her hips into him, wanting more. It was her way of begging.

"I love the way you beg."

She panted. "I didn't say anything."

"You don't have to say it, I feel it." He growled.

He stroked her faster; her clit was stiff and rubbing his penis. It felt so erotic, and it made him harder, and he stroked her faster. She cried out softly. She was close and driving him wild. Covering her mouth with his, he wanted her to yell her release into his mouth. He couldn't move his hands; this feeling was too good.

Royce stroked, and Rosita tightened her loins at the same time. His legs were trapped between her thighs, and he was on his toes. She was squeezing her thighs together, and he felt her squeezing his manhood. Royce lost it, and she screamed as the friction between them burned. He held her lip in his mouth as she yelped, arching her body and his off the bed. Damn, she was stronger than she looked. Her orgasm was like dynamite exploding. He felt it when she squeezed the life out of him. Her body was shaking and shuddering, and her nails were deep in his back. He was going to have marks to show for that one.

He pulled one arm out at a time, kissing her softly until she got her body under control. "You're a wild woman that makes me lose my control."

"I'm sorry. I don't mean to. I've . . . I've never been made love to. Am I doing something wrong?"

Royce rolled over on his back, bringing Rosita to lie on his chest. He thrust his hips. She felt him still inside her, and he was still hard.

"No, baby, you're doing everything right. You've made me the happiest man, and I don't mean sexually. I love *you*."

Rosita moved, and she felt him throbbing, jumping. "Round three?" she asked, smiling.

"Only if you're up for it."

"I believe you're already *up* for it," she teased.

She began to unhook her corset from the front. Royce watched and rubbed her thighs, making little circles with his fingers. She unhooked the last hook and threw the corset to the floor.

Royce spread his hands across her stomach and rubbed. He saw some marks left by the corset, and he caressed her stomach and chest and her breast. Having the best view, he played with both of them, pinching her nipples, and she sucked in her breath. She could feel him throbbing between her legs. She started rocking her lower body, back and forth, and felt his hand tighten on her breast—oh, so he liked that. It was her turn to explore, learn, and experience something new.

"I like this outfit the best. I want to dress you in jewels naked so that I can make love to you in them."

He gripped her hips and twisted them, showing her how to gyrate her hips. He sucked in his breath when she moved and twisted just the right way. She splayed her hands on his torso and rose and dropped slowly, riding him like a horse. Rosita rocked back and forth on her knees, making him cry out with pleasure. She wondered what he'd do if she went faster. She gripped his thighs and bounced up and down. Royce drew his knees up against her back so she could lean back on them. He held her hips and helped her bounce up and down faster. She leaned forward and kissed his chest. It was his turn to grip the sheets. She licked his tight nipples, and his eyes flew open wide. She bounced on him and licked, feeling him stiffen, so she learned that men's nipples were sensitive too. He gripped her breast and squeezed.

"Oh, woman, you are bringing me to my knees," he said slowly and sensually.

"I like that. Now I want you to scream for me."

"You are a quick study."

"I have a good teacher," she said, grinning.

Rosita rocked back and forth and rotated her hips at the same time. She thought Royce was going to come up off the bed. Rosita bounced up and down harder and gasped each time, feeling him so deep within her walls. She wanted to make him scream for her. So she rocked back and forth faster and faster. Royce grabbed her hips and slammed into her raising his hips off the bed. She whimpered at his thrusts. He held her up by her butt cheeks and gyrated his hips, making circles within her canal.

"Oh, yes . . . yes . . . yes," she screamed.

He held her and repeated gyrating his hips and thrusting. Watching his manhood disappear, in and out, he listened to her whimpers of pleasure. It pushed him to another climax with his wife.

"Oh, yes, baby, I feel it too. Now I want you to come with me."

Royce plunged and gyrated until he felt his wife stiffen. He was in control when he felt her shake. Giving in, he dropped back to the bed, slamming deep into his wife, growling his release. He felt her wetness dripping around his limp member and rolling toward his body. He knew he had to get out of the condom. Flipping them, he pulled out of her grabbing the condom that was sliding fast.

He came out of the bathroom and found his wife spread eagle naked on the bed. Damn! This woman was going to be the death of him on his wedding night. She didn't know how much that look was enticing him again. But worse, she was going to be sore and didn't know it. He dropped down on the bed next to her.

"Would you like to take a bath with your husband, and tomorrow we can do one of those couple massages?"

"A bath together?" she asked, crinkling her nose.

His wife was back to her shy self. "Yes, together," he said, leaving the bed.

Royce fixed the bath for them. Unhooking her necklace, he laid it on the nightstand. He scooped up his wife from the bed, who was nodding toward sleep. They would soak in the warm water and then sleep holding each other like they'd been doing for months. Except for clothes, he could now sleep holding his wife, naked for the time being. And knowing things would be a little different when they got home. He stepped into the warm water and submerged both of them. He liked the massive tub for two. Royce sat in the water with Rosita between his legs. She sat in the water with her arms across her breast.

Royce chuckled. "Are you embarrassed to be naked in the tub with me?"

"No, it just feels strange."

"You've shared four orgasms with me, and sitting in a bathtub is strange."

She dropped her head like talking about it made her shameful. Royce turned her around in the water to face him. He draped her legs across his hips and pulled her forward.

"Baby, nothing we do together is dirty or shameful." He lifted her chin. "We are husband and wife, and we love each other. I would never ask or want you to do anything that makes you uncomfortable. Do you trust me?"

Rosita nodded her head, "I trust you. I . . . I feel so . . . I don't know how to explain it when you touch me. I like it when you touch me, and I want to touch you everywhere."

Royce was absorbing her words, and it was affecting him. He started to grow in the water. Rosita wanted to touch him before, and he'd refused her. He'd refused her because of what she'd told him about Marguerite's father. The bastard used her to masturbate and perform oral sex. He didn't want to remind her of those days.

Rosita was practically sitting in his lap, and she felt him hard between them. All she wanted to do was to touch him there. She moved her hand in the water and grabbed it.

"Rosita! You don't have to do that."

"I thought you said nothing we do was dirty."

"It's not. I just . . . don't want you to compare what we do to what happened before."

"This is so different, and I know that you love me. And now I know why you wanted me to wait. You're nothing like him. I only want to touch; I want to feel you."

Royce exhaled and relaxed, palming her face and kissing her. She moaned and gripped him tighter, squeezing him, and he kissed her harder. Exploring her mouth with his tongue, she responded with passion. It caused him to throb in her hand. Oh no, he needed to think of something else. Or he would be pounding his wife in the tub without a condom.

He kissed her softly and pulled away, seeing passion brewing in her big brown eyes. "Baby, I need to tell you some things about me."

She loosened her grip but still held him in the water. "Like what?"

"My job, you need to know the truth." He paused and waited for her to give him her undivided attention. She had a puzzled look on her face. "I'm not the regional manager for GCH. I own all eight of them."

"But you work there. Why would an owner work there?"

It was his turn to tell her a story. Royce started his story with the beginning, admitting how he'd worked at a Starbucks years ago, and yes, he did get fired. He talked about Freddie, and he'd been the cause all those years ago. And then he told her about the lottery ticket and how he'd purchased the GCH franchise.

"You mean to tell me that you're a millionaire and live in an apartment above a garage?"

"Yes, remember when I took you there and told you that I'm a simple man? I didn't feel the need for a big house. Now I have a reason. I was waiting for my bride, my family. I've been waiting for you and Marguerite to fill my life with joy and happiness."

"I thought it was your parents who were rich. They have a nice house, fancy cars, and those trips you took."

"I told you my parents weren't rich."

"I thought you just told me that to shut me up. So you're rich, and that was how you could afford those trips, the first-class tickets, and my birthday present to Hawaii," she said nervously.

"No, baby, we're rich. What's mine is yours and Marguerite's. I know that you loved me for me, the simple man."

Rosita gasped. "You didn't borrow that necklace, did you? And those are all . . . real . . . diamonds?"

Royce chuckled. "No, I didn't borrow the necklace, and yes, those are real diamonds. Don't you remember standing in the living room at Ms. J's? I asked you if you wanted a necklace to go with the diamond earrings. You told me yes, which means you are now my queen, and Marguerite is our princess."

Rosita shivered. She shivered for two reasons: one, she just found out her husband had a secret identity, and second, the water was cold. They'd sat and talked for over an hour. Now things were making sense. Bit and pieces of several conversations were jumbling around in her head. The phone call for Hawthorne Incorporated, the conversation she overheard about his personal life, and the spending of money like it would never run out.

Royce felt her shivering, and he was cold too. He turned the knob to let out the cold water and refilled the tub so they could bathe and get some sleep.

Chapter Twenty-Two

Royce woke up, and Rosita wasn't wrapped in his arms. He had a feeling of where to find her. He rolled out of bed and went in search of his wife. She wasn't in the living room. He rushed back, checking the other bedroom, and it was empty. For a moment, he was frantic until he saw the curtain sway at the patio. He pulled the curtain back and saw her sitting outside drinking coffee.

"Roy! You're naked."

"And you are dressed and out of bed. Why didn't you wake me?"

"Do you know how cute you are when you're sleeping?"

"No, I don't."

"Go and put on some clothes," she barked.

"Why? I want you back in the bed."

"My body aches. I thought we were getting a massage."

"Baby, I'm so sorry. I'll get dressed, and we can get some breakfast first. Why don't you call Mom and Dad to join us?"

Royce noticed that Rosita changed colors. Was she embarrassed again? He dropped down next to her chair. "Are you embarrassed because our parents will know we were having sex?"

She dropped her head. "Yes, am I that obvious? I can't face them." She looked up at him. "Did you say *our* parents?"

"Yes, you're the daughter they never had. Do you know how excited they are for us and to have a granddaughter?"

Rosita exhaled and said she'd call Samantha . . . *Mom*. Royce left her, laughing to himself. He liked his wife being a little shy because they'd never have a dull moment. He spotted the necklace lying next to the bed, this baby needed to be put away in the room safe. Did he need to tell her that the necklace cost a quarter of a million dollars? Nah! He'd get a safe deposit box when they got home, then eventually a wall safe when they bought a house. After he dressed, he asked Rosita for the original box. Rosita told him that his parents were already downstairs in the restaurant and waiting for them.

The happy couple hugged and kissed Samantha and Adam. Samantha made a joke, telling them that they didn't expect to see them before dinner. Rosita blushed and choked on her coffee. Being a bad son, Royce told his mother that he promised his wife a couple's massage to work on her sore muscles, and he got kicked under the table for his remark.

Samantha thought a massage was a good idea. Adam waved his hands in the air because he wanted to pass on that activity. Adam told them they were staying on the island for several more days. Royce asked Rosita if she wanted to have some fun with the older people for an outing and dinner. She wanted to know what kind of outing. Adam burst out that the helicopter tours were the best fun. He wouldn't mind doing that again since there were multiple tour options.

Royce surprised his parents, saying that they'd spend some time on the island before heading back to Maui. The hot tub could wait. He wanted to spoil Rosita and make sure she enjoyed her vacation as well as their honeymoon. Royce, Rosita, and Samantha headed to the Spa and left Adam in charge of booking a helicopter tour.

Rosita snapped more pictures than possibly necessary. Her first time in a helicopter was breathtaking, and she didn't want to forget one moment. She fell in love with the waterfall they flew over. Even though they were on their honeymoon, Rosita was ecstatic about touring Pearl Harbor, Diamond Head Crater, and several other tourist attractions with her in-laws. She didn't mind spending her days with family and her nights wrapped in her husband's arms.

After spending two extra days on Oahu, Royce was ready for some alone time, day and night with his bride. The next morning Royce and Rosita stopped at his parent's suite to kiss and tell them bye. Royce made a comment about relaxing in a hot tub and received a punch in the arm from Rosita.

Adam affirmed his appraisal for their nuptials. He hugged his son tightly and told him how proud he was. While the guys talked, the ladies had their own undertaking. Samantha reminded her of their conversation at the airport, telling her that she knew he'd come around. She already knew that he loved her; she just couldn't explain it. The first sign was when he brought a girl home to meet his parents. Samantha hugged Rosita tight and kissed her on the cheek, promising they'd come to Detroit and visit them soon.

After the short flight, Royce and Rosita were in the rental and headed back to the Chateau. Rosita loved her time on the island of Oahu, but she hadn't forgotten about several conversations, which caused her to blush often.

"I can't believe you said those things to your mother about sex."

"My parents are cool, and I feel comfortable talking or saying something sexual to a certain extent. I would tell you a funny story, but you may not think it's funny. Let's just say that my mother has chastised me as an adult about practicing safe sex."

"Was it about me? I hope your parents didn't think because I have one child, I would get pregnant on purpose just because you have money."

"My parents knew we weren't having sex."

"Really? You told them before we visited them for the holidays?"

"No, it wasn't like that. I had a talk with my dad about you."

Rosita didn't know whether she should be upset or flattered. Turning her head, she looked out the window. She wanted to ask for details of the conversation. Did he discuss that he wanted to get married or that he didn't?

Royce wanted to know what she was thinking. It was noticeable that she was upset with him because he'd discussed their personal issues. Were they going to have their first fight as husband and wife? He wanted to stop at the store before they got to the house. But what he really wanted was to get to the house, unwind, and hold his wife, maybe naked in the hot tub. He didn't want to have to leave again, so he pulled into the store's parking lot.

Royce was a gentleman and opened his wife's door. She sat still as a block of stone. Hell yeah, she was upset.

"Baby, please don't be mad at me. If you give me a chance to explain, it's not what you think. We can talk about it at the house in the hot tub, drinking a couple of beers."

"I don't have a swimsuit. You never told me where we were going." She said, folding her arms across her chest.

"What I had in mind, you don't need a swimsuit, but I do have your bikini in my luggage."

Rosita turned and looked at him with squinted eyes. She exhaled and got out of the truck, but not before he stole a kiss.

They sat in the hot tub, and Royce explained to Rosita how he felt about their situation. He'd inadvertently told him that they weren't having sex. His dad said that he thought that he had strong feelings for her because he wanted to wait for something special between them.

Rosita was feeling better after he explained and that his parents never thought anything terrible about her. He told her that his mother's action of chastising him had been a long time before he'd even met her.

"Baby, as much as I want to enjoy making love to my wife all day and night, I want you to have fun. We came to Hawaii to celebrate your birthday. I want you to be able to tell anyone who asked that you did more than take a helicopter tour. So, tell me, what would you like to do?"

"Well, I did experience a sunrise on top of a mountain, best day ever."

"You mean it was better than getting married at sunset."

"Oh no, that's in my top five best things."

"Best five?"

"Yes, the first four were orgasms as Mrs. Hawthorne."

"Wow, you really know how to swell a guy's head."

"Yes. I guess I do, considering that I feel something swollen poking me. I know how to swell a couple of things. Why don't you tell me more about putting the hot tub to good use today, and tomorrow you can take me to play on a Jet Ski? After that, I'm sure you can find something interesting for us to do."

"I like the way you think."

Royce made a mad dash inside and returned to find his wife had already removed her bikini. It was lying on the side of the hot tub. He stripped off his swim shorts, and Rosita's eyes bucked. Would her husband always be ready? Stepping down into the hot tub, he pulled his wife against him. He kissed her on the neck while he slid his hand between her legs. He toyed with his wife until she whimpered in his ears. When he knew she was ready, he rolled on a condom. Rosita straddled him, sliding down, moaning as they descended into the hot tub. He held his wife until they were sated, beyond satisfaction.

Royce woke before Rosita the next morning, and he stood over the bed and watched her all curled up. She'd made him a happy man the evening before. They not only christened the hot tub but practically every room in the house. It was his turn for an achy body. She was insatiable. He'd met his match in the bedroom, or she'd gone so long without sex that she was playing catch-up. He wanted to let her sleep and sneak and check his email. Although he promised he wouldn't do any work, just a quick peep wouldn't hurt. Toby hadn't called with any emergencies, so everything must be going well.

He opened a couple of emails from Toby, which were the same for everyone in managerial positions.

And then he noticed an email from an unknown person with a subject title of 'Sunrise.' He almost deleted it, thinking it was spam. Then he remembered the mountain and giving out his email address. He opened the email and found several pictures attached. They were beautiful. His favorite picture showed him down on one knee holding Rosita's hand, and the rising sun silhouetted behind them. There were multiply pictures of him holding her in his arms after picking her up and swinging her around. He wondered if he should share them or surprise her later. If he shared them now, she'd know he was monitoring work, okay surprise her later. He loved surprising her and decided to do something grand with the photos. There were two other unknown emails, and he figured they must be from the other people from the mountain. The mouse was hovering over the next email when he heard a noise coming from the bedroom. Quickly he hit the exit button and closed the laptop.

Rosita bounced into the kitchen, and Royce poured her a cup of coffee. He kissed her and passed her a cup. She shook her head at her naked husband.

"Good morning, Sunshine."

"Morning," she said, smiling shyly.

Rosita wasn't used to the whole naked and walking around one bit. She didn't have a robe. So she wore her bikini cover-up. Royce licked his lips. He had a good view of a pair of brown nipples peeping through the netted material.

"What are you grinning at?"

Royce didn't answer. Instead, he pinched a nipple feeling it stiffen. "This . . . mmm."

Rosita sat her cup on the countertop and smacked his hand away. She covered her breast with both her hands. "You wouldn't see them if I had a robe."

"Hell, I'm thinking of hiding this cover-up so that you'll have to walk around naked."

"Never."

"Never?" He asked with a shocked look on his face.

"You know that isn't going to happen once we get back home. We have a three-year-old, remember?" Rosita said, like she had a strange thought.

"I know, and that is why we have to take advantage of this while we can."

"Roy, what are we going to tell Marguerite when she gets older and asks questions . . . I mean? She's bound to figure out that you're not her real father," she asked, worried.

"We will tell her the truth that I'm not her biological father, but I've been her loving Daddy since she was two," Royce said, genuinely.

"I like that," Rosita said, moving closer to her husband.

Royce clutched the bottom of the cover-up and pulled it over her head, grabbing her breasts in his hands, and squeezed. Leaning over, he licked a nipple and pulled it into his mouth. His wife responded just like he wanted her to. She craved his touch as much as he enjoyed watching the emotions spread across her face. She wrapped her arms around him pushing her breast deeper into his mouth. He sucked on her nipple and gripped her butt, drawing her closer to his hardened body. Lifting her by her butt, she wrapped her legs around his waist. She ground up against him. His cock was stiff, and he wanted his wife right now. He turned around, so her butt leaned up against the counter. Yanking the drawer open, he felt around the inside of it until he found what he sought. Holding a breast in his mouth, he walked the few steps until he reached the table. Slowly, he laid her down.

"Oh, baby, we missed the kitchen yesterday."

Royce rose and tore open the packet with his teeth. Quickly, he rolled on the condom and rubbed it against her. He slid a finger inside her while he toyed with her clit with his swollen member. His fingers slid easily. She was ready. Replacing his finger with something better, he pushed, and she accepted him smoothly. Royce started his day by making love to his wife on the kitchen table. Life couldn't get any better than this was his thoughts as he exploded with pleasure. He loved holding his wife and feeling her body rack with shudders as she climaxed in his arms.

Royce was scrubbing Rosita's back in the shower, and she couldn't stand it any longer. She had to know.

"Can you please tell me why there was a condom in the kitchen?"

Royce chuckled and kissed her shoulder. "I . . . ah put them all over the house. So I'd be prepared everywhere, and any time I wanted to put a smile on my wife's face."

"So, where did you hide one in the shower?"

"I didn't, so you need to behave. I want us to fix that problem when we get home."

"You want me on birth control?"

"Yes, we can go to a doctor together and discuss what type would be better. I want to enjoy my wife for a little while before we have something growing in here." He rubbed her stomach with soapy hands. He slid them up her body and cupped her breast. "I want to enjoy my wife for a little while before I share these."

He embraced her from behind, kissing her neck and shoulder. Something was growing between them. She leaned her head back into his chest, moaning, and rubbed her butt against him. She caressed his arms that wrapped around her, barely feeling the light splashes of water because he was standing closer to the stream. Her breathing hardened, just thinking of them bonded together in the shower. Royce pinched and toyed with her nipples. He wanted to make love to his wife right now in the shower. Bending his knees, he slid his swollen manhood between her legs. Rosita shivered and squeezed her thighs around him. She liked how he felt next to her skin. It was hard but soft, silky smooth. The feel of him throbbed between her legs. He rocked back and forth, letting her feel him slide gently between her thighs.

"Oh, Roy." She panted.

"Oh yes, baby, this is what I want you to feel. I want to enjoy my wife with nothing between us."

He pumped his hips forward, feeling her warm folds sliding across his hardened penis. He slid back and forth, touching her clit and feeling her shudder in his arms.

"Squeeze your thighs, baby. I want you to feel me."

Rosita squeezed her thighs as tight as she could and hooked her ankles. Royce slid back and forth, faster and faster creating a force and friction. Rosita leaned into him, whimpering, and grabbed one side of the shower wall with her hand. Royce moved his hands to her thighs. He gripped a thigh with one hand and slid his other hand between her legs. He rubbed her clit, making her cry out. He'd never been in this position, and it was erotic and a turn-on. He felt like he was masturbating and giving his wife pleasure all at the same time.

He felt his body giving in, and she began to shudder. This carnal vibe was a new sensation for him that he'd never experienced. God, if only he could slide inside her. He wanted to feel her warm canal wrapped around his stiff shaft. His thoughts, along with this sensation, pushed him over the top. Rosita's thighs tightened and she slumped forward, screaming, clawing at the shower walls. Royce wrapped his arms around her as he exploded, and his head fell back with a howl, liquids spewing against the shower wall.

He held onto Rosita with one arm to keep her from falling to the shower floor. His other hand was braced against the wall while he got his breathing under control. After a minute, all he could do was slink down to the floor. He pulled Rosita into his lap as he sat on the shower floor. The warm water was beating down on both of them. Neither of them could talk; they were breathing too hard. Damn! He hadn't intended to do that, but she felt so good. He loved the feel of her skin rubbing on him. He wanted to feel his wife without a condom.

Rosita was the first to recover. "I can't wait to go home and see a doctor." She laughed lightly.

Royce bent his head, laughing at his wife. Damn! Neither could he. He kissed his wife and asked her if she could stand because he needed five more minutes. She shook her head, no.

An hour later, they pulled into the Marina, where Royce knew they could rent some Jet skis. They played on them for most of the day. Rosita spotted some people gliding in the air hooked to some ropes. She asked Royce what they were doing. He explained to her that they were Parasailing, asking her if she wanted to try it. Shaking her head excitedly, she didn't know when she'd get to do this adventure again. Rosita wanted to sample everything.

When they returned the rented Jet skis, Royce asked the attendant where they could find the Parasailing boat dock. They were given directions to a different part of the Marina. When they reached the right area, there was a small line. Royce went into the office to purchase their tickets. He noticed on the bulletin board that they did special requests. Royce only had one question for the cashier. He found Rosita watching a group of people piling into a boat about to leave.

"Are we going with them?"

"No, that group is full. We have a couple of hours to kill before we go out. Do you want to grab a drink?"

"Sure."

Royce led them to a restaurant/bar at the Marina. He ordered them a couple of beers, and they headed to the patio to watch the activity on the water. He straddled a bench, and she sat between his legs.

"I meant to ask you a question?"

"What, baby?" He answered, holding the beer in one hand and his other hand rubbing her thigh.

"How did my swimsuit get in your luggage?"

Royce laughed. He wondered how long it would take for that question. He exhaled before he spoke. "I asked Ms. J to find it for me. Please don't be mad at her. I couldn't go digging through all your drawers looking for it."

"That makes sense since she was the reason that I washed both my swimsuits. She asked me where we were going, but I had no idea. So she suggested that I wash all my warm-weather clothes. But I forgot about packing a swimsuit. I had no idea you wanted to take me to Hawaii, but I'm glad that you did."

She folded her arms across her chest. "Do you think from now on, you can stop keeping things from me?"

"I don't think I need to keep secrets from you anymore. You know everything now. Except you can't go shouting about it at work."

"I don't talk about anything personal at work anyway. And you were the one that announced that I was your girlfriend. I would never have told a soul."

Royce told her that Toby was the only person that knew he was the owner, but not about the lottery. He let her in on the secret about the new office, and he told her how special it was and why he chose it. Holding her hand and caressing her fingers, he told her about his first evening. Afterward, he confessed about how miserable he'd been feeling without her in his life. While he kissed each fingertip, he told her that he loved her and wanted to make her happy. He said he wanted to see a smile on her face every day. Rosita felt like crying, she never imagined in a million years that she'd be this lucky. She found her Prince Charming, or perhaps, her daughter had found her Prince Charming, and he loved both of them. She didn't realize tears were rolling down her cheeks until Royce kissed her face.

"Don't cry, baby." He turned her around to face him. She draped her legs across his thighs.

"These are happy tears."

Royce cupped her face and wiped her cheeks with his thumbs, kissing her lips. Rosita didn't know if she could be happier than she was right now and after that mind-blowing sex in the shower. It wasn't even sex. There was no name in her vocabulary for what they did. But whatever it was, she wanted more of it.

"Ah, honey . . . sweetie . . . what do you call what we did in the shower? Because I don't think it was sex."

Now it was his turn to be shy and embarrassed. He hung his head. "I have no earthly idea. I've never even seen that done on a porn movie."

"You watch porn?" She asked, speaking low.

"Baby, every red-blooded male has watched some porn in their lifetime. I have you now, so I don't need to watch it again." He kissed her fingers again. "Why did you ask about the shower? Did you like it as much as I did?"

Rosita blushed. "Yes, I'm tingling just thinking about it. Is that normal? Am I supposed to feel like this?" She asked shyly.

"Yes, it's normal. And no, we aren't doing that again until you are fully protected. You don't know how close I came to penetrating you."

Royce talked and teased his wife while they drank their beers. She was getting more comfortable talking about sex and asking questions. He looked at his watch and told her it was time to go. They left the bar and walked back, holding hands to the Parasailing boat dock. He asked her if she brought the camera. She patted her purse, thinking that she didn't want to miss any Kodak moments where he was concerned. He was thinking about the beautiful pictures of the island from the sky.

The man helped them into the boat, and another man began hooking them into a harness. Rosita removed the camera from her purse before passing it away. The driver asked for their camera and snapped a few pictures after the harness was connected. Using the company camera, the driver took pictures of them ascending into the air. They were rising with the help of a parachute. The speed boat skimmed across the water as they climbed. The boat sped through the water, and it took Rosita a few minutes before she realized they were heading into the setting sun. She'd been looking down at the boat as it got smaller and smaller the higher they climbed. Royce was taking pictures of the island and the settings around them. Rosita grabbed his hand, shrieking when she saw the sun start to dip.

"Oh my God, Roy . . . Look! The sun is going down. You did this on purpose, didn't you?"

"Yes, baby, I wanted us to have one more different experience of a sunset.

"I love you so much," Rosita told him.

She wanted to kiss him, but they were positioned side by side in a harness. Royce grabbed her hand and brought it up to his lips.

"I love you too, baby."

Holding hands, they watched the sun drop into its hidden depths. Rosita hated when the wench started to pull them back toward the boat. When they were safely in the boat and their harnesses removed, Rosita embraced Royce. She told him how wonderful he was, and she was the luckiest woman alive to have him. They returned to the Chateau, changed clothes, and went out to dinner.

Early the next morning, Royce researched activities and tours. Over coffee, they discussed which tours she liked and wanted to do. She selected three that she thought would be exciting. After Royce booked the excursions, they dressed and rushed out of the house to catch a boat for a whale watching tour. Initially, Rosita was scared and held tightly onto Royce on the boat. When the tour guide announced that a whale was nearby, and Rosita saw a tail in the air, her fear disappeared and excitement took over. Royce laughed as she snapped a dozen or more pictures, including a selfie with the whale. Royce was jealous and said his arm was longer, and was able to capture another selfie with both of them and the whale in the background. Several hours later after a heartily late lunch, they enjoyed a submarine tour.

Rosita wasn't upset about the next morning's early tour, especially since it included breakfast aboard the yacht. Actually, the thought of a yacht cruise brought back a memory of their sunset cruise. This one didn't include a sunset, but it should be just as memorable. The yacht cruise would take them around the island and to the neighboring island of Molokai. After arriving at Molokai, they'd board a helicopter for an exclusive view of the majestic sea cliffs. Rosita was blown away at the ruggedness, yet alluring site. Royce recognized the sparkle in her eyes as she clung to the window, looking out. After the helicopter tour, they would eat on the island before returning to the yacht.

As soon as they boarded the yacht, Royce grabbed her hand and rushed off to their assigned cabin. This cruise may be short, but extremely different from the other. They shared a small bag because dinner was a dress-up affair. They had an hour to kill before dinner would be served, and Royce wanted to spend the time wisely. While Rosita was in the bathroom, he stripped and lay naked on the bed. Rosita didn't need to be a mind reader to know what was on her husband's mind. Quickly she undressed and joined him in the bed. Sex aboard a yacht that was moving fast through the water, was most definitely an experience neither one wanted to miss.

After a blissful round of sex, a hot shower, together, they dressed and went to dinner. They joined 18 other people in an immaculate formal dining room. Rosita was glad that Royce made her pack a couple of nice dresses for the trip, and even happier that she brought her beautiful necklace. The other women that sat around the table screamed money. Rosita was shy and felt out of her element. Royce, on the other hand, talked and held a conversation. They were the only black couple, and one man wanted to know what he did for a living. Boasting, Royce told them that *they* owned eight coffee shops in Detroit. After he said they, Rosita held her head up and joined in the conversation.

After the last two days of exploring the island and partaking in the tours and excursions, Royce was ready for some downtime. Rosita asked for an evening of good food and entertainment. She said the food was superb, and the dancing and music were a bonus.

Royce whispered in her ear as they walked out to the truck after attending another Luau. He wanted to spend some time on the beach tonight. He still had his visions of making love to his wife at the water's edge. It was his last fantasy before they went home. They had one more day of honeymoon/vacation, and he had one more thrilling adventure planned.

The following day, Rosita woke before Royce. She fixed the coffee pot and thought back to the day before. She'd never had her cup of coffee. And she wasn't about to let her sex-crazed husband deny her today. Sitting at the table in her cover-up, smiling. There wasn't a room in the Chateau that she could go in and not think of him. Even beaches would have a new meaning for her. Can you say doggy style underwater?

Rosita blushed, drinking her coffee, an image floating before her eyes. She was on her knees, and she kept slipping in the sand. It was hilarious. For a moment, she thought he was going to drown her ass. She climaxed, and he did too, falling onto her back, which made her fall face first underwater. He pulled her up, laughing. Slowly they crawled up on the beach out of the water. They lay on the beach, looking up at the stars and talking. Rosita started to shiver, and Royce suggested they warm up in the hot tub before going to bed. She was surprised that he didn't suggest another round in the hot tub. She'd thought about it.

She was on her second cup of coffee when Royce showed up naked as a jaybird in the kitchen. He kissed his wife on the way to the coffee pot.

"Good morning, Sunshine."

"Morning," she said with a big smile on her face.

He fixed his cup and sat at the table. She was still blushing. "What are you so happy about this morning?"

"Oh, I was just thinking that my husband is trying to kill me on my honeymoon." She jested.

He laughed, almost spitting coffee out of his mouth. "I was not trying to kill or drown you. You're the one trying to kill me. I can't keep up with my sex goddess."

Royce sipped his hot coffee. "Are you ready to have some fun on the last day of our honeymoon? You know I like the sound of that better than a birthday celebration."

"So do I. What plans do you have other than trying to drown your wife?"

"It's a surprise."

"Roy, I thought you weren't going to do that anymore."

"Well, I guess it doesn't have to be a surprise. I wanted to take you riding on a motorcycle."

"Oh, really! I forgot you know how to drive those things."

"Baby, you don't drive a motorcycle. You ride a motorcycle. Are you afraid of motorcycles? I remember you jumping when I cranked mine up."

"I don't think I'm afraid. If I can fly in the air by the seat of my pants, then I can ride with you. Isn't it like riding a Jet Ski?"

"Yes, it's similar."

"Good, then you can let me drive?"

"No, motorcycles are a little more complicated than driving a Jet Ski."

Royce told her to get dressed before he took her on the table again. She took off, running to the bedroom. He leisurely finished his coffee. On the way to the bedroom, he met Rosita coming out wearing some skimpy shorts and a short t-shirt. He turned her around and nudged her into the room. If only, he thought.

He pulled her t-shirt over her head. "Baby, this is not what I meant for today. If you dress like this, I'll either kill someone for staring or kill us from me trying to rub your thighs."

"But I've seen girls dress like this riding on the back of motorcycles." She pouted.

Royce pushed her shorts down over her hips, admiring her lace bra and matching bikini panties. He caressed her sides and licked his lips.

"Since you're out of your clothes . . . I think I'll take advantage of this situation." He picked her up and tossed her to the middle of the bed, and pounced.

Two hours later, they were at a dealership that rented motorcycles on the island. Royce rented a Harley that had a backrest. He didn't want to worry that Rosita would fall off. They grabbed the two helmets, and now they were almost ready. First, he explained to Rosita a few details, instructing her on holding on and signaling him if something was wrong. Too bad the rental company didn't have helmets with built-in communicating systems. If Rosita liked riding, he'd get helmets at home and they could talk to each other while rolling down the highway.

Royce loaded a few necessities into the saddlebags. He convinced Rosita to wear her swimsuit under her clothes, and he'd brought beach towels from the house. His plan was for them to tour the island by bike along the coast. Royce gave her one last kiss before he cranked up. Rosita sat on the bitch seat, grinning. He was glad that she was adventurous and not afraid to try things. He pulled out of the parking lot and headed down the street at an average speed. She gave him thumbs up, letting him know that she was okay. Although, she held him tight around the middle, with her eyes closed.

They rode for about twenty minutes before she opened her eyes and started to admire the scenery. After she felt more comfortable, she sat up straighter and held on by gripping the sides of his shirt. She was beginning to like riding the bike. They stopped after an hour at a roadside café. Rosita asked if they were going to eat, and Royce told her no. He only stopped to make sure she was okay or if she needed to stretch her legs. They continued to a pineapple plantation for a tour and lunch. Rosita remembered the grilled pineapples they ate on the secluded island. She was looking forward to eating more.

Royce and Rosita enjoyed the tour and lunch. Rosita ate more than two pieces of grilled pineapple this time. They climbed back on the bike after Royce told Rosita that he had one more adventure, which was a surprise. They rode for another forty-five minutes before he stopped again.

"Okay, baby, you can strip now."

"What? Strip, what are you talking about?"

Royce took off his boots and jeans, putting them in the saddlebags. He put on his swim shoes and grabbed the beach bag, holding up Rosita's cover-up.

"We're going on a hike to a waterfall. Get naked, baby." He laughed after seeing the expression on her face. "Okay, I'm joking, but you should take off the jeans and shirt."

He pulled her swim shoes from the bottom of the bag. She looked around to see if anyone was watching. No one was paying her any attention. They were gathering their items for the hike as well. When Rosita was ready, Royce pulled her along to catch up with the group. The hike wasn't long, but the scenery around them was spectacular. They walked through the lush tropical rainforest to reach the waterfall. Rosita was in awe of the beauty, taking multiple pictures along the hike. The guide explained all the foliage around them and pointed out areas where people could jump safely into the water pool from various rock ledges. Royce was already removing his shoes.

"Rosita, are you coming with me?"

"You're crazy if you think I'm jumping in that water. Drowning me on the beach is nothing compared to that."

"Don't you trust me? I promise I won't let anything happen to you. Maybe I want to kiss you under the waterfall. I would love to touch you under the waterfall."

"You're so tempting, but I prefer the safety of dry land. You jump, and I'll take your picture."

Royce walked to the ledge, and Rosita stood to the side. He jumped, and Rosita held down the button. She almost panicked because it took too long for him to resurface. She moved closer to the edge and called his name frantically, and Royce resurfaced in a different spot, waving to her. She exhaled loudly and shook her fist at him.

Laughing at her, he dove under the water. Rosita watched him swim like a fish. She thought of Marguerite and how she'd watched her learning how to swim. She could imagine both of them swimming here. Her breath caught in her throat as she watched Royce swim toward the waterfall. And several bikini-clad women followed him.

"Oh no, they didn't," Rosita said out loud.

Royce disappeared behind the waterfall, and Rosita watched the women dive underwater a few feet before the waterfall. She strained and stretched, trying to see behind the waterfall. The water flow was constant and thick. She couldn't see anything but held her breath like she was underwater. It wasn't a minute later that she exhaled. Royce emerged, swimming through the waterfall and in her direction. Bobbing up out of the water, he treaded below her. He waved for her to come in and patted the water in front of him. She shook her head no and laughed. He gave her a pouty face and extended his arms.

He mouthed, "I love you, and I'll protect you." He blew her a kiss.

Rosita saw the women again, and she didn't appreciate that they were stalking her husband in the water. Royce looked up, and she'd disappeared. Rosita reappeared minus her cover-up and shoes. He patted the water, where he wanted her to jump.

Rosita mouthed, "I love you." She closed her eyes and jumped.

She popped out of the water like a cork. Royce had his arm around her, and she was spitting water.

"Baby, you forgot to close your mouth and hold your breath."

Rosita had her arms around his neck and tried to catch her breath. "You . . . didn't tell me . . . that part."

"Baby, you've been at enough of Marguerite's lessons to know that."

"I know . . . I was upset. I saw those women follow you under the waterfall."

"I hope you didn't think I wanted them? You know I only have eyes for you. How about we go under the waterfall? I have an . . . idea."

Royce held onto Rosita. He showed her how to paddle and hold onto him. They made it through the stream of water. It was a small cave, and most of the area was shallow with rock ledges. Royce hoisted Rosita onto a ledge where she sat underwater. He stood in the water between her legs, pushing a few strands of hair out of her face. She had that wet look that drove him crazy. Royce palmed her face and kissed her. They had a better view of the outside world from the cave. Royce slid his hands between her legs under the water.

"Roy, you can't do that here. Somebody might catch us," she said between his kisses.

"Ah, baby, you got to live a little." He slid his finger inside her bikini bottom.

Royce kissed and teased his wife. She moaned into his mouth as he slid his finger in and out. She gripped his biceps for support.

"Ah, Roy, yes . . . yes."

Rosita couldn't move like she wanted to. The ledge was short, and she was afraid of slipping off. She was at the mercy of Royce. And he wasn't letting up. If they got caught, she was going to kill him. Royce was focusing on pleasuring his wife and didn't see the woman until after she popped up in the water.

"Umm . . . you guys want some company?"

Rosita froze with a shocked look on her face. It was one of the women that had stalked her husband, and she looked at the woman with venom.

"Hell, no!"

"What the . . . fuck?" Royce asked, at the same time, Rosita answered.

"Too bad," she said and swam out of the cave.

Royce laughed, and Rosita punched him in the shoulder. "Get me out of here."

Rosita didn't think it was funny. Some crazy ass woman wanted to partake in a threesome. Of course, a man would be flattered and think it was funny. Not to mention it killed her approaching orgasm. He needed to be punished. Royce lifted her off the ledge and held her in his arms.

"Love you, baby. I'll take care of you when we get back to the house, or I'll let you ride me on the motorcycle."

"I'm not doing anything else with you in public," she said, trying to sound mad.

Rosita wanted to squirm out of his arms, except she was at his mercy again. He had to get her back to dry land.

"Gimme a kiss, baby," he asked with a smile on his face.

"No!"

"Oh, so you're gonna play a Marguerite on me, huh."

Royce tickled her, and she slipped down in the water. She screamed until she realized that she was standing on her own two feet in waist-deep water.

"Gimme a kiss."

"If I do, will you promise to get me out of here and back to dry land?"

"Baby, I'd promise you the world."

Rosita closed her eyes, crossed her arms in defiance, and puckered. Royce crossed his arms, watching her, waiting for her to open her eyes. He had a smirk look on his face. She didn't ask for the world. In actuality, she rarely asked for anything, and that was what he loved about her. He knew she didn't care about the money. She loved him for him.

Rosita had been puckered for a while, and her face was tired. Her eyes twitched, and she started to get worried. What if he'd left her? She didn't hear any splashes in the water. Opening one eye, she peeped. Royce was standing in the same spot, watching her with a big grin on his face. Her shoulders dropped, knowing that she couldn't pretend to be angry at him. She'd actually been having fun until the threesome lady showed up.

"I thought you wanted a kiss?" She asked sarcastically.

"I asked you to *give* me a kiss. Will you always be so difficult?"

"When I need to be."

"Good girl, I want you always to be yourself. And put me in my place if I do something wrong."

Royce pulled her into his arms and kissed her. He told her to hold on, and they left the cave. Rosita was delighted to be back on dry land. They joined the group that was sitting at some picnic tables. The guide provided them with drinks and snacks.

Soon, they were on the bike, heading back to the Chateau. They needed to pack, and she insisted that Royce go on a scavenger hunt and find all the condoms he'd hidden all over the house. They had an early flight out of Maui. She didn't have the luxury of having an extra day off this time. Unfortunately, she was due back at work the day after they returned. Rosita wanted to hug and kiss her little girl because this was the first time they'd been separated. It wasn't the same, just seeing her and talking to her on a computer, she missed her terribly, and Royce missed her too. He'd bought her a stuffed pineapple at the plantation. Thankfully, it wasn't six feet tall and didn't need to be shipped home. Home now had a whole new meaning. She wouldn't have to sleep alone again unless Royce was out of town on business.

Chapter Twenty-Three

$\mathcal{R}$oyce pulled the SUV into the garage. He ran around and opened Rosita's door, picking her up out of the truck. Slapping at his hands, she pleaded for him to put her down. He held her tighter and walked through the back door of the house. They walked into the living room, greeted by noisemakers, and showered with confetti. Ms. J decorated the living room with welcome home newlywed paraphernalia. Marguerite was jumping up and down.

Royce kissed Rosita. "Welcome home, baby!"

Rosita squirmed until he put her down. She picked up Marguerite, kissing her and swinging them around.

"Oh my, I think you've grown since we left. Mommy missed you so much."

"I missed you too, mommy." She kissed her mother and reached for Royce, "Daddy!"

Royce kissed her on the top of her head in her mother's arms. "Hey, baby girl."

Royce looked over at Ms. J, who had tears in her eyes. A few steps later, he was lifting her off the floor, and she shrieked. He hugged her and kissed her on the cheek. "I love you, Ms. J., thank you."

"I love you too, son. And what are you thanking me for."

"For picking up strays."

"Put me down, you're making me cry." She wiped the tears from her face.

Royce put her down, and Rosita ran into her arms for a hug. Rosita had only known her for a short time, but she felt like she was with a real family. She knew what Royce had meant. He'd told her the story about how they met, and she'd accepted her and Marguerite without a second thought. She'd been a stray, and Royce had picked her up. They were both wiping tears. Ms. J had gone all out and cooked a meal worthy of a Sunday dinner, including a miniature wedding cake. It was the perfect little reception for them to share.

Royce helped Ms. J clean up the kitchen while Rosita got Marguerite ready for bed. They chatted, and Royce talked about Hawaii, even though he'd spent three weeks there with her and his parents. Ms. J told him how proud of him she was, and she was truly happy for them. She told him she'd had a premonition the same night she found them all cuddled up on the sofa.

"What are you talking about? How could you have foreseen this?"

Ms. J pulled out her phone and found the picture. "I forgot to send this to you."

Royce looked at the picture. He remembered that Rosita and Marguerite had only been at Ms. J's for a couple of weeks. It was the first time he'd put Rosita to bed. Smiling, he sent the picture to his phone. He kissed Ms. J on the cheek again and told her he wanted to read a story to his daughter.

Royce read a story to Marguerite until she fell asleep. He felt Rosita watching him from the doorway. He turned around, and she was dressed in her favorite baggy pants and a sweatshirt. Most men would prefer their wives dressed in sexy lingerie. Oh, he liked the sexy lingerie as well. But he also thought she was sexy as hell just like she was, plain and simple.

Dropping the book on the floor next to the chair, he stalked toward his wife. He wove his hands in her soft hair and pulled her toward him. He laced his wife with soft kisses, whispering to her, telling her how much he loved her. She wrapped her arms around his waist, and she felt his love poking her. She walked backward slowly toward her room, kissing and walking. They stopped walking when her legs reached the bed. Rosita fell back on the bed, and Royce followed, dropping his arms to the bed so he wouldn't crush her. Royce caressed her face looking at her with all the love he felt in his heart. Rosita had seen the same look on his face before he proclaimed his love to her. She didn't doubt that they both lusted for each other. And more so, she didn't doubt that he'd have ever used her. She knew now that he'd loved her enough to ask her to wait. He doubted himself.

Rosita smiled. "How long do you think it's going to take Marguerite to realize you're sleeping in this bed? Considering that she never woke up in the middle of the night and climbed in bed with me."

Royce kissed her. "I hope she doesn't realize it too soon. I would have insisted she stay in bed with her mother. If I'd known then what I know now, I would have locked my doors."

"No, you wouldn't. You said yourself that you didn't want her crying at a locked door."

"True and I have another wicked idea right now. I want to hear my wife moan and scream in my bed. Come on, let's sneak out of the house like a couple of teenagers."

Rosita pushed Royce off her and bounced off the bed, running. Royce chased his wife out of the house to the stairs that led up to his apartment. Royce was nervous and fumbling with the keys to open the door. He planned to pick Rosita up and carry her across his threshold. She jumped on his back and held on. She rode piggyback to his bedroom, where they tore each other's clothes off.

For the first time, Royce made love to a woman in his bed. An hour later, they lay holding each other. Royce told her they could start looking for their own house. He wanted something close to Ms. J so she could continue to keep Marguerite.

They lay in the bed, and Royce asked Rosita what her wishes were in a house. Rosita shrugged her shoulders because she had no idea. She commented that Ms. J's house was the nicest house she'd ever lived in. Living in foster homes meant that she had to share a room with one or more girls. Truthfully, she never imagined that she would ever be in this situation, where everything and anything could come true. Royce held her in his arms and rattled off ideas of having several bedrooms, a theater room where Marguerite could watch her movies, and a big beautiful kitchen full of top-of-the-line appliances. He already knew that Rosita liked to cook and she was good at it.

Rosita nodded in agreement, and then she asked if she could have a sewing room. She'd learned to sew in one of her foster homes and spent many days, making her own clothes. Royce leaned up, saying that she didn't have to sew her own clothes and that she could buy whatever she wanted. Rosita smiled, telling him that she knew that, but it was fun and she could teach Marguerite and together they could sew doll clothes. Royce liked that idea, saying 'yes.' He would make sure the ladies had a sewing room and all the sewing machines they wanted. They had time to get with a real estate agent and began searching for the perfect house.

They had talked long enough that Rosita was nodding off to sleep. Before he forgot, he had one other request. Royce asked Rosita to come and work at the office with him, since she is an owner now and beyond the pay grade of a team shift leader. However, Rosita said she wouldn't leave Janell without a shift leader. She'd leave as soon as a new person was trained to take her position.

Royce woke with Rosita snuggled against him. He had another epiphany. It had been enjoyable kissing her good morning and leisurely having coffee. He should have known this was the woman for him because only true love would fix his problem. She was the first and only person he desired to wake up with and wake up holding. He kissed her awake because she'd left everything in her bedroom in Ms. J's house. In the near future, they'd be able to lead normal lives instead of getting up at the crack of dawn, just to open a business.

They'd have a home of their own and their jobs at the main office downtown.

Royce dropped Rosita off at the back door, just like clockwork. Kissing her, he told her that he'd see her later. Now he felt depressed, and he didn't want to let her go. As soon as he got to the office, he'd send Janell an email to start training a new shift leader.

They decided to keep their marriage a secret until Royce announced that he was the owner and not the regional manager. Rosita pulled off her rings and put them on the chain around her neck. She hid her necklace inside her shirt before going into the building. Unlocking the door, she waved goodbye to Royce, closing the door behind her. Rosita hit the alarm code on the keypad and headed to the break room to lock up her purse.

As soon as she opened the door, people screamed, *"Congratulations."*

Rosita yelped and backed out of the room, holding her heart. Janell was the first to hug her.

"Oh my God, Rosita, I should have known he'd propose. It was so beautiful. When is the wedding? Do you have a date yet?" She asked questions rapidly.

"What . . . what are you talking about? How did you know?" Rosita was stunned.

"Girl, it's all over YouTube."

"What's on YouTube?"

"Your proposal! We recognized you. Didn't you know?"

Janell opened her phone and went to the app. She showed the video to Rosita. Rosita plopped down in the nearest chair, dropping her head in her hands. Oh well, there went that secret, and now she needed to call Royce. Her co-workers grabbed her out of the chair so they could get hugs and offer her congratulations. She looked around the room. They'd decorated the breakroom, and all the staff was there. Everybody from all shifts had gotten up to surprise her.

They still didn't know she was married. A couple of the ladies grabbed her hand, looking for a ring. She stammered and told them she left it at home. Rosita reminded them that they had to get ready and open up. They grinned, saying the store was ready since they had to do something while waiting on her to get to work.

Rosita thanked them profusely. She'd been worried that she wouldn't be accepted so openly being with Royce. Of course, all his staff respected him enormously. How were they going to feel when they found out the truth? When her heart stopped racing and she could breathe, she sent Royce a text.

Rosita: Roy, they know. They all know. Did you know we were on YouTube?

Rosita stuffed her phone in her pocket, figuring she'd hear from Royce soon enough. She got extremely busy with the morning rush hour, working the drive-thru.

Royce went back home and climbed the stairs. He lay down and slept for another hour. The alarm went off, and he dressed in a nice suit and went to work at his new office. He walked in, and Toby came out into the hallway and propped up against the door frame.

"Welcome back, boss," Toby said with a big smile on his face.

"Thanks, man. So tell me, what did I miss around here?"

"No, I think you need to tell me what I missed. You have something to tell me."

"No, nothing other than I had a wonderful vacation," Royce said, looking away.

"Oh, really, then I think you need to see something in my office."

Toby chuckled to himself. Apparently, his boss and friend didn't know that the secret was out. He typed on his computer, brought up a video, and turned the screen around. A soft breeze could have knocked Royce over. There he was visible as day on one knee proposing to Rosita with the silhouette of the sun rising behind them.

"Holy shit! Rosita is going to kill me. I didn't know anything about this. I only saw some pictures in an email. I better warn her."

"I think it's too late for that. How do you think I knew about it? They were planning a surprise party for her this morning."

Royce dug his phone out of his jacket pocket. He hadn't looked at it all morning. He hit the button and the screen popped up, a message from Rosita. "They know." Royce dropped his head.

"So, buddy, when is the big day?" Toby asked, laughing.

"We got married in Hawaii," Royce said low.

"Hawaii? Congratulations, man, I'm so happy for you."

"I think I better call my wife."

Royce sat at his desk and called Rosita's cell. It rang a couple of times and went to voicemail. He called the mainline.

The manager grabbed the phone, "Gourmet coffee house, Midtown, how can I help you?"

"Janell, what are you doing there?"

"Oh, hey boss, congratulations on your engagement. Oh, you remember that *bomb* I mentioned a while back. *Boo-yah!*"

He laughed, "Well, Janell, I have another *bomb* for you. You need to find and train a new shift team leader. My *wife* is going to be working at the office with her *husband. Boo-yah!*"

"Oh, boss, I'm so happy for you guys. She didn't tell me that part."

"Well, can I speak to my wife, please?"

Royce heard Janell yelling for Mrs. Hawthorne to come to the phone. He laughed out loud. Oh yeah, he was going to be in big trouble. Rosita grabbed the phone, sounding like she was out of breath. She kept repeating, they know, they know. Royce exhaled and listened to his wife. He told her it would be okay. Janell knew everything, and he was sure she'd spread the word. Their secret was out of the bag, and the downtown location probably knew too. Oh well, that's what he gets for trying to keep secrets.

After hanging up the phone, he opened his emails. He checked all the emails from the strangers on the mountain. Then he saw the pictures and the link to the YouTube video. There were thousands of hits on the video. He opened up a message to his mother and sent her the link. She'd be excited to see his proposal the whole world was already looking at.

Royce had plenty of work emails that he needed to view, except he'd received an email from the wedding photographer. He looked at each picture and swelled with pride all over again. The photographer had captured Rosita's face as the guys removed her hood. She had love tattooed all over her smile. Royce wanted to print all the pictures and make a wedding album but decided they'd do it together. He called Toby into his office to see the wedding pictures.

Rosita kept her promise and stayed on as team leader until the position was filled. Janell thought it was proper that they give her a big send-off. Her coworkers threw her a congratulatory party. None of them figured that the couple needed wedding gifts. Janell wanted her gifts to reflect her new position, so her gifts included a poster-sized collage of pictures from the time she started working until the present. Various coworkers had pictures on their phones from fun times at work to disasters. It wasn't funny at the time when the coffee machine clogged up and coffee and grinds exploded all over everyone. Her other gifts included some wall art with a coffee theme, an organizer for her desk, a picture frame, a coffee mug from the Midtown location, and a personalized trophy coffee mug that said, '*Rosita, The Best Team Leader Ever.*'

Janell pulled her to the side. "I want you to know that I'm so happy for you and Royce. We all wish you the best. The gifts are so you won't forget us."

Rosita smiled. "You know that you are the closest person to me having a best friend. I could never forget any of you, or my time working with you. Besides, I'm only going to be across town, and I'll see you at the management meetings.

Royce felt like his life was finally in order, and it was time to make the announcement. Royce called a meeting with all his managerial staff. He revealed the truth that he was the CEO of Hawthorne Incorporated, and he owned the three local Gourmet Coffee House's as well as five others. During his speech, he told them he felt closer to his staff because he'd trained and worked alongside most of them. Royce let them know how much he appreciated their loyalty and support. And that he firmly believed in promoting within the company first. He announced that he was in the planning stage of opening several more locations locally and within the state. Instead, of resentment or anger, the management team cheered.

Rosita showed up for work on her first day, with no idea what she would be doing. Royce surprised her, by removing a cover off a plate mounted on the wall. Rosita thought she was going to cry. Next to her name was the title, Operations Manager. Royce kissed her and led her inside her new office. There were multiple surprises waiting for her. Even though he let her select the desk she wanted, he added a few other items to her office. He knew that Toby wouldn't be making many unexpected visits to her office, so he purchased a nice little comfortable sofa for her office. It could also serve as a place for Marguerite to sleep if she came to visit or spent time with her parents. He told her after she'd settled in she could open the folder on her desk and see what her duties and responsibilities were.

Excitedly, Rosita decorated her new office with the items from her friends, with the help of Royce. He was much better with a hammer and nails to hang her pictures. When he was finished with his chore, he wanted a reward.

"I think I deserve something for being your handyman, and I don't want a kiss," Royce said backing toward the door, unbuttoning his shirt. He turned the knob on the bolt lock.

Rosita was swinging back and forth in her comfortable swivel chair, smiling. She wondered why her door had a bolt lock on it. Now, she knew it was so she and her husband could be frisky at work.

Royce finished unbuttoning his shirt and began on his pants, heading to the couch. "I thought we could celebrate your first day," he said and pushed his shoes off, letting his dress pants slide down his legs, and stepped out of them.

"I thought this was illegal. Are you sure we should be doing this at work?" She said rising from her desk, pulling her blouse over her head. Thankfully, her skirt had an elastic waist, and she pushed it down her hips. Seductively, she walked across the room, wearing her bra and panties.

"Nothing is illegal for us; we're married. And I can't wait until we have to work late one evening, and do this in my office with the sun setting," Royce said, sitting on the couch, pulling her into his lap.

"Have I told you today that I love you?" Royce said, unhooking her bra.

"Yes, you told me right after I screamed in your ear from an orgasm, and then Marguerite knocked at the door."

"Well, sweetheart, you can scream silently, but I doubt that anyone will come knocking at this door. I love you so much, and thank you for coming into my life."

"I love you more than I can express, and you have to thank Marguerite for bringing us into your life."

"I have a plan to thank her for the rest of her life. I never realized how rewarding a child can be, and I look forward to the rest of our future," Royce said softly and laid Rosita on the couch, covering her body.

Epilogue

The happy couple spent the next three months living with Ms. J until they found the house of their dreams only a few blocks away. Rosita thought it was too big and had too many bedrooms. Royce kissed her and said he wanted to fill it with children. Royce fell in love with the house because of the pool and the pool house. His favorite item in the backyard was the attached hot tub.

Royce and Rosita were living a happy life. He suggested that Rosita learn how to drive. And for Marguerite's fourth birthday, Royce officially adopted her. She became Marguerite Ariana Hawthorne. Royce continued to grow his empire. He expanded into several other cities in Michigan and opened three additional GCH's in Detroit.

He and Rosita were also working on building their family empire. Marguerite was ecstatic with a sister nine months after her fourth birthday. And two years later, Royce found out he was about to have his first son.

This story isn't the last of Royce and his family. You'll get to see him when he shows up again. You get to meet his cousin, Chase Luttrell, who happens to be a single father. He has to learn how to adapt after the death of his wife.

About the Author

She is a native Louisianan and an avid reader and writer of romance. She lives with her husband and two cats. Her stories take you on an adventure while the characters find love and romance. She hopes you're amazed by intrigue, chaos, and perplexity. Finding love is not always easy, but when you do, hold on tight. Read my words, feel my words!

Social Media Accounts

Visit my website: www.nonagallien.com

Follow me on Instagram: https://www.instagram.com/Nonagallienauthor/
Like my Facebook page: https://www.facebook.com/Nonagallien/
Follow me on twitter: https://twitter.com/NonaGallien

I can also be reached via email: nonagallien@gmail.com